D0144105

When Teddy Came to Town

to Town

a novel

Tyler R. Tichelaar

Marquette Fiction
Marquette, Michigan

When Teddy Came to Town

Copyright © 2018 by Tyler R. Tichelaar

All rights reserved. No part of this book may be used or reproduced by any means, graphic, electronic, or mechanical, including photocopying, recording, taping, or by any information storage retrieval system without the written permission of the publisher except in the case of brief quotations embodied in critical articles and reviews. Inquiries should be addressed to:

Marquette Fiction

1202 Pine Street

Marquette, MI 49855

www.MarquetteFiction.com

ISBN-13: 978-0-9962400-5-5

Library of Congress Control Number: 2018903135

Printed in the United States of America

Cover Photo: Greg Kretovic

Author Photo: Greg Casperson

Cover and Interior Design: Larry Alexander, Superior Book Productions

www.SuperiorBookProductions.com

"To be yourself in a world that is constantly trying to make you something else is the greatest accomplishment."
— Ralph Waldo Emerson

Principal Characters

Fictional Characters

Matthew Newman—Reporter for the *Empire Sentinel* of New York City and former Marquette resident.

Delia Newman Richardson—Matthew Newman's married sister who lives in Marquette.

Roger Richardson—Delia Richardson's husband.

Lydia Richardson—Roger and Delia Richardson's daughter.

Rowena Richardson Robillard—Roger's sister.

Reginald Robillard—Rowena's husband, of the Philadelphia Robillards.

Martha—The Richardsons' servant.

Mrs. Honeywell—The Richardsons' cook.

Lysander Blackmore—Lydia Richardson's fiancé.

Richard Blackmore—Father to Lysander, deceased at time of novel.

Joe Sweet—Boyhood camping companion to Matthew Newman and George Shiras.

Madeleine Henning—Friend in youth to Matthew, Delia, and Roger; she drowned in Lake Superior during a boating excursion on July 4, 1876.

Mordecai Whichgood—Visiting Methodist preacher.

Cecilia Whichgood—Mordecai Whichgood's daughter.

Carolina Smith—Wealthy wife of Judge Smith.

Josiah Pritchard—Matthew Newman's editor at the *Empire Sentinel*.

Historical Personages

The Players in the Roosevelt vs. Newett Libel Trial

The Plaintiff:

Theodore Roosevelt—Former president of the United States, accused by George Newett in his newspaper, the *Iron Ore,* of being a drunkard.

Lawyers for the Plaintiff

W.S. Hill—Marquette lawyer.

James H. Pound—Detroit lawyer.

William H. Van Benschoten—New York lawyer.

Witnesses for the Plaintiff

A.W. Abele—Ohio businessman who met Roosevelt during his 1912 campaign stops.

Lawrence Abbott—Secretary to Roosevelt during his 1909-1910 African trip.

Lyman Abbott—Father to Lawrence Fraser Abbott, Roosevelt's secretary. A theologian, editor, and author.

James E. Amos—African-American former bodyguard of Theodore Roosevelt. Later a special agent for the FBI.

Robert Bacon—Former U.S. Secretary of State.

Joseph E. Bayliss—Member of Michigan House of Representatives and witness to Roosevelt's 1912 campaign when he passed through Sault Ste. Marie, Michigan.

Arthur D. Bevan—Attending physician to Roosevelt when he was shot.

Albin Z. Blair—Former Rough Rider and Ohio judge.

George B. Cortelyou—Personal secretary to President McKinley. Later Secretary of Commerce and Labor, Secretary of the Treasury, and Chairman of the Republican National Committee.

Lucius F. Curtis—Member of the Associated Press.

Oscar King Davis—Secretary of the Progressive National Party (the Bull Moose Party).

Admiral George Dewey—Admiral of the U.S. Navy.

William B. Dulany—Confidential messenger to Roosevelt during his presidency.

Edwin Emerson—Journalist and a former Rough Rider who served as Roosevelt's regimental clerk.

Gilson Gardner—Washington Representative of Scripps newspapers.

James R. Garfield—Former Secretary of the Interior, son to President James A. Garfield.

Lawrence Hill Graham—Journalist and former Commissioner of the Interior for Puerto Rico.

Edmund Heller—Served as naturalist for large mammals for the Smithsonian-Roosevelt African expedition of 1909-1910.

Alexander Lambert—Roosevelt family physician.

William Loeb, Jr.—Presidential secretary to Roosevelt.

John B. Murphy—Wisconsin surgeon who attended to Roosevelt after he was shot.

Truman H. Newberry—Former Secretary of the Navy.

John Callan O'Laughlin—Washington correspondent for the *Chicago Tribune*.

Gifford Pinchot—Former chief of the United States Forest Service.

Henry Rauthier—Assessor for the City of Ishpeming, Michigan.

Jacob A. Riis—Danish-born reporter and author of *How the Other Half Lives*. Roosevelt enlisted him in helping to reform the police department in New York City.

Presley Rixey—Former Surgeon General of the U.S. Navy. A personal physician to Presidents McKinley and Roosevelt.

George Emlen Roosevelt—Theodore Roosevelt's first cousin once removed. Member of banking firm Roosevelt & Son.

Philip Roosevelt—Theodore Roosevelt's first cousin once removed. A newspaper reporter.

W. Emlen Roosevelt—First cousin to Theodore Roosevelt. Member of banking firm Roosevelt & Son. Father to Philip and George Emlen Roosevelt.

William P. Schaufflee—Traffic manager for the M.A. Hanna Company of Cleveland and witness to Roosevelt's campaign in Ohio.

Albert Shaw—Journalist and academic.

James Sloan—Secret Service guard to presidents from Theodore Roosevelt to Harry Truman.

Charles W. Thompson—Correspondent for the *New York Times* who campaigned for Roosevelt in 1912.

Frank H. Tyree—Bodyguard to Roosevelt in the White House.

General Leonard Wood—Physician to Presidents Cleveland and McKinley. Organizer of the Rough Riders with Roosevelt.

The Defense

George Newett—Owner of the newspaper the *Iron Ore*. Accused Theodore
   Roosevelt in an editorial of being a drunkard.

Lawyers for the Defense

William P. Belden—Ishpeming lawyer.

Horace Andrews—Ishpeming lawyer.

Witnesses for the Defense

George Martin Miller—Claims he has seen Roosevelt drunk on many
   occasions, including at Speaker of the House Joseph Cannon's
   seventieth birthday party.

Anonymous—Numerous people who wrote depositions claiming to have
   seen Roosevelt drunk.

The Judge

The Honorable Richard C. Flannigan—an Upper Peninsula of Michigan
   native and former resident of Marquette residing in Norway, Michigan.

The Jury

Robert Bruce—A fifty-four-year-old woodsman from Powell Township.

William Fassbender—A twenty-eight-year-old farmer from Marquette.

John Fredrickson—A thirty-one-year-old miner from Negaunee.

William Garrow—A twenty-six-year-old miner from Diorite.

Thomas Howard—A forty-nine-year-old farmer from Chocolay Township.

Andrew P. Johnson—A sixty-one-year-old farmer from Humboldt
   Township.

John A. Johnson—A thirty-six-year-old farmer from Skandia Township.

W.H. Mathews—A thirty-one-year-old mining office clerk from Ishpeming.

Gus Paulson—A thirty-two-year-old blacksmith from Wells Township.

William Pryor—A twenty-seven-year-old locomotive fireman from
   Marquette.

Joseph Robear—A twenty-five-year-old teamster from Ishpeming.

William Sharpe—A thirty-three-year-old teamster from Negaunee.

Reporters Covering the Trial

Harry Atwell—*Chicago Tribune* photographer.

L.F. Curtis—Associated Press.

J.H. Dunnewind—*Detroit Free Press.*

Richard Fairchild—*Chicago Record-Herald.*

Chris Haggerty—Associated Press.

Carroll McCrae—*Toledo Blade.*

Homer Guck—*Houghton Mining Gazette*, Houghton, Michigan.

Other Historical Personages who are characters or referenced

Will Adams—Marquette playwright who suffered from ossification. Died in 1909.

Byrne, R.P.—Confederate Civil War Veteran who lives in Marquette.

Byrne, Samuel E.—Brother of R.P. Byrne who fought for the Union in the Civil War.

Fred Cadotte (Bawgam)—Indian guide for George Shiras.

Mrs. Charlton—Wife to D. Fred Charlton, Marquette architect who designed the Marquette County Courthouse where the trial takes place.

Robert Dollar—Millionaire known as the Grand Old Man of the Pacific. Former resident of Upper Michigan for whom Dollarville, Michigan, is named.

Mrs. W.S. Hill—Wife to Roosevelt's Marquette attorney.

Robert "Bob" Hume—Caretaker of Presque Isle Park.

Chief Charles Kawbawgam—Last Chief of the Chippewa, buried at Presque Isle.

Charlotte Kawbawgam—Wife of Chief Kawbawgam and Daughter of Chief Marji Gesick.

Jack LaPete (Jacques LePique)—Brother-in-law to Chief Kawbawgam—part-Indian, part-French-Canadian and Irish.

Chief Marji Gesick—Father of Charlotte Kawbawgam. Responsible for leading the white men to the iron ore deposits in Upper Michigan.

Bessie Mather—Daughter of Henry Mather and Mary Hewitt Mather.

Henry Mather—Brother-in-law to Peter White.

Kate Mather—Half-sister to William Gwinn Mather and niece of Henry Mather.

Mary Hewitt Mather—Wife of Henry Mather, sister of Ellen Hewitt White.

William Gwinn Mather—Nephew to Henry Mather and half-brother to Kate Mather.

Carroll Watson Rankin—Marquette author of *Dandelion Cottage*.

Reynolds, Alfred Owen—Toddler son of Maxwell and Frances Reynolds.

Reynolds, Frances Jopling—Granddaughter of Peter White and niece to Frances Shiras White. Married to Maxwell Reynolds.

Reynolds, Maxwell—First cousin to George Shiras III. Resides next-door to him.

Frances White Shiras—Wife to George Shiras III and daughter to Peter and Ellen White.

George Shiras II, or Jr.—U.S. Supreme Court Justice who summers in Marquette.

George Shiras III—Son of George Shiras II. An eminent naturalist and wildlife photographer. Host to Roosevelt while in Marquette.

John R. Van Evera—Former warden of the Marquette Branch Prison, in the crowd when Roosevelt speaks in Marquette.

Ellen Hewitt White—Wife of Peter White.

Morgan White—Son of Peter and Ellen White.

Peter White—Marquette pioneer, father-in-law to George Shiras. Died in 1908.

Byron Williams—Master of Ceremonies for the press men dinner at the Marquette Commercial Club.

Constance Fenimore Woolson—Aunt to William Gwinn Mather and Samuel L. Mather. A popular novelist who wrote about the Lake Superior region.

Joseph Zryd—Violinist in late nineteenth century Marquette. (The author's great-great-great grandfather.)

Stewart Zryd—Spanish-American War veteran. Son of Joseph Zryd.

Roosevelt Campaigning in Marquette on October 9, 1912

PROLOGUE

ON WEDNESDAY, OCTOBER 9, 1912, former U.S. President Theodore Roosevelt, who now styled himself Colonel Roosevelt, based on his past military experience, arrived by train in Marquette, Michigan. He was there to campaign as the Progressive "Bull Moose" Party candidate for the presidency of the United States.

An estimated six thousand people turned out to see Roosevelt—most would not be able to hear him because the crowd was so thick. Throngs of people squeezed into the train yard surrounding the depot and on both sides of Front Street near the makeshift platform erected for him in downtown Marquette.

Among Roosevelt's listeners was George A. Newett, editor of the *Iron Ore*, a newspaper published in the city of Ishpeming, some fifteen miles west of Marquette.

Because Newett and his paper were staunch supporters of the Republican Party, Newett was already inclined to have an unfavorable view of Roosevelt's speech. Newett was angry that Roosevelt had broken with the Republican Party after it had nominated incumbent U.S. President William Howard Taft over himself for its presidential candidate. Roosevelt had then decided to form his own Progressive Party and be its candidate. The result had been division within the Republican Party since many of its members chose to support Roosevelt.

No doubt many other Republicans present were not fans of Roosevelt, but regardless, the enormous crowd was thrilled to see a former U.S. president. The only other president ever to have visited Marquette had been President Taft the year before, so regardless of Roosevelt's politics, the community saw it as a day worth celebrating.

Although Roosevelt had never before visited Marquette, he knew several of the local politicians, including George Shiras III, who summered in Marquette and had served as a congressman for Pennsylvania in Washington, D.C. Roosevelt and Shiras had developed a friendship because of a bill Shiras had introduced to protect wildfowl. Roosevelt shared Shiras' conservation interests, and since they had met, he had taken great interest in Shiras' efforts to photograph wildlife. Now seeing Shiras in the crowd, Roosevelt shouted to him, "Did you get your beaver picture yet?" Shiras shouted back that the glass plate had not yet been developed. Then Roosevelt's attention was diverted away from his friend, and in a few more seconds, he was ready to give his speech.

A presidential candidate's speeches are notorious for pointing out what is wrong with his opponent's position on various issues, and Roosevelt's speech that day was no different. He spoke out boldly against the steel trust, which he blamed for taking over the Republican convention and preventing him from getting the presidential nomination. But today Roosevelt was in steel country. Marquette County's economy relied on its iron mines, which shipped ore to the great cities of Pittsburgh, Cleveland, and Buffalo, where the ore was turned into steel. In fact, George Newett's newspaper, the *Iron Ore*, was named for the community's bread-and-butter.

Roosevelt did not let Marquette's interests in steel dissuade him. Instead, he addressed the situation directly. Speaking without hesitation, he declared, "The steel trust is here in Marquette County, and its attorney, the congressman against whom—"

"That is not true!" a man interrupted him.

The man was John Van Evera, former warden of the Marquette Branch Prison, and a strong supporter of the Republican Party.

Roosevelt, without blinking an eye, shot back, "You stand for theft and you stand for lying and false witness bearing. Another thing I will give you a chance to deny: that every paper influenced by the steel corporation in Marquette and by the standpatters is against us in this county."

Van Evera replied, "I am not afraid of a Bull Moose."

Roosevelt continued, "It is perfectly natural that you should object to hearing the truth told about the side you are championing; and it is perfectly natural that you should come here to try to interrupt a meeting in which I am exposing the falsities and misinterpretations of your side."

"Then tell the truth," persisted Van Evera.

Roosevelt continued, naming local politicians, including Horace O. Young of nearby Ishpeming, who was currently a member of the Michigan State House of Representatives. "Mr. Young is the ex-attorney of the Steel Trust, and his law partner is attorney for the Steel Trust now. I understand, sir, that I am telling you the truth; I speak here from the information given me; but when I speak of the Chicago convention of last June, I speak of what I know. You are supporting the receivers of stolen goods, and a man engaged with the theft; and if you are a man of intelligence and education, you are acting as dishonorably as if you were supporting a man who had stolen a purse. Now you ask to hear the truth. You have heard it. A man who approves of the commission of theft, or who brazenly defends it, is no better than the thief himself."

Roosevelt continued his speech without any further interruptions. When he was finished, the crowd applauded, and soon the former president was off to his next stop on the campaign trail. Meanwhile, the local newspapers' headlines declared:

'Big Bull Moose's' Tour a Continual Triumph

Upper Peninsula Turned Out More Than 40,000 People Wednesday to Welcome the Great Progressive Chieftain

He Was Seen and Heard in Marquette County by Larger Throngs Than Ever Before Had Greeted a Great National Leader

All that said, Roosevelt had already given several speeches that day, and his voice had been somewhat raspy, which caused some people to wonder, especially when he became so animated while responding to Mr. Van Evera's charges, whether he might have been intoxicated.

George Newett did more than wonder. He went home and wrote the following editorial, which appeared in the *Iron Ore* on October 12, 1912.

The Roosevelt Way

According to Roosevelt, he is the only man who can call others liars, rascals and thieves, terms he applies to Republicans generally.

All that Roosevelt has gained politically he received from the hands of the Republican Party.

Had he won in the Republican convention in Chicago, then the Republican Party would still be a good party, and all others would have been made up of liars and thieves and scoundrels generally.

But if anyone calls Roosevelt a liar he raves and roars and takes on in an awful way, and yet Roosevelt is a pretty good liar himself. Where a lie will serve to advance his position, he employs it.

Roosevelt lies and curses in the most disgusting way; he gets drunk, too, and that not infrequently, and all of his intimates know about it.

What's the use mincing things with him when he maltreats everyone not for him?

Because he has been president gives him no privileges above other men and his conduct is just as deserving censure as is that of any other offender against decency.

How can Roosevelt expect to go unlashed when he maliciously and untruthfully strikes out at other people?

It's just as Mr. Harlan said, he's the greatest little fighter in the country when he's alone in the ring, but he acts like a madman if anyone dares criticize him. All who oppose him are wreckers of the country, liars, knaves and undesirables.

He alone is pure and entitled to a halo. Rats! For so great a fighter, self-styled, he's the poorest loser we ever knew.

Two days later, October 14, would be a doubly fateful day for the former president. Roosevelt was continuing his campaign, traveling that day from Chicago to Milwaukee. He was already experiencing a sore throat from all the speeches he had given, but he planned to give another that evening. That same day, he would be handed a copy of Newett's editorial by Oscar King Davis, his party's secretary. After reading the article, Roosevelt whispered to Davis, "Let's go after him." Then, while en route to Milwaukee, the former president sent instructions to Henry M. Wallace, the Progressive national committeeman from Michigan, to retain a lawyer and file a libel suit against Newett.

Once Roosevelt arrived in Milwaukee, he went to the Gilpatrick Hotel, where the hotel owner, a supporter of Roosevelt, provided dinner for him. Word quickly got out that Roosevelt was dining at the Gilpatrick. When he prepared to leave the hotel for Milwaukee Auditorium, where he would give his speech, he found a crowd outside, clamoring to see him.

Roosevelt got into the open convertible waiting for him at the hotel entrance. At first, he sat down, but when the crowd cheered for him, he stood to acknowledge and wave to his supporters.

Suddenly, a gunshot was heard. A man, standing just seven feet from Roosevelt, had drawn a revolver from his vest and shot the former president.

The bullet struck Roosevelt in the chest and knocked him back down into his seat.

The would-be assassin was John Flammang Schrank, a former saloonkeeper from New York who had become profoundly religious. He had followed Roosevelt from New Orleans to Milwaukee. Schrank would later claim he had been writing a poem in the night when the ghost of President William McKinley appeared to him. McKinley had asked Schrank to avenge his death and pointed at a photograph of Roosevelt.

Schrank was immediately arrested. He would later maintain that he had nothing against Roosevelt and he had not intended to kill "the citizen Roosevelt," but rather "Roosevelt, the third-termer," claiming that President McKinley had told him to shoot Roosevelt as a warning to other third-termers. Schrank would be diagnosed by doctors as suffering from delusions and insanity. He would then be committed to the Central State Mental Hospital in Waupun, Wisconsin, for life.

As for Roosevelt, the bullet had lodged itself in his chest, but first, it had penetrated his steel eyeglass case and passed through the folded fifty pages of his speech in his suit pocket. Being a hunter, Roosevelt had a good knowledge of anatomy; because he was not coughing up blood, he knew the bullet had not sunk far enough into his chest to hit his lung, so he refused to go to the hospital until after he gave his speech. His motorcar proceeded to the Milwaukee Auditorium.

When Roosevelt took the stage in the auditorium, he began to address the crowd by saying, "Friends, I shall ask you to be as quiet as possible. I don't know whether you fully understand that I have just been shot; but it takes more than that to kill a Bull Moose. But, fortunately, I had my manuscript, so you see I was going to make a long speech, and there is a bullet—there is where the bullet went through—and it probably saved me from it going into my heart. The bullet is in me now, so that I cannot make a very long speech, but I will try my best."

The former president went on to deliver his speech, and although at times his voice was hardly more than a whisper, he spoke for ninety minutes, and when he had finished, he was cheered by the crowd. Only then did he agree to be taken to the hospital.

At the hospital, Roosevelt was attended by his personal physician, Dr. Terrell. An x-ray showed the bullet lodged in Roosevelt's chest muscle; the bullet had also broken his fourth rib. Dr. Terrell determined that because the bullet had not penetrated Roosevelt's pleura, it would be less dangerous to leave it in place. The former president would carry the bullet inside him for the rest of his life. Because it would hinder his ability to exercise, it would cause him to gain significant weight in his later years.

Roosevelt remained in the hospital for a week. During that time, one highlight of his stay was receiving a photograph from his friend George Shiras. On the back was inscribed the note, "Here is the answer to your question!" It was a nighttime photograph of a beaver gnawing on a tree trunk.

Although the election would be held on November 5, only three weeks away, Roosevelt's opponents, President Taft of the Republican Party and Democratic nominee Woodrow Wilson, both halted their own campaigns out of a sense of fair play while Roosevelt was hospitalized. Once Roosevelt was released from the hospital, all three candidates resumed their campaigns, although Roosevelt himself would only make two more speeches before Election Day.

Roosevelt would not garner enough votes to be elected president, although his 4.1 million votes surpassed the 3.5 million of his Republican opponent, Taft. Because Wilson's 6.3 million votes won him the electoral vote, he would be sworn in as twenty-eighth president of the United States.

With the election over, Roosevelt would quickly turn his attention to his lawsuit against George Newett.

Newett's charge that Roosevelt was a drunkard had not been the first accusation made to that effect. Several reasons existed for these accusations. First, Roosevelt had a very animated presence when he spoke. His voice boomed and he liked to wave his arms about. He did this largely so the people in the back of the crowd could see and hear him, but it often led to people thinking his behavior somewhat erratic and possibly influenced by alcohol. Second, Roosevelt usually gave multiple speeches a day on the campaign trail and he had to speak so loudly to be heard by the massive crowds that his voice often became quite hoarse and, sometimes, it even sounded like he slurred his words. Finally, the prohibition of alcohol was being hotly debated across the country, but Roosevelt remained uncommitted on the issue. When he was asked for his opinion on prohibition by reporters, he often shrugged off the question or muttered a barely audible response. This attitude made people speculate that he was not in favor of prohibition, the reason being that he was a heavy drinker himself. None of these speculations, however, had sufficient support to prove Roosevelt was a drunk.

George Shiras' beaver picture

Tired of all the accusations about his drinking, Roosevelt decided he would make an example of the *Iron Ore* and its editor. On October 25, 1912, his lawyer, James H. Pound of Detroit, filed an extensive Declaration of Intention in Marquette County, and four days later, Pound filed the following formal and detailed complaint:

> That the said defendant, George A. Newett, did upon October, the twelfth, A.D. 1912, publish the following false, scandalous, malicious and defamatory words...."The Roosevelt Way."
>
> That the entire article is libelous. But that Theodore Roosevelt waives all claims for damages for any of the libels contained in said article, except the words, "Roosevelt lies and curses in a most disgusting way. He gets drunk, too, and that not infrequently and all of his intimates know about it."
>
> That Theodore Roosevelt does hereby begin an action of Trespass, in the Circuit Court for the County of Marquette and claims as his damages, the sum of Ten Thousand Dollars.

Newett then hired his own lawyer, William P. Bedell, of Ishpeming, and filed the following response to Roosevelt's allegations of libel:

> Take notice, the defendant will give in evidence and insist in his defense that the words charged in the plaintiff's declaration, were published in good faith, without any malice, and under circumstances creating a qualified privilege, vis.: That at the time the plaintiff was a candidate for the office of the President of the United States, and that as such candidate his public conduct and his fitness for said high office were properly subject to discussion as matters of common and general interest.
>
> And the said defendant will further give in evidence and insists in his defense, the plaintiff had been and was guilty of the facts and acts charged and imputed to him in the publication.

Newett and Bedell now set out to prove that what Newett had printed was true. They began by collecting depositions to support the statement that Roosevelt often became drunk. Upon hearing of their actions, Roosevelt convinced the court to order that the depositions not be made public until the time of the trial, scheduled to begin at the Marquette County Courthouse on May 26, 1913. A great deal of media attention and interest would build throughout the nation as the trial approached.

"To announce that there must be no criticism of the president...is morally treasonable to the American public."
— Theodore Roosevelt

George Newett (left), who wrote the libelous editorial "The Roosevelt Way."
The other man is believed to be Richard Fairchild, reporter for the
Chicago Record-Herald.

MONDAY
MAY 26, 1913

Publicity Photo of Theodore Roosevelt

"The unforgivable crime is soft hitting. Do not hit at all if it
can be avoided; but never hit softly."

— Theodore Roosevelt

CHAPTER 1

"**H**E SAYS HE'S NOT GOING," said Delia Richardson, returning to the breakfast nook where her brother Matthew was finishing his scrambled eggs.

"Why not?" Matthew asked, although he didn't need to. He could well imagine what his brother-in-law's reason would be.

"He says it's too early in the morning and he can't afford to be late at the office," Delia replied. "Plus he has a headache."

Matthew grimaced and then sipped his coffee. He knew Roger had a hangover and didn't want to move any faster than he had to this morning.

"And you know how he feels about Roosevelt," Delia continued, as if needing to defend her husband. "He blames Roosevelt for dividing the Republican Party. If it weren't for Roosevelt, Wilson wouldn't be in the White House now."

"Perhaps," said Matthew, "but it isn't every day a former U.S. president visits Marquette, and especially not for a reason that evokes international interest."

"You can't reason with Roger sometimes, Matthew," said Delia, sighing. "You know that."

Matthew didn't comment. Instead, he said, "What about Lydia? Doesn't she want to go?"

"Lydia?" Delia laughed. "She's rarely up before nine. I've warned her that once she's the lady of the house, she won't be able to lie in bed all day. I hope Lysander breaks her of that habit after the wedding."

"When do I get to meet this future husband of hers?" Matthew asked.

"Oh, he's coming over for lunch today," said Delia. "He seems to be here all the time now. It's hard to imagine that my little girl will be getting married in just six more days. I'm so glad you're able to be here for the wedding. How lucky that the Roosevelt trial gave you an extra incentive to come. I'm sure your editor was thrilled to have a reporter on his staff who's from Marquette."

"Yes, he was," said Matthew. Had his editor not given him the assignment, Matthew might have found an excuse not to come for the wedding, but he wouldn't hurt Delia's feelings now that he was here by admitting that. "Well," he said, changing the subject, "should we get going? I don't want to be late if I'm going to get my scoop."

"I'm ready. I just have to put on my coat," said Delia, stepping into the front hall. Matthew stood and for a moment wondered whether he should carry the dishes to the sink, but he knew Delia would only scold him. "That's why we have servants," she would say. Still, being a bachelor, Matthew was used to waiting on himself. Nor would he ever want to have servants.

In another second, he was in the hall with his sister and reaching for his own coat.

"You know I hate that you don't live in Marquette," said Delia, "but it is nice that you can come home to visit and get paid for it."

"When I left Marquette," Matthew admitted, "I never imagined I'd return here to report on a libel trial involving an American president."

"Isn't that the truth," said Delia, opening the front door and stepping outside. "It's a beautiful day. It feels like summer finally."

Matthew thought it was still a bit chilly out, but it was only quarter after seven. Roosevelt's train was to arrive at 7:45, and it would take a good twenty minutes to walk from Roger and Delia's house on Marquette's east side to the train depot. Roger could have driven them in his automobile, but since he had decided not to go with them and needed to go to his office, he would be using it himself. Since Roger did not open his office until nine o'clock, Matthew knew his brother-in-law had no reason to worry he'd be late; he was only being difficult, but Matthew did not mind walking, and years ago, he had quit taking offense at Roger's mood swings.

For a few minutes, Matthew and Delia walked along in silence until they came to Ridge Street and turned west toward the downtown. Then Delia remarked, "I wish Frances were here so I'd have a chance of getting to meet Roosevelt."

Frances was the daughter of the late Peter White, one of Marquette's founders and most successful businessmen. He had become known as the Honorable Peter White for his political services and Marquette's Grand Old Man for his many acts of philanthropy. White had died five years before, leaving his house to his only surviving child, Frances, and her husband, George Shiras III. Shiras was a former Congressman, an internationally famous wildlife photographer, and the son of Supreme Court Justice George Shiras II. In his home, Shiras would be hosting Colonel Roosevelt—as he preferred to be called since he was no longer president—and many of those who were coming to Marquette to testify on his behalf. Unfortunately, Frances was out East at the moment with her children; she had been unable to change her plans to return in time for the trial and play hostess to the former president.

Delia had scarcely finished her wish to meet Roosevelt before she and Matthew heard a motorcar approaching them from behind. When the driver honked his horn, it startled Delia. Matthew turned around to see that the automobile had stopped just feet behind them and its driver was waving at them.

"Speak of the devil," muttered Delia, who had now also turned around.

"Matthew! I thought it was you!" exclaimed George Shiras III, quickly climbing out of his vehicle and rushing forward to shake Matthew's hand.

Matthew laughed and shook his old friend's hand—he couldn't quite say they were friends now, but they had been once, and he felt pleasantly surprised. "It's good to see you, George," he said. "You must be on your way to pick up Colonel Roosevelt."

"Yes," said George. "I'm a little early, but I didn't want to take any chances. I didn't know you were in town, Matthew."

"He's here to report on the trial," said Delia.

"I should have known," said George.

"Isn't that something," Delia added, "an all-expenses-paid trip to his hometown for business?"

"You must be on your way to the depot then," said George. "Would you care for a ride? Of course, I'll have to bring Theodore back home with me so I can't give you a ride back, but you're welcome to a ride there."

"Oh, think of it, Matthew," said Delia, laughing. "We get to ride in the same car Colonel Roosevelt will be riding in."

Matthew felt he should decline, but Delia seemed too pleased for him not to accept.

"Let me help you in," said George, and he gave his hand to Delia as she stepped up into the automobile and settled herself in the backseat.

"Thank you, George," said Matthew, now climbing into the front seat while George went around to get in on the driver's side. As they started back down the street, Matthew thought about how many years it had been since he had seen George or felt friendly toward him.

"I understand Frances didn't come home. I saw your niece, Frances Reynolds, yesterday," added Delia, using Peter White's granddaughter's name in full to avoid confusion between her and the aunt she was named for, "and she said Frances wouldn't be coming home. I don't know how she could miss the opportunity to be hostess to a former president."

"Well, Frances has met Theodore plenty of times in Washington so the magic of his presence has worn off on her, I guess. And the servants are more than capable of making sure he and all our other guests will be comfortable."

"Other guests?" said Matthew. "Who else will be staying with you?"

"Who isn't?" said George, as he started the car moving west along Ridge Street. "Sixteen people total, all of the rest of them witnesses also; Gifford Pinchot for one, and Edmund Heller—he traveled with Theodore in Africa—and then some of the other witnesses will be staying with some of my relatives."

Matthew knew the Whites and Shirases were related to half the wealthy families living on Ridge Street so he didn't bother to ask which other relatives.

"I never thought I'd see the day when so many famous people would be coming to Marquette," said Delia. "I understand President Garfield's son is coming too as one of the witnesses."

"Yes," said George. "And Jacob Riis, the reformer—he's a great friend of Theodore's—and also some of Theodore's bodyguards and Secret Service men and his former cabinet members."

"Matthew knows Jacob Riis," Delia mentioned.

"You do?" said George, surprised.

"Yes," Matthew replied. "Years ago, I spent an evening with him and Roosevelt walking the streets of New York City when they were trying to stop police corruption when Roosevelt was the police commissioner there. He's quite an interesting man, Riis."

"That he is," said George. "I don't know him that well, but I know Theodore thinks the world of him. And so you've obviously met Theodore before as well."

"Yes," said Matthew, "but it's been several years now so I doubt he remembers me."

By now they were at the corner of Front Street. George turned to drive down the hill through the downtown to the train depot.

Matthew could not help staring at the towering Savings Bank with its clock as they approached Washington Street. It was the tallest building in Marquette, six stories, though only four stories faced Front Street. In New York, it would have been dwarfed by many other buildings, but here, it gave Marquette a metropolitan flair, especially for a small city that had been home to less than ten thousand people when the bank had been built in 1891, several years after Matthew had moved away. Marquette had certainly changed from the frontier village Matthew had known when he had come here as a young boy soon after the Civil War.

Front Street in Marquette, circa 1913. The Savings Bank is the tall building with the clock tower on the left.

"I wonder whether there'll be a crowd," said Delia.

"I doubt it," said George. "It's awful early in the morning."

"You never know," said Matthew. "It is a former president coming to town, after all."

"Oh, everyone in Marquette is excited," said Delia, as they approached Main Street and George turned toward the depot.

There was a crowd, not anywhere near the six thousand who had crowded the depot area when Roosevelt had spoken there while campaigning the October before, but probably two hundred people were standing about, waiting for the train scheduled to arrive within a quarter of an hour.

George parked his vehicle. Matthew and Delia quickly thanked him for the ride before he was approached by a policeman, who was obviously there for security purposes. The officer wanted to discuss Roosevelt's exit in George's vehicle.

Delia and Matthew now joined the crowd of curiosity-seekers, several of whom they knew—with a population of nearly twelve thousand, almost everyone knew everyone else in Marquette, and if they didn't know someone, they knew the same people that person knew. Matthew's wait for the train was quickly taken up by old acquaintances greeting him and asking him how life was in New York. A few minutes later, the sound and then the sight of the train's approach drew everyone's rapt attention.

The spectators felt excitement and a little impatience as they waited for the train to come to a full stop. Once it did, some railroad employees disembarked from it and a few police stepped forward so the Colonel wouldn't be mobbed by the crowd. A few men stepped off the train—Matthew recognized most of them as witnesses—prominent men he had met when reporting in Washington; he had even interviewed one or two of them himself in the past—the social reformer Jacob Riis; James Garfield, son of former President Garfield and Roosevelt's Secretary of the Interior when he had been in office; also Gifford Pinchot, former chief of the United States Forest Service; Robert Bacon, former Assistant Secretary of State; and George Cortelyou, Roosevelt's former Secretary of the Treasury, who had also served as Postmaster General and Secretary of Commerce at different times. In all, about twenty of Roosevelt's intimate friends had come with him to testify at the trial, a few of them even being Roosevelt cousins. People in the crowd, however, did not recognize most of these men by their faces, so it was not until Colonel Roosevelt himself stepped off the train that a few young women squealed with excitement and then applause broke out for the former president. The crowd was not large, but Roosevelt was welcomed warmly by everyone.

In a moment, Roosevelt was surrounded by reporters and spectators. Normally, Matthew would have pushed forward to get his scoop, but he did not want to abandon his sister on the platform, so he stood back, trying to hear what he could.

After generously answering several questions about the trial, which Matthew unfortunately could not quite hear, Roosevelt finally said, "That's enough questions for now. There will be plenty of time for more as the trial progresses. Thank you for your warm greeting."

"Thank you, Mr. Roosevelt," said several reporters as the police tried to move back the crowd so Roosevelt could depart. At some point, George had made his way through the crowd, and he was now guiding Roosevelt toward his automobile.

"I have the car waiting just over there," Matthew heard George say, taking Roosevelt's arm to guide him in the right direction.

"Mr. Roosevelt, won't you take just one more question?" shouted a reporter.

Roosevelt smiled but waved him off, though he shook hands with many well-wishers as he headed toward the automobile. He was now only ten feet away from Matthew and Delia so they could hear what he said.

"Mr. Roosevelt," said a local man as Roosevelt shook his hand, "my wife and I would be honored if you would join us to see *The Prince of Pilsen* at the opera house on Thursday night."

Roosevelt smiled at him and graciously said, "I much appreciate the offer, but I am here on business, not for my own enjoyment, and I do not want my presence at social activities to affect the course of justice, so I must respectfully decline. Plus, I think it would be best given the circumstances surrounding this trial that no one confuses my going to see *The Prince of Pilsen* with drinking Pilsener beer."

The crowd roared at the joke, for the confusion between the words Pilsen and Pilsener was a well-known trademark of the popular play. Clearly, Roosevelt had seen it before. But while the mix-up between a Cincinnati brewer and a European prince made for good comedy onstage, a mix-up between a drunkard and a former president was not so funny in real life. Matthew, however, was very fond of the play, so he made a mental note to take Delia to see it later that week.

Other invitations for the former president followed, which Roosevelt also kindly turned down—from dinner invitations to an offer of free tickets to see the high school's production of another popular play, *The Chimes of Normandy*. Roosevelt's cheerful and gracious manner of refusal left no one feeling slighted, and Matthew marveled at how everyone clearly liked Roosevelt, inviting him into their homes as if they knew him personally. He suspected Delia would have invited the former president to dinner herself if she could get him alone, but she was too proud to make an invitation likely to be refused in public.

After one more thank you, Roosevelt said, "I must go with my host now and meet with my attorneys before the trial begins. I wish you all a good day." Then with Secret Service men and police closing in around him, Roosevelt made his way down the path the crowd had opened up for him, and soon he was beside George Shiras' automobile.

Shiras had the honor of opening the door himself for his illustrious friend, and then Roosevelt climbed into the back of the automobile, followed by the naturalist Edmund Heller and Frank Tyree, who had been Roosevelt's bodyguard while he was president and seemed to be playing that role again today. Once everyone was seated and comfortable, Shiras walked around the automobile to take a seat behind the wheel.

Apparently, some other vehicles were also waiting—perhaps those of George's relatives, since the rest of the witnesses soon piled into them after a few introductions and a bit of confusion over who should ride with whom and what to do with the luggage.

Just as Matthew thought George would now drive off, he saw his former friend lean back and say something to Roosevelt. Then Roosevelt turned, looked straight at Matthew, and said, "It's good to see you again, Mr. Newman. You must visit George and me while I'm here."

Matthew was stunned by the remark. He had often been assigned to cover stories concerning Roosevelt when he was a police commissioner in New York City, but that had been nearly twenty years ago. Matthew certainly hadn't expected Roosevelt to remember him. Was George trying to put in a good word for him so he could get a better story for his newspaper? Matthew wouldn't put it past George to show him such kindness—but was it kindness, or some form of compensation to make up for the past? Did George even realize he had anything to compensate for? Well, truthfully, perhaps George was the one he should compensate for the jealousy he'd held inside all these years.

Matthew would question George's motive later, but for now, all he could think to say was, "Thank you, Colonel Roosevelt. It's a pleasure to see you in my hometown."

Roosevelt flashed his famous smile, and then the automobile was heading toward Front Street, and in another minute, the entire caravan for the plaintiff was out of sight.

"How exciting, Matthew," said Delia, squeezing his arm.

"I can't believe Colonel Roosevelt even remembers me," he replied.

"If you get to go over to George and Frances' house to see him, you must tell me all about it," she said.

"I doubt he'll have time to see me personally," said Matthew. "George was just trying to be kind."

"There's nothing wrong with that," said Delia.

"No," said Matthew, taking out his pocket watch to check the time. He wanted to make sure he had plenty of time to write up a story about Roosevelt's arrival. "Well, we should get back. Are you ready to head home?"

"I suppose," said Delia. "None of the stores are open yet, and I don't need anything anyway. What do you want to do until the trial starts? It starts at two, right?"

"Yes, but I need to write up a story about Roosevelt's arrival and maybe something about Marquette itself to send to my editor today," said Matthew. "After I do that, though, we can have lunch together, and then I can get to the courthouse early enough to wire my story before the trial starts."

"You are going to take me to the courthouse with you?" asked Delia.

"Yes, that's another reason for us to get there early. There are seats reserved for the press, but I imagine a crowd of people will be wanting to get in."

"Then we'll have an early lunch and camp out on the steps if need be so I get a seat," Delia replied.

With that decided, brother and sister linked arms and headed home, following the route Roosevelt had just taken.

The Mining Journal, May 26, 1913
Marquette businesses tied Roosevelt into their ads during the trial,
as if to suggest he endorsed their merchandise.

CHAPTER 2

B Y THE TIME MATTHEW AND Delia were back home, Roger had already left for his office, but Lydia was still in bed. It was past eight-thirty, but it was none of Matthew's business how late his niece lay abed. Perhaps she just wanted to get her beauty sleep so she'd be ready for the wedding on Sunday.

"Oh, I forgot that Lysander is coming by for lunch. I hope we'll still have enough time to get to the courthouse early," said Delia.

"We just have to," said Matthew. He was always punctual if not early, especially when it concerned his reporting duties. He would not disappoint Josiah Pritchard, his editor at the *Empire Sentinel*, by missing even one moment of the trial.

"Well," Delia replied, "he should be here a few minutes after twelve. That's when he usually takes his lunch break at the bank, and he'll have to be back to work by one, so we can leave by then. We should be there by one-thirty certainly."

Matthew grimaced and got a bit of a knot in his stomach. The trial would not start until two; half an hour should be enough time to wire his story and find their seats, but he'd have rather had an hour to be safe.

"All right," he said, trying to remain calm. "I better go up to my room now and write my story."

"Wouldn't you be more comfortable downstairs?" asked Delia. "You could use Roger's study."

"No, my room is fine," said Matthew. The servants would be wandering in and out of the downstairs rooms, and frankly, their presence always made him feel nervous and distracted.

Five minutes later, Matthew was seated at his desk in the guest bedroom and scribbling away. He didn't have much material from Roosevelt's arrival, but he tried to fill space by creating a human interest story out of the northern city he called home.

> Former U.S. President Theodore Roosevelt arrived in Marquette, Michigan, on Monday morning, May 26, to be greeted by a small crowd of onlookers and reporters, all there to welcome the famous politician to their town. Roosevelt is not visiting this northern city for pleasure, however. Rather, he is there to partake in the role of plaintiff in a libel trial. George Newett, proprietor of the Ishpeming, Michigan newspaper the *Iron Ore*, accused Roosevelt of being a drunkard in an editorial following Roosevelt's campaign stop in Marquette last October. Roosevelt has filed suit against the newspaperman for blackening his good name.
>
> Whatever the outcome of this infamous trial will be, the ugliness of the allegedly libelous charge is offset by the beautiful setting where the case will play out.
>
> Marquette is a small but proud city on the shore of Lake Superior. In the last couple of decades, it has become known as the Queen City of the North. Despite a population of just under twelve thousand, the city is home to many of the most important mining, lumber, and banking magnates in the United States. It is also the summer home of former Supreme Court Justice George Shiras, Jr. In fact, Justice Shiras' son, George Shiras III, the award-winning photographer of nighttime wildlife and a frequent contributor to *National Geographic* as well as a former member of the U.S. Congress, will host Roosevelt at his home. Shiras and Roosevelt have been good friends for a number of years due to their shared interest in wildlife and conservation issues....

As Matthew wrote, he could not help but marvel that the enthusiastic young George Shiras he had known as a boy had grown up to be a famous conservationist, photographer, and even politician. Matthew imagined George largely had his father-in-law, Peter White, to thank for that, as well as his father and grandfather, who had been enthusiastic fishermen in their days. George had been lucky compared to Matthew and his father, who had rarely found time to go fishing, at least together. They'd had the family store to run, so the two of them could never leave it unattended except on Sunday, and then only for church. Matthew's mother had forbidden them to go fishing on Sunday afternoons, saying it was a sin, and Matthew's father had silently kept the peace by agreeing with her.

Matthew had loved his father dearly, but he had often wished the store was not like a noose around their necks. He had sometimes imagined—though he felt such a thought might also be a sin, and more so than fishing on Sunday—that he would have preferred to have Peter White as his father. Mr. White always seemed to have time to go out to his camp or to do anything he wanted, even though he owned a bank and an insurance agency and was involved in who knew how many other business ventures. Peter White was successful enough that he could pay people to run things when he was away—Matthew's father was not so fortunate.

As a young boy, Matthew had seen Peter White around town, though he had not known rightly who he was, being still too young to care who was prominent in Marquette in those days. It wasn't until he was eleven and working as a clerk in his father's store that he truly got to know Mr. White.

Matthew vividly remembered that first meeting with Marquette's Grand Old Man, although no one considered him grand yet, being only forty, but Peter White was already rich, owning the bank and having just built his fine home on Ridge Street—the first of several mansion-sized houses. It had been during that meeting that Matthew had also first been introduced to George Shiras III.

To the best of his memory, Matthew thought it was the summer of 1870 when he and George had met. He had been working alone in the store, so it must have been lunchtime; his father had probably gone into the family dining room behind the storefront to eat with his mother and sister while Matthew watched the counter; Matthew would eat later when his father came to relieve him. It was then that Peter White entered the store with another man and two boys.

Mr. White had been in the store before, but Matthew's father had always made it a point to assist him personally. After all, Mr. White had no shortage of money to spend, so Mr. Newman wanted to please him all he could.

But today, Matthew didn't have time to duck through the back door and into their living quarters to fetch his father because the youngest boy in the party, who couldn't be more than six, marched straight up to the counter and proclaimed to Matthew, "I want a fishing pole!"

"You do?" said Matthew, amused by the boy's eagerness. "Well, I think a fishing pole is a very fine thing to want."

"I'm going to catch a big trout, like this," said the boy, and he spread his arms so wide that Matthew doubted a trout that size could be found in Lake Superior.

Peter White, who had now joined his son at the counter, said, "Hello. It's Matthew, right?"

"Yes, sir," said Matthew, starting to feel nervous.

"I don't know if you know my son, Morgan," said Mr. White, smiling. "He likes to exaggerate, so I think he'll make a wonderful fisherman someday."

Mr. White's humor instantly put Matthew at his ease.

"My papa's going to teach me to fish," Morgan told Matthew. "Do you go fishing with your papa?"

Matthew hesitated and then frowned a bit before saying, "No, but I wish I could."

"Why don't you?" demanded Morgan.

"Because my father and I have to take turns watching the store, so I usually go fishing alone or sometimes with a friend."

"Oh, so what kindsa fishing poles do you got?" Morgan asked, either uninterested or satisfied with Matthew's explanation.

"I'll show you," said Matthew, stepping out from behind the counter and over to the wall where all the fishing paraphernalia was kept.

"Wow, Papa. Look at all of them. I like this one," said Morgan, reaching up to grab one off the wall. Peter White grabbed it first before his son could knock it over.

"That one's a bit large for you, Morgan," said Mr. White. Then he turned to Matthew. "Do you have anything Morgan's size?"

Matthew drew their attention to a smaller fishing pole designed for boys.

"But that one's small," said Morgan, smirking his disapproval.

"It doesn't matter," said Matthew. "What matters is—"

"It does, too," Morgan interrupted, "because I need a big one to catch a big fish."

"Hold on, Morgan," Mr. White said. "Let Matthew finish his explanation before you protest."

"Morgan," said Matthew, squatting down to be at the boy's eye level, "you don't need a big pole to catch a big fish because the pole just stays above the water. It's the hook the fish is interested in—or actually what you have on the hook to lure him in—and that should be a big juicy worm. As long as you have some juicy worms, you can catch the biggest fish in the lake."

"Oh," said Morgan, nodding his head up and down as if this all made perfect sense.

"Yes, sir," said Matthew. "The bigger and juicier the worm, the bigger the fish you'll catch."

"George knows how to dig for big juicy worms," said Morgan, gesturing toward the other boy in the store. Matthew looked over at the boy while Morgan continued to speak. He realized George must be about his age. He also noticed that George had been watching them. "George says you have to get worms when they're out crawling around at night. Then you can sneak up on them easily because they can't see you in the dark."

"Well," said Matthew, turning his gaze back to Morgan, "I would say that George knows his worm business very well. With this fishing pole and the worms your friend George will help you find, I think you'll catch a mighty fine-sized fish indeed."

Peter White laughed and then asked, "What do you think, Morgan? Should we get this fishing pole?"

"Yes," said Morgan, jumping up and down.

"We'll get some of these fishing hooks too," Mr. White told Matthew, selecting a packet of them.

"Very good, sir," said Matthew. He took the fishing pole and the hooks over to the counter and began to write out an invoice so Mr. White could pay for them.

A few minutes later, Morgan had his fishing pole in hand and was pretending to cast it. When the boy nearly knocked over a display, Mr. White quickly took the pole from him and said, before his son could protest, "Morgan, let's go outside with it. You can practice casting it better out there."

Matthew smiled gratefully at Mr. White for preventing an accident in the store. Mr. White winked at him, and then father and son departed while the other two in their party brought a few items up to the counter to purchase. Matthew did not know who the man was, but he accepted his payment and thanked him. Then the man turned to George and said, "Son, I'll wait for you outside."

"Okay," said George, as his father turned to leave. Then he set some fish hooks on the counter and dug in his pocket for his wallet.

"You did very well with Morgan," said George. "He can be a handful sometimes."

"Well," said Matthew, "I imagine we were too when we were his age."

"True enough," said George. "I'm George Shiras by the way." He gave Matthew his hand to shake. As Matthew took it, he looked George straight in the eye and saw sincere friendliness there that made him like George instantly.

"I'm Matthew Newman," Matthew replied. "Are you new to Marquette? I've never seen you around here before."

"No, not really new. My father comes up here fishing every year and my grandfather too. They've been coming up here since Marquette was founded, and now this year I'm joining them. We're from Pennsylvania; not Mr. White and his son, though. They're from here."

"Yes," said Matthew. "Everyone knows Mr. White. But Marquette's a long way to come from Pennsylvania just to go fishing."

"It is," said George, "but we love the scenery up here and my family has gotten to know Mr. White and his family very well so we keep coming back. That, plus I think our Scottish blood naturally yearns to be farther north. There's nowhere like the rugged coast of Lake Superior."

"I have to agree with you," said Matthew. "My family came here from New York. I was probably about Morgan's age when we got here, so I barely remember New York now. I know I wouldn't want to live anywhere else than Marquette."

"You're lucky that you get to live here year-round," George replied. "So how much do I owe you?"

Matthew totaled the items being purchased and then George paid him.

"Well, I'm sure I'll be in to get some more hooks soon," George said when their transaction was concluded. "I always manage to lose a few."

"We all do," said Matthew, smiling.

"George, are you coming?" asked his father, sticking his head back in the door.

"I better go," George said, and he again reached his hand across the counter to Matthew. "It was a pleasure meeting you, Mr. Newman."

"Same here," said Matthew, feeling a little intimidated by George's good manners.

And then George departed, and Matthew was left with an inexplicable feeling that he had just met someone very important in his life, although he couldn't say why.

"I still like George, even now," he said to himself as he put down his pen and stretched his hands to avoid writer's cramp. He'd been at his trade so long that he could easily whip out copy while thinking on another topic. He quickly read over what he had written and made a few tweaks to it, but he found he was more focused on hoping he would see George again this week than on the upcoming trial. Somehow, he was starting to think maybe he owed George an apology, although George might not even know it.

"Matrimony always is a lottery."
— *The Prince of Pilsen*

CHAPTER 3

MATTHEW HAD LAIN DOWN TO take a little rest after writing his column. He had half an hour until lunchtime, and he was exhausted from traveling, not having arrived in Marquette until almost suppertime the day before. A nap would ensure he didn't fall asleep during the trial this afternoon.

A few minutes before noon, Martha, the maid, knocked on his door and said, "Sir, luncheon is being served."

"Thank you," Matthew called through the door. Then he got up, quickly combed his hair, and put back on the suit coat he had removed earlier so he wouldn't wrinkle it while lying down.

Two minutes later, he was entering the dining room where he found his sister and niece already seated, along with a young man who had his back to him.

"There's Matthew," said Delia, upon seeing him. The moment she spoke, the young man stood and turned around, quickly offering Matthew his hand. "Pleased to meet you, sir."

Matthew was struck by how tall he was—he exceeded Matthew's height by a couple of inches—and Matthew couldn't help noticing his abundantly dark, thick hair, and the mustache that slightly curled at the ends. The word "nefarious" popped into Matthew's head, but he instantly dismissed it, politely smiled, and said, "You must be Mr. Blackmore."

"Lysander, please," Lydia's fiancé replied. "After all, we're about to be family, and if you don't mind, I'll call you Uncle Matthew like your niece does."

Matthew did mind, but he did not say so. In truth, he had never felt much like an uncle, not having been around for any of Lydia's childhood. But he nodded his head in acceptance. Then he stepped over to the empty chair and, seating himself, said, "That soup certainly smells good."

Martha had been dishing out the soup as he entered, and she now set a bowlful in front of him.

"Thank you," Matthew said, taking his napkin and placing it on his lap. "Isn't Roger joining us?"

"No, he usually doesn't come home for lunch," said Delia. "He prefers to eat downtown. Sometimes he takes his clients out for lunch and a drink."

Matthew was not surprised, especially by the drink. Turning to Lysander, who had also reseated himself, he said, "So, I understand you're a banker."

"Yes," Lysander replied, spreading his napkin on his lap. "It's a good business. Plenty of money to be made handling other people's money."

"I daresay," said Matthew, who had many times reported on bank failures, especially during the Panic of 1893 and its aftermath. He was no fan of bankers nor speculators.

"Lysander is Nathan Kaufman's godson," said Lydia, "so he got a good foot into the banking business that way." Matthew knew Nathan Kaufman had been the founder of the Savings Bank downtown. The Kaufmans were an upstart family—beginning with a family store and eventually rivaling Peter White in Marquette banking. There had been a time, Matthew remembered, when they were no more prominent than his father had been.

"I see," said Matthew. "I seem to remember your father from when I lived here—didn't he have a business of his own for you to take over?"

"He was in real estate mostly," said Lysander, "but he and mother have both passed on now—Dad a few years ago and Mother last winter. Uncle Nathan—he isn't really my uncle, but he and my father were close friends, you understand—he made sure I had a good position. Father and I never really saw eye to eye on things, so it was for the best I didn't work with him."

"I'm sorry for your loss," said Matthew. He didn't see any sign of mourning among the young man's attire, and to marry just a few months after your mother's death seemed too soon to him, but then, he reminded himself, these days, sincerity and sentiment counted for little, unlike in his mourned-for nineteenth century.

"Thank you," Lysander replied. "In any case, my parents left me their house and plenty of land, so be assured that your niece will be well-provided for."

"I am thankful for that," said Matthew. From all appearances, Delia was well-provided for also, but Matthew often questioned whether Roger's money could make up for the obvious lack of affection between them. He hoped that would not be the case for Lydia.

"Lydia tells me you're a reporter in New York," said Lysander. "I'm afraid I've forgotten the name of the paper, however."

"*The Empire Sentinel*," Matthew replied. "Yes, I've been with it for most of my career. I started out at a couple of smaller newspapers, but I've been there for twenty-two years now."

"And you're here to report on the Roosevelt trial?" asked Lysander.

"That's right."

"Do you think it's true—the rumors that Roosevelt is a drunkard?" Lysander asked. He took a sip of his tea, but his eyes peered mischievously over the rim of his cup as he waited for Matthew to answer.

"I don't think it's my place to speculate on it," Matthew replied. "As a reporter, I have to focus on the facts and keep my opinions to myself."

"Well, Mr. Newett certainly doesn't think that way."

"Mr. Newett wrote an editorial, which is an opinion piece, of course," Matthew replied. "I will say this, however. Like any man, I am sure Roosevelt has his flaws, but I reported on Roosevelt many times when he was police commissioner for New York City. I even once had the honor of walking the police beat with him and Jacob Riis when they were cleaning up the corruption and moral depravity in the city. I think Roosevelt a very good, moral man for that reason. I'm also very impressed with his conservation efforts."

Lysander smirked. "A waste of good land if you ask me. Just wait until oil or gold or something is discovered in those parks—then all ideas of conserving them will be forgotten."

"Hopefully," said Matthew, "that will never happen since no one will have the right to mine or drill in them."

"Money speaks louder than pretty landscapes," Lysander replied. "You just wait and see."

"Lysander knows a lot about land," Lydia chimed in. "He learned it from his father, even though he decided to go into banking; in fact, he inherited several rental properties from his parents, and he's involved in the mortgage business through the bank."

"And his parents left him a beautiful home just around the corner," added Delia. "It has such beautiful wallpaper. Your mother, Lysander, had such good taste."

What do I care about wallpaper? thought Matthew. He suddenly felt as if his sister and niece were ganging up on him to convince him of Lysander's good qualities—although those qualities all centered on how wealthy and fashionable he was.

"Thank you, Mother," said Lysander. Matthew felt the urge to slap him for calling Delia that. "And my home will be even more beautiful once it has a new mistress."

Lysander flashed Lydia a smile, which she returned. Matthew told himself to stay calm. He had to admit Lysander was moderately handsome, and his financial portfolio seemed sound, but he still couldn't see what the attraction was for Lydia. He felt like the man was just feeding her a line to get something from her—probably a strengthened position in society. Roger's family had always been among the foremost in Marquette society, and the more Matthew thought about it, the more certain he was that he had heard rumors that the late Mr. Blackmore had been less than honest in his dealings. He had come to Marquette without a penny to his name in the mid-1870s, as Matthew recalled, but he had quickly amassed a fortune. And hadn't there been some story about a lawsuit over a bad deed he had sold to Mr. Longyear? Matthew had also heard, most likely from his mother, that when several of Marquette's wealthiest men had formed the hunting and fishing club north of Marquette—the Huron Mountain Club—Mr. Blackmore had been denied membership. The Kaufmans had also not been allowed in, so what did that say about Lysander having Nathan Kaufman for his godfather? In any case, by marrying Lydia, perhaps Lysander was trying to whitewash the Blackmore name.

"Matthew, you should see the beautiful wedding gown Lydia will have," said Delia.

"I imagine I will see it on Sunday," he replied.

"It's white, of course, but it has little pink roses around the neckline, and...."

And Matthew quit listening at this point. Wedding preparations did not interest him, and as the others discussed them, his thoughts turned to the upcoming trial; he just occasionally muttered a reply to something his dinner companions said to be polite.

Once he had finished his soup and sandwich, Matthew scooted back his chair and said, "It's almost one o'clock. We'd better get going if we want to get you a seat at the trial, Delia."

"Would you like to go with us, Lydia?" Delia asked.

"No," Lydia replied. Then she turned to explain to Matthew, "My maid of honor is coming over and we're going downtown to do some last minute shopping for the wedding."

"I need to go upstairs and freshen up before we go," said Delia.

"Hurry up then," said Matthew. "I have to wire my story to the *Sentinel* before the trial starts."

"Where will you send a wire from?" Lysander asked.

"At the courthouse," Matthew replied. "They're supposed to have several extra telegraphs set up there, which reminds me, I better go upstairs to fetch my story. Excuse me."

Matthew rose from his seat, but before he could leave the room, Lysander said, "I'd be happy to give you a ride to the courthouse on my way back to the bank."

"Oh, that's out of your way, Lysander," said Delia.

"Nonsense. It will only take me a moment," said Lysander, smiling.

Matthew could see the young man was trying to ingratiate himself with his future mother-in-law. *Perhaps,* Matthew thought, *I'm just imagining things, but something about this young man just doesn't sit right with me.* Nevertheless, he said, "I won't refuse a ride then since it'll save us time. Thank you, Lysander."

"My pleasure," Lysander replied.

Matthew and Delia now went upstairs to get ready. Lydia and Lysander were still in the dining room when Matthew came downstairs five minutes later. He could hear them whispering in the dining room, but tempted as he was to enter it, he stayed in the hall. The last thing he wanted was to see Lysander and his niece locked in a lover's embrace. He was relieved when Delia came downstairs a minute later before the maid found him hiding in the hall.

"We're ready, Lysander!" Delia called, walking past the dining room without looking in. Martha now appeared in the hall to help Delia on with her hat and gloves. Meanwhile, Lysander took his time saying his final goodbye to Lydia. Matthew was about to holler that they better get going just as the young man appeared in the hall.

"Thank you again for the ride," Matthew said, trying to contain his irritation. Lysander simply nodded, which caused Matthew to note the glazed look in his eyes.

"We'll be home for supper, Lydia," Delia called from the hall. "I left instructions with Mrs. Honeywell, so you don't need to worry about it." Mrs. Honeywell was the Richardsons' cook.

"Okay, Mother," Lydia hollered back rather than coming out into the hall to say goodbye.

The Marquette County Courthouse, scene of the Roosevelt Trial.
Pictured here on the day of its dedication September 17, 1904.

CHAPTER 4

B Y AUTOMOBILE, IT WAS ONLY a five-minute drive from the Richardsons' house to the Marquette County Courthouse where the already famous Roosevelt vs. Newett trial was about to commence. Matthew was grateful for the ride, and equally grateful that the open automobile and its noise made conversation impractical. The less he had to speak to Lysander, the less likely he would say something he would regret.

"What a crowd!" exclaimed Lysander as he pulled up in front of the courthouse. Matthew climbed out and then helped Delia down while Lysander continued to gaze at the flood of people gathered on the courthouse's front steps and lawn. "What a waste of time just to see a former president," he added.

"Thank you for the ride, Lysander," said Delia, leaving Matthew unsure whether she had heard her future son-in-law's remark.

Lysander tipped his hat and flashed his irritating, ingratiating smile. Then he roared off in his automobile. Rather than voice his opinion about Lysander to his sister, Matthew decided they better just get inside the courthouse as quickly as possible.

Taking Delia's arm, Matthew walked her up the sidewalk. As they approached the stately building, Matthew was struck by how large and grand it looked. How much Marquette had changed since his childhood! When he had come to Marquette as a young boy just after the Civil War, Marquette had hardly been more than a frontier town. Its courthouse had been a fairly new structure, a two-story wooden building with shuttered windows and a pillar-supported portico. But in 1904, it had been torn down and replaced with this gigantic red-colored Lake Superior sandstone temple to justice that covered an entire city block and was complete with a copper-plated dome, massive columns, and stained-glass windows. While most courthouses had towers and Victorian style embellishments, this modern building proclaimed itself the master of Marquette County and everything within it. In fact, Matthew thought it would easily fit in among New York City's finest municipal buildings, save for its distinctive local stone. Matthew was pleased when he heard a couple of his fellow newsmen remark how surprised they were that such a building should be here in the middle of the Upper Peninsula, which to them was seemingly nowhere.

The courtroom itself would not open until 1:50, but Matthew and Delia entered the building now so he could make his way to the press room where the telegraphs were set up. Fortunately, since the trial hadn't yet started, only one other reporter was there sending a dispatch. Delia found a seat in the press room and waited patiently for Matthew as he wired his story. Then they returned to the main hall and waited for the doors to open. A number of reporters were gathered in the hall and upon the stairs, waiting to enter the upstairs courtroom. Matthew knew the members of the press would be let in first, so he hoped to sneak Delia in on his arm so she could get a good seat ahead of the rest of the crowd. But they had several minutes to wait, and so many women had come to view the trial that Delia kept Matthew busy introducing him to her many friends and acquaintances. Despite her position in Marquette society, Delia was still the open-hearted person she had been as a girl, so she was just as friendly to the wives of miners and dock workers as she was to those married to mining magnates and living on Ridge Street. In fact, Matthew recalled, it was her open-heartedness that had ultimately led to her marrying Roger—something she had not let Matthew talk her out of when he had tried.

When the courtroom doors did open, Matthew took Delia in on his arm, and once she had found a seat, he parted from her, making his way to the seats reserved for the press while she sat in one of those reserved for women, who had been given priority over men.

Matthew found himself impressed by the courtroom, and once he found his seat, he spent a moment looking about him at the walls, ceiling, and galleries. But his attention was quickly drawn to the matter at hand when several gentleman entered the courtroom, causing a stir among his fellow reporters.

Matthew was glad when the reporter seated next to him said, "That one's Newett. The one who looks pale. Those are his lawyers with him."

Matthew could not help thinking he would be pale too if he were being sued by a former president of the United States. However, Newett seemed calm, rather than agitated, as he took a seat at the defendant's table between

Courtroom in which the trial was held.

his attorneys. He sat there stiffly, scarcely moving except when one of his attorneys addressed him. Matthew felt a little sorry for him, but he knew Newett had brought this situation upon himself. Matthew also thought it a shame that, if proven untrue, Newett's libelous statements would reflect poorly on the rest of the press' integrity.

"Did you hear about the insane man?" the reporter next to him now asked Matthew.

"No!" said Matthew, a bit surprised.

"I'm Homer Guck, by the way," said his colleague. "I'm the editor for the *Houghton Mining Gazette*."

"Matthew Newman," Matthew replied, shaking his hand. "From New York—the *Empire Sentinel*."

"I figured you were from one of those big Eastern papers," Homer replied.

"Actually, I grew up in Marquette," said Matthew, "so I'm lucky to be back home to report on the trial, but tell me about the insane man."

"Seems some lunatic wired the judge this morning and told him not to start the trial until he arrived. I've got his name here somewhere," said Homer, searching through his notepad. "Here it is—Jacob Miles. His exact words were 'Don't let this sensational trial continue until I have arrived.' Well, Judge Flannigan turned the message over to Frank Tyree, one of Roosevelt's guards, and Tyree notified the chief of police in Minneapolis, where the wire was sent from. The chief wired back that Miles was insane and had been arrested. I guess they're not taking any chances."

"No," Matthew agreed. "Not after the assassination attempt on Roosevelt last fall."

"It's a shame what an unsafe world we live in now," Homer added. "Roosevelt's a good man. I met him once in—"

But before Homer could finish, everyone's attention turned to the entrance as the bailiff led in the thirty-six prospective jurors. Twelve of them would eventually be chosen for the jury.

The prospective jurors were barely seated before Roosevelt arrived. The former president entered the courtroom flanked by two Secret Service men and accompanied by his own attorneys, James H. Pound of Detroit, William H. Van Benschoten of New York, and William S. Hill of Marquette. Despite Colonel Roosevelt's celebrity status, the room stayed relatively quiet as he took his seat. Everyone present was taking this situation very seriously.

Once Roosevelt's party was seated, the bailiff called the court to order at 2:00 p.m. with the Honorable Richard C. Flannigan presiding.

The first prospective jury member, Mr. Joseph Robear of Ishpeming, was now called forth to be questioned by Roosevelt and Newett's attorneys. James Pound, Roosevelt's attorney, began the interrogation, and it was clear from his questions that he wanted to make certain no one associated with Newett or prejudiced by Roosevelt's statements about the iron industry—the bread and butter of the local community—would be allowed on the jury. Simultaneously, Newett's attorney, William Belden, wanted to make certain no jurors would be influenced by Roosevelt's fame and former positions of power.

Pound began his interview by asking, "Mr. Robear, does the fact that the libel occurred in Ishpeming influence you on this matter?"

"It does not," replied Robear.

"Do you look upon the publication of such a statement about Roosevelt as a joke?" asked Pound.

"No," said Robear. "I wouldn't consider it a joke."

Belden now proceeded with his questions.

"Mr. Robear, would the fact that the plaintiff has been a president of the United States affect you? Would it affect you any different from what you would feel if he was a plain citizen like Mr. Newett?"

"No," said Robear. "That fact wouldn't influence me."

"You wouldn't be influenced by the fact that he has been president?" Belden repeated.

"No, sir," Robear said firmly.

Both Belden and Pound agreed that Robear was an acceptable juror. One juror chosen, eleven seats left to fill, and thirty-five prospective jurors remaining.

Matthew could already see it was going to be a long afternoon.

Next up was Hugo Erickson, also of Ishpeming.

Pound began by rephrasing what would become his standard question. "Would it make any difference to you that one of the party to the suit was a president from the state of New York and the other a neighbor?"

"No," Erickson replied.

"If a newspaper declares someone is guilty of murder or burglary, would you regard it as a joke or a serious matter?"

"Serious," said Erickson.

Pound passed the questioning on to Belden, who asked Erickson, "Do you have a preconceived opinion of the case?"

"No," said Erickson.

"Have you any prejudice as to the right of a newspaper to comment on the actions of a public character?"

"No," repeated Erickson.

"If we should prove that what the defendant wrote against the plaintiff was true, would you have prejudice against the defendant?"

Erickson hesitated. Belden rephrased the question, but Erickson remained uncertain how to answer it.

At Judge Flannigan's suggestion, Erickson was dismissed as a prospective juror.

Next, Charles T. Rutledge, an auto repairman from Ishpeming, was called forth for questioning.

Attorney Pound began his interrogation by asking, "Are you a subscriber of Mr. Newett's paper, the *Iron Ore*?"

"Yes, my father is," said Rutledge. "I know Mr. Newett and repair his automobile."

"Your friendship with the defendant wouldn't bias you in the trial of the case?" asked Pound.

"No, I think I could try it fairly," Rutledge replied.

"What do you think about the law of libels? Is it a joke or a serious matter?"

"I think it is serious," said Rutledge.

"If a man publishes something untruthful about another, you think he should be punished?"

Rutledge's answer, "Yes, I do," was enough for him to be rejected as a juror.

On and on the questioning continued throughout the afternoon. Five potential jurors were dismissed for cause, and two because they simply didn't understand the questions asked of them. One was dismissed because he said he could give a fair decision "regardless of the evidence," which caused a titter of laughter throughout the courtroom. A large, blonde man with a drooping mustache could barely speak a word in reply to the attorneys' questions. His lips would move but no words came out. Judge Flannigan allowed him to recover from his stage fright while another man was questioned, but after an hour, the man was still unable to articulate his words and was dismissed. Later, it would be rumored that in the evening he had been seen through the window of a boardinghouse talking with great animation to a friend—he had finally found his tongue.

By five o'clock, the jury selection was not even close to finished. Judge Flannigan dismissed the court, stating that it would reconvene that evening to complete the jury selection. A murmur filled the courtroom as everyone stood up to collect their belongings and depart. No one was pleased to have to come back that evening, but Matthew knew the trial was too important for him not to be present.

Finding his way to Delia's side, Matthew asked whether she would return that evening with him. "I don't think so," she replied. "I'm tired, and I promised Lydia I would help her with some of the wedding preparations after she went shopping this afternoon."

Matthew could see his sister looked exhausted, probably largely due to boredom, despite a few humorous moments over the course of the afternoon.

"Maybe the walk home will wake us both up," said Matthew.

"It'll do me good to stretch my legs," said Delia, "but we won't eat until six. I don't think you'll have time to get back then for the evening proceedings."

"I was thinking the same thing," said Matthew. "If you don't mind, I think I'll just go to the Hotel Marquette for a quick bite. Several of the newsmen are staying there, so I can have dinner with them and get back quickly rather than walking all the way home for dinner and back…unless you mind walking home by yourself."

Delia rolled her eyes at him as if he were being ridiculous. He knew many women would not want to walk unescorted, especially through the downtown, but Delia was of sturdy pioneer stock despite her ladylike appearance.

"I'm sorry I asked," he said, giving her a kiss on the cheek. "I'll see you this evening then."

"What if it's a late night, though?" asked Delia.

"It's not dark until nine-thirty or so now," Matthew replied. "And even if it's later than that, I know my way. I've walked the streets of New York at night, so I'm sure I'll be perfectly safe in Marquette."

"I imagine you're right," said Delia, and then she opened her purse and gave him the house key. "Here—so you can let yourself in if you are late."

"Thanks. I'll see you tonight then," he said, and then Delia headed out the courtroom door.

Matthew heard a group of people laughing, and then looking around, he saw Homer Guck, the newspaper editor from Houghton, in a corner speaking to Colonel Roosevelt with a few reporters gathered around. Matthew walked over to see what was happening.

"I do remember you," Roosevelt was saying to Homer as Matthew approached the little crowd. "You were the fellow who stopped me at the bridge when I was riding into Santiago."

So that was how Homer had met Roosevelt before, thought Matthew. Apparently, they had both served in the Spanish-American War in Cuba.

"Yes," Homer replied. "Do you remember we made you dig your pass out of your boot before we would let you go into the city?"

"You were doing your duty," Roosevelt replied, "and that's what a good soldier does."

"We were stationed there to keep the soldiers from getting into the city and getting drunk," Homer added.

A thoroughly Rooseveltian smile now spread across the former president's face.

"If you were to say that I looked as though I were riding into Santiago after a drink," said Roosevelt, "you would probably be a most valuable witness for the defense."

Everyone got a good laugh from this remark, and then Colonel Roosevelt and Homer shook hands before Roosevelt turned to leave with his Secret Service men.

"I was meaning to ask you when you had met Roosevelt before," said Matthew, going up to Homer.

"I can't believe he remembered me," Homer replied.

"He remembered me too," said Matthew. "I've met him before also."

"When?" asked Homer.

"Join me for dinner and I'll tell you all about it," said Matthew.

And by the time they had reached the Hotel Marquette, Matthew and Homer had shared several stories about their past reporter experiences meeting celebrities.

The hotel's dining room was already packed when Matthew and Homer entered. There wasn't an empty table, but Charles Osborn, reporter for the

Sault Ste. Marie News, who had been sitting on the other side of Homer in the press box, saw them enter and waved them over to two empty chairs at his table. The fourth chair was taken up by another man Matthew didn't know.

"Thank you," said Matthew, introducing himself to Osborn as he and Homer took their seats.

"Pleasure to meet you, Newman, and this is Mr. Sloan," said Osborn, introducing the other man at the table.

"Just call me Jim," said Mr. Sloan, reaching to shake Matthew and Homer's hands.

"Jim, are you a reporter like Osborn here?" asked Homer.

Jim laughed, which momentarily perplexed Matthew, but then Osborn explained, "Sloan here is a Secret Service agent."

"Oh, I see," said Matthew. "Then you must know Colonel Roosevelt very well."

"I do," said Sloan. "I was with him through most of his presidency, and then I was with President Taft, and now I'm working for President Wilson."

"Then you have my great admiration," said Matthew. "I imagine it's quite a dangerous job to protect the president."

"It is," said Sloan, "but I'm sure being a reporter isn't without its dangers."

"That's true," said Matthew. "I've been lucky, but I've had a few friends who have been roughed up by gangs and thugs when they've tried to print a story someone didn't want told."

"You never hear about problems like that here in Upper Michigan," said Homer.

"Are you ready to order?" asked the waiter, suddenly coming up to their table. Matthew hadn't even seen a menu, but Sloan and Osborn knew what they wanted, so Matthew waited for the others to order and then decided he'd have meatloaf like the rest of them to make it easy on both the waiter and the cook.

By now, the dining room was filled to capacity—so many people were talking that Matthew found it difficult to hear his dinner companions. Sloan was saying something about how he had never seen Roosevelt drink more than one or two drinks at any given time in his life and he would tell the jury so. Osborn and Homer were asking him questions about the Secret Service, but Matthew was suddenly feeling exhausted, and the noise in the room didn't help, so he was mostly silent.

Then Matthew realized a young man was standing beside him.

"Gentleman, may I join you?" he asked. The man was tall and had an impressive mustache. His clothes looked expensive, too. He seemed familiar, but Matthew didn't think he was a reporter.

"Of course," said Osborn. "It's a beastly crowded place, but there are two empty chairs at that table."

The man grabbed the two chairs from the other table without asking permission and pushed them up to Matthew's table. "My father-in-law will squeeze in too," he said.

And then Matthew turned and saw his brother-in-law. Instantly, now that he had context, he recognized the young man as Lysander Blackmore—how could he have not recognized him?

All the men scooted over their chairs, making room for Lysander and Roger. Roger weaseled his way in between Matthew and Homer, and as he did so, he pointedly told Lysander, "I'm not your father-in-law yet."

"No?" said Sloan. "What does this mean? Is there a wedding in sight?"

"On Sunday," said Lysander, beaming. "I'm Lysander Blackmore." And he shook hands around with everyone as he added, "And I am to marry the beautiful Lydia, daughter of this here gentleman, Roger Richardson."

At this announcement, congratulations were given and glasses raised before Matthew got the chance to ask his burning question, "What are the two of you doing here?"

"That's a rude question," said Osborn, laughing.

"Not at all," said Lysander. "Matthew is to be my uncle. His sister is married to Roger here."

"That's right. You did tell me you were from Marquette," said Homer to Matthew.

"To answer your question, Uncle Matthew," said Lysander, "your brother-in-law and I come here frequently for drinks after a long day at the office."

"I could use a drink right now," muttered Roger.

"We already placed our order," said Osborn, "but I'll try to flag down the waiter."

"Roger," said Matthew, "I won't be coming home for supper. The jury selection is going to continue tonight so I came here for a quick bite to eat instead."

Roger was now flagging down the waiter himself so he didn't seem to hear Matthew. "Bring me a Scotch," he told the waiter.

"One for me also," Lysander added.

"So what do you do here in Marquette?" Sloan asked Lysander.

"I'm a banker," said Lysander, launching into a discussion on the stock market without even bothering, Matthew noticed, to ask Sloan what kind of work he did. Matthew considered Sloan's work far more interesting, so he would have preferred to hear about it.

By the time the waiter brought the food, Matthew was becoming tired of listening to his niece's fiancé.

"Shouldn't you get home to dinner?" asked Matthew when Roger ordered a second drink.

"I'm the master of the house. They'll wait for me," said Roger. "So what's the prospect looking like? Is Roosevelt making a fool of himself yet?"

"It's only jury selection," said Homer.

"The man is insufferable," Roger continued. "He single-handedly destroyed the Republican Party—it's his fault that lily-livered Wilson got elected."

"Yes," said Homer, "but Roosevelt's still a man of principles."

"Principles?" said Roger. "He's a drunkard. You can bet your bottom dollar on that."

It takes one to know one, thought Matthew, but he said, "I wouldn't be so sure, Roger. He has a host of powerful friends here to testify in his favor."

"He probably bought them all off," said Roger.

"What's that?" asked Sloan, suddenly turning his attention from Lysander to Roger. Matthew felt a pain in the pit of his stomach. Here was his brother-in-law badmouthing a former president of the United States to his bodyguard.

"Man's a drunk," said Roger. "Why, I was there in the crowd when he came through Marquette. He waved his arms around like a madman."

"He just gets very animated when he speaks," said Sloan, calmly.

"Ha!" said Roger.

"Mr. Sloan," Matthew told Roger, hoping to calm him down, "was President Roosevelt's bodyguard at the White House. He's in the Secret Service and now works for President Wilson."

But Roger wasn't even listening; he was too busy guzzling down his drink, and then he was shooting off his mouth again.

"I hear he's staying with that Shiras," said Roger. "*The bird man*. Takes photographs of birds and thinks he's something special. Well, I could tell you a few things about the Shiras family, so it doesn't surprise me any that Roosevelt is staying with him. Why, my family came from Pennsylvania, not far from where Shiras grew up. We've known those Shirases for a long time—they were brewers for generations in Pennsylvania. Why, old George probably has a still in his house. Why else do you think Roosevelt wants to stay with him?" And then Roger laughed at his own joke.

"I don't know Mr. Shiras very well," said Sloan, "but I can guarantee you that Colonel Roosevelt has never been drunk a day in his life."

"You can't guarantee that," said Roger. "Ain't no one that's been with him every day of his life."

"He's a man of honor, sir," said Sloan. Matthew could see Mr. Sloan's nostrils beginning to flare. Should he crawl under the table before Sloan threw Roger across the room? No, then he would miss a good show.

"Honor," said Roger, not knowing when to shut his mouth, "is just a fancy word people bandy about to hide their true intentions."

Lysander laughed and said, "I have to agree with my father-in-law there. I guarantee you that anyone who goes around talking about honor is not to be trusted."

"I think we better head back to the courthouse now," said Homer, checking his pocket watch.

"Yes, I think so," said Osborn.

"Let me tell you, sir," said Sloan to Roger, "that this lawsuit is the result of libel, and what you are saying now is libel as well. You don't know Colonel Roosevelt, so you have no business speaking about him in such a manner." Mr. Sloan now rose to his feet. For a second, Matthew feared Sloan would grab his brother-in-law by the throat.

Osborn and Homer quickly jumped to their feet.

"We better get going," said Homer.

"Let's go, Jim," said Osborn, putting his hand on Sloan's arm.

"I'm not afraid of no Bull Moose," said Roger, half-quoting Van Evera's words during the campaign stop last fall.

"Then you're a fool," Sloan replied.

"Then you can just get yourself out of this dining room," Roger told him. "This is where I drink, and this is my town, so you have no business speaking to me like that."

"Come on, Jim," said Osborn, pulling on his arm. Sloan shook him off. Matthew looked at his brother-in-law, sitting there with his graying hair and middle-aged paunch, glaring at a man who could have twisted him into a pretzel.

"Dad, let's get going," said Lysander, now standing up. "I'm hankering to see my Lydia." He pulled out Roger's chair with Roger still in it.

Perhaps Roger now finally realized he was pushing his luck. In any case, he stood up and said to Lysander, "You're paying for the drinks," and then he turned and walked out of the dining room.

"We better go before we're late," said Matthew.

Sloan reached down to find where he had placed his hat beneath his chair. Osborn and Homer looked relieved.

Matthew and Lysander dug in their pockets for some money.

"It was good to see you again, Uncle Matthew," said Lysander, tossing a few coins on the table.

"You'd better get Roger home," Matthew replied.

"Don't worry. I know how to handle him," said Lysander, winking, and then he also turned and walked out the door.

A couple of minutes later, after paying their bills, Matthew and his three companions also exited the building. Matthew was relieved to see no sign of his in-laws on the street.

Matthew couldn't say he had enjoyed dinner, but he was glad a physical altercation had been prevented. Not that he wouldn't have liked to see someone give Roger his comeuppance, but it would have been an embarrassment to Delia. Besides, Matthew suspected now that Sloan had only wanted to intimidate Roger a little. He was sure Secret Service men were well-trained in self-control. Nevertheless, he felt the need to apologize for Roger's behavior as the four of them walked back to the courthouse.

"I'm afraid my brother-in-law isn't very rational when he drinks too much," said Matthew.

"It's forgotten," said Sloan so firmly that Matthew didn't dare to continue.

"The meatloaf wasn't bad," said Osborn, trying to lighten the mood.

"Mine was quite flavorful," Homer added.

"Tomorrow night I'll try the chicken," Osborn added.

By now they were quite close to the courthouse and joined a steady stream of reporters and would-be onlookers making their way toward it along Baraga Avenue.

"There's Teddy," said Homer, pointing out the plaintiff as he rode up in an automobile with George. Matthew recognized Jacob Riis and Frank Tyree riding with them. By the time Matthew and his companions reached the courthouse block, the Roosevelt party had climbed out of the vehicle. Matthew was planning to walk past them and go up the courthouse steps when he heard George holler, "Matthew, there you are!" Matthew turned and saw George approaching him. Roosevelt, meanwhile, looked like he was in deep conversation with his lawyers, who had come to the vehicle to greet him.

"Hello, George," said Matthew, feeling awkward over how pleased George looked to see him.

"I'm starting to think the jury selection is going to take longer than the trial," George joked. "Anyway, I was hoping to invite you to dinner tomorrow night. Roosevelt and Jacob Riis both say they know you from back when Roosevelt was a police commissioner, and they'd like to see you if it's convenient for you. I hate to take you away from your family, but—"

"I'd be dee-lighted," said Matthew, mimicking Roosevelt's well-known speech inflection. And he meant it. He felt awkward around George, but what reporter would turn down such a chance to talk to Roosevelt? And he had always liked and admired Riis.

"Good," said Shiras. "It won't be anything too fancy—Frances isn't home you know, but we'd love to have you."

"I'm honored to be invited," Matthew replied, "especially when I know you have a houseful of guests."

"And Delia won't mind?" asked George. "I'd invite her, but I didn't think she'd be comfortable being the only woman in a houseful of men."

"I'm sure she'll understand," said Matthew, "and besides, she's very busy helping my niece get ready for her wedding on Sunday."

"Oh, yes, the wedding," said George, and then his face dropped. "Delia and Roger were kind enough to invite me, but I'm afraid I'll have to miss it.

With Theodore here, I need to entertain him, and he wishes to avoid most social affairs, so bringing him to the wedding would be out of the question. I'm hoping to take him out to our camp[1] in Deerton for the weekend, so he can see where I've taken my wildlife photographs. I'd invite you along if it weren't for the wedding."

"I'd love to join you," said Matthew, "but no, I can't miss the wedding. I've been an avid follower of your photography experiments, though." Calling them "experiments" seemed like an understatement to Matthew as soon as the word left his mouth. George was famous for his wildlife photography. He had been the first photographer published in *National Geographic,* and his photographs had been so popular that photography had since become one of the magazine's regular features. George had also won awards for his photographs at the 1900 World's Fair in Paris and the 1904 World's Fair in St. Louis. The judges had been fascinated by how he had set up cameras in the woods near his camp so that whitetail deer would trigger them at night and let him get a good photo of them—something he never could have done in person without scaring them off.

"But you will come to dinner then?" Shiras repeated.

"Yes," said Matthew. "I wouldn't miss it." And Matthew gave George's hand a shake, thinking it very decent of George to invite him; of course, George probably didn't know that...

"Well, we better get in there," George said, interrupting Matthew's thought. "The sooner it starts, the sooner we can go home to our beds."

Matthew and George walked into the building together. Roosevelt and most of the witnesses and spectators had already entered the courthouse. George went up into the gallery seats reserved for male spectators since the women had been given the best seats below. Matthew found his seat beside Homer Guck in the press section.

"I see you're friends with the big wigs," said Homer, poking Matthew in the ribs.

"I'm sorry; I didn't mean to ignore you," Matthew replied, not having noticed that when George started speaking to him, Homer had left his side.

"Who is he?" asked Homer.

"George Shiras III. Colonel Roosevelt is staying at his house."

"Oh, the wildlife man," said Homer.

---

1   "Camp" is a common term used in Upper Michigan for a cabin in the woods.

"Yes, and a former member of Congress. He introduced the migratory bill to protect wildfowl during Roosevelt's presidency. They're good friends because they're both big believers in conservation."

"But how do you know him?" Homer asked.

"I—" Matthew hesitated. "George and I kind of grew up together. He used to spend his summers in Marquette when he was a boy. His father is George Shiras, Jr., the former Supreme Court Justice, and he and his father used to come up here fishing every year. Eventually, he married a local girl—Marquette businessman Peter White's daughter, Frances. They inherited Peter White's house—that's where Roosevelt is staying."

"Oh, Peter White," said Homer, stretching out the name and nodding knowingly. Everyone in Upper Michigan knew of Peter White.

Judge Flannigan now called the court to order and the jury selection process reconvened.

Several more prospective jurors were called forth for questioning. Some were approved, some rejected. Ultimately, nine more prospective jurors would be added to the original thirty-six in the quest to find twelve who would be approved by the attorneys for both the plaintiff and the defense.

The highlight of the evening would be when August Brodin was called forth. He caused a stir by entering the courtroom wearing a Bull Moose pin on his lapel. Two dozen reporters all wanted to get photos of it.

Although George Newett had decided not to attend the evening jury selection, his absence did not stop his attorney, Mr. Belden, from doing his job. Assuming that the Bull Moose pin meant Brodin was a supporter of Roosevelt, Belden did not want Brodin on the jury, as he made clear.

"Have you ever had cause to dislike the defendant?" Belden asked Brodin.

"None that I can remember," Brodin replied.

"Was there ever anything about you printed in the *Iron Ore*?"

"No, nothing."

"You dislike Mr. Newett, do you not?"

"I don't think of him," Brodin answered.

When Belden asked him how he felt about the case, Brodin admitted he had strong feelings, and that was enough for Judge Flannigan to agree to dismiss him.

Charles Thoren of Negaunee was called forth, but the white-haired eighty-four-year-old was considered to be unable to deal with the strain of the jury's requirements.

Several other men were dismissed for saying they already had strong opinions of the case that only evidence could change.

At 9:30 p.m., when the jury selection was still not complete, Judge Flannigan agreed to a short intermission, and then the selection continued until about 10:30 p.m.

Finally, the twelve jurors were determined to be:

Joseph Robear of Ishpeming, a twenty-five-year-old teamster

William Fassbender of Marquette, a twenty-eight-year-old farmer

Robert Bruce of Powell Township, a fifty-four-year-old woodsman

William Garrow of Diorite in Ely Township, a twenty-six-year-old miner

William Pryor of Marquette, a twenty-seven-year-old locomotive fireman

Thomas Howard of Chocolay Township, a forty-nine-year-old farmer

John A. Johnson of Skandia Township, a thirty-six-year-old farmer

W.H. Mathews of Ishpeming, a thirty-one-year-old mining office clerk

William Sharpe of Negaunee, a thirty-three-year-old teamster

Gus Paulson of Wells Township, a thirty-two-year-old blacksmith

Andrew P. Johnson of Humboldt Township, a sixty-one-year-old farmer

John Fredrickson of Negaunee, a thirty-one-year-old miner

Judge Flannigan now gave the jurors instructions, telling them they were under the direct charge of Undersheriffs Bennett and Jamerson while the court was under session. During the evening jury selection, Sheriff Moloney had been busy setting up a dozen cots in the anterooms of the courthouse where the sequestered jurymen would sleep until the trial's conclusion. It was the first time a jury had ever slept in the courthouse, but the precaution was being taken so the men would not be influenced by any communication with the public. The jurors would also have to eat their meals under the supervision of court officials, and they would not be allowed to see any newspapers.

Judge Flannigan completed his instructions to the jury by saying, "Keep your minds open until the conclusion of the testimonies. You are not to discuss the case with anyone—not even among yourselves—while the trial is in progress. If anyone tries to communicate with you in any way to try to influence your judgment, you must report it to the court immediately. While here, you may write all the letters you like, but you may not receive any letters that are not first inspected by the court officers."

With that, Judge Flannigan stated, "The trial will begin tomorrow morning at nine o'clock. This court is convened." It was 10:40 p.m.

As the jurors were led off to their sleeping quarters by the undersheriffs, Matthew, his fellow reporters, the plaintiff, the defendant, their attorneys, and all the spectators quickly rose to their feet. They were all glad to stretch their legs and make their separate ways home to their beds.

When he exited the courthouse, Matthew was surprised to find that several would-be spectators, who had not been allowed into the courtroom due to its having reached full capacity, were still waiting outside the courthouse just to get a glimpse of Colonel Roosevelt. Clearly, the interest in this trial was only growing.

The twelve final jurors (seated).
The two men standing are likely the undersheriffs.

"I invited three boy companions between the ages of nine and twelve to accompany me on a one night's visit to the mouth of Dead River, several miles north of town. The enterprise was to be undertaken without the assistance of guides or elders, so prone to interfere with the freedom of youth."
— George Shiras III,
Hunting Wild Life with Camera and Flashlight, Vol. 1

CHAPTER 5

As Matthew walked toward the street, he saw George and Colonel Roosevelt climbing into George's automobile. He waved to them, but they did not see him in the dark.

While thinking how kind George had been to invite him to dinner tomorrow night, Matthew made his way to the street and then turned right, heading north on Third Street. When he got home, he would write up his story about the jury selection so he could wire it to his editor in the morning. It would be a late night for him, so as he walked, he started to think about how he would word his article so he could get a head start on it; however, he quickly found his thoughts turning to George Shiras.

In their youth, there had been quite a friendship between Matthew and George, a friendship that still seemed to live in George's breast after all these years. Perhaps that was because George had never known there was a reason for that friendship to die. If George knew the reason, he certainly wouldn't be so eager to invite Matthew over for dinner.

As Matthew climbed the hill on Third Street, which would eventually take him to where he would turn east toward the lake and his sister's house, he realized it was still quite warm out. It was almost summer, and it made him remember another summer night, more than forty years ago—during that same summer when he had first met George.

George had made a few more visits to Matthew's father's store after their initial meeting, and soon, Matthew had found himself sharing fishing tips with George, although it was quickly apparent that George knew far more about fishing than Matthew did. Once or twice, George came in with his father. In those days, George Shiras, Jr. was just a middle-aged lawyer; it wouldn't be until 1892 that he would become a Supreme Court justice. Years later, Matthew had used it to his advantage that he had known the justice since his boyhood to get a couple of interviews with him while he was on the Supreme Court.

In any case, Matthew was always pleased when George came into the store with or without his father. He enjoyed hearing George's stories, especially the one about how he had gone camping in the wilderness for ten days past the Huron Islands with some Indian guides. Matthew envied him, having never been able to escape for more than a day from working in the store. Nor had he ever been more than a few miles from Marquette since his family had first come to town. One day when he told George this, George asked him, "Would you like to go camping with me tomorrow night?"

"Uh, I'd have to ask my folks," Matthew replied. "Where are you going?"

"Just overnight to the mouth of the Dead River."

"Will your father mind if I go?"

"He's not going. I want it to be a boys' adventure, so I'm inviting you and a couple of other boys—four of us total."

"Sure, that sounds like fun," Matthew said. Actually, it sounded exciting beyond words—to get away from the house and store and his family overnight seemed like a dream come true. Not that he didn't love his family, but a boy reaches an age when he wants to have adventures.

"Great. Here's what you need to bring," said George, launching into a list of supplies.

Matthew still had to broach the subject with his parents, but fortunately, his dad walked into the store from the backroom at that point, and before father or son could say anything, George said, "Good morning, Mr. Newman. I would like your permission for Matthew to go camping with me and a couple of my other friends tomorrow night."

Matthew's father seemed a bit surprised by this request, but he smiled and said, turning to his son, "I don't see why not. I can manage the store in the morning until you get back."

George then filled Mr. Newman in on all the details so he wouldn't be worried.

"It sounds like great fun," Mr. Newman had replied, "and it's about time Matthew learn to be a man and do things for himself."

Matthew didn't like that remark so much—not that it wasn't true; he knew it was true—but he liked to think he was a man already.

Fortunately, George departed before Matthew's mother appeared in the store. The moment Mr. Newman told her he had given Matthew permission to go on a camping trip, she tried to nix the idea, saying there was no way her son was going camping overnight with "just a couple of ruffian boys and no parents."

"Relax," Matthew's father had told her. "It'll do the boy good. I went camping myself when I was his age."

Mrs. Newman now saw it was two against one and she was likely to lose. She didn't repeat that Matthew couldn't go, but all through dinner that night, she worried and kept reminding him of what to do if he cut himself and to be careful not to ruin his shoes by getting them wet—which could also make him sick—and a host of other feminine fussings she mistook as real concerns that only made Matthew want to escape from her all the more. By comparison, Delia scarcely said a word at dinner, and only later, at bedtime, did she say to Matthew, "I wish I could go too." He frowned and said, "No girls allowed," and that was the end of that.

The next day when the appointed time had arrived, Matthew could barely contain his excitement. And he could scarcely believe it when a one-horse wagon arrived with three boys in it—one of them being George. However, a man was driving the wagon, which made Matthew fear there would be adult supervision after all.

"Climb in," said George. As Matthew did, George introduced the other two boys, Robert "Bob" Hume and Joe Sweet. Matthew already knew them from school. Then George explained that his father had hired the driver to bring them up to the Dead River where they would be dropped off. Matthew had no problem with a ride to the campsite, so long as they would be alone once they reached it—adults tended to prohibit boys' freedom.

There wasn't any real road to the Dead River in those days—everything was basically wilderness a block or two north of Ridge Street, but there was a rough dirt wagon road along the lake, just wide enough for a one-horse wagon to make its way along the lakeshore. It got the boys within a mile of the Dead River anyway. From there, they thanked their driver, collected all their paraphernalia, and loaded down with blankets, tent canvas, and pots and pans, they set off for the mouth of the Dead River.

They found it easiest-going to walk along the forest's edge near the beach, and the walk did not feel long since they joked all the way about how many fish they would catch and how brave they would be if they saw a bear.

Soon, they had reached the river. They quickly selected a campsite far enough away from where the river met the lake that it wouldn't get washed away by the tide. Then, first things first, according to the list of priorities in a boy's world, they decided they would build a fire before putting up the tent. Soon they were scurrying about the forest looking for tree branches dry enough to burn. George's father had given him some matches, and once the wood was all assembled and several dead leaves added to the pile to get the fire going, George struck a match and ignited the blaze. Fortunately, enough sandy beach existed between the boys' campsite and the forest that there was no danger of starting a forest fire. The boys had felt a bit defeated before leaving when even their fathers had insisted they not bring any axes, guns, or anything else they might hurt themselves with, and it didn't hurt any to hear repeated warnings from their mothers not to go into the shallow river from fear they might get carried out into the lake. But as soon as they had a blazing fire going, they felt their manhood had been restored to them.

Once the fire was steadily burning, Joe was left to watch that it didn't go out, while the others erected a tent. None of the boys had ever put up a tent before—at least not without the assistance of his father—but somehow it would be managed.

They did quite well, in fact, until one stubborn pole refused to stand up straight enough.

"It doesn't matter," said Matthew. "The canvas will still go on."

And it did, though no one could claim it looked aesthetically pleasing once it was accomplished.

"It's sagging on the ground," said Bob.

"That's okay," George replied. "We can tuck our feet into the extra part to keep them warm tonight."

"Good idea," said Matthew, knowing they had each only brought one blanket, which might not be enough since even in summer in Upper Michigan, the temperature at night could drop into the forties.

But the evening air was warm and pleasant now, and soon the boys were indulging in fishing in the river. Each one felt quite pleased with himself, and as young boys do, they bragged to each other about the sizes of the fish they caught, each claiming his catch was the superior one. One day they would likely grow into old men who told tall fish tales and taught their sons to do the same.

When the boys started to get hungry, they set about cleaning their fish so they could cook them over the fire. They decided they would also make flapjacks for supper, but too late, they realized the lard and the butter had been left behind. Matthew had been responsible for the lard, so he felt terrible about it, but George told him not to worry.

Joe set about making flapjacks anyway—they had to be peeled, or rather scraped off the bottom of the frying pan, and they came out in burnt crumbs, but they worked as a sort of breading for the equally burned fish, and no one complained since they all had sweet-tooths and there was plenty of syrup, bread, jam, and cookies to go with them. Besides, if their fish were a bit chewy, they knew they had a nice beefsteak they were saving for breakfast.

"But we have no lard or butter, so the beefsteak will stick to the pan too," said Bob.

"We can let the pan soak in water overnight to clean it," Matthew suggested.

"The beefsteak will still stick to it," Bob objected.

"We can skewer it on a stick and cook it over the fire," said George.

"That's a great idea," said Joe, and Bob readily agreed. Matthew had to admit that George was obviously the brains of this expedition.

They all felt so content with the success of their dinner—as they perceived it—that even though they knew their mothers would have told them not to, they decided to take a swim in Lake Superior to burn off the excess energy they had gained from eating. Developing stomach cramps from swimming too soon after their meal wasn't really too much of a concern because Lake Superior was so cold none of them could stay in the water for more than ten minutes anyway. That was just enough time for them to get wet and cold, and then have an excuse to huddle around the fire to warm themselves as the night grew cooler.

Soon they were wrapped in blankets around the fire, trying to get warm. Dusk had now approached, and they were looking up at the first stars when they heard a distant roaring coming from the forest behind them.

"Is it a bear?" asked Joe, looking startled.

"Bears don't sound like that," said Bob, laughing.

"It sounds more like wind," said Matthew.

"But wind doesn't roar, though it does make a whooshing sound," Bob replied.

"What if it's a forest fire?" asked Joe.

"It could be," George admitted.

"What if it's headed this way?" exclaimed Joe. "If we go to sleep, we could all wake up burned to death!"

"If you burn to death," Bob noted, "you won't be waking up."

"Shh, just listen," said George.

They all listened and then shivered with fear—or perhaps the shivering was just from the night air—though the fire was throwing off plenty of heat.

"I don't see any smoke coming from the woods," said George, and he got up and walked toward the forest to get away from their own fire on the beach, "and I don't smell any either."

The wind now began to shift, and in a couple of minutes, the sound ended. The boys were not knowledgeable enough yet to realize it had merely been the sound of a rapids on the Dead River, carried to them on the wind, which had now changed direction.

The boys turned to talking about all of the big things they would do when they were older. Bob wanted to stay in Marquette and become a policeman. Matthew said he wanted to write great adventure stories like those he had read in magazines. Joe said he didn't want to write about adventures but have real ones, so he would go and explore Alaska. George said he wanted to photograph wildlife; everyone else thought this the dullest of their chosen occupations, but he said he would do it anyway.

After a while, as they kept talking, Joe found it hard to keep his eyes open, and when he fell off the side of the log he was seated on, the others admitted they were tired too. They thought the fire would just burn itself out, so they made their way into the tent. Bob insisted he wanted to sleep in the back of the tent. Joe wanted to argue with him, but he was too tired to say much, so he slept second from the back. Matthew slept next to Joe, with George on his other side by the doorway. Matthew did not want to seem afraid, but he was glad to know that if a wild animal came into the tent, he would not be the first eaten—he would have rather seen Bob or Joe be eaten over George, however. George said he didn't mind sleeping by the door because then he was closest to the fire, and if he got cold and the fire went out, he could get up to throw more wood on it.

George's good intentions aside, he was soon snoring with the rest of the boys. By midnight, the fire had burned out, and the boys were snuggling up with their blankets over their heads to keep warm.

"Bears! Bears!"

The cry woke the boys from their lethargy.

For a moment, Matthew thought it must be Joe overreacting since he was the youngest, but then Matthew realized George was kneeling over him and yelling, and then George was struggling to climb over him and his companions.

In a moment, all four boys were awake and scrambling over each other in the tent.

"Where is he?" Bob asked.

"Quiet," said George. For a second, none of them moved. Then George bravely looked out the tent door.

"I think he's gone," said George, "but I saw his paw under the side of the tent. He stole the beefsteak."

Joe turned pale at these words. Not because he wanted breakfast, but because the beefsteak had been stored in the tent right behind his head.

"I'm going to kill that bear!" exclaimed Bob.

By now, George had crawled out of the tent, and the other boys quickly followed him, though none of them took Bob's comment seriously. They certainly weren't going to wrestle a bear for their breakfast.

But once Bob was out of the tent, he pulled a revolver from his pants and shot it into the air.

"What was that?" Matthew exclaimed, not having seen Bob's action.

"It's a gun!" Bob replied.

"Bob," George scolded, "I told you that you couldn't bring any weapons on this—"

"I brought it to protect us from bears," said Bob, cocking his revolver again.

"You didn't let me finish," George replied. "I was going to say, 'But I'm glad you did.'"

"You can't kill him, though," said Matthew. "He's long gone by now."

"What should we do?" asked Joe. "I can't go back to sleep now."

"I could chase him down and shoot him," said Bob.

"What good would that do?" asked George.

"It would get us back our breakfast," Bob said.

"I'm not eating a beefsteak full of bear slobber," said Joe.

"Neither am I," said Matthew, "and besides, that bear probably wolfed it down before we were even out of the tent."

"No, he wouldn't have," said Bob, grinning. "He's not a wolf. He'd have to *bear* it down."

Joe thought this remark hilarious, but Matthew did not appreciate being corrected. He was already sensitive about word choices, years before he would even think about newspaper reporting.

Ignoring his companions, George walked to the fire, which only had a little smoke rising from it now.

"George, light the fire again," said Joe.

"All right," said George, thinking that would keep the bear scared off.

Meanwhile, Bob started pacing with his gun along the edge of the forest.

"I think I see him," said Joe, peering into the woods where he was imagining all kinds of wild animals now staring back at him.

"Where?" asked Bob.

"There—can't you see his eye?" asked Joe.

"Those are fireflies," Bob scoffed.

"I wouldn't be too sure," Joe replied.

"Joe, bring me some leaves," said George.

Joe looked reluctant to go close enough to the woods to fetch stray leaves, so Bob quickly collected a bunch in his hands, despite having to carry his revolver also.

"Well," said Matthew, sitting down on a log by the fire, once Bob gave George the leaves and George had gotten the fire going, "we have no breakfast now."

"It's too early for breakfast anyway," said Bob. It was still dark out.

"Maybe we should take turns keeping watch until morning," George suggested.

"I'm not going back into that tent or to sleep," said Joe.

"We could just lie on the beach and take turns keeping watch," said Matthew.

The boys agreed to this. Bob and Matthew were brave enough to go back into the tent and remove all the blankets to bring them closer to the fire. Then they all made a pretense of lying down, but they were actually leaning up on their elbows like Romans at a state dinner, all too afraid to enter into a more vulnerable state.

"I'll just make sure I keep the fire going," said George, who remained sitting on a log and poking at it with an ember.

"I'll keep watch with my gun," said Bob, moving onto his stomach so he could face the forest and aim his revolver directly in front of him.

Matthew was half-afraid that Bob was more dangerous than the bear, but he didn't say anything.

"I'm hungry," said Joe.

"I wish I'd shot that bear," said Bob.

"Why?" asked George. "He'd have swallowed that beefsteak down before you could stop him."

"So? Then we could have had bear meat for breakfast," said Bob.

"We have nothing to cut it with," said Joe.

"I brought my pocketknife," said Bob. "You always have to be prepared."

Matthew decided to close his eyes. Maybe sleeping would be better than listening to Bob. He must have quickly drifted off because he felt startled awake when a log fell into the fire, and then he realized it was almost daylight.

"Over here!" hollered Bob.

Matthew turned and saw George walking over to where Bob was standing a few feet from the side of the tent.

"Bear tracks," Bob pointed out, using his revolver as a pointer.

Joe now got up and ran over to look at them.

"They're too small for a bear," said George.

"Must've been a coyote then," said Bob.

Matthew stood up now and called to his companions. "Let's pack up and head home! I'm starving, and the sooner we get back to Marquette, the sooner we can have breakfast."

They all agreed to this, and after a quarter of an hour, the fire was extinguished, the camping gear collected, and the boys were walking back to Marquette. They arrived at their homes several hours before the wagon intended to retrieve them could set out to collect them. They arrived before their parents had even gotten out of bed.

What a group we were, thought Matthew as he turned up the driveway to Delia's house. He was still chuckling to himself when he let himself in and went upstairs to his room.

The Marquette Daily Mining Chronicle, May 27, 1913
The *Chronicle* mistakenly said that Belden, not Andrews,
cross-examined Roosevelt.

TUESDAY
MAY 27, 1913

"My acts were plainly moral!
The facts I do not conceal.
He forced on me a quarrel
And then it was steel to steel."
— *The Prince of Pilsen*

CHAPTER 6

MATTHEW HAD NOT GOTTEN MUCH sleep, but the trial would keep him and all the onlookers wide awake the next morning, for Roosevelt would be the first to testify.

Delia had decided she would go with Matthew that morning, and Roger, since the trial was to start at the reasonable hour of nine o'clock, agreed he would drop them off at the courthouse on his way to work. Matthew was glad for the ride after the late night so he wouldn't have to rush as much that morning.

They arrived at the courthouse just fifteen minutes before the trial was to begin. Matthew was fortunate to have just enough time to wire his story quickly to his editor and find his seat beside Homer Guck before Roosevelt entered the courtroom.

"Good morning," Homer greeted him. "I think this will prove to be an interesting day."

"I believe so," Matthew agreed as Judge Flannigan entered the courtroom.

In another minute, the court was called to order. After a few preliminaries, Roosevelt's attorney, James Pound, made his opening remarks to the jury.

"Gentlemen of the jury," said Mr. Pound, "the plaintiff in this case is a native of New York, which has, in fact, been his home the major portion of his life. He has had the same uneventful life that the average city boy has, but when he reached the dignity of manhood, the age of which has been set for one thousand years by the English as twenty-one, and he was permitted to assume full citizenship, he was called upon to discharge and to execute sundry and diverse trusts reposed in him as a representative of the people, in the first place of his native state, and the people of the United States afterwards. The highest gift given any American citizen was placed upon his shoulders by a great majority.

"Now then, gentlemen of the jury, when he had discharged his duties as president of the United States, and became again a plain American citizen, this man, then in the prime of manhood, chuck-full of vigor, made up his mind for the good of humanity, that he would explore the dark continent of Africa.

"Upon his return, he became again a common ordinary citizen and so he desired to remain, until a certain crisis forced the plaintiff to take either a negative or an affirmative position. The result was that he became a candidate for the high office he has held. During the campaign, he had occasion to go to different parts of the country, and while in the state of Wisconsin, in the city of Milwaukee, at a time when he faced a very serious crisis, he was apprized of the fact that the defendant in this case had published of and concerning him, what he claims, and what I claim, his representative, a wicked base, malicious, and unjustified libel.

"Now, gentlemen of the jury, it was the defendant in this case, who at the hands of the plaintiff, when he was in power—"

"Objection!" shouted Mr. Andrews, counsel for the defense, not wanting Pound to mention that Newett formerly had been a postmaster and received his appointment from Roosevelt during his presidency.

"Objection sustained," replied Judge Flannigan.

"I say," continued Mr. Pound, thinking it best to reword his statement, "the defendant was without any justification. He must have been in a condition of mind where he did not have the fear of God before him.

"Gentlemen, the man I represent, as plaintiff in this case, is not a man without fault, but of strong heart and noble aim.

"Then, without justification, this libel was maliciously made, and it will appear in this case that this man did not know anything of the facts that he charged at the time, and that he has continued in the position he assumed by attempting to justify this base fabrication."

When Pound completed his opening speech, the defense gave its opening remarks, clarifying that Newett had good authority to back the statement he had made in his newspaper—as the defense intended to prove.

Now came the moment everyone had been waiting for—Colonel Roosevelt was called as the first witness. After being sworn in, Roosevelt took a seat in the witness box, and his attorney, James Pound, began to question him.

Throughout the questioning, Roosevelt seemed unintimidated by the situation. He answered quickly, and occasionally, he became so excited that his voice grew higher and he gestured with his hands—such vigor in his speech may have been what got him into trouble in the first place, but no one would have suggested he was intoxicated today. Instead, everyone in the courtroom listened with great interest.

Mr. Pound began his questions by asking, "What is your name, please?"

"Theodore Roosevelt," the colonel replied.

"You were born where?"

"I was born in New York City, October 2, 1858."

"Your home during your boyhood was where?"

"New York City in the winter," Roosevelt replied, "and in the country in the summer, the adjacent country."

"You finished your studies about what year—I mean as a scholar, of course?" asked Mr. Pound.

"1880."

"And at that time did you take a degree?"

"Yes, I took a degree."

"From where?"

"Harvard," said Roosevelt, slightly smiling as if proud of it.

"After graduating from Harvard, what did you devote your attention to?"

"Writing, and I went into politics."

"What was the first connection you had with politics?" asked Mr. Pound.

"I was elected to the legislature in the fall of 1881, and re-elected in 1882, and in 1883."

"The legislature of what State?" asked Mr. Pound.

"Of the State of New York."

"During that time," continued Mr. Pound, "and as a part of your duty, did you become acquainted with a number of government men that were somewhat new to you?"

"I did," said Roosevelt.

"Just a moment," the defense's attorney, Mr. Andrews, interrupted. "We object to that, as irrelevant, incompetent, and immaterial."

Mr. Pound turned to Judge Flannigan and remarked, "I am not going to pursue it any further."

"We object to it," Mr. Andrews repeated, clearly wanting it struck from the record.

"I think I am entitled to that much," Mr. Pound replied.

Judge Flannigan turned to Mr. Pound and said, "I have some question about it, Mr. Pound."

"Do I understand," asked Mr. Pound, "that in case of an adverse ruling, an exception is given as of course, or do we have to take it?"

"You have to take it," replied Judge Flannigan.

"Please give me an exception," Mr. Pound requested.

Matthew, who had reported on not a few court cases, knew an exception meant that the lawyer did not agree with the court's ruling and he would try to have it overruled by a higher court later. The exceptions were needed to make it clear the lawyer whose objection was overruled did not concede on the matter. While Matthew could see the reason for exceptions, he wondered how many other objections there would be since he personally didn't see any reason for this particular one that Mr. Andrews had just made.

Mr. Pound now continued his questioning. "After your service as a member of the legislature, what was the next matter that you were associated with, in connection with the government in any way, either municipal, state, or national?"

"I was appointed Civil Service Commissioner in the spring of 1889," Roosevelt answered. "I served until the spring of 1895. I then was appointed police commissioner. I was president of the police commission of the City of New York until the spring of 1897. I was then appointed Assistant Secretary of the Navy, under President McKinley, and I served until the spring of 1898. I then resigned to accept the position of Lieutenant-Colonel of the Volunteer Cavalry, commonly called the Rough Riders, in the war with Spain. I served through the fight at Santiago, in which the regiment lost—"

"I object to that," Mr. Andrews stated.

Matthew knew that mention of casualties would likely build up sympathy for the colonel with the jury. Mr. Pound seemed to understand that as the reason for the objection as well, so he skipped over the matter and asked, "And after Santiago?"

"I was promoted to be colonel."

"How many times were you under fire?"

"I was—"

"I object to that as irrelevant and immaterial," stated Mr. Andrews.

Matthew was surprised by Pound's question. Then again, perhaps he deliberately wanted to build up sympathy for the colonel. Even if the defense objected, the jury would have still heard the question.

Judge Flannigan didn't seem too concerned about the objection, saying to Mr. Pound, "I will hear you. Why do you think that is competent?"

"I think it is a part of the man's history," Mr. Pound replied.

"You may take the answer," Judge Flannigan agreed.

Roosevelt then proceeded. "I was under all the fire there was in Cuba. I was in the Las Guasimas fight, and in the Santiago fight, in which the number of—"

"I object to this statement," repeated Mr. Andrews, unwilling to give up.

"That will be sufficient," Mr. Pound said, turning to Roosevelt. "At the expiration of the contest in Cuba, where did you go—were you mustered out?"

"The regiment was mustered out in September 1898 at Montauk Point," Roosevelt replied, "and I was elected governor of New York that same fall."

"How long did you serve in that office?"

"I served for two years; and while governor, in the spring of 1900, I was nominated as vice-president with President McKinley, and served as vice-president until in September 1901, when President McKinley died because of the bullet wound inflicted by Czolgosz. I then became president, and I served the three-and-a-half years of the unexpired term for which President McKinley was elected. I was nominated and elected president in 1904 and served until March 4, 1909."

"Now, Mr. Roosevelt," continued Mr. Pound, "after the expiration of your term of office as president, what did you next devote your attention to?"

"Two weeks and a half after I left the White House," said Roosevelt, "I went to Africa, as the head of the Smithsonian expedition for the National Museum—an expedition to collect natural history material for the National Museum at Washington. I was a year on that expedition; I was eleven months in Africa, entering at Mombasa, on the east coast, and going into the middle of Africa, and down the Nile. I then spent about two months in Europe, and came home, reaching home in June, 1910. Since then, I have been connected with *The Outlook*."

Matthew remembered well Roosevelt's series of magazine articles in *The Outlook*. In them, Roosevelt had promoted progressive principles against elitism and in favor of honest and efficient politics and democracy.

"In that connection with *The Outlook*, have you had occasion to travel somewhat over the United States since your return?"

"It was independent of that connection," Roosevelt replied.

"You have, though?" repeated Pound.

"I have traveled back and forth across the United States since I returned."

"Now," asked Pound, "did you ever live in the West?"

"I did."

"Tell me when."

"From 1883 to 1896."

"What portion of the West were you in?" asked Pound.

"I lived on a cow ranch in the short grass country of the Little Missouri."

"In what state?"

"In what was the Territory of Dakota when I went in there," said Roosevelt, "but now is the state of North Dakota. I lived there at intervals for two or three years during the major part of the time, but for the latter part of that time, I was only out a few weeks or a few months each year."

"Now," continued Mr. Pound, "during the year 1912, did matters so shape themselves that you participated in the campaign of 1912?"

"I participated in it," Roosevelt affirmed.

"In the month of October 1912, were you in the state of Wisconsin?"

"Yes."

"I call your attention to the date October 11, 1912. Do you remember that date?"

"If you can identify it by some incident," Roosevelt replied. "I don't remember that date."

"I ask you to look at this paper, and look at the date, if you please?"

"Yes," said Roosevelt as Pound handed a copy of the *Iron Ore* to him—the very issue of the paper that had contained Newett's allegedly libelous editorial.

"Did you ever see a copy of that?" Pound asked.

"I did."

"With reference to October 11, this date, as near as you can tell, when was it that you saw that?"

"It was within a few days," Roosevelt replied, "but I cannot remember whether it was before or after I was shot."

"I move to strike out the answer," Mr. Andrews objected.

No sympathy wanted for gunshot wounds, thought Matthew.

Judge Flannigan, however, thought otherwise, stating, "The answer may stand."

"I except," Mr. Andrews persisted. "I move to strike out the latter part of the answer, relating to when he was shot, as incompetent, irrelevant, and immaterial."

Turning to Judge Flannigan, Mr. Pound stated, "I only offer it as fixing the date."

"You have an exception, Mr. Andrews," Judge Flannigan stated. "Let the answer stand."

Mr. Pound now resumed his questions. "Where were you when your attention was first called to this article?"

"That is what I am not sure of," said Colonel Roosevelt. "My memory is that I was in Mercy Hospital at the time, but it may have been before I had gone there. That is the only reason I mentioned about being shot, that I don't remember."

"Mercy Hospital is where?" asked Mr. Pound.

"I object to that as immaterial in this case," said Mr. Andrews.

Matthew could not see the point in such an objection. Apparently, Judge Flannigan agreed with him.

"The objection is overruled."

"Note an exception," said Mr. Andrews.

Mr. Pound turned back to Colonel Roosevelt and asked, "What is the answer?"

"Mercy Hospital is in Chicago."

"You are in doubt as to the other place, where you say you were shot," said Pound. "Where were you shot—what city?"

"I object to that," persisted Mr. Andrews. "I don't think that fixes any date, and the evident purpose is, it seems to me, to put in here something entirely foreign to justice, in this case."

"It is strictly competent," Mr. Pound calmly insisted. "He identifies it in connection with one or the other of two places."

"What do you expect to claim for this testimony?" Judge Flannigan asked Mr. Pound.

"Nothing more," Mr. Pound replied, "than to fix the division of time beyond peradventure."

"For that one purpose," Judge Flannigan stated, "you may take the answer."

"Note an exception," said Mr. Andrews.

Mr. Pound nodded to Colonel Roosevelt for him to proceed.

"Milwaukee," Roosevelt answered.

Mr. Andrews refused to give up, declaring, "That has no relevancy to this case."

"We have ruled on that proposition," said Judge Flannigan, "and you have an exception."

Mr. Pound continued, "Calling your attention to this article, did you read it?"

"I did," said Roosevelt.

"How did you feel about it?"

"I felt indignant," said Roosevelt, his color slightly rising.

"Were you at that time able to recall the gentleman whose name is at the head of this sheet as the owner?" asked Mr. Pound.

"I think not," said Roosevelt.

Mr. Pound now turned to the counsel for the defense and asked, "You gentlemen do not raise any question about this paper, do you?"

"No," said Mr. Belden, taking over for Mr. Andrews. Matthew hoped that meant the questioning could continue without so many interruptions.

"I think," continued Mr. Pound, "we may as well here as any place introduce this, and I will offer this article in evidence."

"There is no objection to that," Mr. Belden agreed.

"I will read that portion of it," continued Mr. Pound, "which I deem to be pertinent, from the article under the caption 'The Roosevelt Way.' I will offer in evidence the head of the editorial page down to and under the flag."

Judge Flannigan confirmed, "You may read to the jury at this time just what you offer."

"For identification," said Mr. Pound, "I will read: '*Iron Ore*. Two Dollars per year in advance. George A. Newett, Publisher. Entered at the Post Office at Ishpeming, Michigan, as second class matter. Saturday, October 12, 1912.' Now I read as to the libel:

The Roosevelt Way

According to Roosevelt, he is the only man who can call others liars, rascals and thieves, terms he applies to Republicans generally.

All that Roosevelt has gained politically he received from the hands of the Republican Party.

Had he won in the Republican convention in Chicago, then the Republican Party would still be a good party, and all others would have been made up of liars and thieves and scoundrels generally.

But if anyone calls Roosevelt a liar he raves and roars and takes on in an awful way, and yet Roosevelt is a pretty good liar himself. Where a lie will serve to advance his position, he employs it.

Roosevelt lies and curses in the most disgusting way; he gets drunk, too, and that not infrequently, and all of his intimates know about it.

What's the use mincing things with him when he maltreats everyone not for him?

Because he has been president gives him no privileges above other men and his conduct is just as deserving censure as is that of any other offender against decency.

How can Roosevelt expect to go unlashed when he maliciously and untruthfully strikes out at other people?

It's just as Mr. Harlan said, he's the greatest little fighter in the country when he's alone in the ring, but he acts like a madman if anyone dares criticize him. All who oppose him are wreckers of the country, liars, knaves and undesirables.

He alone is pure and entitled to a halo. Rats! For so great a fighter, self-styled, he's the poorest loser we ever knew.

When Pound had finished reading, he turned to Colonel Roosevelt and asked, "You are now fifty-four years of age, as I figure it out?"

"I am," said Roosevelt.

"I ask you, since your arrival at the age of manhood, what is the fact as to whether you have ever been under the influence of intoxicating liquors or drugs?"

Finally, thought Matthew, *we're getting to the main point of this trial.*

Roosevelt spoke clearly and without hesitation. "I have never been drunk or in the slightest degree under the influence of liquor."

"Now," said Mr. Pound, nodding as if to commend the witness for his answer and encourage him further, "I wish you would describe in your own way to the jury, what, if any, use you make of liquors, spirituous or malt, since your manhood, in your recollection."

"I do not drink either whiskey or brandy, except as I shall hereafter say, except as I drink it under the direction of a doctor; I do not drink beer; I sometimes drink light wine."

"Let me ask you right there, have you ever indulged in porter on any occasion?"

"I never drank liquor or porter or anything of that kind," Roosevelt replied. "I have never drunk a high-ball or cocktail in my life. I have sometimes drunk mint juleps in the White House. There was a bed of mint there, and I may have drunk half-a-dozen mint juleps a year, and certainly no more."

"All at one time," asked Pound, "or was it just a—some people here may be in the courtroom for the first time, and I desire you to state the facts."

"I never drank but one mint julep at a time," said Roosevelt. "I doubt if I have drunk a half-dozen a year; I doubt if I drank a dozen during the entire seven-and-a-half years there; since I left the presidency, in the four years since I left, I remember I have drunk two; one at the Country Club in St. Louis, where I simply touched a mouthful, and one at Little Rock, Arkansas, where there was a dinner given by the governor of the state and others, and they passed a loving cup of mint juleps, and I drank from that as it passed."

"What is the fact," Pound continued, "I may be too anxious about it—but I want to know whether there was ever a time that you drank two mint juleps inside of one day of twenty-four hours; would that much time pass between the half-dozen you have tasted in the four years you were drinking in the White House?"

"I should say, Mr. Pound," replied Roosevelt, "it would be perfectly possible for me to take that much on some occasion in the past thirty-four years or nearly, to drink two mint juleps together, but I don't think so: I think not."

"Now, you say you occasionally drink light wine; will you just describe the amount?"

"I don't like beer," Roosevelt explained, "and sometimes I will go to a friend's house where they will ask me to drink beer or whiskey, but instead of drinking beer or whiskey, I will drink light wine, a glass or two glasses. At home, at dinner, I may partake of a glass or two glasses of white wine. At a public dinner, or a big dinner, if they have champagne, I will take a glass or two glasses of champagne, but I take it publicly just as much as privately."

"While you were president of the United States, will you tell us what the fact was as to whether there were a number of dinners, three or four annually, known as state dinners?" asked Mr. Pound.

"Yes," said Roosevelt.

"Or diplomatic dinners?"

"As you understand," Roosevelt explained, "there are in the White House every year three or four dinners, sometimes more, which are called state dinners, regular functions to which members of Congress, foreign ambassadors, and others are invited. I also dined, as every president does once a year, with each member of his cabinet, and at those dinners, as far as I remember, without exception, there was champagne. Outside of that, in the White House, I have drunk light wine, and not usually at all if we were alone; if there were guests, I might drink a glass or two of light wine, and I might not drink anything; and in the White House, I never touched brandy or whiskey except as I have described it in connection with the mint juleps or under the doctor's direction."

"Just one question right there," said Pound. "Has there been, since your experience in Cuba, anything that occurs to you occasionally in the way of illness or chills?"

"Oh, I have had, ever since the Cuban campaign, I have now and then had a slight attack of fever, and which will be brought on usually by over-exertion," said Roosevelt. "I had a couple of attacks of fever in Africa. I had one attack when in the Rocky Mountains; in the Rocky Mountains when I had an attack of fever, it lasted two or three days, and then it came on again; and in the first attack of it, the doctor gave me a drink of whiskey, but I told him I didn't think it did me any good, and when the relapse came, I asked him not to give it to me, and I took hot tea instead. In Africa, the expedition took with it a case of champagne, a case of whiskey, and a bottle of brandy. I never touched one drop of either the champagne or the whiskey. The champagne was used purely for certain members of the party who got dysentery and fever towards the end of the trip, and it was also used for certain elephant hunters and traders and missionaries whom we met who were sick with fever or dysentery, and it was only used for such purposes. The whiskey was used chiefly for such purposes, but some members of the party drank it otherwise. I never touched a drop. The brandy bottle—I was the only person that drank from the brandy bottle."

Mr. Andrews, who must have felt he'd been silent for too long, now stated, "I think this is not responsive to any questions asked."

"Yes," Mr. Pound clarified. "I asked him what the experience was in Africa."

"You may proceed," said Judge Flannigan, "and you have an exception, if you care for it."

"I except to the ruling," Mr. Andrews replied.

At Mr. Pound's nodding, Roosevelt now answered the question again. "The only brandy I drank was at the time of my two fever attacks. I drank in those two fever attacks, by direction of the doctor, about seven tablespoonfuls. I think most of it was in the first fever attack; and then I told the doctor, Dr. Mearns, when the second fever attack came on—"

Mr. Andrews burst in, "The conversation with the doctor I ask to have excluded."

"That probably would not be proper," Mr. Pound replied.

Roosevelt forged ahead, finishing his answer. "After the second fever attack, I refused to take any more, and took tea, and during the eleven months that I was in Africa, the only liquor, brandy or whiskey that I took were those seven tablespoonfuls of brandy."

"How many men were in your party that started with you from Mombasa?" Mr. Pound asked Roosevelt.

"Five."

"Was it added to by guides or others as you traversed the country?"

"That," asserted Mr. Andrews, "is objected to as immaterial."

"You may have an exception," said Judge Flannigan.

Matthew thought by now that even Judge Flannigan must be growing tired of Mr. Andrews' objections.

"Two other men," Roosevelt answered, "two professional elephant hunters, joined us."

"Where was it that you left Africa proper before you reached Egypt?" asked Mr. Pound.

"Khartum."

"You went in at Alombasa and came out of Africa at Khartum?" Mr. Pound asked to clarify.

"Yes."

"From Khartum, your progress down to the Mediterranean was by what method?"

"It was by railroad. At Khartum, I was met by my wife and daughter and son and various friends and certain newspaper men, who continued with me until I came home."

"In the basket of champagne, how many bottles would be included?" Mr. Pound asked, now getting back to the real issue at hand.

"You mean the case of champagne?" Roosevelt asked.

"Yes."

"I don't know," Roosevelt admitted. "I never saw it."

"What I am getting at," Pound explained, "was it six or eight or ten or twelve bottles?"

"I couldn't tell you," said Roosevelt. "I don't know how many bottles there were."

"I understand you that you do not claim to be a prohibitionist or total abstainer?"

"I am not," said Roosevelt.

Here, Matthew could not help but think about the efforts across the nation to make prohibition of alcohol the law of the land. While he knew most people used alcohol responsibly, and he occasionally enjoyed a glass of it himself when with friends, he would not particularly miss it. More importantly, he thought that people like his brother-in-law, Roger, might be pleasanter if they didn't have access to it—and by extension, that would make easier the lives of everyone they knew.

Mr. Pound now asked Colonel Roosevelt, "How would you describe yourself as a user of any kind of liquor, free, or—"

"I use—"

"Just a moment," Mr. Andrews interrupted.

Ignoring his opposition, Mr. Pound continued his question. "How would you describe yourself as a user of liquor, either spirituous or malt, as to being a free consumer of them to excess or abstemiously?"

"That is objected to because it is leading and incompetent," insisted Mr. Andrews.

"That seems to be clearly competent," Judge Flannigan replied. "I will give you an exception."

"Will you allow me to make my statement as to how much I use?" Roosevelt asked.

"Go ahead and state it," Mr. Pound confirmed.

"I can begin," said Roosevelt, "by saying that I am not a total abstainer, but that I am very abstemious, very abstemious in the use of wine at all; that I know of no man in any profession—"

"Just a moment," said Mr. Andrews yet again.

"Well, that may not be material," Mr. Pound agreed.

"I ask that that be excluded," Mr. Andrews continued, "and ask that the jury be instructed not to consider it."

Judge Flannigan had to agree this time. "The last answer will be stricken out, the last part of it," he said, turning to address the jury. "Now, gentlemen of the jury, as this suit progresses, if a question is answered and the Court strikes out that answer, you will disregard the answer; it will drop right out of your minds."

Matthew smiled. Such a direction was only likely to make it stick in their minds more. Mr. Andrews had finally succeeded with one of his objections according to the court record, but that didn't mean he had succeeded with the jury itself.

"Now," Mr. Pound continued his questioning, "you may just describe your consumption of liquor in the last fifteen years."

"When I went to Cuba—"

"May I suggest, if the Court please," interrupted Mr. Andrews, although adding, "I don't want to interrupt Colonel Roosevelt unnecessarily, but it seems to me this matter has all been gone over, and while it may be entirely competent, I doubt the advisability of repeating it."

"Repetition sometimes becomes necessary on account of interruptions," Judge Flannigan stated, looking rather sternly at Mr. Andrews. Matthew and a few others in the court could not help letting out a muffled snicker at this remark. Judge Flannigan, ignoring the disorder, turned to Colonel Roosevelt and said, "You may go on."

"Just describe it in your own way," Mr. Pound told his witness.

"When on the campaign in Cuba," Roosevelt continued, "I drank nothing. I had no whiskey or brandy with me. Before I left, several people sent me whiskey and brandy bottles, and I asked the colonel of the regiment, Colonel Wood, what he would do with it, and they were turned over to the hospital. Since coming back, I have told you how much I drank in the White House. That same statement applies when I have been home, and applies while I was governor. May I describe the routine of the White House?"

"As briefly as you can," Mr. Pound agreed. "I think we would all like to know that."

"I would get up in the morning at about eight," the colonel began, "breakfast with Mrs. Roosevelt and the children; walk around twenty minutes, walking around the White House grounds; from there go down to the office where my private secretary, Mr. Loeb, was, and take up—"

This time, Mr. Pound interrupted the colonel, but only for clarification. "The offices were where with reference to the capital?"

"The office is connected with the White House, about two hundred feet away. I would take up my work with Mr. Loeb and answer the mail, and senators and congressmen would come in. I would have a cabinet meeting; every moment would be occupied up to about one o'clock. At one o'clock, unless I had shaved myself, I would be shaved, in a little room between the room where I sat and the room in which Mr. Loeb sat. I would quite frequently, instead of shaving myself, get somebody to shave me, because then I could do work while I was being shaved. I had to economize every spare moment. Mr. Loeb, or sometimes a senator or congressman or someone else, would come in and see me while I was being shaved. Usually, Mr. Loeb was in at the same time, and I would dictate letters to him, and then as soon as I was finished shaving, I would go and wash my hands, Mr. Loeb usually coming in with me and I giving dictation or answering questions as I was finishing washing my hands. Never, on any occasion on any day, in the entire time that I was in the White House, had I ever touched a drop of anything prior to lunch, never under any circumstances."

"Then what followed?" asked Mr. Pound.

"I would go over and lunch with Mrs. Roosevelt, and sometimes with guests."

"Did the lunch immediately follow your ablutions?"

"As soon as I washed my hands, I would walk right across the terrace and take lunch with Mrs. Roosevelt. Often, there would be people there, and almost always, because I had some business to do with them. If Mrs. Roosevelt and I were alone, we had only tea or milk or water, whatever it was, at lunch. If there were any guests, there would usually be light wine on the table.

"Immediately afterwards, I would again go back to be with Mr. Loeb and finish up the work, and I would go over with any head of a department or anyone who had anything to put before me in connection with the government service. At four in the afternoon, or as near that as possible, I would go out for a ride or for a walk or play tennis, and then stop and get back about six. I would then take up the mail that had accumulated in the afternoon and answer that and do any other things that there were to do. I would then spend half an hour with the children, and bathe and dress for dinner. If we dined alone, we had no wine and no liquor of any kind on our table. If there were guests and it was a small affair, we would have light wine, of which I have spoken: if it was a state dinner, there would be champagne. If we were alone, as soon as dinner was over, I would again go back to the office, or get Mr. Loeb or some head of a department or any other man with whom I had business up to my library and go over the business with him. And after a cabinet dinner or state dinner, as often happened, I was pressed with work; I would work perhaps half an hour or three-quarters of an hour after coming back to the White House. I would then usually sit down and read some book entirely disconnected with my work, so as to get the work out of my head before I went to bed. I would go to bed at about twelve; that was the usual time I was able to go to bed; and at that time, not infrequently, Surgeon-General Rixey, who was my doctor during those seven-and-a-half years, would be in to see me, when I would go to bed, and get up and breakfast as I have described. On these trips through the country—"

"Just a moment," Mr. Pound interrupted. "I want to finish up with the White House now. During that seven-and-a-half years when you were in Washington, from the time you arose at eight o'clock in the morning up till you went to bed at twelve o'clock at night, were you constantly engaged in business excepting the time that you took for recreation?"

"Excepting the time I mentioned for recreation," Roosevelt explained, "and excepting the half hour I mentioned when I was with my own family, I was engaged every minute of the day in business, and not excepting those times, I was always in sight and in touch with either the members of my own family for the half hour or thereabouts that I have spoken about, or Mr. Loeb and the other people who were associated with me, and that included the two hours' walk that I took. For instance, the Secret Service men were always in attendance; and whenever I went out for any reason, they would go out with me. When I went to church, one of them would follow some little distance behind, and when I went out in the evening on any occasion, they would follow with me. When, for instance, Speaker Cannon had a seventieth birthday celebration in the evening, on that occasion, Mr. Loeb went with me. We keep a record in the White House of the particular hours at which I left the White House and came back to it. When I went to Speaker Cannon's reception, the card shows that Mr. Loeb and I started at about 9:20, with Jim Sloan, the Secret Service man; we went there to the reception and came back about eleven o'clock. At that particular reception, as he was from Jim Sloan's district, Mr. Sloan, the Secret Service man, accompanied me out to the carriage and asked if he could stay, as he had friends there. Mr. Loeb said yes, that he was going home with me, and he went home with me.

"And at that reception, as at the cabinet dinners, as at every other occasion, I never touched a drop of whiskey or brandy. At that reception, I drank a glass of champagne and I ate a sandwich, and I drank the glass of champagne in proposing Speaker Cannon's health on his seventieth birthday."

"I think," said Mr. Pound, "the jury would like to know to whom you refer as Secret Service men."

"They are men furnished by the United States Government for the protection of the president. Secret Service men are two men, or several men, allotted to follow the president around and prevent assassins and cranks from getting at me. For instance, I would not allow them at one time to go to church with me."

"Just a moment," said Mr. Andrews, using his favorite expression. "I don't think that is competent."

"I don't care to go any further than that," said Mr. Pound to placate Mr. Andrews before turning to his next question. "You said you enlisted in the army as lieutenant-colonel of the First Cavalry?"

"Yes."

"What was your rank when you were mustered out?"

"I object to that as immaterial," Mr. Andrews proclaimed.

Mr. Pound, not batting an eye, replied, "I insist that it is entirely competent. Of course, the only object I have is to show if there was any promotion, bearing on the impairment of the man's health and bearing on the man's life."

Judge Flannigan ruled, "I think the position in life of the plaintiff is competent and material here."

Colonel Roosevelt, now with an affirming look from Mr. Pound, continued. "I was made colonel; I was recommended for brevet rank, and for a medal of honor, and I came back acting as brigade commander, in command of the brigade."

"You say brevet...."

"I was recommended as brevet brigadier general," Colonel Roosevelt clarified.

"Now, you began to state, and I diverted you a moment ago, in regard to certain trips that you had made. Now, if you will take that up in point of order during the time of your residency, or anterior to that, and describe what there was in the shape of drinking, I will be much obliged to you."

"First, occasionally," said Roosevelt, "but still more as president, I traveled over the country, following exactly the precedents of Mr. Cleveland and Mr. McKinley and my predecessors in the presidency. On those trips I never, while on the cars, touched any liquor or any wine, except just before I went to bed at night; if it was a short trip, I touched nothing whatever, but if it was a long trip and the strain, especially on my throat, was very severe, after undressing at night, on the advice of Surgeon-General Rixey, and Dr. Holbrook Curtis, I would take either one or two goblets of milk with a teaspoonful of brandy in each; I would usually take that and then read for twenty minutes in bed by the electric light, and then I would sleep perfectly, and be all fresh the next morning. And on these trips on the average day, which meant nine days out of ten, I would touch nothing during the day of any kind. For instance, that was the case passing through Michigan last fall; it was the case in Ohio last year. I would touch nothing of any kind until I went to bed, and if it was a short trip, I would take nothing at all; if it was a long trip, and my throat began to get exhausted, I usually then took either one or two tumblers of milk with a teaspoon of brandy in each tumbler. On occasions on that trip, I would stop at some friend's house. For instance, in Toledo, Ohio, after my speech, I went to the house of Mr. Shepley, to meet Mayor Whitlock. Mayor and Mrs. Whitlock were there, and Mr. and Mrs. Shepley and Regis Post and myself. On that occasion, Mr. Shepley asked Mayor Whitlock and Mrs. Whitlock and all to take a little supper, and there was champagne. I drank a glass, and then found that they had a pitcher of milk, and then I took milk and doughnuts instead."

"That suited your appetite better?" asked Pound.

"That suited my appetite better," Roosevelt agreed, "and I should say on an average on those trips there would be about once a week when there would be some experience like that."

"When you had a hard day or a long trip," asked Pound, "does that mean the distance, or how about the speeches that you were called upon to make, or both?"

"It means both the distance and the speeches. It is very difficult for anyone, who has not been through it, to realize the strain that there is in such a trip. For instance, I remember in Kansas in two days I made thirty-seven speeches. I began each day with a speech before breakfast, and on each day, I finished my last speech at eleven in the evening, making nineteen one day, eighteen the preceding day, and often the speeches were in railroad yards; we were running races with railroad trains going by, and whistles blowing; often speeches out in the open air, where there was no chance to save my voice, but I had to try to reach the people on the outside of the crowd who had come from a long distance and who I felt were entitled to hear me if they could, and it was as exhausting an experience as could possibly be, generally; and every man who speaks like that must take care of himself all that is possible."

"Did you feel it was a duty you owed to the people that you should exert yourself to make yourself heard and understood?"

"I object to that," broke in Mr. Andrews, "as leading, immaterial, and irrelevant."

Mr. Pound rephrased his question, "Why was it that you exerted yourself to the degree that you did?"

"There was no point in my going unless I used my voice to make myself heard," said Roosevelt.

"Were you two or three times in the legislature?"

"Three times," Roosevelt confirmed.

"Did you have any experience in New York in relation to the mayoralty?"

"I ran for mayor in 1886, and was defeated by Abram S. Hewitt and Henry George."

"Another question on the subject of these state dinners," continued Pound. "At these state dinners, state whether your consumption of champagne did or did not exceed, at the utmost, two glasses?"

"It would be either one or two glasses."

"During the last fourteen years, for medicinal purposes or otherwise, how many drinks of whiskey have you had, to your best recollection?"

"Except as I have testified," Roosevelt replied, "in connection with the teaspoonful of brandy in the milk at night, and excepting as I have testified to in connection with the mint juleps, and on the advice of doctors, I believe that in the last fifteen years, I have not had a dozen. I have not taken whiskey a dozen times."

"I ask you, even on these trips, how many times have you in the last fifteen years carried even a small flask of whiskey with you?"

"For the last fifteen years, I have never carried a whiskey flask, or a brandy flask with me. In the days on the ranch, we never had whiskey on the ranch, but I used to then have a pocket flask of brandy, which I would keep for accidents, but I never used it, and have never used it, and I abandoned carrying it, and I have not carried it for twenty years."

"When you were on the ranch, did you frequent saloons, or have any occasion to?" asked Mr. Pound.

"I never went into a saloon; I don't believe that I ever went into a saloon in the western country except where it was at a little hotel, where the only two rooms would be a kitchen and a dining room where you had the dining table and everything else."

"And bar, too?" asked Pound.

"In the room with the bar: and I don't ever remember of drinking at a bar; certainly not for fifteen or twenty years, and I do not remember more than once or twice going into a saloon, and as far as I can remember, not at all in the last fifteen or twenty years."

"You said that you were in the city of Milwaukee—"

"I had no whiskey or brandy in my possession at that time or on any of these trips."

"You said you were in the city of Milwaukee. Did you get out of there without swallowing any lager beer?"

A few people in the courtroom laughed here, knowing how famous Milwaukee was for its beer. In fact, at least one German, Mr. Rublein, had come from Milwaukee to Marquette and set up a brewery that produced the local favorite, Castle Brew.

"On this occasion, yes," said Roosevelt, himself smiling.

"I think you covered it," added Mr. Pound, "but I want to be sure; just one question, whether what you have said of the fifteen years; does that also apply to your methods during the year 1912 in the campaign as well as the rest of the time?"

"It applies exactly," said Roosevelt. "What I have said about the trips while I was president applies exactly to the trips since I have been president, including 1912."

"Now I call your attention to the state of Ohio," said Mr. Pound. "What is the fact as to whether you made a personal canvass, as strong as you were able, for that state?"

"I did, for nine days; I was nine days in the state."

"Without any surplus words, tell us how you traversed the state, from what point you entered, and to what point you went, whether V-shaped or parallel, or how?"

"We went around the state, and I think with certain zigzags," said Roosevelt. "We went across the north of the state to Toledo, through the middle and eastern parts, and then the western part of the state to Columbus, and then to Cleveland, and I then spent Sunday with Mr. Garfield at his home, and continued the trip; I think on Monday was the last day. It may have been Monday and Tuesday."

Matthew knew the plaintiff had witnesses who had been present at Roosevelt's various campaign stops in Ohio; they were ready to testify he had not been drunk during any of that stretch of the campaign, hence the questions about Ohio.

"Did you make an address to the constitutional convention in the state of Ohio?"

"I made an address to the constitutional convention."

"About how long before or after the campaign trip for the delegation was that?"

"That address was made in February. I went to Columbus—I had prepared the address five or six days in advance; I went to Columbus and stayed at the house of Dr. Washington Gladden; I made the address and came home. I should say it was a month later that I made my speech in Carnegie Hall, which was practically the opening of the primary campaign—Carnegie Hall, New York."

"There was a time in your life," said Mr. Pound, changing the subject, "that you thought you had wasted it on the law business, I believe?"

"I studied law for a year after leaving college," answered Roosevelt.

"What I want to ask you is this: as a part of your education curriculum, were you a member of debating societies, or anything of that kind, so as to get a special training as to public speaking, or have you had to rely upon your own experience?"

"No," said Roosevelt, "I never got any training in public speaking until I ran for the legislature."

"Did your first experience come as a candidate?"

"I think my first experience did not come as a candidate. I think it came when I was in the legislature."

"You mentioned Dr. Rixey. Will you kindly tell me a little in detail who Dr. Rixey is and was, and how he came to be connected with you?"

"The head of the medical department of the navy is called the surgeon-general of the navy," Roosevelt explained, "just as the head of the medical department of the army is called the surgeon-general of the army: and the president usually has either the surgeon-general of the navy or the surgeon-general of the army as his attendant—sometimes, some army or navy doctor other than the surgeon-general.

"When I became president, Dr. Rixey was surgeon-general of the navy under President McKinley and was President McKinley's family doctor. He had attended President McKinley through his shooting when he died, and he was transferred to me and became my family doctor all during the seven-and-a-half years that I was in the White House. There was an occasional time when he would be absent from Washington on official business. I think I sent him once for three months to the Philippines on official business, but when he stayed in Washington, he was with me on most of my trips. I should say that he must have been with me nine-tenths of the time that I was president, and he used then to see me every day and often many times a day, and he looked after me to keep me in—"

"He would see you at what times?" Mr. Pound interrupted for the sake of clarification.

"Oh, it would depend; if he thought that I needed attention, he would see me before breakfast, and wait and see me after dinner."

"How late at night has he been at the White House?"

"Twelve or one o'clock; he would wait sometimes and come up after dinner if there was something—you see, the president has got to go on with his business; he can't be sick; he has got to go on with his business; and if I had any trifling ailment, he would have to be with me; if I had an attack of indigestion or anything of that kind, he would have to see that I could go right on exactly as if I didn't have it."

"A sort of physical insurer of the president?" suggested Mr. Pound.

"Exactly," Roosevelt confirmed.

"Your family doctor at home in New York, at that time and for many years, has been who?"

"Dr. Alexander Lambert," said Roosevelt. "He has been a close personal friend and the family doctor, and has been on trips with me."

Here Mr. Pound paused for a second, then said he had no more questions. Colonel Roosevelt was requested to remain on the stand while the defense cross-examined him.

While many of Roosevelt's supporters hoped Mr. Belden, who seemed more mild-mannered, would be the attorney to cross-examine, Mr. Andrews willingly stepped forward. But despite his previous string of objections, he spoke more calmly to the former president than people at first might have expected.

"Colonel Roosevelt," he began, "you have told us your age, and that your boyhood was mainly spent in New York?"

"In New York," Roosevelt confirmed. "My boyhood was mainly spent in New York."

"That is you spent the winter-time perhaps in the city, and the summer time at your country place?"

"At my father's," said Roosevelt, "where he had a country place."

"By that," said Mr. Andrews, "you mean a place outside of the city where the family spent the summer?"

"It was generally a farm where the family spent the summer."

"You have never lived in the state of Michigan, have you?"

"I never lived in the state of Michigan," Roosevelt confirmed.

"And have never in the last eight or ten years been here, except upon a flying trip?"

"Excepting on a comparatively short trip; I was several days here when I was inspecting the Naval Militia."

"That was how many years ago?"

"I think it was fifteen years ago."

"So that I would be correct in saying that within the last ten years, you have scarcely been within the state excepting upon a short flying trip?" asked Mr. Andrews.

"Excepting upon short visits through the state, usually to speak."

"Your acquaintance in Marquette County is somewhat limited, is it?" asked Mr. Andrews.

"It is limited," Mr. Roosevelt agreed.

"Do you know any of the residents here?"

"I know Mr. Shiras."

"Who?" Mr. Andrews asked to get clarification.

"Mr. George Shiras."

"And nobody else?"

"I have known Mr. Shiras better than anyone else, but I have met various men from the northern peninsula."

"Do you remember anybody else that you know in Marquette County?"

"I know Mr. Hill."

"He is your attorney?" Mr. Andrews confirmed.

"My attorney."

"You have known him since this case began?"

"No, I think I met him last year."

"Did you know him at that time?"

"There were several gentlemen got on board the train while I was passing through here," Roosevelt explained, referring to his campaign stop last October that had started all this trouble for him.

"He may have been one of them?" Mr. Andrews persisted.

"I think he was one of them, sir, but I am not sure."

"That was your only acquaintance with Mr. Hill?"

"Yes," Roosevelt confirmed.

"Mr. Shiras is really a resident of another state entirely, and comes here sometimes in the summer; is that correct?"

"I don't know," said Roosevelt.

"But you don't understand that he makes his home here all the time, do you?"

"I couldn't answer that; I know that his grandfather and father were here, and that he has been here, but I don't know whether he lives here or not."

"Or whether he lives here in the winter time?" asked Mr. Andrews.

"I know that he is off on hunting trips, natural history trips a great deal, both summer and winter, and my understanding is that he is in Washington in the winter, but I may be mistaken."

"It was in Washington that you made his acquaintance?"

"I made his acquaintance I think when he was in Congress, but my chief friendship with him sprang from the fact that he is a student of natural history, and so am I."

"Mr. Shiras was in Congress from Pittsburgh?" asked Mr. Andrews.

"In Congress from Pittsburgh," Roosevelt agreed.

"Do you know that that is his present home?"

"I don't know; I have been told so."

"During the time that you have related to the jury, your main occupation has been that connected in some way with politics, has it not?"

"At which time during the last fifteen years?" asked Roosevelt.

"During the time you specifically related to the jury, beginning with your career in the legislature?" Mr. Andrews clarified.

"Beginning with my career in the legislature," Roosevelt explained, "I should say I was as much a writer and historian as I was a public servant, until I went to the Spanish War, but while I was governor and president, of course, those were my main occupations."

"Since that time, since your return from Africa, you have been engaged with *The Outlook*, that is a publication in New York City?" asked Mr. Andrews.

"I have."

"And somewhat in politics also?"

"And in politics also, and might I amend my former answer? As I explained, I was for about thirteen years a great deal on my cattle ranch in the West."

"That was prior to the time I speak about?" asked Mr. Andrews.

"Well, it was subsequent to my being in the legislature."

"It was?"

"It was; it began the last year I was in the legislature."

"Now," said Mr. Andrews, changing the subject a bit, "your acquaintances and vast number of associates while you were in Washington on business and in the city of Albany were men also engaged in politics?"

"A good many of them were, and also practically every historian and naturalist to be found in the neighborhood of either Albany or Washington."

"You had among your acquaintances and associates a great many senators, did you not?"

"I knew almost every member of the Senate of the United States," Roosevelt confirmed.

"You received them in the White House, and were invited to their homes?"

"I received them in the White House. Only on rare occasions did they invite me to their homes."

"You knew also and associated with and received a great many congressmen, did you not?"

"I received all the congressmen that came."

"And on your trips, you were received by them and entertained more or less?"

"Sometimes."

"On most of the trips?"

"Entertained by them, no," said Roosevelt.

"You would be met by them?"

"I would be met by them on the trips while I was president—congressmen, senators, governors, private citizens, all met me."

"You were banqueted on those trips frequently?"

"It would depend upon what you mean by frequently," said Roosevelt cautiously.

"You went to various banquets?"

"Yes."

"On nearly all of those speaking trips that you speak of?" persisted Mr. Andrews.

"On almost all the speaking trips while I was president, there would be public banquets."

"Now," said Mr. Andrews, "since that time, you have been entertained in various homes of public men during the trips, such, for instance, as the home that you mentioned in Toledo?"

"Mr. Shepley," said Roosevelt. "I don't think you would call him a public man."

"Well, at other places, you have been entertained by public men on these trips?"

"Only rarely," said Roosevelt. "I was much more apt to be entertained by private citizens."

"Do I understand you to say that during all that time you never took anything in the way of intoxicants?" asked Mr. Andrews now finally getting to the real point of his questioning.

"What do you say, sir?" asked Roosevelt, a bit surprised by Mr. Andrews' switch to straightforward questions.

"If you took anything in the way of intoxicants, it was mainly a little brandy and milk?" asked Mr. Andrews, softening his tone a bit.

"No, you didn't understand me to say that," objected Roosevelt. "You understood me to say that about spirituous liquors."

"I will confine it to spirituous liquors," said Mr. Andrews. "The only spirituous liquors you took in the main, that is in general, would be a little brandy mixed with milk?"

"A teaspoonful in a tumbler of milk, at night," Roosevelt confirmed.

"And nothing else?"

"Nothing else."

"And that you never, in fifteen years, drank more than a dozen glasses of whiskey?"

"Oh, I didn't drink a dozen glasses of whiskey in fifteen years," said Roosevelt, smiling at catching Mr. Andrews' error.

"Perhaps I have exaggerated it?" said Mr. Andrews, unable not to smile himself as if they were just playing a game.

"Yes," said Roosevelt, nodding his head.

"You never drank any whiskey, then?"

"No, I have said that in the fifteen years, outside of the teaspoonful of brandy that I have given you, and outside of the mint juleps of which I have spoken, it would be probably an over-statement to say that a dozen times I have drunk whiskey on the occasion of having a fever attack or some occasion like that, but I never drank a glass of whiskey on those occasions; the doctor would give me usually a little bit in a little tumbler with the lines graduated on it."

"A little graduated glass?" Mr. Andrews clarified.

"Yes."

"In that perhaps a teaspoonful or something like that?"

"A small amount; I couldn't tell you how much."

"And that you never took any whiskey or spirituous liquors except on the prescription of a doctor?"

"Excepting as I have described, I never did."

"And you never, as I understand you, drank a high-ball?"

"No," Roosevelt confirmed.

"And you never have drunk more than five or six glasses of mint juleps in a year?"

"I have said I didn't average as many as five or six glasses in a year; I don't believe I ever drank as many as half-a-dozen glasses in a year, and you know those are not tumblers; those are small glasses of mint julep," said Roosevelt, unwilling to give Mr. Andrews any ground.

"I don't know about the glasses you speak of," said Mr. Andrews to be difficult. "Do you understand that mint julep is made of whiskey?"

"So I understand; made either of whiskey or brandy."

"Now your main drink, if you drink anything," said Mr. Andrews, switching topics, "is a little light wine?"

"The main spirituous drink, if I drink anything, is a little light wine."

"By light wine, what do you mean?"

"I mean so-called white wine," said Roosevelt. "California white wine, or Sauterne, and sometimes at home a couple of wine glasses of Madeira instead of white wine."

"It would be either white wine or Madeira wine?" Mr. Andrews confirmed.

"Yes."

"Any other kinds of wine?"

"I may have drunk a glass of sherry occasionally, but very occasional."

"Any others?"

"As I have described, at banquets or at the big dinners."

"I am asking about light wines."

"No."

"No red wine?" Mr. Andrews persisted.

"I don't drink red wine," Roosevelt flatly stated.

"You don't drink any red wine?"

"I wouldn't say I never drank any red wine. I may have been at some place where they passed around a glass of red wine and I may have touched it to my lips, but I don't like it; I don't drink it."

"You don't keep any wine of that kind in your house, do you?"

"Red wine?"

"Do you keep wine in your house?" asked Mr. Andrews, generalizing.

"Yes."

"Do you keep brandy?"

"Brandy and whiskey, both."

"All right in your home?"

"I keep it at the house."

"Did you keep brandy and whiskey and wine and all these liquors in the White House?" asked Mr. Andrews.

"I did; I inherited President McKinley's cellar, too."

"I ask the Court to strike out that which is not responsive to the question asked," said Mr. Andrews, not surprisingly—after all, he had been pleasant for quite a long time now.

Judge Flannigan, however, agreed it was not relevant and told the stenographer, "You may strike out that part of the question."

"Note an exception, please," said Mr. Pound, having to give his opposition back as good as he got. "I think he may state that he continued—I think it is competent for the witness to say that he continued the system that he found."

"If the witness answers that way," said Judge Flannigan, "that he continued the system in the White House, it will be received."

"May I amend my answer?" asked Colonel Roosevelt.

"If you cannot answer directly," said Mr. Andrews, frowning, "amend it any way you want to."

"I can answer it directly, certainly," said Roosevelt.

"I ask the question—" began Mr. Andrews.

But Mr. Pound objected, "Wait a minute; let him answer it."

"I simply ask," repeated Mr. Andrews, "did you keep liquors in the White House while you were president?"

"I continued the custom I found in the White House," repeated Roosevelt, "and kept liquors in the White House."

"Did you keep two butlers to take care of liquor in the White House?" Mr. Andrews asked.

"Not to take care of the liquor in the White House; they did that incidentally, as they had done it under the previous administration."

"I ask that that be stricken out as not responsive to any question I asked him," Mr. Andrews again insisted.

"That answer may stand," said Judge Flannigan.

It was hard to read the judge, but Matthew suspected he was getting tired of Mr. Andrews' antics.

That did not stop Mr. Andrews from asking his next question. "Now, you frequently go to banquets?"

"Yes."

"You drink wine and champagne there?"

"I drink champagne or white wine; I prefer light wine, white wine."

"Or both?"

"Very rarely."

"You do sometimes?"

"I doubt if I do, but it would be possible on some occasions that I have drunk both."

"Do you drink brandy at the banquets?"

"No."

"Have you ever drunk brandy at a banquet?" Mr. Andrews groped.

"I never have," Roosevelt replied without hesitation.

"Nor anywhere else?"

"Except as I have described," Roosevelt said, showing a touch of frustration in his tone with Mr. Andrews' repeated questions. Matthew could not blame him; the questioning was becoming circular to an extreme now.

"A teaspoonful in a glass of milk?" Mr. Andrews persisted.

"A teaspoonful in a glass of milk," Roosevelt repeated.

"Do you know Scotch whiskey?"

"I have seen it."

"Do you keep it in your home?"

"That I could not tell you. I know we did keep both Scotch whiskey and rye because the guests at my house when they come are asked at dinner whether they wish whiskey, and I know they used to be asked whether they wished Scotch or rye; whether we have it now or not, I do not know."

"In addition to keeping it, you offer and serve liquors in your home to your guests, do you?"

"I do," said Roosevelt, not blinking at the question.

"Mr. Roosevelt, has that been your custom a good while?"

"I think it has been my custom ever since I have had a home, but that I am not sure of; in the first—"

"I think that answers the question," Mr. Andrews said, trying to cut off the colonel.

Judge Flannigan, however, turned to Roosevelt and said, "You may proceed."

"It is possible it has only been my custom since I was governor or president; inasmuch as I never drink whiskey or brandy, I cannot be sure of it. I think that we had whiskey or brandy in the house before I was governor or president; I know we have had it since."

"Is that all the answer you care to give?" asked Mr. Andrews, as if thinking the plaintiff's responses insufficient.

"That is the answer," confirmed Roosevelt.

"When did you first meet Mr. Pound?" asked Mr. Andrews, now switching his tactics.

"The first time I remember meeting him was last fall."

"Do you know a Mr. Wallace of Detroit?"

"Yes."

"What is his business?"

"I don't know."

"Who had charge of the beginning of this suit, if you know?"

"That I cannot tell you," said Roosevelt.

"Don't you even know who began this lawsuit?" asked Mr. Andrews, his tone feigning exasperation with Roosevelt's response.

"I was in Mercy Hospital, laid up with the shooting when the suit was begun," Roosevelt said calmly. "This libel was brought to my attention after I had been shot."

"Do you know?" repeated Mr. Andrews, not even bothering to object again to the mention of the gunshot wound.

"I am telling you. You asked me if I didn't even know that; I am telling you why I didn't know."

"Do you know who began the suit?" Mr. Andrews repeated yet again.

"I do not," said Roosevelt firmly.

"Do you know that Mr. Wallace had charge of it?"

"I knew that he knew of it, whether he had charge of it or not."

"Do you know whether he had charge of the employment of counsel?"

"That I cannot say."

"Had you met Mr. Pound up to that time?"

"I may have met him: I may have met him before that time on a trip in Michigan."

"Have you any memory of it?"

"I don't remember whether I even met him or not. I met hundreds of people then."

Mr. Andrews grimaced and paused, then asked, "Was Mr. Pound employed by you?"

"Is he employed by me now?" asked Roosevelt to clarify the question.

"Was he originally employed by you?"

"You mean personally?" asked Roosevelt.

"Yes, sir," Mr. Andrews confirmed.

"In person, no. I was in Mercy Hospital on my back."

"I simply ask you whether you personally employed Mr. Pound. Can you answer that directly?"

"Of course it is possible that they asked me—it was by my direction that he was employed, but I didn't see him personally."

"Did Mr. Wallace have charge of the beginning of this suit?"

"Not that I know of."

"You don't know of any connection he had with it?" Mr. Andrews pushed.

"I know he was consulted about it."

"There were printed in the newspapers interviews in which Mr. Wallace stated that he had charge of the case, and that the Progressive organization of this state had charge of it. Have you seen those interviews?"

"I have not."

"Have you borne the expense of the matter of taking testimony and all that kind of thing in this case yourself?"

"Yes," said Roosevelt, nodding.

"You have?"

"Yes," Roosevelt repeated.

"And it has not been done under the direction of the organization here in Michigan?"

"It has not been."

"Have you in person had charge of it?"

"Mr. Pound has had charge of it," said Roosevelt.

"Just Mr. Pound?"

"Yes."

"I think that is all, Mr. Roosevelt," said Mr. Andrews, returning to his seat.

Matthew and the crowd were surprised Mr. Andrews had quit so suddenly. Although he had tried to trip up the former president a few times, tried to twist his words, he had not been as deliberate or aggressive as might have been expected given his objections during Mr. Pound's questioning.

Roosevelt now waited as Mr. Pound returned to perform his re-direct examination.

Clearing his throat, Mr. Pound began, referring to himself in the third person, "As I understand it, you have no recollection of having seen Mr. Pound either in Milwaukee or Chicago prior to the beginning of this suit, which was sometime in the month of October?"

"I have no recollection of it, Mr. Pound," Roosevelt replied.

"As matter of fact, you communicated, when you had sufficiently recovered, your desire directly to Mr. Pound by letter, did you not?"

"I did," Roosevelt confirmed.

"That is objected to as leading and incompetent," insisted Mr. Andrews. "The letter is the best evidence."

"The objection is," clarified Judge Flannigan, "that the letter would be the best evidence, Mr. Pound."

"That is right," Mr. Pound agreed, "and I do not propose to go into the contents of the letter. I am only wanting to know whether the witness assumes the responsibility of direction."

"I assume full responsibility of the direction," said Colonel Roosevelt, "and no organization has any responsibility, excepting myself, or has paid, or will pay a dollar."

"Have you directed all the proceedings from that time up to the present," asked Mr. Pound, "so far as the proceedings is concerned?"

"I have directed all proceedings," Roosevelt stated. "I have communicated with you, and you have communicated with me direct. The only exception has been where I have communicated with Mr. Bowers and Mr. Van Benschoten as counsel in New York City."

"And the reason for that was," asked Mr. Pound, "they were there in New York, and you were not accessible to me?"

"The reason was," said Roosevelt, "you were in Detroit; I wanted a lawyer that I could consult at once on any phase of the case that came up without your coming on from Detroit."

"And you were directed to get counsel close at hand?" asked Mr. Pound.

"I had to get counsel close at hand. I consulted you as to whom I should have," clarified Roosevelt.

Mr. Pound now stated that he had no further questions. Judge Flannigan then told Colonel Roosevelt he could finally leave the witness stand. His testimony had been the longest of any that would be included in the trial, but it had also been the most important for setting the trial's tone. Some observers were disappointed that the testimony had not been more sensational. Unless witnesses could be brought forth now to prove that Roosevelt had lied on the stand about how much he drank, it did not look good for the defense. Nevertheless, Mr. Andrews maintained a calm and suave air, as if he had the plaintiff right where he wanted him.

Believed to be Roosevelt's lawyers:
(left to right) James H. Pound, William H. Van Benschoten,
and William S. Hill

Marquet
Histor

Cliffs at Presque Isle Park

"Preserve it, treasure it,
as little altered as may be for all time."
— Fredrick Law Olmsted on Marquette's Presque Isle Park

CHAPTER 7

THE DAY'S TESTIMONY WAS FAR from over. Save for a break for lunch, both sides continued to examine and cross-examine witnesses throughout the morning and the afternoon. Each witness called was for the plaintiff and answered in a straightforward manner all the questions posed to him. Most of this testimony was designed to prove that Roosevelt's physical vigor, his perfectionism in his work, his strenuous exercising, and his overall capacity to do a tremendous amount of work would not have been possible in one who, according to Newett's statement, "got drunk and that not infrequently."

Henry Rauthier, the assessor for the city of Ishpeming, was called to testify that George Newett was indeed the owner of the *Iron Ore*—a testimony that was more of a formality to identify the defendant and make certain he was responsible for what had been printed.

Several doctors also came forward to testify to the former president's good health. Dr. Alexander Lambert, the Roosevelt family's physician and Roosevelt's intimate friend of thirty years, took the stand, followed by Dr. Presley Rixey, the former U.S. Surgeon General, whose official duties during both President McKinley and President Roosevelt's terms of office were largely devoted to guarding and maintaining the president's physical wellbeing. Dr. Rixey had attended Roosevelt at many state dinners at the White House, so he testified to the president's drinking habits on the rare occasions when he did drink—testimony that coincided with what Roosevelt himself had said.

A sworn deposition by Chicago surgeon Dr. Arthur Bevan was also introduced as evidence. Dr. Bevan had examined Roosevelt following the assassination attempt. In his deposition, he stated:

> I should say that after receipt of the gunshot wound, Colonel Roosevelt remained in an unusually normal condition as far as his heart and his nervous system were concerned. He had more or less

irritation in breathing, and absolutely no nervousness or excitement, he slept like a child, his nervous system was perfectly placid and under complete control, and the entire picture was entirely and absolutely inconsistent with that of a man who used liquor and was suffering from a gunshot wound of the character received by the colonel. I have taken care of a large number of gunshot wounds, some in men who drank, others who had been temperate, and have had the opportunity of studying both groups of cases very carefully. I know from this experience that Colonel Roosevelt's condition during the period while he was at the Mercy Hospital under our care and suffering from the gunshot wound, was such as to be absolutely inconsistent with his being a drinking man or a man who had ever abused himself with liquor.

Another deposition by Dr. John Murphy, also a surgeon in Chicago, likewise confirmed that save for his gunshot wound, Colonel Roosevelt had been in excellent physical condition, which would not have been the case were he a drinking man.

Other witnesses that day included Gilson Gardner, a newspaperman whose duties for many years had caused him to follow Colonel Roosevelt's movements closely. He had attended many public functions where Roosevelt had been a guest, and he testified that he had never seen Roosevelt under the influence to the slightest degree during any of these social events.

However, the man who stole the show during his testimony was Jacob Riis, the well-known sociologist, social reformer, and writer. After Riis had published his book *How the Other Half Lives* in 1890, Roosevelt had been so impressed that he had sought out Riis. Together, they had patrolled the police beat in New York to ensure that the police were doing their jobs and to stamp out crime and corruption in the city. Riis had been born in Denmark and migrated to the United States in 1870, at the age of twenty-one. He had never quite lost his accent, but he could write in English better than most native speakers.

Matthew could not help but like Riis. He had liked him ever since he had first met him and accompanied him and Roosevelt one night to report on their efforts to clean up the streets of New York City from corruption. Matthew knew that, like Roosevelt, Riis was sincere in his desire to help Americans, and especially his fellow immigrants, rise above poverty. He now won over the hearts of the jurors and all the courtroom spectators by his answers to the attorneys' questions.

When asked whether Roosevelt had ever been under the influence of alcohol while in his presence, Riis, with full gusto, exclaimed, "Oh, Lord, no!" When asked whether Roosevelt ever used coarse or profane language, Riis sharply stated, "Mr. Roosevelt is a gentleman." When asked whether his acquaintance with Roosevelt had been intimate, Riis stated, referring to their first meeting, "I made him my brother then and there, and he has been so ever since." When Mr. Pound asked him, "What is the fact as to whether or not you were in sympathy with one another as to various ideas of public work at that time?" Riis replied, "I just loved the man."

No one could help smiling at Riis' unabashed and sincere affection for the plaintiff. Most men, Matthew thought, would be lucky to have such a friend as Riis to vouch for them.

When the day's work concluded at five o'clock, it was apparent the trial would persist for several more days since numerous witnesses were yet to be called.

After Judge Flannigan dismissed the court, people slowly began to file out of the courtroom.

"I'll see you tomorrow," Homer said to Matthew, who nodded and added, "Have a pleasant evening." He did not want to tell Homer that he had been invited to the Shiras home for dinner that night. Matthew almost felt guilty that he would get more time in Roosevelt's presence than his fellow reporters.

Matthew made his way to Delia, who said, as they passed into the hall, "I hope Roger remembers to pick us up," but before they could get outside, George came up to Matthew and said, "We're going to take Theodore out to see Presque Isle Park if you'd care to ride with us. I'm afraid I only have room for one in the vehicle, however."

Delia, not feeling slighted and understanding it was a great opportunity for Matthew to ride with the former president, smiled and said, "Go ahead, Matthew."

"We have some time before dinner so we thought we should make the best of it," George said quietly so people in the crowd would not overhear him, "and then you can just come home with us for dinner."

"That would be splendid," said Matthew, thinking it such a treat that he momentarily forgot the awkwardness he always felt around George.

"Good," said George. "We're parked over there." He pointed to Main Street where his car was waiting. Roosevelt and Tyree were already walking toward it.

"I see Roger over there," said Delia, gesturing toward Third Street, "so I'll see you later tonight, Matthew."

"Thanks, Delia," said Matthew, kissing her on the cheek. "Have a good evening."

Brother and sister parted, and in another minute, Matthew was climbing into the front seat of George's automobile, directly in front of Colonel Roosevelt.

"I'm pleased to see you again, sir," he said to Roosevelt, shaking his hand before entering the vehicle.

"I'm glad you could join us, Mr. Newman," said Roosevelt. "I remember well that night you walked the streets of New York with Jacob and me, and the wonderful story you printed in your paper after that."

"It was my pleasure to print it," said Matthew. "I knew then you would do great things for New York, and I couldn't have been more pleased to see all the things you've since done for our country."

"We all must do our work," said Roosevelt. "That's the most important thing about life. To find good work to do to benefit our fellow human beings."

"Here we go," said George, taking his seat and then starting to move the car forward. "I believe Jacob Riis and a few others will be following us," he added for Matthew's information.

As George pulled his automobile out onto Third Street, Matthew fell silent, not sure what more to say to the former president. He was on this little excursion as a friend, not a reporter, and so he did not wish to be rude and ask questions of the great man. But finally, out of curiosity, he asked, "Colonel Roosevelt, what do you think of Marquette?"

"It's a fine city. I can see why George has spent so much time here, although it's not Oyster Bay, of course," said Roosevelt, referring to his New York home. Matthew smiled, appreciating the colonel's good humor.

"Look at that beautiful building," said Roosevelt as they came to the corner of Washington and Third Street. "What a roof it has."

"That's the City Hall," said George. "It is quite a noticeable structure." Matthew had to agree. Its giant domed roof made it stand out, and it was, as Mayor Nathan Kaufman had said at the time it was dedicated in 1895, "a city hall to last forever."

The Marquette City Hall

George now turned the vehicle onto Washington Street toward Lake Superior so Roosevelt could get a glimpse of the downtown he had not yet seen having come down Front and then up Baraga Avenue to the courthouse previously.

"We have several fine performers who come to our opera house," Matthew informed Roosevelt and Tyree.

"Yes, I hear *The Prince of Pilsen* is being performed there this week," remarked Roosevelt, while waving back at people who had stopped on the street to wave and gape at him. "But I'm afraid the crowd would be too overwhelming for me. Everyone would be so busy trying to get a glimpse of me that they wouldn't enjoy the performance."

"Too many references to beer in that play anyway," Tyree added. "Still, it's a great play."

"It is," said Matthew, turning to address George. "I'm hoping Delia will go with me."

George drove down toward the lake, and for a minute, Matthew felt a bit embarrassed about the mess that was the lower harbor, full of coal and docks and ships, but George said, "We'll be enjoying some beautiful scenery in a few more minutes."

Soon they had left the city industries behind, and once they passed the Waterworks building, George turned up the hill on Ridge Street, drove past his house and several other fine homes, and then turned onto Pine Street, passing residences for several blocks as they went down a hill. Then they made their way along a wooded road until they reached Lakeshore Boulevard, which ran along Lake Superior and made its way out to Presque Isle Park.

"My father-in-law, Peter White, had this road built," George told Theodore, "and he planted all these Lombardy poplars along it to make it scenic."

"He was a wonderful visionary from all you've told me," said Roosevelt, "and from what I know, myself. Why, I remember when he came to see me while I was president—he wanted funding to celebrate the fiftieth anniversary of the locks at Sault Ste. Marie, although you'd hardly know his purpose since he spent most of his time entertaining everyone in Washington with his stories of his days when he was a young man here and Marquette was a frontier town."

"And he got his funding, didn't he?" said George, smiling.

"He did indeed—$15,000 I believe it was. How could Congress refuse him? He had a particular charm about him that few men can claim. I would have loved to see him here in his native environment."

"He would have loved to have hosted you," said George. "I'm not one to believe in ghosts, but I have to admit sometimes I feel his presence still in the house. I'm sure wherever he is, he's delighted to know you're a guest in his home."

"I noticed the city library is named for him," said Roosevelt.

"Yes," said George. "He loved Marquette, and he did a lot for its development. He thought nothing of helping to fund a church roof or our city's Father Marquette statue. But the library and Presque Isle Park are definitely his two greatest legacies to the city."

"When George and I were boys," Matthew added, "we'd go camping up in that area, but there was a lot of swamp so you could only get to the park by boat, and it wasn't even a park then; it belonged to the Coast Guard, but Mr. White changed all that."

"I guess," George added, "you could say he was a conservationist like you and me, Theodore, since he thought Presque Isle would make a splendid park for the city and he foresaw how Marquette would keep growing north, which now a quarter of a century after he bought the park, has proven to be true. The city commission didn't want anything to do with the park when he tried to give it to them. They said it was too far from town, so no one would ever go there; to prove them wrong, he built this road out to it. Eventually, the city decided to run the streetcar line out here too, and now, especially when everyone is buying automobiles, crowds of people are constantly going out there to go swimming or have picnics."

By now, they could all see the new Lake Superior & Ishpeming Ore Dock was in view. It rose above the road, serving as a sort of grand entrance to the park.

The Lake Superior & Ishpeming Ore Dock, built in 1912

Roosevelt shook his head at the sight of the massive dock, larger than any he had seen in Marquette's lower harbor.

"Is it for iron ore?" asked Roosevelt.

"Yes, it's a pocket dock," said George. "There was another one built of wood back in 1896, but it wasn't strong enough for all the ore, so they constructed this one in the last couple of years. It's the first reinforced concrete dock ever built, and it's considered quite the engineering marvel—it's definitely the greatest ore dock ever built."

"And how exactly does it work?" asked Roosevelt.

A ship was pulled up alongside the dock, so George explained how the trains would come from the mines south of Marquette and ride up onto the trestle that went over the road. They would make their way to the end of the dock, and then the train cars would unload the iron ore into the dock's pockets. Once full, the pockets would then tip down to become chutes that let the ore slide down them into the hulls of the ore boats.

"Yes," said Roosevelt. "I can see that chute there is open."

As they approached the trestle, they could actually hear the ore pouring into the ship.

"Then the ships are off to Cleveland or Buffalo or Pittsburgh," Matthew added, "where the ore is converted into steel."

"It's a great marvel," said Roosevelt. "This iron country has made our nation a world player in industry and trade. In fact, George, your father-in-law proved that to me by bringing all the financial figures with him when he came to Washington to convince us the Sault locks deserved an anniversary celebration. But what most amazes me is that this iron country is not more heavily populated."

"It's the brutal winters that keep people away, right, George?" said Matthew.

"That's the truth," said George. "They keep me away. Six-foot snowbanks and wind chills of forty degrees below zero." And George raised his shoulders to give a good shiver at the thought.

"I believe it," said Frank Tyree. "The winters in Oyster Bay can get cold like that too now and then."

Roosevelt laughed and said, "Cold weather keeps a man tough."

"Even so," said Tyree, "I'm glad to live in West Virginia now." Tyree was now the United States Marshal for that state, but he'd spent plenty of time at Roosevelt's Oyster Bay home on Long Island when he was in the Secret Service.

By now, George had driven under the railroad trestle and they had officially entered Presque Isle Park. George explained that the park's French name meant "almost an island," but the locals had come to call it familiarly "The Island."

George turned to the right to take the road around the park, and as he did so, they all got a view of the ore dock's other side.

"It's a beautiful lake," said Roosevelt. "It's so large that one would never know it wasn't an ocean."

"The park is beautiful too," remarked Tyree. "The trees are so green— almost in full leaf already."

"It is really quite untouched," said Matthew. "It was intended to be preserved as a natural park."

"Yes," George added. "My father-in-law asked Frederick Law Olmsted to give his recommendations for maintaining it. Theodore, you knew Olmsted, didn't you?"

"Oh, yes," said Theodore. "He was very active in the creation of many of our National Parks, and he also designed Central Park and many other parks in various cities."

"Well, he was a friend of the Longyears, who used to live in Marquette," said George. "He did the landscaping for their mansion, so while he was here, my father-in-law asked him to take a look at Presque Isle. When he did, he thought it so beautiful that he said it should be left exactly as it is, not destroyed by manmade innovations."

"I think he was absolutely right," said Roosevelt as George drove them up a small hill. At the top of the hill was a grassy clearing that looked down over the lake, and near the center of the clearing was a giant stone, at least a yard tall and propped up on a foundation of other smaller stones. The main stone was unique because two-thirds of it were composed of black granite, but a stripe of red granite ran through its middle.

"This," said George, stopping the vehicle, "is the grave of Charles Kawbawgam. He was the last Chief of the Chippewa Indians in this area. He died about a decade ago, and his wife, Charlotte Kawbawgam, is buried here with him. She was the daughter of Chief Marji Gesick who first showed the white men where the iron ore outcroppings were. They say Marji Gesick later regretted leading the men to the shining rocks and felt like a curse had been placed on him for it."

"Superstition," muttered Roosevelt.

Grave of Charles and Charlotte Kawbawgam

"My father-in-law was good friends with Kawbawgam, so I remember him well," George continued. "When Marquette was founded back in 1849, Kawbawgam let several of the early settlers stay in his lodge house that first winter. It was then he became good friends with my father-in-law, who was only nineteen at the time. Another time, my father-in-law got lost in a snow-

Charles Kawbawgam, last Chief of the Chippewa (1799-1902)

storm and the chief found him and gave him shelter. After that, my father-in-law built him a house here by the entrance to Presque Isle. They stayed close friends until the end."

George now started up the vehicle again and they continued around the park, taking the road down its forest-covered hills with trees so thick you could not see Lake Superior, though it was only a few dozen feet away.

"Down there are the Black Rocks," said George. "You can't see them from the road, but they're a geological marvel, the only rocks like them in the country. We don't have time to go look at them now, but maybe we can come out to see them some other time."

In a few more seconds, they came around another curve, and then, there was the lake before them again. The road was now very close to the edge of the lakeshore, so Roosevelt could see many of the interesting rock formations, including the arched rock, along the shoreline.

"Here's the pavilion," said Matthew. "It used to be out on Partridge Island where J.M. Longyear placed it for private parties, but later, he decided to have it moved to Presque Isle—they moved it in winter, when the lake was frozen, using horses to pull it over the ice."

"That sounds like quite an undertaking," said Frank Tyree.

"This open area over here," said George, pointing to his left and inland, "I've often thought would be a good place to have a zoo. I'd want it to be all local animals—white-tailed deer, bear, raccoons, maybe even some ruffed grouse and pheasants," he said. "I'm afraid the younger generation doesn't get out into the woods like they used to, and I'm not a fan of hunting like you are, Theodore, but I think it would be nice for the children to come and see the animals here."

"That sounds like a wonderful idea," said Matthew. "Marquette should have a zoo. There isn't one anywhere in Upper Michigan to my knowledge."

"And who is this gentleman?" asked Roosevelt, seeing a man waving at them from the front yard of a house.

"That's Bob Hume," said George. "He's the park's caretaker. I'll introduce you to him."

Shiras slowed down the car as they approached Mr. Hume. The caretaker's smile quickly turned into a look of shock when he saw who was in the vehicle.

"Bob, allow me to introduce you to Colonel Roosevelt," said George.

"Welcome to Presque Isle, sir," said Bob, reaching toward the colonel and giving him a hearty handshake. "It's an honor, sir."

"Let's stop here so I can stretch my legs a moment and hear more about the park from this young man," said Roosevelt, his joke causing Bob to beam since Bob was well past fifty. In a moment, George had turned off the motor and the party was climbing out of the vehicle.

Robert Hume, Caretaker of Presque Isle Park

"And, Bob," said George, "you probably remember Matthew Newman."

"Hello, Bob," said Matthew.

It took Bob a moment to recognize the boy he had gone camping and to school with so many years before, but then Bob laughed and said, "I do," giving Matthew's hand a hearty shake. "We had many fine adventures together as boys, the three of us, and poor Joe."

"Poor Joe?" said Matthew. "Why, what's become of him?"

"Drank himself to death," said Bob. "He's been dead a few years now."

"I'm sorry to hear it," said Matthew.

"Drink is the devil's business," added Bob, turning his attention back to Colonel Roosevelt. "It's a shame, too, sir, that it's the same business that has brought you to Marquette. I don't blame you for being angry to have such a lie spoken about you."

"Thank you," said Roosevelt. "I appreciate your support."

"I've seen liquor cause all kinds of problems in my past line of work as a policeman," Bob added. "I won't let anyone bring a drop of it into the park."

"Very wise," added Roosevelt approvingly.

"Bob, this is Frank Tyree, Colonel Roosevelt's former bodyguard," George added as Frank walked around the car to shake Bob's hand.

By now, the vehicle that had been following them had pulled up as well. In a moment, Dr. Lambert, Dr. Rixey, and Jacob Riis had all gotten out along with their driver, Maxwell Kennedy Reynolds. Mr. Reynolds was not only George's first cousin—because their mothers had been two of the four Kennedy sisters whose marriages had resulted in nearly all of Marquette's well-to-do families on Ridge Street being related—but he was also married to Frances Jopling, Peter White's granddaughter, making him George's nephew-in-law. George had enlisted his Reynolds relations in helping to host many of the witnesses who had come to testify at Roosevelt's trial, and they had been delighted to assist.

"I've been reading about all of you in the newspapers," Bob Hume said as he was introduced to everyone in the party and shook their hands. "But I never thought I'd get to meet all of you."

"Well," said Roosevelt, "George insisted I come and see your beautiful park. He's told me how Olmsted said it should be kept as natural as possible, and you've done a fine job making sure it has stayed that way."

"Thank you, sir," said Bob Hume. "It's a big job for one man, but I'm fortunate that the people of Marquette love it, so they help me take care of it by not littering or being destructive. I've rarely had a problem at all."

"Bob is also the one who found the stone for Chief Kawbawgam's grave," said George.

"Yes," said Bob. "When it washed up on shore, I thought it was such a distinctive stone that I decided it would suit the old chief. A geologist offered me $1,000 for it, but I refused. I told him it was for Charley Kawbawgam and no one else. After all, Kawbawgam was a good friend to me when I first became caretaker here; you know he used to live over near the entrance to the park, so I saw him regularly. Peter White, well, he was the chief's good friend too, so I'm sure he would have been happy with my using the stone to honor him."

"Bob," George added, "has been busy cultivating a herd of wild deer here on the island."

"Really?" said Roosevelt.

"Yes, sir," said Bob, "although I'm not sure how wild they are anymore. I'm afraid I spoil them by putting out food for them."

"I'm hoping we'll have deer in my zoo someday, too," George said.

The caretaker's house at Presque Isle where Bob Hume lived

"Have you ever seen any moose here on your island?" asked Roosevelt.

"I can't say I have myself," said Bob, "although one or two people claim they have, but if so, they must have snuck on and off the island while I was asleep. There are only a handful left in the state now I understand."

"Well, you can say now that you have seen a moose here," Roosevelt added, smiling widely, for his question had been so he could make a joke. "A bull moose."

Bob Hume laughed. "Yes, sir," he said, "and may I add that I wish I had seen one in the White House this year as well."

"You do?" said Roosevelt. "Well, that's very kind of you."

"It's a shame, this trial, sir," said Bob. "We're delighted that you've come to Marquette, but we wish it was under better circumstances."

"Thank you," said Roosevelt. "You're very kind."

"It's a real shame, especially since I understand you got the news about that editorial in the *Iron Ore* right after you were shot."

"I did," said Roosevelt.

"Bob has a gunshot wound himself," said George.

"Really?" said Roosevelt. "Tell me about it."

"It was back in the summer of 1899," said Bob. "I've always been a city employee, working mostly in the parks, but I'm also a police officer, and I was once even the chief of police for Marquette. Anyway, Officer Odette and I were responding to a burglarized house call. We were just passing the block between Ridge and Arch Streets when four thugs came around the corner. One thrust a pistol in Officer Odette's face, seized him by his collar, and said, 'Thumbs up.' Odette threw off the fellow with his left arm and grabbed his pistol with his right. The thug meanwhile fired, but because of how Odette had thrown him, the bullet hit me. I pulled out my own gun at that moment, but I don't remember what happened next since I was wounded and a bit in shock. Apparently, the crooks ran off and fired a few more shots at Odette, who chased them for about fifty feet. He said we both fired at them, although my memory of it isn't clear. Once they had run off, Odette, realizing he was outnumbered without me, ran back to help me. He said I'd better see a doctor so he managed to help me walk to Sidney Adams' house since it was nearby. Adams' son-in-law, Dr. Dawson, lived there, so I knew he would help me. I must have been a sight because as soon as Mr. Adams opened the door, I fell on the hall floor, saying, "They've got me, I guess." I thought I was a dead man. My memory of what happened after that is kind of muddled. I know they laid me down somewhere and tried to make me comfortable. I remember talking to the reporter who came. By then, the doctor had determined that I had been shot in the back—actually my left shoulder—and the bullet had hit bone, which pushed it down toward my heart. That was what made me fall down in shock initially. The bullet finally lodged itself in the pit of my stomach."

"That's quite a journey for it to make," said Roosevelt. "Mine didn't penetrate anywhere near that far."

"Did they catch the shooter?" Jacob Riis asked Bob.

"No, they never did."

"So they didn't find out the motive?" Jacob persisted.

"I think it was a gambler," said Bob. "We'd been trying to clean up a gambling racket in town. I was only doing my duty, but I guess they thought I was too hard on them, so they wanted revenge. I think the burglary call was fake just to get us out in the open where they could take aim at me and Odette. Anyway, I was quite the sight I believe. My wife came to see me, but I was so certain I was going to die that I had her send for our children so I could see them one last time. When the police chief, Tim Hurley, came, I told him not to wait for me to die, but just to go get the dirty crooks. He promised he would and got together a posse of about twenty people who went to the saloons the gamblers and other suspicious characters were known to frequent. He even raided the houses of prostitution down on Lake Street. By morning, about twenty suspects had been arrested for gambling, but just who shot me was never determined."

"I wouldn't have thought gambling was a problem here," said Tyree, "or prostitution for that matter."

"These gamblers were having a big tournament here, but it wasn't just the gambling that was the problem," Bob explained. "It attracted a bunch of pickpockets and thugs and just plain unsavory characters. We didn't want that sort in our town, so we tried to put a stop to it. We should have started sooner, but we'd never had an issue like that in Marquette before, so I guess we hadn't known what we were up against until it was too late. As for prostitutes, well, you know, there are some in every town, no matter how you try to prevent it."

"It's too bad," said Roosevelt.

"You did your duty, though," said Frank Tyree, who knew what it was to be in the line of danger. "And you look very strong and healthy despite it."

"I am," said Bob, "even though the bullet is still lodged in me."

"I'm not surprised," said Roosevelt. "So is mine. The doctors decided it was safer to leave it in me than to try to remove it."

"And does it bother you any?" asked Bob.

"Only the knowledge that it's there," said Roosevelt. "I don't feel any pain from it anymore. It has been over seven months now."

"It's going on fourteen years for me," said Bob, "and it hasn't stopped me from doing my work."

"Nor I," said Roosevelt. "Right after I was shot, I went and gave the speech I was scheduled to deliver that night before I let anyone take me to the hospital."

"Then you're a stronger man than me," said Bob. "I only walked a block to the Adams' house before I collapsed."

"Yes," said Dr. Lambert, "but your bullet traveled a lot farther, so you were bound to feel it more."

Dr. Rixey and Roosevelt both agreed with Dr. Lambert on this point.

"It doesn't matter," said Bob. "It was worth a few days of pain and being in the hospital to make sure Marquette's streets are safe."

"Yes, we have to do our duty," Roosevelt agreed. "We can't let a few scoundrels stop us."

"I do wish, though," said Bob, "that they would pass these Prohibition laws they keep talking about. Drink just attracts criminals to the area, and people don't know what they're doing when they drink. That's what happened to my friend, Joe. He became so addicted to hard liquor that he couldn't even work, and eventually, it killed him."

"I know," said Roosevelt, his face growing very sad, as if he had known a few victims to alcohol himself. But then he seemed to shake off the feeling and replied, "That's why I don't like these libelous charges against me. All my life I've been a working man, and I will never give into the temptation of liquor when I know my country and my family need me."

"Well said," Matthew replied.

"Well, we should get going," said George. "Mr. Riis and Dr. Rixey and Dr. Lambert have a train to catch. They'll be leaving this evening since they gave their testimonies today, and it's almost dinner time for the rest of us."

"It was a pleasure to meet you, sir," said Roosevelt, again shaking Bob's hand. "It seems we have a lot in common. If George doesn't mind, and if this trial continues into next week, I'd be honored if you would join us this weekend. George is going to take me and a few friends down to his father-in-law's hunting camp to show me where he takes his wildlife photos. We'd leave on Saturday afternoon and come back on Sunday."

Bob Hume's face lit up. "I would enjoy that very much," he said. "Wait until I tell my wife. She'll probably be speechless to think of me spending the weekend with the former president of the United States. Too bad she's gone shopping in town. She would have loved to meet you."

"Give her my best wishes and my compliments on how beautiful your house and yard look," Roosevelt replied.

And with that, all the members of the party climbed back into their automobiles.

"Pleasant chap," said Roosevelt as George drove them out of the park. "We need more committed men like him."

"Bob takes wonderful care of the park," George replied. "He loves it like it's his own child."

"Bob has never been one to refuse when something needs to be done," Matthew added. It had done his heart good to see his old friend.

The party now returned to the Shiras house. Since Maxwell Reynolds lived next door, he waited for the two doctors and Jacob Riis to collect their belongings. Then, after Roosevelt thanked them for coming to Marquette on his behalf and wished them a safe journey, Maxwell drove them back to the train depot.

Meanwhile, Matthew found himself entering Peter White's house, now the home of George and Frances Shiras, a home he had not set foot in since he had left Marquette nearly thirty years ago.

The Peter White House where George Shiras hosted Theodore Roosevelt.
In front of the house are Peter White, his granddaughter Frances Jopling,
and neighbor boy Alfred Kidder, Jr., as shown in the close-up.

CHAPTER 8

SHIRAS, ROOSEVELT, AND TYREE WERE all busy talking about the trial as they entered the house, but Matthew, for just a moment, ignored them and let himself look about the front hall he remembered so well.

The second he saw the staircase, he had a flashback to one of the happiest moments of his life—Frances descending the stairs while he and her father stood watching her, and in another moment, he remembered how he had linked his arm in hers and escorted her outside. They had been off to a party together that night, and Matthew had felt like a young Adonis with Venus on his arm.

"What do you say, Matthew?" asked George, breaking Matthew's reverie.

"Sorry," said Matthew. "What?"

"Where have you been?" laughed Frank Tyree.

"Sorry; I have a bad tendency of writing my news reports in my head, and I was caught up doing that."

"And what are you going to write?" asked Roosevelt.

"Oh, well, if you don't mind, I thought maybe I'd write a human interest piece about your trip around Presque Isle. And, of course, I'll report on the trial. I'll go home and write up my dispatch tonight after dinner to send to my editor in the morning."

"Nothing too personal, though," Roosevelt cautioned. "I don't want any reporters complaining I gave you preferential treatment."

"Understood, sir," said Matthew, nodding.

By now, some of Shiras' other guests, who would serve as witnesses in the next couple of days, came downstairs.

"We thought we heard Theodore bellowing," said James Garfield. "We hoped that meant it was dinner time. We're all starving."

The staircase inside the Peter White Home

"Why don't you gentlemen all have a seat in the parlor and I'll check on dinner," said George.

Matthew, Colonel Roosevelt, and a half-dozen others went into the parlor to have cigars and talk over the day's events at the courthouse. Five minutes later, George returned saying that dinner was served, and the men, although all being gentlemen, charged like bull moose into the dining room.

Parlor of the Peter White Home

In a few minutes, they were all seated, cloth napkins unfurled, servants hovering behind them to give them soup and then their main courses and to fill up their wine glasses as needed. Matthew smiled to see that, like himself, Roosevelt chose to drink water.

"Tell me more, George, about your father-in-law," said Roosevelt once everyone's plate was stacked with roast beef and mashed potatoes. "I'd like to know more about the man whose house I'm staying in. Was he also interested in wildlife photography or hunting?"

"I don't know that there was much he wasn't interested in," Shiras replied. "But he wasn't much of a hunter until his later years. He was always so involved in business that I don't think he found much time until then."

"But did he enjoy hunting?" asked Roosevelt.

"I would say so, but his eyesight wasn't the keenest in the end," replied George.

"That's too bad," said Matthew, who remembered Mr. White as being very active.

"Well, maybe I should take that back," said George. "Perhaps his eyesight just wasn't as keen as Fred Cadotte's. Fred was, and still is, one of my Indian guides, and I swear he can spot a deer from a hundred yards away even in the thickest woods. One day, Fred and my father-in-law were out hunting with me when my father-in-law spotted a deer drinking from a pond. He took aim and was just about to fire when Fred tiptoed up carefully behind him and in a low, tense voice, whispered, 'Don't shoot! It's a man.'

"Flustered, my father-in-law lowered his gun, and then we all peered through the opening between the trees and realized it was indeed a man. He was bent over, scooping up water with his hands and washing his face. He wore a yellowish-brown canvas coat that resembled a deer's hide, so my father-in-law's mistake was understandable. Once we realized the man wasn't a deer, we quietly walked away without being noticed.

"Later, we learned that the man we had seen was Robert Dollar. Yes, *the* Robert Dollar—the Grand Old Man of the Pacific. Few people outside the Upper Peninsula know this, but he briefly lived here in Marquette. In fact, the village of Dollarville, about a hundred miles east of here, is named for him. Anyway, he was engaged in land-looking and timber cruising, so on that day, he was camping nearby. Imagine if my father-in-law had shot him—what a blow that would have been to the world of shipping—there'd never have been a Dollar Steamship Line."

"Lucky indeed," said Roosevelt, "both for Dollar and your father-in-law."

"Yes, we were lucky that Fred was there," said Shiras. "Like most of my Indian guides, he's a real blessing to me."

"I think I remember Fred," said Matthew. "Is he the same man they call Fred Bawgam?"

"Yes," said Shiras. "He was Chief Kawbawgam's nephew."

"Is that the chief whose grave we saw at Presque Isle today?" asked Roosevelt.

"Yes," said George. Then he explained for the benefit of the other guests who hadn't visited Presque Isle that afternoon, "They called Kawbawgam the last Chief of the Chippewa. Although most people call them the Ojibway, which is the French version of their name, while Chippewa is the English version, but I guess Chief of the Chippewa has more of a ring to it. Anyway, Kawbawgam's buried here in Marquette at Presque Isle Park, and it's said he lived to be about a century old. He was married to Charlotte Kawbawgam, the daughter of Chief Marji Gesick. Everyone called him Charley Kawbawgam."

"I guess the natives here were a lot friendlier with the settlers than out West," said Garfield.

"That they were," said Shiras, "and I think maybe the white man treated them better also. Not that there haven't been issues here and there, but I've never known any of the Ojibway around here to be anything but friendly and helpful. I suspect Bishop Baraga had a lot to do with that since he was one of the first white men in this area. He came here from Slovenia back in the 1830s to be a missionary to the Indians. They used to call him the Snowshoe Priest because he would snowshoe all across the Upper Peninsula and even to northern Lower Michigan and out to parts of Wisconsin to preach the gospel and convert the Indians. He was also the first bishop of the Marquette diocese when it was established, and he's buried here in St. Peter's Cathedral. Some say he was a living saint. He cared about the Indians so much that he came to resemble them before he died. In any case, I would say we were fortunate to have him come as an ambassador to the Indians before the rest of us arrived in this area. He was here a good decade, I believe, before Marquette was founded or any of the mines opened."

"Tell me about your other Indian guides," Roosevelt requested. "You said you've had many, and it interests me, considering how they sound as clever as some of the African guides I met when I was on safari."

"One of my favorite guides," George complied, "was Jack LaPete. He was a brother-in-law to Chief Kawbawgam. He had a French father and an Indian mother, and he was born over by Sault Ste. Marie."

"I remember Jack," said Matthew, smiling. "He was quite a character."

"How so?" Roosevelt asked.

George laughed and then explained, "Well, for one, he married an Indian woman—her name was Mary. One day, he bet her that she couldn't swim, even though she insisted she could. So she got in the water, and wouldn't you know it, she drowned. You would think Jack would have been heartbroken over it, but when I expressed my sympathies to him, he just said it had been a bad bet since now he couldn't collect on it."

Roosevelt roared at this. "It must not have been a happy union!" he exclaimed.

"Oh, I don't know about that," said George. "I think Jack was tender-hearted enough. He just knew how to turn a phrase."

Bishop Baraga, the Snowshoe Priest (1797-1868)

"Did he ever marry again?" asked Roosevelt.

"No, I think he was heartbroken, honestly," said Shiras, "and he used humor to hide it."

Matthew thought he could understand that. He had known what it was to lose someone he loved to drowning, but he caught himself before he could get too melancholy and added, "He never married again as far as I've heard, but I believe he still liked the ladies, given how he always found one to party with him once a year."

"Oh, yes," said George. "I'd nearly forgotten about that."

"Tell us," said Garfield.

"Well," said George, "Jack was always a sober and temperate man, but once a year, he decided to have a grand celebration in town. He would put on his best clothes, make his black hair glisten with bear's grease, and go to the stable to select the best-looking horse and buggy. Then he would choose a good-looking girl; it didn't matter whether she was white or Indian, and the girls all knew him, so they were honored to be chosen. The two would then ride around Marquette in that buggy like a king and queen in their royal carriage, waving greetings to everyone. When the ride was over, Jack would return the horse and buggy and give the girl a five-dollar bill."

"Lucky girl!" said Roosevelt.

"I'd say so," Matthew agreed. "I wouldn't even be surprised if Jack got a few kisses from the girls. But he can't still be alive, George?"

"No, he died a couple of years ago," said George, "but even how he died shows just what a character he was. Back in, oh, it must have been about 1893, he came to me one day and said, 'I want to go to Manitoba, in the Red River country, so that when I die, I will be buried there.' I was astonished since Jack had lived on Lake Superior his entire life as far as I knew, and he must have been about eighty by then. When I asked why he would want to move away, he explained that he had long carried with him a secret about himself unknown to anyone else except his mother. It turns out his mother had not been an Ojibway but a Sioux. She had been with her people, camped near the Red River in Canada, when a band of Ojibway warriors abducted her and carried her off to live with the Ojibways at the St. Mary's River over at Sault Ste. Marie. She remained there, where a few years later, she met and married a French trapper, Jack's father. 'Therefore,' she told Jack, 'the Indian blood in you is that of the Sioux, and yet you have lived all your life with the Ojibways, their traditional foes.' Jack said that his mother told him this when he was fifteen, and ever since then, he had kept it in his mind that when the time came for the Great Spirit to call him, he wanted to be buried in the land of his forefathers, and he told me that the time had now come."

For a moment, Matthew was distracted from the conversation, deeply moved that old Jack LaPete should feel so strongly connected to his Sioux ancestors even though he had spent his life among the Ojibway and white men.

"Well," George continued, "Sam Ely and I tried to dissuade him for several weeks not to go. We told him he would be going to live among strangers, but finally, he told us, 'You are denying my last wish,' so Sam Ely said he would raise the necessary money so Jack could make the journey and be cared for in his old age. Sam, motivated by generosity but also a sense of humor, made up a sheet for people to sign their names to, each one agreeing to send a small annual sum of money to Jack. Sam numbered the paper to show each successive year up until the time Jack would be 110. Everyone thought this was funny, but it turned out not to be, really.

"Jack went off to Manitoba, and I would hear from him every once in a while, but as the years went by, the subscribers to his annuity started to die off, and none of us could believe Jack was still alive; we thought maybe he was buried and someone else was dishonestly collecting the money, so I wrote to Jack, asking him to reply to several questions that I knew only he could answer. He couldn't write, but I got back a letter from a friend of his who had responded to all the questions with accurate answers and provided many more details. It wasn't until the winter before last that I got a letter from a Catholic priest saying Jack had finally gone to his reward. He must have been nearly a hundred years old."

"It sounds like these local Indians are long-lived," said Roosevelt, "if both Jack and the Chief you mentioned lived to be a century old."

"Yes," George agreed. "Even Chief Kawbawgam's wife, Charlotte, lived well into her eighties."

"And she was herself a chief's daughter, you said?" asked Roosevelt.

"Yes," said George. "Her father was Chief Marji Gesick, who was also friendly with the white men when they first arrived, although he lived to regret it. You probably remember I said that he thought he was cursed later for showing men from the Jackson Iron Company where the iron ore was."

At that moment, the doorbell rang. George got up to answer it, saying, "I better get it in case it's some reporters—no offense, Matthew—but I don't trust the maid to know how to shoo them away."

Matthew took no offense. He understood that George wanted to protect his guests' privacy.

"Fascinating stories," remarked Roosevelt while they waited for George to return.

"Yes," said Matthew. "I knew several of the guides George has mentioned, and I can vouch that they were all characters, but also strong and goodhearted men."

"Frances is here," said George, stepping back into the room.

Suddenly, Matthew's heart began to pound. If George hadn't been in the doorway, and if Matthew were not himself a civilized man, he might have bolted like one of the deer surprised by George's night cameras. George had told him Frances was in New York, so what was she doing coming home now?

Then George stepped out of the doorway and revealed behind him a young woman who looked like she could be Frances—but just for a moment, until Matthew realized she was clearly twenty-some years too young.

"Colonel Roosevelt, gentlemen," said George, "allow me to introduce you to my wife's niece, Mrs. Frances Reynolds. She's married to Maxwell whom some of you have already met. They live next door."

All the men had risen to their feet when they saw Frances enter, and now the former president went up to her and took her hand. "It's a pleasure to meet you, Mrs. Reynolds," said Roosevelt, "and I can't thank you enough for allowing my friends to stay at your home while they are here for the trial."

"It's completely a pleasure and an honor," Mrs. Reynolds replied. "We've enjoyed having them immensely."

As Roosevelt and Mrs. Reynolds exchanged pleasantries, it gave Matthew a moment to regain his composure. Then he suddenly found himself the center of attention.

"Frances, this is Matthew Newman," George was saying, while nodding his head in Matthew's direction. "I'm not sure if you've met him before, but he's from Marquette—Delia Richardson's brother, you know."

Mrs. Reynolds smiled and said she was pleased to meet him.

Matthew replied, "It's a pleasure to see you. We actually have met before, but you were just a little girl, so you wouldn't remember."

"No, I'm afraid I don't," said Frances, "but Uncle George and Aunt Frances and your sister have all mentioned you to me so many times that I feel like we're old friends."

"Precisely why I invited Matthew to dine with us," said George. "Frances, we were just about to have dessert. Do you want to stay for some?"

"Oh," said Frances. "I just had mine. We just finished supper next door."

"After feeding all those guests," Roosevelt told her, "I think you deserve a second one."

"I won't turn it down then," Frances said, smiling. Meanwhile, George had gone into the parlor and now came back carrying a chair for her. The men quickly scooted over to give her a space at the table, right between her uncle George and Colonel Roosevelt. "I wanted Max to come over with me," she said once she was seated, "but he decided to stay home to put the boys to bed."

The serving girl now came in to clear the dishes and then bring in the dessert as Roosevelt started up the conversation again.

"Your uncle was just telling us about Chief Marji Gesick and how he regretted showing the white men where the iron ore was. George, did he ever get over feeling that way?"

"No, I don't think so, and nor did his daughter," said George. "You see, he was supposed to have a share in the mining company, but he never saw any profits. Years later, his daughter, Charlotte, took the Jackson Iron Company to court to get her father's share. The court sided in her favor, but unfortunately, the company had never been profitable, so I don't think she ever received anything."

"Isn't that how it often goes?" remarked Mr. Garfield.

"There have been a lot of local mines that have gone bankrupt over the years," Frances replied, "yet people keep digging up the Upper Peninsula, and not just for iron ore and copper, but also for gold and silver."

"Really?" said Roosevelt.

"Oh, yes," Matthew said. "There was even a silver mine out at Presque Isle a year or two before Marquette was founded. I remember your father-in-law telling me that, George. I think it only operated for about a year, though."

"I do hope, Colonel Roosevelt," said Frances, changing the subject, "that the trial turns out in your favor."

"Thank you," said Roosevelt. "So do I."

"Theodore gave some incredible testimony today," said George, "and I don't see how Newett even has a case after what all the other witnesses said."

"Even so, I still have to testify," said Garfield. "I didn't come all this way not too."

Everyone laughed, and then Roosevelt said, "Well, I've had enough thinking about the trial today, and also of being cooped up indoors. Do you think it would be safe for me to take a little walk around the neighborhood after dinner?"

"I don't see why not," said George, "and I think the neighbors will be respectful of your privacy."

"Does anyone care to join me?" asked Roosevelt.

Frances and the other guests declined, but George clearly felt he should entertain his guest. Matthew found himself saying, "I should get home to write my dispatch for my newspaper, but I'll walk along with you first since I'm staying in the neighborhood."

"Very well," said Roosevelt. "I admit I'm a bit curious about this fine neighborhood."

"Teddy is Teddy, and there is no other like him."
— Richard Mather Jopling

Jopling, a Marquette native, made this comment when eighteen and writing home from St. Mark's School in Southborough, Massachusetts in 1911 after Theodore Roosevelt visited the school. He was a first cousin to Frances Jopling Reynolds.

CHAPTER 9

FRANCES REYNOLDS SAID HER GOODBYES and was about to walk home when Matthew, George, and Roosevelt stepped outside with her, but she had barely stepped out the door before she found her husband Max walking across the lawn, chasing after their toddler son, little Alfred Owen.

"Max, he's supposed to be in bed," Frances scolded.

"He refused to go to sleep until his mama came to kiss him goodnight," Max replied.

"Maybe he wants his Teddy," said George, grabbing his nephew and picking him up. "He usually has it with him."

Theodore Roosevelt grinned at this comment, causing Matthew to laugh. George looked startled for a moment and asked, "What did I say?"

"He wants his Teddy," said Matthew, again laughing.

"Well, he's right here," said Roosevelt, reaching over and taking the boy from George. Little Alfred Owen seemed startled to be in the hands of the large man, but after a moment, he just beamed at Roosevelt and Roosevelt beamed back. After all, Roosevelt wasn't too unlike his Teddy Bear, considering that the Teddy Bear had been named for the former president by Morris Michtom, a candy store owner in New York, whose wife had made the first one. Michtom had the idea for the Teddy Bear after a celebrated incident in 1902 in which Roosevelt had refused to shoot an old bear because he thought it would be unsportsmanlike. He had then been lampooned by political cartoonist Clifford Berryman for it, and the cartoon was what had given Michtom the idea. Of course, Michtom had gotten permission from Roosevelt to name the Teddy Bear for him.

"He's a fine lad," said Roosevelt after a minute, handing Alfred Owen back to his mother. "I'm glad he has a Teddy Bear."

The original Berryman cartoon showing
Roosevelt refusing to shoot a bear.

"Thank you," said Frances, who found Alfred Owen would struggle with her until she put him down. "He's a fine boy when he's not having a tantrum anyway, which I'm afraid he'll do if he doesn't get his rest. Max, where's Max Jr.?"

"Sound asleep," said Max.

"Good. I wish this one would take after his big brother."

"Give him time," said George.

"Colonel Roosevelt," asked Max, "would you mind if I took a photograph of you with our son?"

"Not at all," Roosevelt replied.

Max ran into the house to fetch his camera while Frances thanked him for the opportunity.

"I don't imagine Alfred will remember meeting you since he's so young," said Frances to Roosevelt, "but I know he'll treasure the photograph when he grows up."

"Well, I hope he does," said Roosevelt.

"It's very kind of you to let Max take your photo," Frances continued. "I know you don't like publicity."

"It's no problem at all," Roosevelt replied. "I'd only be worried if George wanted to take it—I don't need to be on display at the next World's Fair as a wildlife photograph."

Everyone laughed at this remark, and then George added, smiling, "A bull moose—that's one photograph I still have to get."

By now, Max was back outside, and in another minute, the photograph was taken, after some cajoling of Frances to get her to be in it as well.

"Thank you again, sir," said Max, shaking the colonel's hand once the moment was forever captured.

"Yes, thank you," said Frances. "I do wish my cousin Richard were home. He thinks the world of you, but he's away at Harvard right now. He met you when you came to speak at his school a couple of years ago."

"Oh, what school was it?"

"St. Mark's," said Frances. "But he's been at Harvard for a year now. His full name is Richard Mather Jopling."

"Oh, yes," said Roosevelt. "I think I remember him; he told me he was related somehow to George here. He seemed to be a bright boy."

"He is. He's very interested in music, and he writes poetry. He admires you greatly. Well, thank you again. It was a pleasure to meet you."

"The pleasure was all mine," said Roosevelt.

"It was good to meet you, too, Mr. Newman," Frances added.

"The same here," said Matthew, nodding to all the Reynolds family.

"Let's go home now, Alfred," said Frances, taking her son's hand again and leading him home.

Theodore Roosevelt with Frances Jopling Reynolds
and her son Alfred Owen Reynolds

"Max, we're going for a walk if you'd care to join us," said George.

Max looked over to his wife, but she was busy fussing with Alfred, so he smiled and said, "Sure."

In another minute, they had crossed the street and were walking west along Ridge Street's north sidewalk.

"So," remarked Roosevelt, "George was saying I might know a few of the other residents who live in this neighborhood."

"If not, I'm sure George will tell you all about them," said Max. "He and I are practically related to everyone around here."

"Not to my family," said Matthew, though he instantly wondered why he had said it. The thought had just crossed his mind, however, that if he had married Frances, he would also be related to all these other wealthy families. Not that he cared about that; he was no social climber.

"Mr. Newman, you're related to the Richardsons, though, aren't you?" asked Max. "I think that's what Uncle George told me."

"Yes, Delia Richardson is my sister."

"I hear her daughter is marrying Lysander Blackmore on Sunday," Max continued.

"Yes," Matthew replied, not wanting to say more. He wasn't sure claiming a relation to the Richardsons or the Blackmores would be in his favor.

"Who built this tall house?" asked Roosevelt, pointing to one kitty corner from the Peter White House.

"Colonel James Pickands," said George. "He was Samuel Mather's partner in Pickands Mather and Company."

"I recognize the company name," said Roosevelt. "If he's a colonel, I'd also be interested in meeting him. What war did he serve in?"

The Pickands home, built in 1881.

"The Civil War actually," said Shiras, "but I'm afraid James Pickands moved away years ago. You see, his wife died soon after they moved in. It's said the plaster in the house was still wet, which made her come down with pneumonia."

"That's a pity," said Roosevelt.

"She was the daughter of John Outhwaite," added Matthew. "He was a director of the Cleveland Iron Company. His other daughter married Jay Morse, who was a silent partner in Pickands Mather and Company."

"Yes," continued George. "And when Colonel Pickands moved back to Cleveland after his first wife died, he married Seville Hanna, Mark Hanna's sister."

"Oh, yes," said Roosevelt. "Now I remember the Pickands name. Of course, I know Mark Hanna well."

"Wasn't he President McKinley's campaign manager?" asked Max.

"Yes," said Roosevelt, "and McKinley's very good friend, too. When I became president after McKinley was shot, Mark was very gracious to me. I know some say he's a hard man, but he's also a firm friend."

"That's what I've heard too," said George. "I've never really gotten to know him, though I've met him in Washington a few times."

"Well, to finish the story," said Matthew, "when Colonel Pickands died, his widow, Seville Hanna, married Jay Morse, whose wife had also died by then. So you have two best friends who first married sisters, and later, were both married to the same woman."

"Just not at the same time," said Max, laughing.

"Even so, they must have had quite the friendship," said Roosevelt. "That's a fine house there too, that brownstone," he said, pointing across the street.

"Yes, Daniel Merritt built that one," said Shiras. "He moved to Duluth later."

But Matthew was not looking at the Merritt house but the Henning home, now belonging to Judge and Carolina Smith—he could not abide the snooty Carolina Smith. What a shame that his dear friend Madeleine had drowned. If she hadn't, her parents never would have sold their fine house to that snob and moved away.

Matthew was debating whether to mention the Henning family to Roosevelt—he knew Gerald Henning had had his hand in many business ventures back East—but at that moment, a woman approaching from the opposite direction suddenly came to a standstill at the sight Colonel Roosevelt. At least, that's what the four men assumed until they got a few feet closer and her true interest became obvious when she exclaimed, "Matthew Newman, is that you?"

"It is," he said, not recognizing her at first.

The Merritt home, built in 1880

"It's Caroline," she replied. "Caroline Rankin. You knew me as Watson, though."

"Hello, Mrs. Rankin," said George, tipping his hat to her as Matthew recovered his surprise.

"I haven't seen you in years," Matthew said. "How have you been?"

"I'm well," she said. "I didn't know you were in town."

"I'm here reporting on the trial. Oh, I'm sorry, Colonel; let me introduce you to Mrs. Rankin," said Matthew.

Colonel Roosevelt bowed to her. "It's a pleasure to make your acquaintance, ma'am."

"Mrs. Rankin," George told Roosevelt, "is a celebrated children's author."

"Delia sends me clippings whenever you're mentioned in the *Mining Journal*," Matthew told Mrs. Rankin. "And I believe I've read all of your books. I've read *Dandelion Cottage* three or four times. It's a charming story."

"That's quite a compliment," she replied, "that a grown man would read a girls' book so many times."

"Well, I'm still looking for writing tips from you, you know," said Matthew. Then he turned to the others and said, "This woman taught me everything I know about news reporting. She was the first female reporter at the *Mining*

Carroll Watson Rankin, author of *Dandelion Cottage*

Journal, and when I got my start there, I used to ask her to read my stories and give me advice."

"Oh, you were a fine writer," said Mrs. Rankin. "And you got better stories too." Turning to the colonel, she explained, "Being a woman, I was relegated to the society columns while Matthew got to report on the criminal activities and fires—all the juicy stuff."

Dandelion Cottage, source of the 1904
children's book of the same title

"Do you have a penchant for crime stories, Mrs. Rankin?" asked the colonel, smiling.

"Why not? There are female detectives," she replied, "at least in storybooks."

"And well there should be," said George.

"It's so good to see you, Caroline," said Matthew. "We were just going for a walk and hoping Colonel Roosevelt wouldn't be noticed by too many people."

"It's a small town," said Caroline, turning to Roosevelt, "but I imagine most people will be polite and only stare out their curtains at you, sir. I must say it's a pleasure to have you here in Marquette, despite the circumstances."

"Thank you," he replied.

"Matthew, it was wonderful seeing you," she continued, turning her attention back to him. "I imagine you're very busy with the trial while you're here in Marquette, but write me a letter sometime. I'd love to hear from you."

"I will definitely do that," he said. "It was wonderful to see you, too."

The men then wished Mrs. Rankin good day and continued in the opposite direction from her. They had now reached Pine Street, so they turned right to walk north around the high school and then continue on Arch Street walking east to make a circle. When they reached Arch, George had them walk a bit west, first, so he could point out the small dwelling that had been made famous as Dandelion Cottage by Mrs. Rankin's book some nine years earlier.

They then returned to walking back toward the lake. Along the way, George and Max pointed out some of the other fine homes in the neighborhood to the colonel, including those belonging to the Kaufman and Reed families, and then when they reached Cedar Street, they walked north toward Michigan so George could point out the towering home built by Alfred Swineford.

"Swineford," George explained, "built this home when he owned our local newspaper, the *Mining Journal*. He later sold it to the Longyears and moved to Alaska. He was the first resident Governor of Alaska, you know, appointed by Grover Cleveland I believe. He died in Alaska a few years back."

The Alfred Swineford home, built in 1882.

"Well, apparently the newspaper business was prosperous for him," said Roosevelt, admiring the large home.

"It was a good paper at least to get my start at," said Matthew. "I was very grateful for the job. Of course, Mr. Russell was the editor I worked under, and he bought the paper soon after from Mr. Swineford. Caroline and I had many a late night there trying to get the copy finished in time for the newsboys to deliver it."

"It must have been a good experience for you," said Roosevelt, "since you've stuck with the newspaper business all these years."

"Being a reporter is fascinating," Matthew replied. "I get to meet all sorts of interesting people, yourself included, and every once in a while, I feel I can make a difference with a story."

"That you can," said Roosevelt. "I'm against this strain toward yellow journalism in recent years, and men, like Mr. Newett, who print opinions rather than facts, but there's no doubt we need the press if our democracy is going to survive."

"That's true," said Max. "We need someone to make sure there are no shenanigans going on."

"And we need to stand up to reporters when they start the shenanigans themselves," George added, in reference to the trial.

Roosevelt, perhaps not wanting to discuss the trial on a public street, changed the subject by remarking, "But you said that house belonged to the Longyears. I thought you said they were the family who moved their house."

"They did," said George. "They only lived in the Swineford house for a short time while building their mansion. It took up this entire block right here."

George pointed to the block between Arch and Ridge Street, kitty corner to the Peter White House. "All of this property belonged to my wife's grandfather, Dr. Morgan Hewitt. He was the first president of the Cleveland Iron Mining Company, and he built a fine home here, but he only lived in it a few years before he died. Then the Longyears bought the property, tore down Dr. Hewitt's home, and built an enormous mansion—the largest Marquette has ever seen. Bigger even than anything on Cleveland's Euclid Avenue I believe," said George. "I understand Samuel Mather's new house in Cleveland is forty-three rooms, but the Longyear mansion was sixty-five rooms and all built of Lake Superior sandstone."

The Longyear Mansion, built 1892.
It was moved to Brookline, Massachusetts in 1903.

"It must have been quite a sight," said Roosevelt.

"It was," Matthew agreed. The whole block and down the hill was the Longyears' property, and they had the grounds landscaped by Fredrick Law Olmsted."

"That's how my father-in-law got Olmsted to come and take a look at Presque Isle," George reminded Roosevelt.

"And what did your father-in-law think of the house?" asked Roosevelt.

"We all thought it rather ostentatious," George admitted. "After all, my father-in-law built the first home on this street, and everyone decided to copy him by building here, but the Longyears rather went overboard."

"Now," said Roosevelt, "remind me why the home was moved."

"The Longyears' son, Howard, who was just a teenager," began George, "drowned in Lake Superior when canoeing with his friend, Hugh Allen. They were on their way back to Marquette from the Huron Mountain Club—that's where a lot of the people who live around here go hunting and fishing—it's about forty or fifty miles northwest of Marquette. My father-in-law and the Longyears and the Allens were among its founders. Anyway, Mrs. Longyear was grief-stricken by her son's death, and she wanted to build a memorial park to him on the property down there at the bottom of the hill, but the Marquette and Southwestern Railroad also wanted to run a railroad track through there. The city decided it was better to please the railroad than Mrs. Longyear. Infuriated, Mrs. Longyear went on vacation to Paris with her husband, saying she could never set foot in Marquette again after the way the city had treated her over the park. While they were riding down the Champs Élysées one day, Mr. Longyear suggested to his wife—he later told me he was only joking—that they move the house. She decided it was a splendid idea."

Roosevelt laughed at this. "You never know when you're putting your foot in your mouth when you joke with a woman," he said.

"And so they moved the house, block by block," said George. "I forget how many railroad cars it took, but it must have been about sixty. They took it apart and carried it all the way to Brookline, Massachusetts, but when they got it there, Olmsted told them it wouldn't look right on the new piece of property, so it was rearranged, and I believe even more rooms were added then."

"Quite a story," said Roosevelt.

"Who lives here now, George?" Matthew asked, not having been home for a few years and not recognizing the new home on the property.

"This house on the corner belongs to George Burtis. He owns a sawmill. The rest of the property still belongs to the Longyears. I imagine they'll sell it off eventually."

"That's it for our walk, I guess," said Max since they were now across the street from his and George's houses. "I should get home now before Frances starts to wonder where I've gone."

"We should point out the Mather house, though," said George.

"And which Mather is that—does Samuel Mather have a house here too?" asked Roosevelt.

"No, this one was built by Henry Mather, his uncle. Henry's wife was sister to my mother-in-law. They were both the daughters of Dr. Hewitt. Henry and Mary Mather had a daughter, Bessie, who married James Jopling—his brother, Alfred, married my wife's sister Mary."

The Henry Mather home on Cedar Street in Marquette, built 1888.

"You're making my head spin," Roosevelt said. "So many relations, though I suppose it's like that for most families."

"Yes, I imagine so," said Max. "Like I said, between the Whites, the Mathers, the Hewitts, and the Kennedy sisters, George and I are related to just about everyone on this street."

"I don't think I've ever met Samuel Mather personally," Roosevelt added, "but I did meet his son while I was president, at least one of them—Amasa Mather."

"Oh, yes," said George. "I remember that. You invited him to the White House because he had just come home from Africa and India, where he went on safari."

"Yes," said Roosevelt. "He gave me many fine tips since I was planning to go on safari myself as soon as I finished my term as president."

"The Mathers," Matthew added, less interested in hunting big game than in literature, "are also related to Constance Fenimore Woolson."

"I know that name. I'm afraid I haven't read her books, but I know she was good friends with John Hay, my Secretary of State, during my presidency," Roosevelt said.

"Miss Woolson was sister to Samuel Mather's mother," Matthew explained, "and a great-niece to James Fenimore Cooper."

"Now that name I definitely know," said Roosevelt. "*The Last of the Mohicans* is a delightful book."

"Miss Woolson," Matthew continued, "wrote wonderful novels and stories set in the Great Lakes region, including on Mackinac Island and also some short stories that were probably set in Marquette."

"Didn't she commit suicide?" asked George.

"Some people believe so, but she was very ill, and I think she just lost her balance and fell out of her window in Venice," Matthew replied. "It was a real shame because she was a wonderful novelist."

"I read her book *Jupiter Lights*," George replied. "Frances told me to read it, but the female characters in it were too emotional for my taste."

"You should try *Anne*," said Matthew. "That's the one set on Mackinac Island. In any case, we owe her a great debt for making the Lake Superior country known to a wider audience."

"It would have been known anyway," said Max, "because of the iron ore."

"I've never been much for women's fiction," said Roosevelt. "H. Rider Haggard, now there's a great writer. Have you read *King Solomon's Mines*?"

"Yes, I do like a good adventure story, too," said Matthew, smiling, "but not as much as I like to read books set in the Great Lakes."

"Well, I better get home for sure now," said Max. "It's getting dark."

"Yes, I better go home too," agreed Matthew. "I imagine the trial will be another long day for all of us tomorrow."

"It was a pleasure going for a walk with both of you," said Roosevelt, shaking Max and Matthew's hands.

After another minute, they had all said goodnight and gone their separate ways until morning when they would reconvene at the courthouse.

Marquette Regional History Center

Frances White Shiras

"A girlish face smiles at me as it did long years ago.
Oh, sweetheart of my boyhood days! Oh, memory most
dear!"
— *The Prince of Pilsen*

CHAPTER 10

MATTHEW WALKED DOWN RIDGE TOWARD Spruce, where he would turn to head home. As he walked, he couldn't help noticing the Call house beside the Peter White home. It was now the summer residence of George's father, Justice Shiras, but thirty years before, it had belonged to Charles Call, and it was there Matthew had escorted Frances to a holiday party that night so long ago. Frances had actually been the one bold enough to ask him to escort her.

Matthew had been surprised by the invitation—he was hardly a member of the Ridge Street set—not by blood or by social standing. And Matthew did not even know the Calls, although he knew they were well-connected like all the other families who lived up on the Ridge; Mr. Call was Peter White's nephew, his sister's son, and that made him related by marriage to the Mathers and Joplings. Mrs. Call, having been a Kennedy, was related to the Spears, Reynolds, and Shirases. Matthew had, not surprisingly, felt intimidated by Frances' invitation, but he had also felt so honored that he could not refuse it. Plus, he knew how much courage it must have taken her, as a girl, to make the invitation herself—especially when he was not of her social standing and all her wealthy cousins and friends would be there.

Frances' father had not objected when Matthew had shown up to escort her to the party. Mr. White wasn't going since Mrs. White was not feeling well and he preferred to stay home with her, but he was all smiles when he had opened the door to Matthew that night. After all, despite all his wealth, Peter White might have been the most down-to-earth man in Marquette. So down to earth that Matthew now found himself smiling, recalling how he had been told one time, years before, about a children's play that was going to be put on at the Guild Hall at St. Paul's. Several boys were going to play Indians in the play, and Peter White had been there for the rehearsals. Not content with the boys' performance, he offered to show them an Indian war dance. Then he jumped up on stage, bent over, and began prancing about, making hideous war cries to show the boys how it should be done. After such a performance, Mr. White was held in high esteem by all the boys.

Matthew laughed at the memory, and then feeling a little better, he told himself, *I'm not going to think about that party now*, and repressing a painful remembrance, he muttered to himself, "I better get home. I still have to write my dispatch so I can send it in the morning." Then picking up his pace, he was at his sister's house in five more minutes.

Matthew found Delia settled in the parlor, busy with her needlework. He felt relieved when Delia told him Roger had already gone up to bed, though it was only nine-thirty and not quite dark.

"Did you have a nice time?" she asked him.

"Yes," said Matthew. "Colonel Roosevelt and all of his friends are very pleasant. I feel exhausted, though, and I still need to write my article, so if you don't mind, I'll head upstairs and tell you all about it tomorrow morning at breakfast and on the way to the courthouse."

"All right," said Delia, "but I think I better stay home tomorrow. Lydia needs help with so many things. The wedding is coming so fast now."

"I understand," said Matthew. "Then I'll tell you everything about tonight at breakfast, and I'll tell you all about the trial tomorrow night when I get home."

"That sounds good," said Delia, trying to repress a yawn. "I'm tired myself. Good night."

"Good night," said Matthew, and then he made his way upstairs.

For the next hour or more, Matthew diligently wrote his dispatch. Then he undressed, turned off the light, and crawled into bed, but his senses were still excited from the evening, not because he had spent so much time in Roosevelt's presence—though that should have excited him plenty—but because Frances had been present everywhere in her house tonight—he could picture her in each room, sitting in various chairs, playing at the piano, reading a book, eating dinner.

He had not expected he would ever enter the Peter White house again. In fact, if Frances had not befriended him, he never would have expected to enter it to begin with. He had never aspired to being among the elite; neither had Delia, despite her marriage. But when they had all been in their teens, Madeleine Henning, the social leader of the upper class young people in Marquette, had taken Delia under her wing, and that meant Matthew had quickly followed. Roger Richardson, who'd had his heart set on Madeleine from a young age, had not been happy about Matthew joining their circle, but Matthew had never been Roger's rival when it came to Madeleine. She was a charming girl and kindhearted in her way, but also a bit too spoiled for Matthew's taste, though he loved her as a friend. Still, who knew how things might have turned out if Madeleine had not drowned on that Fourth of July evening in 1876? She had fallen out of a canoe when they had all been out upon Lake Superior together, and despite their efforts to rescue her, she had quickly sunk beneath the waves, never to be seen again.

After Madeleine's death, Roger had begun drinking—and it didn't help that Delia blamed him for her best friend's death since Madeleine had fallen out of Roger's canoe. However, Roger's melodramatic expressions of guilt and grief had eventually caused Delia to pity him, and then before Matthew knew it, she was marrying Roger, to their mother's delight, and to Matthew's dismay. Matthew's father was very ill by that point, so he did not voice any opinions on the matter. He would die soon after Roger and Delia's wedding, leaving Matthew in charge of the store and having to care for his mother, who was so heartbroken by his death that she had died just two years later, leaving Matthew, a young man of twenty, in possession of a general store he did not want and with a sister who wanted him to marry into high society like she had.

Matthew had no interest in money or fame; once Delia planted the idea in his head, however, he began to toy with the possibility of such a marriage, but only because, by then, he had fallen in love with Frances. He never would have conceived of aspiring to her hand had mutual grief not first made them good friends.

Matthew and Frances' friendship had commenced in the spring of 1878. Matthew's father had died not long before, and that spring a series of illnesses and especially the diphtheria had been striking down people all over the city. By the time it was over, Frances had lost three younger siblings and her cousin, Ellen White Mather. Two of her siblings, Mark Howard and Sarah, had been little more than babies, but Frances' brother, Morgan, had been a boy of twelve. She was four years older than him, but they had been close companions, and his loss hurt Frances more than she could say. Knowing her parents were devastated as well—her father especially because he now had no son to carry on his name—Frances had held in her grief rather than upset her parents further by expressing it. But after a few weeks, the dam inside her was ready to break, and it happened a few weeks after her siblings' deaths, on a beautiful sunny day in late May when it seemed impossible that sickness could have ever gripped Marquette.

On that day, Frances entered Matthew's store. He had not seen her since Morgan's funeral, and he had not had a chance to speak to her there. In fact, he barely knew her. Delia, newly married then, had insisted he go, as if the funeral were a significant Marquette social affair, but that would not have enticed Matthew. He went because Mr. White had always been kind to him, and he had always enjoyed waiting on the enthusiastic Morgan when he came into the store, so he simply wanted to show the family respect.

Matthew instantly recognized Frances when she entered the store—it would have been hard to miss her since she was dressed in mourning. The store was empty save for her, so he quickly went up to her and pressed her hand, though he was too tongue-tied to say anything. Then he saw her looking at the mourning ribbon he still wore for his father.

"You understand," she said. "I know you do; you understand what it is to lose someone close to you. Morgan often spoke of you—about how you and George had taken him fishing last summer and how he couldn't wait to go again this summer when George comes back to visit. He loved to go fishing, and he—"

And here she broke into tears, and in a moment, Matthew had her in his arms, trying to comfort her. He gave her his handkerchief to wipe her tears and blow her nose. And then the bell rang, announcing that another customer had entered the store. Frances quickly slipped behind a shelf to hide her pain while Matthew waited on his customer.

After the customer left, Frances returned to the counter with some small purchase, and a few days later, she came into the store again, and again the next day, and eventually Matthew got the idea that she might be interested in him. And he began to think he might also be interested in her.

It was hard, however, for Matthew ever to get away from the store. After his father had died, his mother had tried to help with the family business, but Matthew soon realized she seemed to be slipping into some sort of depression or feeble-mindedness that made her forgetful and unable to complete the simplest tasks. Soon, all she did was sit in the parlor and stare out the window, her life slowly slipping away.

Matthew finally hired a smart young man, a few years his junior, to help in the store so he could spend more time looking after his mother without worrying about leaving the store unattended. And now and then, he also used the young man's presence as an excuse to go out and meet Frances for a walk along the lakeshore. Together, they talked about their families, their grief, and the great mysteries of life.

When Matthew's mother died, Frances came to the store the moment she heard the news. She stayed for hours and even helped him and Delia pick out the dress his mother would be buried in. Delia didn't seem to resent Frances' presence, and Matthew saw her attention as a sign that she was clearly his best friend, if not more. He sometimes wondered whether more was possible, but he was never brave enough to broach the subject.

A few years passed like this. In the summers, George would return to Marquette. Matthew liked George. He knew Frances liked him too. But when George went away again, Matthew never corresponded with him. They were both busy, after all. Nor did Matthew ever ask Frances whether she corresponded with George, though he was sure their fathers must stay in touch.

Life continued on, but Matthew now found himself bored with his life, living alone after his mother's death. Going to supper at Roger and Delia's once a week only made him more and more disenchanted with his brother-in-law. The young man he had hired was through school now and in need of more money because he was getting married. Matthew did not want to see him go elsewhere because he did not want to run the store himself. Then one day, after reading a story in the *Mining Journal* that was so poorly written that Matthew knew he could do better, he went down to the newspaper's offices and expressed his interest in being a reporter. He showed the editor, Mr. Russell, a few short stories and essays he had written for school and for his own pleasure, and Mr. Russell agreed to give him a story a week. After a few weeks, there was an opening and Matthew was hired on full-time. His clerk was thrilled because Matthew then promoted him to store manager. Soon Matthew was out, meeting more people as he wrote his news reports. He was constantly interviewing the great men in the town, and they seemed to like him, and that made him think he might just be accepted among them if he were able to convince Frances to marry him.

Matthew had so long tried to repress the thought of marriage to Frances, thinking it would be impossible, that he wasn't quite sure exactly when he fell in love with her. He just knew he had never met a girl like her before, and he doubted he ever would again. But he also knew he could not expect her to marry him if he could not provide for her in the style to which she was accustomed. So he saved every penny he could, and with his clerk's new enthusiasm for the store, they soon implemented new ideas to market their products better and their profits grew. *Someday*, Matthew kept telling himself, *I will be ready to marry Frances, if she'll have me.*

That was the other issue. Even if he could provide for her, would Frances want him? It finally dawned on him that he better ask her, even if they had to have a long engagement. Otherwise, he was just making castles in the air. And Frances was a very desirable young woman, so if he didn't ask her soon, someone else certainly would—someone likely wealthier and more handsome than he—someone he probably couldn't compete with, so he better ask her as soon as he found the courage.

It was that night—the night he went to the White house to escort her to the party—that he decided he would propose. It had been the dead of winter— the party was to celebrate New Year's Eve if he remembered right; Matthew recalled that it had been bitter cold as he walked to the White house, yet he found himself sweating from anxiety when he rang the bell. And sweating even more as he stood in the hall trying to make small talk with Mr. White while Frances was still getting ready.

But then Frances had come down the stairs—a vision of loveliness—and he had helped her on with her coat, and then she had taken his arm, and they had gone outside and started the short walk next door to the Calls' house as Matthew searched for the words and the right moment to ask the question that would decide his future....

Matthew decided to stop the trip down memory lane now. He needed to get his sleep. Tomorrow's trial was what he needed to focus on, and not the dreams of his youth. The past could never be changed, no matter how many times he might wish it could be.

"If I could only get him to disgrace himself.
Suppose I get him beastly drunk?
But you cawn't get a Dutchman drunk, don't you know."
— *The Prince of Pilsen*

WEDNESDAY
MAY 28, 1913

George Shiras III

"Colonel, if this evidence keeps up much longer,
you will begin to believe it yourself."
— George Shiras III to Colonel Roosevelt

Reported in an anonymous biographical sketch of
George Shiras III in manuscript form at the
Northern Michigan University Archives in
Marquette, Michigan.

CHAPTER 11

IN THE MORNING, MATTHEW WALKED to the courthouse. Since Delia was not joining him, he did not feel inclined to ask Roger to give him a ride. Conversation was always awkward, if it even happened, whenever he and Roger were alone together.

When he reached the courthouse, Matthew showed his press pass to the guard at the door and then went into the special room where extra telegraph wires had been set up for the trial reporters. After sending off his dispatch to the *Empire Sentinel*, Matthew made his way to the seats reserved for the press and found Homer Guck already there.

"This is going to be quite a day of testimony, I think," said Homer. "Plus, I've heard some rumors about the primary testimony to be made for Mr. Newett. It seems that Mr. Miller—"

"All rise!" called the bailiff.

"I'll tell you later," whispered Homer.

Matthew nodded, curious, but not so curious that he wanted to risk not hearing the trial or being thrown out for contempt of court because he was whispering.

Judge Flannigan now called the court to order, and soon the next witness for the plaintiff was on the stand.

First up was John Callan O'Laughlin, the Washington correspondent for the *Chicago Tribune*. O'Laughlin testified that he had known Roosevelt since 1893 when he was Civil Service Commissioner and Roosevelt had been Secretary of the Navy. During that time, they would see each other almost daily, sometimes as often as six or seven times a day, and each time anywhere from five to forty-five minutes. Never once in all that time, said O'Laughlin, had he ever thought Roosevelt intoxicated or heard him utter a single swear word. O'Laughlin had known Roosevelt so intimately that when the Spanish-

American War had broken out in 1898, Roosevelt had advised him not to enlist because he had a wife and children at home. Later, after Roosevelt's term as president, O'Laughlin had accompanied him on his trip to Africa as correspondent for the *Chicago Tribune*. He gave additional testimony about being with Roosevelt as he traveled through Europe, giving details of all the habits of the former president's party there, and finally, he described his experiences witnessing the 1912 campaign.

In cross-examination, Newett's attorney, Mr. Belden, asked Mr. O'Laughlin, "Was there not in 1912 among newspaper men a report that Colonel Roosevelt drank and sometimes to excess?" O'Laughlin replied, "There has never been a reputable newspaperman at Washington who has regarded such a report as anything but silly." Mr. Belden objected to this statement and had it struck from the record.

Soon after, an argument ensued about whether newspaper reports concerning Roosevelt's lack of sobriety could be seen as reliable evidence, given that the report in Newett's own paper was being questioned. Belden suggested that Newett himself could testify to the accuracy of such stories, but Judge Flannigan ruled that newspaper stories did not count as evidence in the case since newspaper men themselves might write what was not exactly true.

On this note, the court recessed for lunch.

Matthew had listened with rapt attention, taking notes as needed, throughout the morning's proceedings, but as soon as he felt it safe to speak, he turned to Homer and said, "Can I join you for lunch?" He liked Homer, but he also wanted the scoop on what Homer had overheard about Mr. Miller—something he had not been likely to forget through three hours of testimony.

"Of course," said Homer. "Should we go back to the Hotel Marquette?"

"That's fine," Matthew agreed.

Once they were off the courthouse grounds, Matthew said, "Now, please tell me what you heard about Mr. Miller."

"Well, as you know, he's supposed to be the key witness for the defense—the man who claims he saw Roosevelt drunk at Senator Cannon's reception."

"Yes," said Matthew, confirming he knew all this.

"Well, as far as I know, he's Newett's only witness," said Homer. "At least he's the only who's been named so far, and now it seems like he won't be attending the trial at all."

"Do you know what Miller's occupation is?" asked Matthew.

"I believe he was a press agent in Washington and also a consular agent for the government. He actually claims he saw Roosevelt drunk on more than one occasion."

"That's right," said Matthew. "I heard that he swore in an affidavit that when Roosevelt was asked at Senator Cannon's dinner, 'Will you have a little glass of whiskey, Mr. President?' that he heard Roosevelt reply, 'No, sir; I will have a great big glass of whiskey.' Is he reneging now on those claims? Is that why he won't be attending the trial?"

"Not exactly," said Homer. "I heard from the reporter for the *Mining Journal* this morning that he's fled to Canada. He sent a letter giving his address as being in Winnipeg from now on. Apparently, there's a warrant out for his arrest if he appears in Marquette. He's under indictment for grand larceny. It seems he's bounced a few checks."

Matthew could not help laughing at the irony of this statement. "Larceny is far worse than drinking and swearing," he said.

"I couldn't agree more," Homer replied.

When they arrived at the Hotel Marquette, they met several of their colleagues who were also staying there, and three of them all repeated to Matthew the same thing they had heard that morning from the *Mining Journal* correspondent about Mr. Miller. With Newett's key witness hiding out as a fugitive in another country, it didn't look like he was likely to win his case.

After lunch, Matthew and the other reporters made it back to the court in time to witness the testimony of Robert Bacon, the former ambassador to France. Bacon attested to Roosevelt's sobriety at many social functions he had attended in Washington, as well as when he had dined with the former president in Paris. He had not, however, witnessed the 1912 campaign.

After Bacon was dismissed from the stand, Lawrence Curtis, the financial editor for the Associated Press, took the witness stand. Like his predecessors, he testified to Colonel Roosevelt's temperate habits and the overall cleanliness of his speech. He had attended Colonel Roosevelt daily on his 1912 campaign, so he answered many questions about Roosevelt's use of alcohol during that time. He had seen the plaintiff numerous times throughout the day during the campaign, and he had never seen him drink liquor on the train or anywhere else except when he was with a guest.

Throughout the afternoon, Matthew frequently looked over to see how both Roosevelt and Newett were reacting to the witnesses' various statements.

Roosevelt seemed keenly interested, hanging on every word and frequently nodding his head in agreement with what was said. Newett, however, did not seem very interested at all. Rumors were circulating that he was suffering from a medical condition, but Matthew thought it more likely Newett was ashamed of the hole he had dug for himself; by now, he must realize there was little likelihood he could win the case.

In the middle of the afternoon, a much-needed recess was held. Matthew made his way to the men's room in the courthouse and waited in line as his fellow press men and some of the witnesses took their turns using the facilities. There was little discussion in the washroom since it was forbidden that the press harass or intimidate the witnesses for statements; furthermore, some members of the press held different viewpoints on the case, and no one should discuss anything that the jury might overhear.

When Matthew stepped back into the main hall of the courthouse, he noticed a young lady standing at a distance with a camera, clearly trying to take a photograph of Colonel Roosevelt. Just as the young woman raised her camera, Frank Sloan, Roosevelt's former personal bodyguard, stepped up to her. Matthew expected Sloan would tell her she was not allowed to take any photographs, but instead, he said something to her, then led her forward to Colonel Roosevelt.

"Step aside there, sir," said Sloan to one of the attorneys speaking to Roosevelt. "We need space so this young lady can take a photograph."

Colonel Roosevelt, immediately realizing what was wanted of him, stepped over into the light, and putting on a very dignified air, he waited for the young lady to raise her camera and take his picture. When she had finished, she thanked him. In return, he bowed to her, waved his hand in a sort of salute, and flashed her his thoroughly Rooseveltian smile. When she turned around, Matthew could see she was also smiling with delight at the colonel's kindness.

But this pleasant moment was quickly over, and then it was time for the rest of the afternoon session.

The session began with Truman Newberry, former Secretary of the Navy, taking the stand. Although the Newberry family was from Detroit, the town of Newberry, Michigan, about a hundred miles east of Marquette, had been named in honor of his father, who had been a U.S. Congressman for Michigan.

Newberry began his testimony by saying he had first met Roosevelt in 1896 when he was Assistant Secretary of the Navy and Roosevelt was Secretary of the Navy. Newberry had frequently accompanied Roosevelt in inspecting battleships. They had also attended many functions together, and as with the other witnesses, Newberry could verify that he had hardly ever seen Roosevelt touch a drop of alcohol. He had also been in attendance at Senator Joe Cannon's seventieth birthday party at the Arlington Hotel in Washington, D.C., and he had seen Roosevelt acting perfectly sober on that occasion. Clearly, the tales of Roosevelt's insobriety at the Cannon dinner—especially given that Mr. Miller was not going to testify in opposition—were a falsehood.

Finally, after a long day of testimony, Judge Flannigan dismissed the court for the day.

Just as Matthew was bidding Homer goodbye and getting ready to leave, George came over to speak to him.

"Thank you for coming to dinner yesterday, Matthew," said George.

"Thank you for having me," Matthew replied. "It was an honor."

"I'm sorry Frances wasn't home," added George. "I know she would have loved to see you."

"Give her my best," said Matthew, trying not to sound either cold or emotional.

"I will. Next time you come to Marquette, please let us know and we'll make a point of having you over for dinner again."

"Well, I'm afraid I don't get to leave New York too often," Matthew replied. "It was just a coincidence that I could come this time since the trial is in Marquette."

"You must come to Washington often, though, to report on politics," said Shiras. "We're in Washington all the time, you know. We're rarely in Marquette except in the summer. Do you get to Washington very often?"

"I make a couple of trips there a year," Matthew admitted, not wanting to lie. "But my paper already has a Washington correspondent so I never know when it will be."

"Well, next time you're there, look us up."

"I will," said Matthew.

"Good. Well, I better be going. Theodore doesn't like to be kept waiting. I know he enjoyed seeing you again, though."

"Give him my best," said Matthew.

And then George headed back across the courtroom, and Matthew turned to collect his belongings, all the while thinking, *I don't want to call on them in Washington.*

Jacob Riis

"I know that we are told nowadays that there is no devil;
that he has gone out of business; if he has, I want to know
who is carrying his business on.
We come upon evidences of it every day."

— Jacob Riis, addressing the students at the
Marquette high school, May 27, 1913

CHAPTER 12

MATTHEW WAS STARVING AND EXHAUSTED by the time he had walked back to Roger and Delia's house. He was hoping he had time for a nice bath before dinner, but the second he walked in the door, he was greeted by Delia, who announced, "We have an invitation to attend a luncheon at the Hills' tomorrow."

Caught off-guard, Matthew's brain could not even process whom the Hills might be. "Delia," he said, "you know I'm in town on business to cover the trial. I can't be spending a long time at a luncheon."

"Well," she said, pretending to be highly offended, "I would think that if Colonel Roosevelt has time to attend the luncheon, then you could get away for it."

"Roosevelt? Why is he going? I thought he wasn't attending any social events while he was in Marquette, and just who are these Hills anyway?"

"Oh, Matthew," laughed Delia. "You don't think I'd just invite you to some ladies' luncheon, do you? Mrs. Hill is the wife of William Hill, Colonel Roosevelt's Marquette attorney."

"Oh...that Hill," said Matthew. Mr. Hill had been the least active of Roosevelt's attorneys during the trial, so Matthew thought his temporary lapse of memory was forgivable.

"Of course, you'll attend," said Delia.

"But why would they invite me?" asked Matthew. "Didn't they invite you and Roger?"

"Don't be silly," said Delia. "Agnes Hill knows Roger's a boor, and she also knows how proud I am of my brother, who is reporting on the trial, so, of course, she invited you. I talked it over with her this afternoon and it's all settled. I even connived to get Roger to eat lunch downtown tomorrow so we can have the automobile. Then you can get from the courthouse to the luncheon and back in time."

Matthew had to admit that sometimes Delia amazed him. He had no doubt it was Roger and not himself who was originally invited, but Delia had managed to manipulate everything to benefit him since she knew he would want to report on all of Roosevelt's movements. She truly was a wonderful sister, despite how he had neglected staying in regular contact with her over the years.

"That's wonderful, Delia," he said, and he could not help but give her a kiss on the cheek. "Of course I'll go."

"Now you just have time to wash up for dinner. We'll eat in half an hour. Be sure to wear something nice because Lysander is coming over."

"Okay. Thanks again," said Matthew, and he ran upstairs, despite how fatigued he had felt a few minutes earlier. The invitation to the luncheon tomorrow even made up for having to dine with Lysander this evening.

Half an hour later, Matthew came downstairs and entered the parlor. He found Lysander sitting on the sofa—and the man was not only sitting beside Lydia, but his arm was wrapped around her waist.

Men were not so forward in my day, Matthew thought, *but, of course, they're engaged and will be married in just a few days—and if I'd been more forward when I was younger, maybe I wouldn't be alone now.* He could remember once longing to put his arm around Frances' waist—and not just when they had been dancing at the Calls' party—but he had never dared when not on a dance floor.

"Hello, Uncle Matthew. How did the trial go today?" asked Lydia, blushing slightly when she saw him looking at Lysander's arm.

"Very well," said Matthew, "or at least very well for Colonel Roosevelt. It doesn't look like Newett's key witness is going to pull through."

"Why's that?" asked Lysander.

"Uh!" Lydia let out a little screech. Matthew lost his train of thought for a second as he realized Lysander must have pinched her. When Matthew saw his niece turning beet red from embarrassment, he tried to pretend he had not noticed by continuing to speak. "I guess," he replied, "that Mr. Miller, the key witness who claims he saw Roosevelt drunk at Senator Cannon's dinner, is hiding out in Canada because he's been indicted for grand larceny."

"That's quite a turn of events," said Lysander, finally pulling his arm out from behind Lydia so he could light a cigar. Lydia, seeing his intention, automatically reached for the lighter on the coffee table to light it for him.

"Yes, it was quite a surprise to everyone, I think," said Matthew. "Of course, Roosevelt's witnesses will be testifying for another day or two at least, but it will be interesting to see what happens when it's time for Newett's witnesses to testify because I'm doubtful he'll have any."

"Dinner is served," said Martha, stepping into the room and curtseying.

"Thank you, Martha," said Lysander.

As if he's the man of the house, thought Matthew.

Everyone stood up. Lydia, being the lady in the room, went in to dinner first—on Lysander's arm, of course. Matthew followed, noting Lysander's fine physique as he did so. He wouldn't be an easy man to knock down. Not that Matthew ever would do something like that—he had too much of his Quaker ancestors' blood in him to resort to violence—though, he was sometimes tempted.

Delia was already in the dining room, but Roger was absent.

"I told Roger he didn't have time for a bath before dinner," said Delia, as a way to apologize for his absence.

"Not the long baths he takes," agreed Lydia.

If I knew he was going to take a bath, I would have taken the time to do so, too, Matthew thought.

"You can't blame a man for wanting to relax after a hard day's work," said Lysander. "I often take a bath when I get home from the office."

"Well, but I'm sure you wouldn't keep dinner waiting, Lysander," said Delia.

"Since I'm the master of the house, and the only one of significance, the servants can wait for when I want dinner," he replied. "That's the whole reason to have servants—to wait on us."

"Yes, I suppose," said Delia.

"Uncle Matthew was just telling us about the trial," Lydia told her mother as Martha brought in the soup.

"Yes, tell us all about it," said Delia, turning to Matthew.

Matthew did so, beginning with the controversy over whether newspaper stories could be used as evidence. They all ate their soup while listening to him. He was just finishing up his explanation when Roger appeared.

"Soup on a warm day like this!" Roger exclaimed, sitting down and looking disgusted.

"Yours can't be very hot now," Delia said to him. "We're almost done with ours."

Roger curled up his nose, dipped his spoon into it, blew on it, and then placed the spoon in his mouth. "It's like ice."

Martha chose that moment to return with a platter of corned beef—an unlucky move for her because Roger, pointing at his soup, said, "Take this away! Bring me a salad instead."

"Yes, sir," said the girl, not knowing whether she should bring the corned beef back into the kitchen and then return with the salad or first serve the corned beef and then remove the soup bowls and bring a salad for him.

"I'll carve it, Martha," said Delia, resolving her dilemma. Martha set the beef on the table next to her mistress, and then she collected the soup bowls, including Roger's full one.

Roger frowned at her as she approached him, but Martha managed to suffer his countenance and carry off his soup without spilling it.

"Now, what size slice would everyone like?" asked Delia as she began to carve the meat.

"I can't believe you're doing that," Roger told her, "and all wrong, too."

"Here, allow me to assist you," said Lysander, who, since he was seated next to her, was able to take the knife and fork out of her hand. "It's hard work for a woman."

"Sometimes women have no choice but to do men's work," muttered Delia, fortunately too low for Roger to hear.

"Father," said Lydia, to smooth things over, "Uncle Matthew has been telling us about the Roosevelt trial today."

"Stuff and nonsense," said Roger.

"What is?" asked Lysander.

"This whole trial," Roger replied, handing his plate to Lysander for his share of the corned beef.

"Why's that?" asked Matthew, although he knew better than to encourage his brother-in-law.

"It just is," said Roger. "Roosevelt ruined the Republican Party, and now he's trying to pretend he's some sort of virtuous man."

"I don't think trying to defend yourself against defamation of character is wrong," Matthew replied.

"No, perhaps not," said Roger, "but then he gets some slow-witted people like that fellow Rice to sing his praises, like he's some sort of Greek hero come to save mankind or something."

"Do you mean Jacob Riis?" asked Matthew. "He's hardly slow-witted."

"You can't understand a word he says with that accent of his," said Roger. "All these immigrants should go back to their own countries."

"When did you ever hear his accent?" asked Delia.

"I saw him downtown yesterday, passed him on the street, and he was babbling nonsense."

"I have to admit," said Lysander, "I agree with you. This country was first founded by good hardworking Englishmen, but now they're letting all the riffraff in."

"I suppose you'd prefer it if they only let the English in," said Matthew, "or better yet, if we were still one of Great Britain's colonies."

"Now, now," said Delia, "no political arguments at the dinner table."

Lysander laughed and said, "I'm not sure, Uncle Matthew, that being a British colony would be so bad, but I wouldn't go that far. It's not just the English, but any hardworking people I appreciate—the Dutch for example. But all of these Irish and the immigrants coming from Eastern Europe—not only are they lazy, but they're bringing lice and other diseases into this country."

"Don't they check for lice at Ellis Island?" asked Lydia, but everyone ignored her.

"I believe Jacob Riis came from Denmark," said Matthew, "so you can't lump him in with those people, not that I agree with you. I know several hardworking Irishmen and Slavs in New York."

"Danish or Dutch, what's the difference?" said Roger. "My point is they're letting Rice brainwash the minds of our young people. I heard what he did yesterday, speaking at the high school. I read it in the paper just now while in the bathtub. He told those students that Roosevelt's motto is...."

Everyone waited but Roger couldn't remember.

"Well, some nonsense about how you don't have to try; you just have to be a good person."

"I read it, too," said Delia, "and that's not what it said."

Here Martha reappeared to bring Roger his salad and to carry away the corned beef platter.

"Martha," asked Delia, "will you go find us today's *Mining Journal*? I believe Mr. Richardson left it in the bathroom."

"Yes, ma'am," she said before taking away the corned beef. Matthew couldn't help noticing that Roger didn't even thank her for bringing him the salad. Nor did he ever touch it.

"Jacob Riis," Matthew continued to argue, "has done a lot in New York City to help clean up crime and advocate for improving the conditions of the poor. I actually walked the police beat with him and Roosevelt many years ago when Roosevelt was police commissioner."

"Well, maybe there's a good immigrant now and then who does something right," Roger admitted, "but most of their kind are bringing crime. I don't mind if people come here and adopt our values, but they need to leave their foreign ways in the Old World."

Martha, who must have run upstairs and back, now returned with the newspaper. She was about to give it to Delia when Roger barked, "Give it here!" Martha quickly scurried over to her master and handed it to him.

"Where is it now?" Roger grumbled, searching for the page while everyone ate and waited in anticipation. Finally, he found the article on page ten. "Here it is. Rice is praising Roosevelt, of course, and then he says we should all live by Roosevelt's rules and his—this is it—Roosevelt's motto, 'Better faithful than famous.'"

Lysander here snorted in derision. "What a crock!" he said.

"What's wrong with it?" asked Delia.

"That kind of thinking is what stops progress in this world," Lysander replied.

Matthew thought Lysander's mindset was already enough to stop progress, but he kept his mouth shut.

"Why?" asked Lydia. "I don't desire fame. I'm going to be happy just being faithful—to my husband."

It was all Matthew could do not to spit up his corned beef at this comment.

Lysander, however, smiled and said, "That's fine for my future little wifey," and he gave her a pinch on the cheek, "but the men who think that way are the ones who become drones. They stay with their employers, accepting low wages and being overworked rather than striking out on their own to try to do something big."

"Maybe their employers should just pay them fair wages and help them rise above their stations," said Delia.

"If we did that," said Roger, "who would do the work?"

"Such people aren't bred to think; that's the problem," said Lysander. "Most men are cowards who think obeying orders is the best policy. People who follow get nowhere in life."

"Well, someone still has to do the work," said Matthew, not quite siding with Roger but wondering where Lysander was going with this argument.

"Yes," said Lysander, "and that's why those people never get anywhere— because they believe in such platitudes as 'Better faithful than famous.' That mindset keeps them stuck where they are."

"I'm afraid I'm not following your reasoning," said Matthew.

"Oh, let's forget politics," said Delia. "Lysander, Lydia and I want your opinions on the decorations for the wedding."

And before the prospective bridegroom could object, the two women began to question him about such things as napkins, tablecloths, and seating arrangements. Matthew and Roger both quit listening and turned their attention to their corned beef. Matthew kept thinking what an unfair and ignorant attack Roger had made upon one of the journalists he most admired—not that he was surprised—it was Roger, after all. When Martha came in to take his salad plate, Roger told her to refill his brandy and leave the bottle on the table. He refilled it again during dessert, and a third time when the dishes were cleared away and it was time to retire into the parlor. At that point, he asked Lysander to join him in his office for another cigar and a drink. Matthew noticed that he was not invited to this little gentlemen's party, and although he felt he should take umbrage at being excluded, instead, he just felt relief and willingly joined the ladies in the parlor.

Once Matthew and the women were seated, Lydia picked up a fashion magazine to look at and Delia retrieved her needlework. Matthew, however, had nothing to occupy himself with, so after a moment, he said, "I feel stuffed from dinner. Would anyone care to go for a walk?"

Delia immediately consented, but Lydia refused. "I want to talk to Lysander again before he leaves," she said. *Is she addicted to that scoundrel?* Matthew wondered, but he only said, "I'll go find my hat," and went into the hall.

In another minute, Matthew and Delia were outside.

As they made their way down the front walk, Matthew restrained himself from saying, "I don't know how you can be married to that man, Delia," or worse, "Do you want your daughter to be as miserably married as you?"

"Let's walk along the lake," said Delia, and following her lead, Matthew turned with her onto Arch Street and then they walked down the hill toward the waterworks building.

"Matthew," said Delia, "I keep forgetting to ask whether you'd like to go see *The Prince of Pilsen* with me tomorrow night."

"I'd love to," said Matthew. "I've been meaning to ask you the same thing. I just keep forgetting." At least now he wouldn't have to spend tomorrow evening with Roger—he knew Roger would never want to go to a play.

"Good," said Delia. "I'll have Martha go fetch us two tickets in the morning. Usually, Lydia goes to the theater with me, but she doesn't seem to want to do anything with the wedding coming up. Still, I need a break from all the planning, and I do want to spend more time with you while you're here."

"I'm glad you asked me," said Matthew. "We haven't gone to the theater together in years. It will be just like when we were young and used to go to all the plays at Mather Hall together. Do you remember that?"

"Oh, yes," said Delia. "I miss those days. Sometimes I wonder why we had to grow up at all."

Soon, the two were lost in reminiscing about their childhood growing up in Marquette. Walking north along the lake, it was easy to pretend they were children again, for the beach and lake had not changed much since they had first moved to Marquette. But Marquette itself certainly had, and so had they.

"Oh, life in high society
Is one perpetual lark
For the monkeys on the boulevard
Beat those in Central Park
There are stranger pets in our social sets
Than there were in Noah's ark."
— *The Prince of Pilsen*

CHAPTER 13

MATTHEW AND DELIA WALKED FOR a long time, all around Marquette. It was a pleasant night, not too warm or cold, so they walked longer than usual. Although neither said so, they were not eager to return home and listen to Roger's ranting after all the drinks he'd had at dinner and since then. Consequently, by the time they did return, it was getting dark and they both agreed it was time to go to bed.

As they stood in the hall before going their separate ways, Delia reminded Matthew, "Now don't forget about the luncheon tomorrow at the Hills'. They live at 608 Spruce."

"I won't forget," said Matthew. "How can I when Roger's letting me borrow the car?"

"I'll be glad to have someone to go with," added Delia. "It's hard going to things alone when Roger doesn't feel up to it. Although I imagine you know that feeling, being a bachelor."

"Yes, it can be awkward to attend parties by yourself," Matthew admitted.

"I do wish," said Delia, "you would get married and settle down, Matthew—back here in Marquette, of course."

"But what would I do here?" Matthew asked.

"Couldn't you work for the *Mining Journal* again?"

"And report on mine closings and how the blueberry crop is doing? No thank you. I'm at the center of the business world in New York and I get to travel to Washington and other places now and then. I would be bored with just reporting on local stories."

"Maybe you could open a store here," said Delia. "You have the experience."

"Perhaps someday," said Matthew, yawning, "but it doesn't need to be decided tonight."

"No, I guess not," said Delia, "but I just worry about you being all alone. You deserve someone to love you."

"I'm glad you think so," said Matthew, kissing her on the cheek. "Good night."

"Good night."

Delia turned and disappeared into the parlor to check on Roger. Matthew climbed the stairs, tired from the walk and perhaps more so from Delia's words, "You deserve someone to love you." Most of the time, he never thought about marriage any longer, but now Delia's words kept repeating themselves in his mind as he got ready for bed.

He didn't know who would want him now, an old man of nearly fifty-four, set in his ways, with not much money to his name, but there had been a time, many years ago, when he had almost convinced himself that he had found someone to love him.

As Matthew crawled under the covers, his thoughts went back to that holiday party with Frances at the Call home....

When Frances had come down the stairs, her father had told her how beautiful she looked, and she had kissed him on the cheek. Then Peter White had turned and looked at Matthew and begun laughing.

"What's wrong?" Frances had asked.

"The boy looks awestruck," said Mr. White.

Matthew laughed then and said, "She looks like a Christmas queen in that red dress."

"I was afraid it was too flashy," said Frances.

"Not at all," said Matthew, giving her his arm.

"He likes your dress, Frances, because it matches his cheeks," said Mr. White, winking. If Matthew's cheeks hadn't been red before, they were now.

To relieve his embarrassment, Matthew changed the subject.

"Are Mary and Alfred coming?" he asked, referring to Frances' sister and her husband.

"They've already left," said Frances.

"Well, we should be going then," said Matthew, glad to hear he would be accompanying Frances alone. The Calls only lived next door to the Whites, but it would give Matthew a couple of minutes to have Frances all to himself.

"Have a wonderful time," said Peter White as they passed out the door.

Matthew braced himself as they stepped outside, not because the air was frigid, but because he knew this was his chance to broach the subject.

"I wish Mother wasn't still feeling ill," said Frances. "I hate for her to miss the party. She told Father to go without her, but, of course, he refused."

"That's too bad," said Matthew, his nerves making it difficult for him to know what else to say.

"The doctor came, but he says it's just a cold," Frances prattled on, and Matthew kept saying, "Uh huh" as she talked about her mother's illness, waiting for her to stop so he could say what really mattered, but before he knew it, they were down the walk and had passed along the sidewalk, and now they were turning up the Calls' front walk.

Not knowing how to be subtle, Matthew came to a standstill.

"What is it, Matthew?" asked Frances, looking nervous.

The Call House

"I just wanted a moment alone with you before we go in," said Matthew.

"Oh," said Frances, looking more nervous now. "I wanted one with you too. I wanted to tell you that—"

"Happy holidays!" shouted someone, accompanied by a great whooshing sound. Matthew and Frances turned to see Richard Blackmore coming toward them in a horse and sleigh.

"Hello, Mr. Blackmore," said Frances, just as the sled pulled up in front of them. Frances was friendly to everyone, although Matthew knew the Blackmores were not well-liked in Marquette. No doubt Mr. Call had some business dealings with Mr. Blackmore or he would not have invited him.

"Hello, Frances," said Mr. Blackmore, climbing out of his sleigh. "You're looking lovely this evening."

Why is he using her first name? Matthew wondered. *How rude!*

"Thank you," she said. "But where is Mrs. Blackmore?"

"I'm afraid she has a cold," he replied, "so I've had to come alone."

"My mother has one too," said Frances. "I think it must be going around. My father decided to stay home since she couldn't come."

"Well, that's no fun," said Mr. Blackmore. "I just figured leaving my wife at home would give me a chance to dance with all the pretty girls."

Matthew could see this old man was clearly trying to flirt with Frances, and he did not like it. Richard Blackmore was married, and forty, if he was a day. What was wrong with him, not staying home with his wife like Mr. White had?

"Are you going in?" asked Mr. Blackmore. Before Frances could answer, he was offering her his arm, and she, being too polite to refuse, took it. Matthew, not pleased at all, was left to trail into the house behind them, without even a nod of acknowledgment from Mr. Blackmore. Now when would he find a chance to speak to Frances alone?

Once the three of them were in the door, the servants were there to take their coats. The Episcopalian minister—Matthew didn't know his name—came up to them and said, "Richard, I'd like you to meet Rev. Whichgood. He's assisting at the Methodist church this week while their regular minister is out of town. I didn't want him to have to spend the holiday alone, so I persuaded Mr. Call to invite him and his daughter, Cecilia, to the party."

Mr. Blackmore shook hands with the visiting Methodist minister, but Matthew noticed that his eye instantly went to the minister's daughter,

Cecilia, who stood at her father's side. She looked to be about eighteen, and she made a stunning appearance in a light pink dress gown with little flowers stitched about the waist. It seemed more suited for a spring than a holiday party, but Matthew assumed the girl probably didn't have many party dresses since her father's minister salary likely didn't permit it.

"I'm enchanted to meet you, Miss Whichgood," said Mr. Blackmore, turning and reaching down for Cecilia's hand, which he proceeded to kiss.

Matthew took this opportunity to reclaim Frances' arm and pull her gently into the dining room. He did not want Mr. Blackmore to get any ideas about kissing her hand.

In the dining room, amid an abundant table full of appetizers, they found Frances' fourteen-year-old cousin, Bessie Mather. She instantly engaged Frances in conversation while Matthew took the liberty of collecting a small plate of food for his companion.

"Mother says I can stay up until just after midnight," Bessie said to Frances, her excitement evident in her face and tone. "'Just long enough to see the New Year in and then to bed,' she says."

"You're quite the grown up young lady then," said Frances. "I imagine you'll have many beaux vying to dance for you tonight."

"I hope so," said Bessie. "I especially hope cousin William will dance with me. Don't you think he's very handsome?"

"Yes, I do," said Frances, "though perhaps a bit old for you."

"Old? He's only twenty-seven."

"Twenty-seven!" laughed Frances. "That's twice your age."

"It is not. I'm fourteen, so I'm more than half that, and anyway, when he's thirty-nine, I'll be twenty-six, and then I'll only be two-thirds of his age, so I think if we got married, it would work out."

"You'd probably have to move to Cleveland if you married him," said Matthew, joining in the conversation. He knew William Gwinn Mather often came to Marquette to visit and look into his business interests in the mines, but he also knew that side of the Mather family was firmly entrenched in Cleveland.

"Did your cousin Kate come up to visit too?" asked Frances.

"She did," Bessie said, "but not Sam or Flora."

"Well, it's nice to have cousins coming to visit," said Frances, "even if they're only the cousins of my cousins."

"I agree," said Bessie. "I like all my cousins on both sides of the family."

"Who else is here, Bessie?" asked Matthew. They had not gone into the parlor yet where the dancing was taking place, but between the snacks and the music he could hear playing, Matthew was already feeling in a holiday mood. Some dancing might also help him work up his courage to speak to Frances.

"Well, your sister and Alfred," Bessie said to Frances, and then turning to Matthew, she said, "and your sister and her husband, too."

"That's good," said Matthew. At least Delia would dance with him if no one other than Frances would.

"What about James?" asked Frances, referring to her brother-in-law Alfred's brother, James Jopling.

"Oh, yes, of course," said Bessie. "I do so like his English accent."

"He's closer to your age too, Bessie," said Frances. "He can't be much more than seven years older than you, and you know, cousin marriages are becoming frowned upon, so maybe you should set your eyes on James instead."

"Yes, he's nice," said Bessie, "but Cousin William does have such an elegant mustache."

Matthew could not help laughing at this. He had never understood the fascination with facial hair that all the young men his age were sprouting. He'd always preferred to shave daily rather than have a prickly, itchy beard.

"Where's Bessie?" asked a voice, and then they all turned to see Bessie's mother—and Frances' aunt—Mary Hewitt Mather, enter the dining room. "There you are," she said. "Hello, Frances. I'm glad you could come." Mrs. Mather simply stared at Matthew, as if trying to place him, and then Frances said, "Aunt Mary, this is Matthew Newman. He owns Newman's Mercantile downtown."

"Oh, yes," said Mary, her eyes going to the plate in Matthew's hand. "I see you're enjoying the appetizers."

"Very much so," said Matthew, although he feared she thought he had taken too much.

"Bessie, Mrs. Smith is looking for you."

"What does she want?" spat out Bessie.

Matthew could not help smiling. Carolina Smith was no favorite of his either.

"Don't use that tone with me, young lady, or you'll be going home early," said Mrs. Mather.

"Well, I'm not going to babysit her daughter."

"She doesn't want you to. She wanted to ask you about the new dollhouse I told her you got for Christmas."

"Oh," said Bessie, her face lifting a bit. "All right."

"Excuse us," said Mary, leading her daughter off.

"Have you had enough to eat?" asked Frances, smiling as Matthew put a piece of cheese in his mouth. She had not touched the plate of food he had given her.

"I guess I'm just a little nervous," he said, having consumed all his snacks in a couple of minutes.

"You're my guest," she reminded him, "so no need to be nervous." Then she set down her untouched plate on the table and took his arm, prompting him also to put down his plate. "Let's go meet everyone else."

Matthew realized she thought he was nervous because when she had first invited him to the party, he had expressed that he did not belong with her social set. But she had no idea why his nerves were further heightened tonight.

They stepped into the parlor. For midwinter, the house was quite warm with so many people crowded into it. When Matthew heard the small orchestra switch to playing a Strauss waltz, his holiday spirits lifted. They had barely stepped into the room before he took Frances in his arms and they joined in the dance.

"I don't even have you on my dance card yet," Frances protested.

"You don't need that," said Matthew. "You should be able to remember that I get all your dances."

Frances laughed and replied, "Don't you wish. But I won't let you monopolize me. I'm quite fond of Clevelanders with mustaches, you know."

Matthew smirked and clutched her more tightly around the waist. "Well, if Mr. Mather doesn't mind waiting until I'm tired out, then he can have you."

As they circled about the room, Matthew spotted William Gwinn Mather in a corner talking to his uncle Henry. The young man was quite handsome and distinguished-looking. His father was likely a millionaire, and William would soon be also, probably taking over Cleveland Iron Mining Company upon his father's death since his older brother Samuel had decided to co-found his own company with Jay Morse and Colonel Pickands. Looking at William's elegantly tailored suit and expensive shoes, Matthew wondered why it was that some people had all the luck.

When the dance ended, Matthew agreed to let Frances rest for a moment.

"Mr. Zryd is in his finest form tonight with that marvelous violin of his," she remarked. "I could almost have danced my feet off."

Matthew joined in clapping as everyone applauded the orchestra, and especially the middle-aged Zryd, a Swiss native who had become much requested in Marquette for how he could make people cry and dance for joy with his melodies.

As Matthew escorted Frances off the dance floor, he became aware of how well-dressed the other men in the room were compared to him; his coat was at least three years old, but all of these men looked dressed in the latest fashions. Nor did anyone in this crowd think anything of taking a trip to Europe or building a house with a ballroom, luxuries Matthew doubted he would ever know.

"Hello, Miss White," said William Gwinn Mather, whom Matthew suddenly realized was at his elbow and greeting his dance partner.

"Hello, Mr. Mather," she replied. "It's so nice that you were able to come up for the holidays."

"Well, I spent Christmas in Cleveland you know, but Kate and I did want to see Uncle Henry and Aunt Mary during the holidays."

"And have you heard anything lately from your aunt in Europe?" asked Frances. Matthew knew she meant Constance Fenimore Woolson, whose novel *Anne*, set on nearby Mackinac Island, had been a bestseller a year or two before.

"Aunt Connie?" he asked. "Yes, we received a Christmas card and letter from her."

"My father and mother were so happy to meet her when they were in Italy a few years ago."

"Yes, she wrote to tell us about seeing them— how they quite unexpectedly bumped into each other—in Florence I think it was."

"Is your aunt writing anything new? I so loved her novel *Anne*, especially the descriptions on Mackinac Island, although I thought her heroine was far too good for Heathcote."

William Gwinn Mather
circa 1884

"Oh, she's always writing," said William. "I know she wants to write another novel, but she's also busy traveling and writing short stories. She finds it hard to stay in one place. I can never keep straight whether she's in Florence or London or some other foreign town. Sam keeps track, but I have a hard time doing so."

"It must be wonderful, though, to have an author in the family."

"We have a few of them actually," said William. "You know that James Fenimore Cooper is our great-great-uncle—well, not mine actually, but Samuel's on his mother's side, and of course, all of us Mathers are related to Cotton Mather."

"Well, I wouldn't brag about that," said Frances. "So horrible, those Salem witch trials."

"Who's your friend?" asked William, but before Frances could answer, he gave Matthew his hand and said, "I'm William Gwinn Mather. I don't believe we've met."

"I'm Matthew Newman," said Matthew, returning the handshake. "It's a pleasure to meet you, sir."

"'Sir'? You make me sound old."

Matthew knew the young gentleman was a couple of years older than himself, but that hardly mattered. "I'm sorry, sir."

"There you go again. Just call me 'Will.' You're not the Matthew that sometimes goes fishing with George Shiras, are you?"

"Yes," Frances answered for Matthew. "George and Matthew are good friends; they go fishing all the time when George is here in the summer."

"I'll have to join the two of you this summer then when I come back up," said Will. "I'm afraid I work far too much and could use a vacation."

"Most of us do work too hard," said Matthew, but then he wished he hadn't because he didn't want to broach the subject of his own employment, from fear this dapper young millionaire's son would look down on him. But before Matthew could think how to change the subject, Frances was explaining to Will about all the beautiful items Matthew sold in his general store as if he owned Harrods in London.

"May I have this dance?" asked James Jopling, suddenly appearing and just as suddenly whisking Frances away, leaving Matthew to stand awkwardly beside Will as the music started up again, making it too difficult to talk, even if they could have found anything further to say to one another.

"There you are, Matthew," said Delia, filling Matthew with relief as he turned to see her behind him. Will took this opportunity to nod goodbye and disappear into the crowd. Matthew could not blame him for wanting to escape his mundane company.

"Hello, Delia," said Matthew. "I heard you were here, but I didn't see you anywhere."

"I was out on the patio, getting some air. It's so crowded it's getting stuffy in here."

"And where's Roger?"

"Over at the punchbowl," she said, rolling her eyes and nodding her head in the direction of the beverages.

"Figures," muttered Matthew, but then he realized he shouldn't complain about his brother-in-law, even if his own sister did, so he said, "Actually, I'm rather thirsty after dancing. Would you like me to get you a drink?"

"Thank you," said Delia.

Matthew made his way to the punchbowl and back, ignoring Roger, who was talking to Charles Call. When he returned to Delia's side, he found her engaged in conversation with Carolina Smith. Apparently, Bessie's telling Carolina about her dollhouse had not taken long. The sight of Carolina usually would have made Matthew walk the other way, but he couldn't do so when he had to deliver Delia her glass of punch.

"You're too kind," said Carolina, thinking the second glass she saw Matthew carrying was intended for her. Matthew had already sipped out of it—just to see whether Roger had spiked it, which he fortunately hadn't—but Matthew did not refuse the glass to Carolina. He considered it repayment for how she had three times ordered drapes for her parlor from him, only to return them each time and then finally settle on a pair from another store. It had not been his fault she—or more likely whomever she had hired—hadn't been able to measure her windows properly.

Carolina sipped the punch as she continued speaking to Delia, rattling on about how her neighbors should do a better job of landscaping their yard, which seemed an odd subject with two feet of snow on the ground and likely four more to come before anyone could even start thinking about landscaping again.

Matthew escaped to get another glass of punch, and then he escaped into a corner where he hoped no one would pay attention to him. Who would when they all seemed to be paying attention to Frances? He watched her dance with one man after another until, finally, one of the dances ended with her standing just a few feet from him. Then he managed to speak to her for a moment.

"Frances, I think it's my turn again," he said.

"Oh, I'm sorry, Matthew. I—"

Before Frances could finish speaking, Mary Mather interrupted them. "Excuse me; it's Matthew, right?" she said. Matthew now noticed Bessie behind her. "I notice you haven't had a dance partner for a while, and Bessie here would love someone to dance with."

Matthew looked down at Frances' cousin and said, "I'd be delighted," because he was a gentleman. He never cursed out loud, but that didn't stop him from doing so in his head.

He tried to chitchat with Bessie while they danced, but she kept staring about her, looking for her cousin Will. Finally, Matthew saw that James Jopling was without a partner, so he danced her over to James, hoping James would get the hint and cut in, but no such luck, and so he gave Bessie another spin around the room until the orchestra finally quit playing.

By then, Frances was off in someone else's arms, but fortunately, a young man about Bessie's age now came up to her, and in another moment, she had waltzed off with him.

"So is tonight the night?" asked Delia, whispering in his ear. She did have a way of sneaking up on him.

"I don't know," said Matthew.

"Did you bring the ring?"

"I did, but I—I don't know—I tried to talk to her on the way here, but—"

"Don't put it off, Matthew," Delia warned, "or someone else will snatch her up."

"I know," said Matthew. "It's just—I can't believe she would ever—"

"Think what it would do for your business," Delia continued. "Why, you could sell the mercantile, quit working at the newspaper, and find a good paying job at your father-in-law's bank or in one of his other businesses."

"I'm not interested in her for pecuniary reasons," said Matthew, afraid even to say Frances' name from fear someone might overhear and laugh at his aspirations.

"I know," said Delia, "but just think—you'd be related by marriage to Peter White, and to the Mathers and the Calls too."

Roger now came up to them. He opened his mouth to speak, but instead, he let out a belch.

Delia rolled her eyes.

"What's the matter, Delya?" asked Roger, slurring her name. "It's healthy to let it out."

"It's not healthy to be rude in front of all these fine people," she replied.

"Now don't start that. These people aren't all that much. They didn't start out with anything more than your family did. Why, my mother's family, the Palmers, had money generations before these social climbers."

As he spoke, he swung out his arm as if to encompass the entire crowd under the umbrella of "social climbers." In the process, he succeeded in spilling his whiskey—it clearly wasn't punch—all over Matthew.

"Roger!" exclaimed Delia. "That's it. It's time for us to leave. I'm sorry, Matthew."

"It's okay," said Matthew, wiping himself off with his handkerchief while wondering whether Roger could even walk home. "Let me help you." He discreetly took Roger's arm while Delia walked in front of them. "I ain't that drunk," said Roger, but fortunately, he didn't put up a struggle to escape from them. Together, Matthew and Delia led Roger into the hall. Matthew hoped that when they reached the door, Roger wouldn't make a spectacle of himself by tumbling down the front step.

In the hall, they found Richard Blackmore talking to Cecilia Whichgood.

"Mr. Blackmore," said Delia, to get his attention so he would move out of their way, "it was pleasant to see you again."

"What? Are you leaving?" asked Richard Blackmore.

"I'd stay for another dance or two," said Roger, "but the wife has a headache."

So typical of him, thought Matthew, *blaming someone else*. But he knew Delia probably did have a headache—one likely to last the rest of her married life.

As Richard and Cecilia tried to step out of the way, Roger attempted to pass them and tripped on the rug, half-falling and nearly bringing Matthew down with him.

"Oh, he can't walk home," said Richard, shaking his head. "Let me take you home in my sleigh."

"Oh, it's only a few blocks," said Delia.

"No, I insist. I've been meaning to give some sleigh rides along the lake as part of the party celebrations. Cecilia and I just came from a ride ourselves."

Cecilia blushed and then quickly disappeared into the dining room. While Matthew wondered about the girl's abrupt departure, Delia accepted Richard Blackmore's offer.

"You're very kind," said Delia.

"That's what neighbors are for," Richard replied. He did live only two blocks from Roger and Delia. "What about you, Matthew? Are you leaving too?"

"No," said Matthew.

"Well, do you want a sleigh ride? I can come back for you and Frances when I'm done bringing your sister and Roger home."

For a minute, Matthew didn't know what to say.

"I think Frances would love that," said Delia, poking her brother.

"Ye-es," said Matthew, realizing his opportunity. "So do I. I'll go find her and we'll be waiting when you get back."

"Now's your chance," Delia whispered to Matthew as Richard, who had taken Roger's arm, helped Roger out the door and down the front walk.

"Don't worry, Roger," Richard said, laughing. "I had a few too many myself."

Matthew hoped that wouldn't affect Richard's driving.

Matthew waited until everyone had gone out the front door, and then he went back into the parlor. In a second, he spotted Frances talking to her sister, Mrs. Jopling. Quickly walking up behind her, he said, "I have a surprise for you," and he covered her eyes with his hands, suddenly feeling lighthearted and merry.

"What kind of a surprise, Matthew?" she asked, for she instantly recognized his voice.

"Come see," he said.

Frances looked hesitant, but her sister said, "Go along, Fanny."

"All right, Matthew," she agreed, "but you'll have to remove your hands or we'll never make it through this crowd."

"Okay," he said, "if you promise you'll like it."

"I can't promise that until I see it," she replied.

"All right, fair enough," he said, removing his hands, "but it requires going outside."

"I won't mind that," Frances replied. "It's far too warm in here."

In another minute, he had led her into the hall and found a maid to fetch their coats. As they put them on, Frances asked, "Won't you tell me what it is?" Serendipitously, Richard Blackmore pulled back up in front of the house with the sleigh.

"It's right there in front of your eyes," said Matthew, opening the front door and taking her hand to help her down the stairs.

"The sleigh?" she asked, puzzled.

"Yes, what's better than a sleigh ride?" he replied, and momentarily losing his self-consciousness, he began to sing, 'Jingle bells, jingle bells. Jingle all the way!'"

"'Oh what fun it is,'" she joined in, "'to ride in a one-horse open sleigh.'"

"Hello!" Mr. Blackmore called to them as they started down the walk. "Hop in!"

When Frances realized Richard Blackmore would be their driver, she looked hesitant, but Matthew gave her his hand and she took it, and then he helped her up into the sleigh, quickly scooting in beside her.

"Thank you, Mr. Blackmore," said Frances, remembering her manners. "What a treat this is."

"My pleasure," said Richard. "Wrap yourselves up warm now. It gets cold by the lake."

A large buffalo skin to serve as a blanket was on the seat. Matthew quickly spread it over their laps to keep them warm and comfortable. Then Richard said, "Giddup" and they were off, dashing down Ridge Street's steep hill toward Lake Superior.

"Oh," said Frances, "look at how peaceful the lake is tonight."

"It's surprising it's not covered with ice yet," said Matthew, admiring how the moonlight was shining on its nearly flat black surface.

"It will be soon," said Frances, "although Lake Superior is so large it rarely freezes over, you know."

"I know," said Matthew. "But it'll freeze enough along the shore that soon we can go ice skating."

"Last winter when I asked you to go ice skating, you kept telling me you were too busy," Frances scolded.

"Well, that's about to change," said Matthew, and he placed his hand over hers.

Frances did not reply. She looked inland since Matthew was on the side by the lake.

"It's such a clear night," said Matthew. "We're lucky it's not snowing."

Frances did not reply.

"On nights like this, I almost envy the Eskimos."

Silence.

"I'd so love to live in an igloo," he said, being silly just to get a response out of her.

Still she was silent. And she did not turn her head back toward him.

"Frances," he said.

"I'm cold," she said.

But now she seemed so distant, still looking away from him, that he could no longer be the Matthew he was just moments before, the Matthew who would have wrapped his arm around her. What had just happened? Should he pull his hand away?

Richard turned around to look at them, and that made Matthew pull his hand away quickly. Now he had really fouled it all up, and at that moment, the sleigh jolted. "Oops!" said Mr. Blackmore and turned back around since the horse had nearly pulled them off the trail.

"You're right, Frances. The lake is definitely peaceful tonight," said Matthew, still trying to get a reaction out of her. He wanted her to look at him. He wanted to look into her eyes, and then to put his hand in his suit pocket and pull out the ring, and then to ask her the most important question of his life, and to receive an affirmative answer, and to slide the ring on her finger. But no, proposing in the sleigh would not be the best idea—sure, it would be romantic, but what if they hit another bump and the ring flew out into the snow? Better to wait until the ride was over. Then he would ask her before they went back into the party. But first, he had to get her to warm up to him again.

"Don't you think Marquette is the grandest place in the world?" he asked.

"I do," said Frances, and now she turned her head back, looking forward, though, and not at him directly.

"Of course, that has a lot to do with your father," said Matthew.

No reply.

They had reached Vernon Street now. They had been traveling over snow along the lakeshore where there was no road. Now Richard turned the horse onto Vernon and they were headed back toward town, climbing up another hill.

"Your father," said Matthew, still trying to get her to talk, "without him, I doubt Marquette would be half so grand. I think I respect him more than anyone else I've ever met."

"He thinks very highly of you," said Frances. "He says you're a good boy and a hard worker."

"Thanks," said Matthew, but he hoped Mr. White thought of him as more than a boy.

Vernon Street's hill was quite steep, and for a moment, Matthew wasn't sure the horse would make it to the top, but somehow, it managed, though at a slow pace. And then the moment they reached the top, they were swiftly dashing through the street as the horse tried to regain his momentum.

"Oh!" screamed Frances, a bit surprised by the speed.

"Hang on," said Matthew, putting his arm around her to hold her tightly as they sped past the buildings belonging to Smith Moore Gold Mine.

By the time they had reached Pine Street, the horse had slowed down. Florence looked a bit ruffled, and she pulled away from Matthew.

"Matthew," she whispered, "Mr. Blackmore will see you."

Is that really why she's pulling away from me? Matthew wondered. Of course, Peter White's daughter couldn't allow herself to be seen in a compromising situation, so he removed his arm and discreetly scooted over an inch away from her. Then he said, "Richard, Frances is getting cold. Maybe we should head back now."

"I've got some brandy in my pocket," said Richard. "I don't imagine she'd want some, though."

"No, thank you," said Frances decidedly.

"That's all right," said Richard. "We'll head back. I promised Cecilia another ride anyway."

"Please tell Mrs. Blackmore I hope she gets over her cold soon, and wish her a Happy New Year from me," said Frances.

"Actually, she's in the family way, you know," said Mr. Blackmore.

"Oh, I didn't know," said Frances.

"Congratulations," said Matthew.

"Thanks," said Richard Blackmore.

They had reached Front Street by now. Richard turned onto it to head south a few blocks until they reached Ridge Street. Then he turned the sleigh again to head west, back toward the Calls' house.

"I love all of these grand homes," said Matthew as they went past the massive Breitung and Merritt houses.

"I love living on this street," Frances added.

"Maybe someday," said Matthew, "I will too."

"I'm sure you can if you want to, Matthew," said Frances. "I have no doubt you're going to be a very successful man."

"Really?" Matthew wondered whether that meant she thought one day they might live together in one of these houses because her father would take him into one of his several businesses.

"Yes," said Frances. "I wouldn't be surprised if you ended up owning the *Mining Journal* someday."

"Oh, I don't know about that," said Matthew.

Richard now pulled the sleigh up in front of the Call house.

Matthew got out of the sleigh and then helped Frances down.

"Thank you, Mr. Blackmore," said Frances.

"My pleasure," he said, climbing down from the sleigh himself. "I think I'll go in and warm up for a minute before taking anyone else out."

"It is quite cold out here," Frances replied.

She started to follow Mr. Blackmore into the house, but Matthew, too scared now to be graceful, clutched her hand to stop her.

"Frances, can we wait to go in for a minute?" he asked. He saw Mr. Blackmore pause at the door, holding it open for them.

"All right," said Frances, looking puzzled.

Matthew watched Mr. Blackmore, who realized by now they weren't coming in, enter the house and close the door as he found the courage to speak.

"It's just that…just that I wanted to talk to you alone for a minute. Here, come over here," he said, pulling her from the walkway onto the sidewalk between the Call and White houses where they would be less likely to be interrupted.

"What is it, Matthew?" she asked, looking even more puzzled as he unbuttoned his coat to reach into his suit pocket.

In a moment, he had pulled out the ring, and then—realizing he had not planned this well since he'd be kneeling in the snow—he went down on his knee and started to open the ring case. Only, he hadn't taken off his gloves so he couldn't get it open at first, and then just as he did, Frances said, "No, Matthew. Get up. No. Please."

As he looked up at her, he felt his face constrict with pain. He could not speak. He did not know what to reply.

"Please, Matthew, get up," she repeated, and then she turned sideways, as if afraid to face him.

"All right," he said, hearing how pathetic his voice sounded as he did so.

When she did not turn back toward him, he returned the ring to his pocket, and then he tried to take her hand. She let him, but it was as if he were holding the palm of a lifeless doll.

"Frances, you must know how I feel about you. I—"

"I didn't know you cared that much," she replied. "I'm sorry. If I had known, I never would have invited you to the party tonight. Of course, I invited you before I—"

"But couldn't you come to care about me too?" he interrupted. "I thought you did. I thought we were more than friends."

"We are friends. Good friends. Best friends," she said, turning to face him. "But I only love you as a friend, Matthew. Oh, don't you think I've tried to love you as something more. I did, but…."

And then she began to cry and Matthew felt even worse, as if he were some sort of heel who had hurt her badly, although he didn't understand how. All he had wanted was to shower her with love, with kisses, with affection, and with every pretty thing money could buy.

"I don't understand," he said, standing there feeling confused and helpless. He began to shiver.

"I'm…." She was sobbing now, trying to spit out the words between sobs. "I'm going…to…to marry George."

"George?" For a moment, Matthew couldn't even think who George was.

"Yes," she replied. "I'm sorry. I should have told you sooner. I was going to tell you later tonight. I didn't know how to tell you. He wrote to me at Christmas and asked me. He said he wanted to ask me in person, but he couldn't live any longer without knowing whether there was any hope, and I couldn't keep him in suspense, so I wrote back to him yesterday and told him I would be his wife."

"George," Matthew repeated, stunned. "I didn't even know you liked him."

"Well, I do," said Frances. "I'm sorry."

Matthew didn't know what to say. What did it matter what he said now? All hope was lost.

"I'm sorry, Matthew," Frances repeated. "I didn't want to hurt you. That's why I planned to tell you later tonight, but I didn't know you were going to…."

And she started sobbing again.

"It's okay," said Matthew. "I understand."

He didn't understand, but he was a gentleman, so he forgot about his feelings and tried to console her.

"You're not too angry, are you?"

"No," said Matthew. "I'm not angry at all. You're a beautiful woman. You're free to marry whomever you want. George is a very lucky man."

"Do you mean that?" she asked, looking at him through her tears.

"Of course I mean it," said Matthew. "George is a good man. I don't think I know a better one, in fact." But the voice in his head was saying, *I hate George. If he were here, I would knock him down. I'd make him bleed.*

"Thank you for understanding," said Frances.

"You better stop crying now," said Matthew, "or those tears will turn into ice."

At that moment, the front door of the Call house opened and Cecilia Whichgood stepped outside with Richard Blackmore.

"Father told me 'No,'" Cecilia was saying to Richard, "but he's half-asleep in a corner so he won't know."

"Let's go back inside," said Matthew.

"No, I think I'd rather go home," said Frances.

"Are you leaving already?" Richard called to them.

Matthew half-turned around and waved at him. "Thanks again for the ride! Good night!"

But Richard was already busy, helping Cecilia back into the sleigh, and rather than sitting up on the driver's seat, he took a seat beside her.

"Do you want me to walk you to the door?" asked Matthew.

"No, I live right there," said Frances, although they kept walking together in that direction.

They stopped at the walk up to the house. Frances said, "Good night, Matthew," and then she turned and practically ran to the front door.

For a moment, Matthew stood lost in confusion. Then he turned and walked home, leaving the new year to be rung in by happier people.

Mint Patch New Attraction

———

Washington, May 30.—The White House mint patch, referred to by Colonel Roosevelt in his testimony in the libel suit he is pressing at Marquette, Mich., promises to become as much an object of interest to capital visitors as the Washington Monument or the Library of Congress.

Already tourists are asking the White House police to point out the bed that gave up its fragrant leaves for Colonel Roosevelt's occasional juleps.

The bed, fifteen feet long by four feet wide, is situated beside a lattice-work house used by the White House laundries in which to dry clothes. Although mint always has been within easy reach of the White House porch, the present "patch" was established by President McKinley.

President Taft seldom used it, although it furnished its part to many a refreshing julep served to Mr. Taft's callers. President Wilson also uses it—for garnishing spring lamb.

— *The Mining Journal*, May 30, 1913

THURSDAY
MAY 29, 1913

"Liquor drinking," says Lillian Russell,
"robs women of their beauty.
This, if nothing else, ought to induce women
to give up the pernicious booze habit."
— *The Mining Journal*, June 3, 1913

CHAPTER 14

IN THE MORNING, ROGER, DELIA, and Matthew had just sat down to breakfast when Roger announced, "I won't be home for supper tonight. I'm eating with a client in Negaunee."

"Negaunee!" said Delia. "Well, how will you get there?"

"What do you mean?" asked Roger.

"You told Matthew he could use the car today so he'd be able to get back and forth from the trial to the luncheon at the Hills this afternoon."

"I never said that," said Roger.

Matthew had to admit that Roger had never said it to him, but he had no doubt Roger had agreed to it when Delia had asked him.

"I asked you about it yesterday, Roger," Delia reminded him, "and you said it was fine. You never said anything then about dinner with a client tonight."

"I don't remember ever discussing it with you."

"You did, as soon as you got home last night before supper, and we haven't had any telephone calls since then, so I don't know how you suddenly have this mysterious dinner engagement."

"Delia," said Roger, buttering his toast, and not even bothering to look at her, "sometimes I think you rehearse your conversations with me in your head, and then you think we had them when we didn't."

"Is that so?" said Delia. "Well, regardless, Matthew needs the automobile today. You'll have to take the train."

"You know there isn't a train at that time of the day."

"How would I know that? I never go to Negaunee."

"Well, that's not my fault."

"It is your fault because I did have that conversation with you," Delia insisted.

"It's all right," said Matthew, who had heard enough by now. "I'll just walk there. It shouldn't take me more than twenty minutes."

"Why," exclaimed Delia, "you'll be late and miss the whole thing, and you'll be late getting back to the courthouse too!"

"Then I just won't go if I can't get there in time."

"You could take the streetcar," Roger told Matthew.

"Yes, I could, at least part of the way," Matthew agreed.

"And you could take the train," Delia told Roger as he wiped toast crumbs from his mustache.

"How do you expect me to run a successful business," Roger demanded, "if my clients think I can't even afford my own automobile but have to take the train like any common fellow?"

"Don't worry about it," said Matthew. "It's not that important."

"It is to me," said Delia. "I don't want to have to go to the party by myself."

"It's always all about you, isn't it, Delia?" Roger replied.

"Never mind worrying about it," Matthew repeated, getting up.

"Where are you going?" Delia asked her brother. "You didn't even drink your coffee."

"I just better get going if I have to walk to the courthouse," said Matthew.

"I can give you a ride there at least," said Roger.

"That's all right. I'd rather walk," said Matthew. "Then I can think a bit about what I should write in my next article."

Matthew knew he was pushing his luck by not accepting the ride—he might not have time to send his dispatch before the trial started—but he didn't want any favors from his brother-in-law. It was bad enough staying under his roof; he'd have stayed in a hotel if Delia hadn't insisted he stay with them. Matthew was starting to look forward to returning to New York now; he loved Delia, but he did not love seeing her under these circumstances. Hopefully, the trial would end sooner than originally predicted.

Twenty minutes later, Matthew had reached the courthouse, having enjoyed the chance to walk, stretch his legs, and think about the trial and what he might write today. Covering a luncheon wasn't a very good news story anyway, so he would not mind if he missed it. He could always go to lunch with Homer and the other reporters. But he also knew he couldn't disappoint Delia; he'd figure out how to get to the Hills' house, even if it did mean walking there and back.

Matthew found he only had five minutes when he arrived at the courthouse—just long enough to send his dispatch off to the *Empire Sentinel.* Once that task was done, he squeezed into his seat next to Homer, just in time too, as the bailiff called, "All rise for the honorable Judge Richard C. Flannigan."

After a few short preliminaries, the first witness was called to the stand. Charles W. Thompson was a correspondent for the *New York Times,* and he had also been a member of Colonel Roosevelt's 1912 campaign. Thompson testified that he had been with the colonel throughout the campaign; therefore, it was impossible that the colonel could have become drunk during his campaign visit to Marquette or at any other time during the campaign.

When Mr. Thompson stepped down, A.A. Abele was called. Abele, an Ohio businessman, had met and heard Roosevelt speak during his campaign stops in that state. He said there had been no sign that Roosevelt was intoxicated in any way. Following Abele's testimony, Colonel Roosevelt's cousin's son, Philip Roosevelt, was called. He testified to every type of liquor he had ever seen kept at the colonel's home at Oyster Bay, including different types of whiskey, wine, and champagne, but like everyone else, he confirmed that he had never seen his cousin drunk or take more than one or two glasses of any kind of strong drink in an evening.

Matthew was feeling a bit sleepy as the testimonies continued, perhaps from overexerting himself during his walk that morning, perhaps because he had not slept well after thinking of Frances the night before. He also noticed that George wasn't in the courtroom today. Roosevelt may have been driven here by him, but if so, George had not entered the building. After Matthew had spent so much time last night thinking about Frances, he wasn't sure he wanted to see George today. He hated to admit it, but sometimes, when he thought back to that time, though he tried not to, all the old feelings would come back to him and he would still feel like he was in love with Frances, and....

"We'll take a recess for lunch now," said Judge Flannigan, banging his gavel and returning Matthew's thoughts to the present.

"Are you coming to the hotel for lunch today?" Homer Guck asked Matthew.

"No, I'm afraid not," said Matthew, only just deciding for certain at that moment. "I'm supposed to go to a luncheon the Hills are having for Colonel Roosevelt today. My sister was invited and I guess she finagled an invitation for me."

"Lucky you," said Homer.

"Well, yes, I guess so," said Matthew, stopping himself from confessing that he would rather not go since he knew Homer would have loved to.

"Enjoy your lunch," said Homer. "I'll see you this afternoon."

"Yes, you too," said Matthew, collecting his things and then turning to leave the courtroom.

How will I ever walk to the Hills and back in time? he wondered. *And if I don't get back in time, I might not be let back into the courtroom until the afternoon recess. That would be shirking my duty to the* Empire Sentinel, *but at the same time, I just can't let Delia down. Not after Roger was so nasty to her this morning.*

These thoughts passed through Matthew's head as he stepped out the courtroom door and started down the steps.

"Matthew!" someone shouted, and turning, Matthew saw it was George, waving from where he was seated in his automobile.

Matthew walked slowly toward him. He couldn't walk fast with everyone else spilling out of the courthouse around him, but it gave him a moment to notice that Colonel Roosevelt was climbing into Mr. Hill's vehicle. That must mean George wasn't going to the reception.

"Matthew!" George shouted again. Matthew realized he had not responded to him yet, so he raised his hand and waved to let George know he was coming.

"Hello, George," he said when he was within a few feet of him. "I only have a moment. Delia expects me to join her at the Hills for the reception. Do you think the streetcar can get me there in time? I'm not sure what the streetcar schedule is."

"Delia told me you were going," said George. "She was out in her yard when I happened to drive by, so she asked if I would mind giving you a ride. Of course, I couldn't refuse her."

"Oh," said Matthew, surprised and not sure whether the surprise was pleasant. "Are you going to the luncheon also?"

"No," said George. "Mrs. Hill kindly invited me, but I wanted to get some errands done this morning."

"Then I shouldn't trouble you for a ride," said Matthew.

"It's no trouble at all," said George. "Hop in."

Matthew did as he was told, muttering, "It's very kind of you."

"Don't mention it," said George.

"It was also very kind of you to have me over for dinner the other night," said Matthew as George started up the vehicle.

"Anything for an old friend," said George. "It's too bad you're not staying longer so we can go fishing or camping like in the old days. In fact, on Saturday, if we go out to my camp, I expect you to join us."

"Oh, I couldn't," said Matthew.

"Why not?" George asked, turning onto Baraga Avenue and heading toward Lake Superior.

"I imagine you'll be staying overnight."

"So? The next day is Sunday."

"Yes, and my niece's wedding," Matthew reminded him.

"Weddings are usually held on Saturdays," said George.

"Yes, but when my family heard about the trial and that I was coming for it, they changed it to Sunday afternoon, and I wouldn't want you to rush back on my account. I'd come back on my own, but I don't have an automobile."

"So I've noticed," said George, laughing.

They had reached Front Street now. They were silent for a moment as George looked both ways before venturing to turn.

"Do you know the Hills well?" asked Matthew.

"No. Just to say hello when I see them," said George. "I'm sure Mrs. Hill only invited me because I'm hosting Theodore. I don't know how Theodore chose him for his lawyer. I think Mr. Belden must have contacted Mr. Hill, something like that. Do you know them?"

"No, but I guess Delia does through one of her women's groups or something."

"Most likely," said George. "I sometimes think all the women in this town know each other better than all the men do."

"I think that's probably true," said Matthew. "It seems like they're usually plotting among themselves to get us to do what they want."

"I wouldn't be surprised," said George.

Another moment of silence followed—George didn't seem to mind. They had now turned onto Ridge Street, and again, Matthew was reminded of Frances as they drove past all the houses he and Frances had once walked past together. Then they came to Spruce Street, just a block before Matthew would have seen Frances and George's house. A few blocks later, they had arrived at the Hills' house.

"Thank you again for the ride," said Matthew, noticing several automobiles were already parked in front of the house, as were several others. "It looks like everyone's already here. I'd have been really late if I had walked."

"My pleasure," said George. "Have a good time. But how will you get back?"

"I'll walk back," said Matthew.

"Or Delia will have already arranged a ride home for you that she'll tell you about when you get inside," said George. "That said, I could come back in an hour, and—"

"No," said Matthew, bluntly. "You've done plenty, George."

"I'm happy, like I said, to help an old friend," George replied, and then he put his foot on the gas pedal and nodded his head goodbye.

Why does he have to be so friendly? Matthew wondered as George disappeared into the distance. *Why can't he just leave me be? I haven't even seen him in years. I appreciate it, but....*

And then he took a moment to compose himself before going up the walk to ring the doorbell.

"We'll have a gala day!
Fate sends a prince this way!
Each voice we'll raise
To sing the praise
Of such a noble guest!
With loud acclaim
We hail his name
The brightest and the best!"
— *The Prince of Pilsen*

CHAPTER 15

MATTHEW RANG THE DOORBELL AND waited, but no one answered the door. He rang it again, and finally, the door was opened by Delia.

"There you are!" she said. "Did George give you a ride?"

"Yes, thanks to you," said Matthew.

"Come in; we're ready to eat."

She took his hand and almost pulled Matthew into the dining room.

"There you are," said Colonel Roosevelt. "We were all waiting for you. My stomach was starting to rumble."

"I'm sorry I'm late," said Matthew, although he knew the former president couldn't have beat him by more than a couple of minutes, but everyone had already managed to sit down at a very long table.

"It's no problem," said Mrs. Hill, coming up to play hostess. "We're happy to have you, Mr. Newman. Please take a seat here beside your sister." She walked to a chair and actually pulled it out for Matthew.

"Thank you, Mrs. Hill," he replied, dropping down into it only after Mrs. Hill had sat down herself, as well as Delia.

Matthew looked around as the conversation recommenced—he had clearly interrupted it. Besides Delia and himself, Mr. and Mrs. Hill were hosting Colonel Roosevelt, Gifford Pinchot, James Garfield, William H. Van Benschoten, and a few other guests he didn't recognize. In time, Delia introduced him to them, but he did not remember all their names, save for Mrs. Charlton, whom he knew must be the wife of Marquette's premier architect.

"How did things go at the trial this morning?" asked one guest—Matthew thought he had been introduced as Dr. Cunningham.

"Well, I would say," began the colonel, but before he could say more, Mrs. Hill said, "Now, no talk of business at the table. This is a social event."

Matthew was surprised she would dare chide the colonel, but Roosevelt only smiled at her and said, "Let me offer a toast to Mrs. Hill for this sumptuous feast!" for it looked sumptuous as the serving girls now brought in trays of ham and potato salad and little finger sandwiches and other light summer fare.

Everyone raised his or her glass—Mrs. Hill had decided she would only serve lemonade; certainly no alcohol—and said, "Here, here," and clinked them together.

Because so many people were present, it was difficult for one conversation to predominate, so people spoke to those next to them or in small groups. The food was quite tasty, and Matthew enjoyed a couple of jokes made by those sitting near him, but he also found himself starting to feel sleepy once he had begun to digest his food. Mrs. Hill roused him from his drowsiness when she remarked to Roosevelt, "It's a shame that Frances wasn't here for your visit."

"George told me she wanted to come home," replied the colonel, "but I told him not to let her trouble herself. I'm sure that after all the years we've known each other, any luster I had has long since worn off in her eyes."

"Oh, I don't believe that," said Delia. "Any woman would be honored to have you as a guest in her home."

"Thank you for the compliment, Mrs. Richardson," said Roosevelt, "but I didn't wish to put Frances out. It is more than I could have asked that George and his relatives have so graciously let me and those testifying on my behalf stay in their homes."

"I'm sure we're all happy to do whatever we can," said Mrs. Hill. "This trial has been a true travesty."

"Dear," said Mr. Hill, smiling, "you yourself said we were not to talk about the trial."

"Very true," said Mrs. Hill. "Mr. Newman, I believe you and George have been friends for years. Do you often see him and Frances out east?"

Matthew swallowed the piece of ham he was chewing on and replied, "No, I'm afraid not. I believe they're in Washington or Pennsylvania most of the time, while I'm in New York."

"That's too bad," said Mrs. Hill. "I remember a time when we saw you and Frances together around Marquette so much that we were all surprised when she ended up marrying George."

"Agnes," muttered Mr. Hill.

"Oh," she said, as if realizing she had said too much.

"Mr. Newman," said Roosevelt, as if intentionally trying to end the awkward moment, "used to see plenty of me in New York, however. He even walked the streets with Jacob Riis and me one night when I was police commissioner there. He's a fine reporter, and you should all be proud that he's one of your native sons."

"We are proud," said Delia. "Marquette's a small city, but we feel we still have some greatness here."

"All towns do," said Mr. Garfield. "I believe there is greatness to be found everywhere when you look for it."

"There is certainly plenty to be admired about Marquette," said Roosevelt. Matthew wondered whether the colonel truly meant it or he was just being polite, but then he went on to say, "It may not be the size of New York or Washington, but Marquette's a beautiful city, full of green trees and all those distinct sandstone buildings, like nothing I've ever seen elsewhere."

"We have Mrs. Charlton's husband to thank for much of that," said Mr. Hill.

Roosevelt turned inquiringly to Mrs. Charlton.

"Mr. Charlton," explained Mrs. Hill, "is Marquette's best architect. He is responsible for many of our finest buildings, including the courthouse where your trial is being held."

"Indeed," said Roosevelt. "Then, please, Mrs. Charlton, give my compliments to your husband. It's a fine big building, grand to an extreme, and far better than many of the courthouses I've seen that look more like New England churches than temples to justice."

"Thank you," said Mrs. Charlton. "Fred will be very proud to hear such praise. I wish he could have come today, but he's always so busy at his office."

"Mr. Charlton also built the Longyear mansion," said Matthew, "the building on the corner across from George's house that we were telling you was moved to Massachusetts."

"Oh, yes," said Roosevelt.

"And he built the opera house," said Delia. "We'll be going there this evening, Matthew and I, to see *The Prince of Pilsen*. Will you be going, Colonel Roosevelt?"

"No," said the colonel, "I'm afraid not. I don't want people to accuse me of having an interest in Pilsener beer." Matthew had already heard this joke at the railroad station—and so had Delia, though she must have forgotten it because she joined in the laughter with everyone else, for the play was well known for how Pilsener beer was confused with the Prince of Pilsen in the play.

"The Decoration Day ceremonies are also being held at the opera house tomorrow, I believe," said Dr. Cunningham.

"Yes, but I won't see those either," said Roosevelt. "I was asked to speak there, and if circumstances were different, I would have gladly done so, but I think it best I remove myself from all activities so I am not accused of trying to win over public opinion during the trial."

"Well, I hope you enjoy your time here in Marquette, regardless," said Mrs. Hill.

"I am so far, given how many kind people I've met," said Roosevelt, flashing his famous smile.

"Good," said Delia. "We're not all like Mr. Newett."

"To tell the truth," said Roosevelt, "I rather feel sorry for the man. He was just repeating what many others have accused me of, but I had to take a stand before more people tried to ruin my reputation."

"As well you should," said Mr. Hill, siding with his client.

"Enough talk of the trial now," said Mrs. Hill. "It's time for dessert."

The serving girls now brought in homemade ice cream with fruit toppings. Everyone exclaimed how scrumptious it was, and then talk turned to dessert recipes and then the weather, and before they knew it, the dinner hour had passed pleasantly and it was time for everyone involved in the trial to return to the courthouse.

Roosevelt on Suffrage

At the pageant in the Metropolitan opera house on the night preceding the parade Colonel Roosevelt made a straight-out woman-suffrage speech. Suffrage conditions, according to this conspicuous convert to the cause, have changed enormously in sixty-five years:

"A meeting like this would have been impossible sixty-five years ago. The idea of the mastership of man over woman has changed to the idea of equal partnership between man and wife, and the loftiest type of family life that I know is in the homes where that equality is accepted as a matter of course.... In no state where suffrage has been tried has it done damage and in every state it has bettered social and industrial conditions. All the arguments against it are duplicated in the arguments against manhood suffrage a century ago."

— *The Mining Journal*, Tuesday May 27, 1913,
excerpted from a speech Roosevelt
made prior to traveling to Marquette

CHAPTER 16

MATTHEW WAS ONE OF THE first to excuse himself from the dinner party, knowing he would need extra time to walk back to the courthouse. He briefly spoke to Delia before departing, agreeing to meet her at the Clifton Hotel for supper that evening before the play, and then he found his hat and said his goodbyes.

"We could squeeze you into our vehicle," Mr. Hill offered.

But Matthew declined, not wanting to crowd Roosevelt, by saying, "I think I need the exercise after that fine lunch. Thank you so much for the invitation, and for your hospitality, Mrs. Hill." And then, after a little bow and a kiss on the cheek for Delia, Matthew got a head start on the others, who would regardless reach the courthouse before him due to that modern wonder, the automobile.

For a minute or two, as he turned onto Ohio Street and headed west, Matthew felt lighthearted, but then the remark Mrs. Hill had made began to fester in his head. She had meant nothing by it—she had just been thinking out loud really—but it had hurt nevertheless to know that people still recalled his friendship with Frances; apparently, he hadn't been the only one who had thought it would grow into something more.

Matthew's thoughts went back again to that New Year's Eve when Frances had told him she would marry George. He had been devastated that night, but in the morning, he had told himself it was a new year and anything might happen—perhaps she would change her mind. He had kept telling himself that for several weeks.

They had been lonely weeks. For a long time now, he had stopped by the White house or Frances had come into the store, at least once or twice a week, but nearly a month passed before he saw her again.

Matthew had been thinking of her one morning, dreaming of what might have been until a customer had come into the store, a customer with quite a large order. Matthew was in the middle of helping him when he heard the bell ring and looked up to see Frances enter the store. For a moment, their eyes met, but then she disappeared behind a display. Matthew focused on finishing up with the customer, all the while aching to speak to her. But by the time that customer was satisfied, another had entered, and then another. It must have been a good half hour before the store was empty again, save for Frances and himself.

Matthew could see her in the corner, pretending to be deeply interested in some women's gloves. He approached her, clearing his throat to warn her he was near, but she did not turn around. Finally, he walked up behind her and reached to put his hand on hers, which was propped up on a shelf, holding a glove. He heard her sniffle, and then she turned around and he saw that she was crying.

"I'm sorry, Matthew," she said.

He looked into her eyes for a moment and saw how much she was hurting. Then he pulled out his handkerchief and gave it to her to dry her eyes.

"You have no reason to be sorry," he replied. "I'm the one who's sorry."

She wiped her tears and then asked, "You're not angry at me? You haven't come by the house for a month. I—"

"No, I'm not angry," he replied.

Neither spoke as she continued to wipe her eyes.

"I'm glad," she said, handing him back his handkerchief. "Are we still friends then?"

"I would like to think so," said Matthew, "but…I don't think it's advisable."

"Then you are angry," said Frances.

"No, I mean, I'm hurt. I…."

And then the question burst from him: "Why George?"

"You mean, why not you?" Frances replied.

"Yes," said Matthew. "I'm not angry at you. I'm not angry at George either. I guess you don't even have to answer my question. I know George is a wonderful fellow. I just—I just wish I wasn't so…inferior."

"Inferior?" said Frances, her eyes growing large.

"Yes," said Matthew. "George is a man of action. He's always out hunting and fishing and doing photography, and he's involved in politics. What do I have to offer by comparison? With him, you'll be traveling and doing all sorts of exciting things. All I do is sit here in this store, or in a room alone writing for the *Mining Journal.* Heck, if I were you, I'd have picked George too."

"Matthew, you are not inferior. You're just different. You're more bookish, and George is more outdoorsy. One isn't better than the other."

"If that's true, then why did you pick him over me?" Matthew repeated, his eyes looking down at the floor to hide the hurt in them.

"I don't know, Matthew. You can't explain love."

"Is it because he'll fit in better with your society friends?" Matthew asked, looking up as he now allowed himself to feel anger.

"No, of course not."

"You'll never know want with George," Matthew continued. "I imagine that's part of it. He can provide for you better than I can—more than that, he can give you fancy trips to Europe and buy you expensive things, and—"

"Matthew, do you really think I'm that petty and small?" she asked, and he could hear the pain in her voice. Then he felt like a heel again.

"I'm sorry, Frances."

"I came here wanting us to still be friends," she said, looking directly at him, her eyes red. "I didn't think you'd turn on me, Matthew. I thought you'd at least try to be happy for me."

"I am," said Matthew, and then he could not help but grab her and hold her to his chest. "I am happy for you. I want you to be happy—even...even if it's at the sacrifice of my own happiness."

She let him hold her for a moment, but then she broke away.

"You can do all the same things as George, Matthew," she said, pulling out her handkerchief to wipe her eyes. "You've told me that you feel trapped by this store. That you want to write for a major newspaper, maybe even write a book, and see the world. Go and do it! Why don't you go and do it?"

Her tone was so demanding that it shocked him, leaving him speechless.

And then she turned and stormed out of the store, slamming the door behind her so hard that the building shook and a couple of items fell off a shelf.

Out of habit, Matthew quickly walked over to pick up the fallen merchandise, but before he could put it on the shelf, he began to cry.

"I thought," he told the departed Frances, "that with you by my side, I would have the courage to do all those things."

And then he was silent.

Now, walking up the courthouse steps, he felt the same pain he had then. The pain was usually not this strong anymore—over a quarter of a century had passed, and he repressed such memories most of the time, scarcely thinking of Frances even once a month, but being here in Marquette had seemed to stir up the old feelings. He would be glad to return to New York soon.

He entered the courthouse now and quickly made his way upstairs. As he reached the top of the stairs, he saw the courtroom's doors had already closed.

"Did they start already?" he asked one of the guards in the hallway.

"I just shut the door," the guard replied, but the man must have recognized him because he slightly opened the door and allowed Matthew to slip through. "Thank you," said Matthew, ignoring everyone in the courtroom who was likely staring at him as he found his seat while the bailiff called, "All rise!"

Gifford Pinchot was the first witness to testify that afternoon. He had worked under President McKinley and then Roosevelt as chief forester for the United States. He had often traveled and been away from Washington, but despite that, he testified to all the drinks he had ever seen served in the White House, and he stated that when he was in Washington, he saw the president so frequently that Roosevelt could not have been drunk without his knowledge.

Next to take the stand was Lawrence Abbott, publisher of the magazine *Outlook*, for which Roosevelt was a contributing editor. He had known Roosevelt since 1886, and been particularly intimate with him through the magazine since 1910. Never once had he seen Colonel Roosevelt intoxicated.

James Garfield, son to the late president and former Secretary of the Interior, came forth next to testify. When Garfield was asked by the plaintiff's lawyer to describe how liquor was used in the White House during his father's presidency, Mr. Andrews objected for the defense, but it was overruled. Garfield then went on to describe his intimacy with Roosevelt when he was himself Secretary of the Interior, as well as the intimacy between their families, including his visiting Roosevelt frequently at his home at Oyster Bay. Garfield concluded that he had seen Roosevelt under great strain while in Washington, and he had also seen him during times of relaxation, including horseback riding with him on trips in the West. Plus, he had been with Roosevelt during the campaign in Ohio. Overall, it would have been impossible for Colonel Roosevelt ever to have been intoxicated in his company without his knowledge.

Next on the stand was Edmund Heller. He had gone on safari to Africa with Roosevelt. He testified that during that time he had never seen the colonel take a single drink. The defense tried to argue that because Mr. Heller had been ill during the trip, Roosevelt could have drank on side trips he took without Heller being aware; the defense also suggested that Heller was so busy caring for the animal skins collected that he was not frequently with the colonel. Matthew could only smirk as he listened to this reasoning. Surely, Heller would have noticed drink on Roosevelt's breath even if he had been away from him for a couple of hours.

O.K. Davis, Secretary of the Progressive National Committee, next testified to knowing Roosevelt during his years as a newspaper correspondent. He had first met Roosevelt in 1898, and he had often reported on events at the White House. Davis had, of course, also been on the 1912 presidential campaign tour, and his testimony matched those of previous witnesses when he stated it would have been impossible for Colonel Roosevelt to have indulged in any kind of liquor without his knowledge.

When five o'clock came, everyone felt it had been quite a long day of testimony, and they were all grateful to have the court adjourned. Tomorrow was Decoration Day, so there would be no courtroom proceedings out of respect to military veterans. The trial would recommence on Saturday morning, but only last until noon. Since Roosevelt's witnesses had not yet all been called to the stand and none of Mr. Newett's had yet testified, it was speculated that the trial would run over into Monday if not longer.

"We'll just have to wait until Saturday to see what happens," remarked Homer to Matthew as they prepared to leave the courtroom.

"Yes," said Matthew. "It does look like the trial might still take two weeks as initially suspected."

"It's interesting, though," said Homer. "I'm sure you've seen plenty of big trials like this out east, but to the editor of a country daily like myself, it's really fascinating. The thing is I've been reading about all of these great men all these years, but when you see them in person and hear them speaking, you realize they are just common ordinary human clay like the rest of us."

"That's true," said Matthew. "We're all human."

"Even Gifford Pinchot wasn't as tall as I expected him to be," went on Homer, "nor was his nose as long. Garfield, too, is but a regular, ordinary-looking sort of a chap. The colonel comes up to expectations when you have a talk with him, although he isn't as large a man physically as one expects to see."

"No," Matthew agreed. "It's his commanding appearance that makes him seem larger than life."

"Very true," said Homer. "I wouldn't want to get on his bad side, but he's a gentleman through and through. He has every right to take Mr. Newett to trial, and yet, I don't think he's being vindictive, just trying to reestablish his reputation."

"I fully agree," said Matthew. "Well, I better be going. I'm taking my sister to see *The Prince of Pilsen* this evening."

"Have fun," said Homer. "I'm catching the last train back to Houghton for the holiday, but I'll be coming back tomorrow afternoon in time for the big dinner. Will I see you there?"

"What dinner?" asked Matthew.

"The one for all the pressmen in town—that means you and me."

"Oh, yes," said Matthew, who vaguely remembered some mention of it when he had gone to lunch with a few of his fellow reporters earlier that week. "When and where is it again?"

"The Marquette Commercial Club. Tomorrow night at six."

"Right," said Matthew. "I'll see you there, then."

"Okay. Have a good holiday," said Homer.

Matthew wished him the same and then quickly made his way out of the courtroom. He was glad he had agreed to meet Delia at the Clifton Hotel for dinner because he never would have been able to walk all the way to her house and then downtown for dinner and still make it in time for the play this evening.

Marquette Opera House

THURSDAY MAY 29

HENRY W. SAVAGE Offers
THE ALL STAR CAST

IN A
BRILLIANT REVIVAL
OF

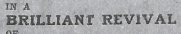

AMERICA'S
BEST MUSICAL COMEDY

With "Jess" Dandy as Hans Wagner

AND THE FOLLOWING POPULAR FAVORITES

Bernard Ferguson	Frederick Lyon	John O'Hanlon
Edna Pendleton	Norma Brown	Mary C. Murray
Bobby Woolsey	Campbell Duncan	Ellen Crane
Evelyn Hall Mead	Wm. Sternberg	Dell Walker
Lottie Kendall	Dorothy Delmore	

and 60 others including the CITY GIRLS, BATHING GIRLS and SEA SHELL GIRLS. Special PRINCE OF PILSEN ORCHESTRA under the direction of EMIL BIERMANN.

PRICES—Box Seats, $2; Lower Floor, except last 4 rows, $2; Last 4 rows Lower Floor, 1.50; First 2 rows Balcony, $1.50; Balance Balcony, $1; Gallery, $.50.

Seats on sale at Bigelow's Tuesday, May 27th at 8:30 a. m.

Marquette Regional
History Center

May 29, 1913 ad from *The Mining Journal* for *The Prince of Pilsen*

CHAPTER 17

MATTHEW ARRIVED AT THE CLIFTON Hotel about 5:20 p.m., five minutes later than he had told Delia he would. He found her waiting on the hotel's porch for him. Unlike some women, she did not mind being alone for a few minutes without a male escort. After all, she was well-known in Marquette, had many friends, and because, or in spite, of her husband, no man would have offended her.

The Clifton Hotel, circa 1910

"I'm sorry I'm late, Delia," Matthew apologized as he stepped up to her. "I'm afraid I don't walk up these hills as fast as I used to."

"Neither do I," she replied. "It's not too busy yet so we can get a good table, and we have lots of time before the play starts."

The opera house was on Washington Street, just around the corner and half a block from the hotel, so thankfully, they would not have to rush to eat.

The host quickly seated them, and then a waiter came to take their drink order.

"So what did you do all afternoon?" asked Matthew once they were again alone.

"Just listen to Lydia stress over how fat she is," said Delia, rolling her eyes.

"Fat?" said Matthew. "She's skinny as a beanpole."

"I know," said Delia. "Plus, I told her that men like women with curves, but apparently Lysander told her he finds thin women more attractive, so she's trying to lose weight for their wedding night."

Matthew sighed and then found that he couldn't hold himself back from remarking, "I hope she knows what she's getting into. There's bigger problems in married life than being a few pounds overweight."

"That's for sure," said Delia. "But he seems to be affectionate toward her, and I know he'll be a good provider."

"Even Roger is a good provider," said Matthew.

Delia ignored him and became focused on the menu until the waiter returned to take their order.

Once they had both told the waiter what they wanted and he had returned to the kitchen, Delia said, "You seem rather down. Is something wrong?"

"No," said Matthew. "I'm just tired. Sitting all day and taking notes on the trial can be exhausting, and now I'll have to write another dispatch tonight. Even if it's Decoration Day tomorrow, my editor will be expecting me to send information."

"But it's what you wanted," said Delia, "to report on big stories. Isn't that why you left Marquette in the first place?"

"I guess," said Matthew.

"If you're too tired," Delia added, "we don't need to go to the play."

"No, no. I want to go. You know I love a good musical."

"You weren't upset at lunch by what Agnes said, were you?"

"What?" asked Matthew, pretending he had no idea what she meant.

"You know what," Delia replied. "What she said about you and Frances."

Matthew took a deep breath and exhaled. "Delia," he said, "that was what—nearly thirty years ago? Please give me credit for being able to move on with my life."

"All right," she said, casting her eyes down on the table. "I didn't mean to upset you."

"You didn't upset me," he replied, softening his tone. "Like I said, I'm just tired, and it's noisy in here, and there's a lot of cigar smoke too."

"Yes," said Delia. "Maybe you should step out to get some fresh air."

"No," he said. He wouldn't be so rude as to leave Delia alone in a public place even for a minute.

"Then tell me how the trial went today."

"All right," said Matthew, and he filled her in on the day's events until the waiter brought their food.

Dinner itself was not remarkable. The food was all right. Matthew had the Lake Superior whitefish, something he had loved when he used to catch them himself and cook them over an open fire, but this whitefish was dry and over-embellished with seasoning. Fancy hotel restaurant or not, no substitute existed for home cooking. Delia had some sort of pasta dish with tomato sauce. Matthew knew she had a nervous stomach—likely acquired from years of living with Roger—so he hoped the pasta wouldn't give her a stomach ache during the play.

While they ate, Delia told him all over again about the wedding preparations and the particular frustrations of the last few days dealing with the caterers, the florist, the seamstress, and the two bridesmaids who had had a spat and were now not speaking to one another. And then there was Roger, who wanted to have a bachelor party for Lysander, which Delia was opposed to, but which she didn't know how to put a stop to.

Matthew pretended to be interested since he felt he had been rude to Delia when they first arrived. Nevertheless, he was glad when he looked at his pocket watch as they finished dinner and saw it was almost time to go. He'd had enough chattering over women's things.

"We only have fifteen minutes before the show starts," he announced.

"Oh, we better get going then," she replied. She took a last drink of her wine as Matthew stood up, and then he pulled out her chair for her. Within the next minute, he had waved down the waiter and quickly settled the bill;

then they stepped out onto the hotel's porch, arm-in-arm, and were on their way to the opera house.

As they turned the corner onto Washington Street, they saw a crowd of people gathered outside the opera house. Several carriages and even a couple of automobiles were drawn up in front of it. Delia waved to someone she knew, and then she and Matthew approached the door.

Attending the theater was one of Matthew's favorite activities, and he had been in fine opera houses before—not only the famous Metropolitan Opera House in New York City, but its predecessor, the Academy of Music. He had also frequented Tony Pastor's theater, as well as more recently the Winter Garden and the newly opened Princess Theatre, and when he had traveled, he had always made it a point to attend theaters elsewhere. But despite the grandness of all those other theaters, he was always very pleased to see how fine the Marquette Opera House was. When he had been a young man in Marquette, he had attended shows at Mather Hall, but that building was now but a memory. After Matthew had moved away, Peter White and John M. Longyear had gotten together to fund the Marquette Opera House, constructed in 1892. It soon became a regular stop for touring theater troupes and even attracted such celebrities as Lillian Russell, who had come in 1909 to perform in her hit play *Wildfire*.

Matthew and Delia now passed through the brownstone theatre's Romanesque arch and entered the lobby. Delia presented their tickets to the usher, and then they went upstairs to a box seat in the balconies. Usually, Matthew would have paid for a floor seat or whatever was affordable, but he should have known his sister would pay for the most expensive seats in the house. As they made their way to the balcony, Matthew was struck by the theater's size and its grand Italian Renaissance style with the same kinds of plush seats that filled Madison Square Garden, allowing 900 people to partake in the opera house's festive atmosphere.

Matthew had only been in the opera house once before, in 1906, when he had come home to visit. At that time, one of Marquette's own, Will Adams, had produced his own original operetta, *Miss D.Q. Pons*. Adams had been much loved in Marquette for his humor and ability to transcend his medical issues—the poor man had suffered from ossification since his late boyhood, and by the time his operetta had premiered, his body was as hard as a statue. On opening night, he'd been wheeled into the opera house on a portable bed. Matthew recalled how during the final curtain call for *Miss D. Q. Pons*, the crowd had shouted, "Author! Author!" Then realizing Adams could not come out to greet them, the audience members had rushed the stage to congratulate him on his play's success. Just a few years later, Will Adams' life had been cut short at age thirty-one. Matthew now pondered what Adams might have accomplished had he lived, or whether he would have accomplished much at all if he had not been driven on by his disease to persevere. It was a mystery how God decided to hand out talent and mix it with life's difficulties. *Perhaps,* Matthew thought to himself, *I would not have gone to New York and become a good reporter if circumstances had been different.* Others, like his brother-in-law, seemed to do nothing of merit with their lives—of course, Roger ran a business, but he had inherited it from his parents, and he did little else except drink and be a burden on his wife.

Marquette Opera House where *The Prince of Pilsen* was performed.

They were in their seats now. Delia was busy introducing Matthew to someone seated on the other side of her, but the theater was so full and noisy that he could scarcely hear what was being said. Finally, Delia turned back to him and they read the program, commenting on it to each other. The play was being performed by a touring company so they did not know anyone in the cast, but the newspaper had written up the play so Delia told Matthew what she had learned from the article she had read earlier.

"It's said to be an all-star cast," said Delia, "though I don't know who all these actors are."

"Jess Dandy is playing Hans Wagner," said Matthew. "I've seen him in productions in New York."

"Yes, and Lottie Kendall is the dashing widow."

"I think the widow's my favorite character in the whole play," said Matthew. "Or at least the song about her."

"Isn't Lottie Kendall the one who sings 'Ta-ra-ra Boom-de-ay'?"

"No, I think that was Lottie Collins," said Matthew. "She died a few years ago."

"Oh, well, it's a production by Henry Savage, so it's bound to be good," said Delia.

"Yes," Matthew agreed. "I saw his production of *The Merry Widow* a few years ago and it was fabulous."

"I envy you getting to go see all those plays on Broadway," said Delia. "I love our opera house, but I'm sure it's nothing to the theaters you've been to."

That was true, but the theater's lights now dimmed, so Matthew did not respond.

"It's too bad Colonel Roosevelt couldn't come," Delia whispered, "but I can understand why he wouldn't want to, given the play's subject matter."

The overture now began, and Matthew felt the chills start up his spine like they always did whenever he saw a favorite show. Then the curtain rose on a beautiful scene depicting the French Riviera.

"I would so love to go to France," Delia whispered. "When we first got married, Roger promised to take me on a European tour, but he always has excuses for why we can't go yet."

Matthew didn't reply. He loved his sister, but he wanted to watch the show, not listen to her, so he was not going to encourage her.

In another minute, he had forgotten Delia—and Roger—as he was reintroduced to the International Hotel in Nice, filled with waiters and valets ready to do anything necessary to please their wealthy customers—plus, behave like pirates to pad their own pockets. Among the hotel's guests was a wealthy brewer from Cincinnati who made Pilsener beer. Through a misunderstanding, partially due to his heavy German-American accent, the hotel staff mistook him for the Prince of Pilsen, while the brewer thought they were calling him the Prince of Pilsener, as a tribute to his excellent beer. Audiences loved the simple brewer's American sense of being more important than he really was, thinking the fame of his beer had now spread to Europe. Of course, there was a real Prince of Pilsen in the play, and soon enough, the prince discovered he was the victim of a case of mistaken identity. However, the prince decided to play along, not revealing his true identity but letting everyone think the brewer truly was the prince; that way the true prince could woo the brewer's beautiful daughter without her being prejudiced in his favor because of his royal lineage.

Matthew had to admit the plot was rather silly, but he was a sucker for these European-style comic operettas, enjoying not only the works of Gustav Luders, the composer of *The Prince of Pilsen*, but also those of Franz Lehar, Victor Herbert, and Reginald De Koven. Matthew actually had quite a large phonograph record collection and frequently listened to such musical gems from *The Prince of Pilsen* as the "Heidelberg Stein Song," "The Widow," and "The American Girl."

Tonight, however, Matthew was struck by the show's irony. Halfway through the first act, the Heidelberg students' song made him think of Roger:

> Better than riches of worldly wealth is a heart that's always jolly
>
> Beaming with happiness hope and health and warmed by love divine.
>
> But sweeter than kisses we win by stealth are the hours we give to folly
>
> So come let us clink but first let us drink one toast with the brimming "stein."

Roger clearly preferred his stein over his wife's kisses or any worldly wealth, and as far as Matthew was concerned, hours spent drunk were nothing short of folly. He much preferred to have his senses about him and use his time more productively.

And then, as the first act drew to a close, came one of Matthew's favorite songs, and he couldn't help but laugh because its lyrics were so true:

> There's the weepy, creepy widow
>
> In the sable garb of woe!
>
> She's a helpless, hopeless creature

As she wants us all to know.

When the life insurance is paid

And "weeds" will speedily fade

She's a dreamy, scheme-y

Peaches and creamy

Do-come-to-see-me widow

A peaches-and-creamy

Do-come-to-see-me widow.

Matthew had experienced more than his share of widows interested in him in recent years. Several of his married friends in New York had started to lose family members, leaving them with widowed sister-in-laws or cousins. More than once, Matthew had found himself invited to a dinner party where it was soon evident that matchmaking was intended, but neither the attractive women, nor the rich ones, had come away with any hopes of becoming Mrs. Newman. No, Matthew had given up on marriage many years ago. Perhaps, he often thought, he had never even desired to be married—at least, that's what he now told himself, and it was true for the most part. There had only been Frances whom he had ever thought he could marry; all the other women seemed more interested in what he could do for them—provide for them— than interested in him or his thoughts or interests. He had never seemed to attract the intelligent ones he might have built a life with—he would gladly have provided moral support to a wife who was a suffragette or wanted a career, and he had known a few fine newspaper women, but most had been nearly young enough to be his daughters when he had met them. No, instead, he had always attracted the needy ones, the kind who were seeking a husband to become the center of their universe, whose whole purpose in life would be to bring him his slippers or cut his steak for him, and who would then whine when he didn't give them sufficient attention. Such a suffocating life was not for him. After now watching how the weepy-creepy widow schemed to get her hands on the Prince of Pilsen, whom she mistook the brewer for, Matthew congratulated himself that he had escaped matrimonial bondage.

The widow's song was followed by a couple of more songs, plus the dueling scene, and then the first act was over. The curtain closed and the lights came on, and before Matthew's eyes could even adjust, Delia turned to him and said, "There's Carolina Smith!"

And before Matthew could even recollect whom Carolina Smith was, Delia was out of her seat and walking toward the woman. Matthew turned to see a woman just a few years older than himself, dressed in a green opera gown and a mink stole, despite it being quite warm in the opera house, and he wondered how he could have forgotten her haughty look even for a second.

"Carolina, it's so good to see you," said Delia. "You remember my brother, Matthew, don't you?"

Matthew stood and stepped toward Mrs. Smith, giving her a slight bow. Carolina Smith simply stared at him and flared her nostrils, immediately giving him flashbacks to all those damn curtains she had kept returning to his store.

"Hello, Mrs. Smith. It's good to see you again," said Matthew. After all, he was a gentleman, and sometimes being a gentleman meant telling a hideous lie. He had never liked her, always thought she was a snob. He still didn't feel guilty about letting her drink from that glass of punch he had already sipped from at the Calls' holiday party so many years before.

Carolina only nodded, as if fully aware that it was good to see her.

"What do you think of all this excitement that's come to Marquette?" Delia asked her.

"What excitement?" Carolina asked.

"Why, the Roosevelt trial, of course."

"It's unfortunate," said Carolina, sighing. "All those riff-raff politicians coming to town for such a circus; it's ridiculous, if you ask me. I don't for a second doubt that *that man* is an alcoholic. Why, everyone knows it."

"Everyone thinks they know it," Matthew corrected her. "That's the point of the trial—to see whether it's true."

"A waste of the taxpayers' money," she replied.

"Justice is never a waste," said Matthew, feeling less and less inclined to behave like a gentleman while speaking to her.

"What could you possibly know about it?" Carolina asked.

"Matthew," Delia interceded, "is a reporter for the *Empire Sentinel* in New York. He's here to cover the trial. He's been sitting through all the sessions."

"I see," said Carolina.

"I'm also here to cover the general opinion of the local population," Matthew added. "Mrs. Smith, do you think most people in Marquette really do believe that Roosevelt drinks and swears a lot?"

"It's not for me to speak for others," she replied, "but I can tell you that if my late husband, Judge Smith, were still alive, he would be completely disgusted that such a man dared to call himself a Republican after the way he left the convention and formed his own party.'"

"But Roosevelt doesn't call himself a Republican any longer," said Matthew. "That's why he formed the Progressive Party."

"And destroyed the Republican Party in the process," Carolina replied. "Woodrow Wilson never would have been elected if it weren't for Roosevelt. I say there isn't a paper in this country that could say anything bad enough about Roosevelt to make me feel sorry for him."

"Roosevelt isn't asking for sympathy," Matthew replied, "just justice. If the tales of his drunkenness aren't true, no one has the right to slander him."

"He's just a bully like Newett said, and he's proving it by going after Newett," Carolina concluded. "Excuse me, now. I must go speak to Mrs. Kaufman."

Delia and Matthew let her pass them without even saying goodbye, and then they returned to their seats.

"She hasn't changed any," said Matthew.

"No, she's always had very youthful skin," Delia replied.

"I meant her attitude. She's always been a prig."

"Oh, Matthew, shush. What if someone hears you?" said Delia.

"It might be good if someone in this town finally said what he thinks."

"Well, I admit Carolina can be difficult to take at times," said Delia, "but I want to stay on her good side. I couldn't bear it if she didn't invite me to her annual Christmas party. Everyone is always there."

"I didn't know she invited housekeepers and stableboys."

"Whatever do you mean?"

"You said, 'everyone.'"

"You know what I mean," said Delia, grimacing.

Matthew wanted to say, "Oh, you mean everyone who is a snob," but he held his tongue. He might not have held it for long, however, if the lights had not now dimmed.

Once the curtain rose again, Matthew found it difficult to enjoy the second act. It had been a long day and the air in the opera house felt stagnant, so he was having trouble staying awake. As the confusion over who was the brewer of Pilsener beer and who the true Prince of Pilsen was resolved, Matthew began to long for his bed. Only his favorite song, "The American Girl," kept him awake during the second act:

> The American girl is a girl to love
>
> Wherever her home may be!
>
> She may be light or she may be dark
>
> But she always is fair to see.
>
> The American girl I'll gladly toast
>
> To the sound of the popping cork.
>
> But I still insist that first on the list
>
> Is the girl from old New York!

Matthew had met enough American girls, in Marquette, New York, and many other places, but the years had long since passed since he had felt so enthusiastic about women. Now he wondered what had happened to that young boy who had been ready to fling down his coat like Sir Walter Raleigh so Madeleine Henning could walk across it. And the young man who had actually fantasized about fist-fighting George so he could have Frances all to himself. Had that passionate youth ever really existed except in his imagination? Whatever romantic ideals he'd had in his youth had clearly vanished with the passing of the years.

Soon, everything on stage had come to a happy conclusion; all the couples were together and likely to be quickly wed, and Matthew, realizing how far from a musical comedy his own life was, reemerged into the real world. He tried patiently to wait as Delia spoke to all of her acquaintances, and then, finally, they were back outside on Washington Street. A bit too brusquely, Matthew took his sister's arm and led her away from the crowd and down the block to Front Street. Once in more open space, he felt he could breathe again, and he enjoyed feeling the evening's coolness, free from the theater's stale air.

Delia began discussing the play with him—who had sung well, whom they thought might have come in late for his cue, and who had been badly cast; they agreed on how fine the costumes were, and how impressive the sets had been, and both said it had been a fine evening, which Matthew had to agree was true, despite how tired he felt and their short run-in with Carolina Smith.

"I'm so glad Roger didn't come tonight," said Delia once they had walked halfway home. "He would have spoiled it for me, moaning and sighing throughout the whole production."

"I'm glad to know I'm better company," said Matthew, smiling.

"I miss you so much, Matthew," she replied, squeezing his arm. "I don't know why you don't come home to visit more often."

"My work keeps me busy; you know that," Matthew replied, feeling a bit guilty for saying so. He knew family should come before work, but that was easier said than done.

"You don't have anything to spend your money on," said Delia. "You must have quite a bit put away by now. I'm sure you could retire soon and move back home."

"Maybe in a few more years," he said, unwilling to commit himself. Truthfully, he was not fond of his new editor at the *Empire Sentinel*. Returning to Marquette might not be such a bad idea. He missed seeing Lake Superior each day, and despite Roger, he would like to see Delia more. But...there was also Frances and George; he wouldn't want to get too involved with them, which he feared would happen if he returned home.

"Well, at least tomorrow the trial isn't being held, so I'll have you all to myself for the whole day," said Delia when they had reached the front walk to her house. "You will go to the Decoration Day ceremonies with me tomorrow, won't you?"

"Yes, and we should go to the cemetery also," said Matthew.

"Oh, I would love that. Roger will never go there with me. I always have to take care of his parents' graves as well as Mother and Father's. He always claims he has a headache or something, and Lydia complains that planting flowers is so dirty." Delia laughed at this remark, but she quickly hushed herself once she inserted the key in the front lock and opened the door.

"I'll see you at breakfast then," said Matthew once they were in the front hall. "Good night."

"Good night, Matthew. Thanks again for taking me to the play."

"My pleasure," he replied, and then he turned and went up the stairs while Delia went into the parlor because the light was on in there and Roger was likely asleep in his chair, possibly with a spilled glass of vodka in his hand or a cigar hanging out of his mouth.

Matthew felt light-hearted as he got ready for bed. The play had cheered him up more than he realized and the "weepy-creepy widow" song was stuck in his head.

When he climbed into bed, he heard the brewer's signature line like he was hearing it for the first time: "Vos you ever in Cincinnati?" The brewer had acted like Cincinnati was the center of the universe. How funny that a brewer could be mistaken for a prince and would think nothing of being praised as the Prince of Pilsener beer. Americans—even German-born ones like the brewer—were notorious for wanting to give themselves lofty titles, from entrepreneurs calling themselves Soap Kings to young ladies at state fairs competing to be Queen of Corn. Their ancestors had fought for freedom from the yoke of tyranny, but how quickly their descendants had reverted back to worshipping those with titles—look at all the American heiresses who had rushed off to Europe to marry dukes and counts, as if having such a husband made you a somebody.

Over the years, Matthew had amused himself in quiet moments by imagining what people would say if he interviewed them. He had conducted so many interviews as a reporter that he could often anticipate people's responses. Now he amused himself by imagining what it would be like if he were to interview the Cincinnati brewer in *The Prince of Pilsen.*

"Why do you think you should be known as the Prince of Pilsener?" he asked.

"Because my beer is the best," the brewer responded.

"And making good beer is enough reason to be considered a prince?"

"It is if my beer is the best."

"And that's enough for you?"

The brewer looked at him, puzzled.

"Vot do you mean?" he finally asked.

"I mean, making the best beer gives your life enough purpose?"

"Vy, yes. Vell, I have my family, of course. I'm very proud of my daughter—my son, he's given me a heap of trouble, but he's a good boy, too."

"But you never wanted to do anything else except brew beer?"

"I like beer."

"So do lots of people, but aren't there better things you could do in this world?"

"Millions of people like beer. It's a good thing to make. It makes people happy."

"It also makes them drunk," said Matthew.

"Vat's vrong with forgetting your troubles for a little vile? It don't hurt nobody."

"It does," said Matthew. "My sister is married to a drunkard. He's made her life miserable."

"But not everyone is a drunkard. Most people just vant to have a good time."

"And what is the point of having a good time? Aren't there better ways to occupy oneself—ways that are more productive to society?"

"Say that again. I don't quite catch you."

"Wouldn't people be better off building hospitals or caring for the poor or pursuing some other good cause? And don't you realize that alcohol has a lot to do with the causes behind poverty? Economic freedom is one of the freedoms we should have in America, but it can't exist when men impoverish their families by buying too much alcohol, which also impairs them so they can't work, thus leaving their children to starve."

"I'm just von person," said the brewer. "I can't fix all those things, but I can make people happy vith my beer."

"Happy and useless," Matthew replied. "How many great man have been ruined by drink—or just by being accused of drinking too much, like Roosevelt has been?"

"Vot kind of crazy talk is all this?" demanded the brewer. "There's something vrong with a man who can't enjoy a drink now and then." And then Matthew imagined the brewer storming off in anger.

"This trial is making me cynical," Matthew told himself.

And then, as he lay there, he remembered he had forgotten to write his dispatch for the newspaper when he got home. Now, he would have to get up early to do it—he was too tired right now—but even so, he began writing it in his head until he drifted asleep.

WORLD DISCUSSES TEDDY'S MINT BED

Civilized Nations Send for Information About That White House 'Julep' Garden.

WASHINGTON, JUNE 5—APPARENTLY PRETTY NEARLY every civilized nation in the world has been stirred by the discovery of the mint bed in the White House grounds, the existence of which was revealed by the testimony in the Roosevelt-Newett libel suit.

That mint bed suddenly has attracted more attention than the possibility of war with Japan or changes in the new tariff. A large number of newspapers, including foreign publications, have wired or cabled explicit instructions to their Washington correspondents for a detailed story of the bed.

The demand is for exact information as to who planted it. Which president found the most use for it? In what corner of the White House grounds is it situated? What are its precise dimensions? How affluent a crop does it produce? Who has personal charge of it? Does it require assiduous cultivation? Is the crop used for any purpose other than the preparation of the celebrated beverage of old south? Who mixes 'em? Does the president, a southern man, abide by the drink of his fathers? And so on down to fractions of fragments of information.

So far the information collected by those besieging the White House has not been extensive. The attack of the correspondents has been general, and nearly everybody employed about the place has been interviewed except President Wilson.

The attitude of those interviewed has been that the contents of the president's back yard is nobody's business but Mr. Wilson's. It is admitted, however, that the bed is there and that it lies somewhere ferninst [sic] the corner of the back porch; that it is not bigger than about ten by twelve and that President Wilson, who is as abstemious as the testimony would prove Colonel Roosevelt, and almost as tremendous a worker, uses mint only in connection with lamb. If he wants a drink, which is seldom, he prefers Scotch, according to one authority.

One aged employee, who is from the old south, said people who entertained the idea that a president would or could be a regular devotes [sic] of mint juleps, gave him a pain.

"A mint julep is not intended as an intoxicant," he said. "While liquor is used in making it the mint julep is intended primarily as a refreshment, to be sipped and enjoyed and lingered over, and no gentleman of the south ever cared for more than one in an afternoon or an evening.

"Why, man, two or three of them drank in a hurry will make one deathly sick. I know because I have seen it tried by northern men who had heard about the julep but did not know how to drink it," said this White House employe [sic].

— *The Mining Journal, June 6, 1913*

FRIDAY
MAY 30, 1913

"I wish the men would do something besides extend congratulations.
I have asked President Roosevelt to push the matter of a constitutional amendment allowing suffrage to women by a recommendation to Congress.
I would rather have him say a word to Congress for the cause than to praise me endlessly."

— Susan B. Anthony,
in response to a telegram Roosevelt sent her on her eighty-sixth birthday in 1906

CHAPTER 18

MATTHEW WAS UP EARLY THE next morning so he could get his dispatch written before he went down to breakfast. Once done writing, he tucked the paper in his pocket, hoping he and Delia would have time to stop by the Western Union office before going to the Decoration Day ceremonies at the opera house that morning.

As Matthew could have predicted, Roger refused to go with them. "A man deserves a day off," he grumbled when asked. "And none of my family died in the Civil War or the Spanish-American one, so what do I need to go for?"

"To show respect for those who did die," said Matthew, "and for those who have fought for our freedom."

"Freedom!" scoffed Roger. "Wars are all about economics. No one cared about freeing the slaves; the South just wanted to keep its cotton-picking workforce, and the North just wanted to save face when the rebels decided to leave the Union, and that business down in Cuba—it was all blown out of proportion to sell newspapers, although I wouldn't expect you, given your profession, to admit it. Sometimes, though, I wonder how you can call yourself a newspaperman when you're so clueless about how the world really works."

Sometimes, Matthew wondered why he did not take a fist to his brother-in-law's jaw, but the strain of Quaker blood he had inherited from his grandparents kept him fairly peaceful. Still, if ever there was a man who could tempt a pacifist to violence, it was Roger Richardson.

"It's all right. You stay home and rest, Roger," said Delia. "We're going to go to the cemetery anyway, and I know you won't enjoy that."

Needing to get in the last word, Roger shook his head and muttered, "Wasting my money on flowers the dead don't even know you're planting over them." And then he got up and poured himself a drink. It was not yet nine o'clock.

Matthew wanted to remind him they would be planting flowers on his parents' grave, but he didn't bother; he suspected Delia cared far more about Roger's parents than he did.

Soon after breakfast, Matthew and Delia set out on foot—they did not dare ask Roger to let them use the automobile. After a quick stop at Western Union, which had stayed open because of the need for the trial reporters to send their dispatches, brother and sister walked to the opera house for the Decoration Day ceremonies.

"It's too bad there isn't a parade today," said Delia, "but I guess I can understand it. The Civil War veterans are all around seventy years old or more now, and I imagine marching is getting to be too much for them."

"That's true," said Matthew. "It's hard to believe so many years have passed since the war."

"Do you even remember it?" asked Delia. "I don't."

"No, I don't really," said Matthew, "but I do remember Father coming home in his uniform, and how when Mother saw him coming up the road, she ran and jumped up into his arms so quickly that I thought she'd knock him over, but he just swung her around in a circle and they hugged and kissed and laughed for what seemed like the longest time."

"I wish I could remember that," said Delia. "I do remember seeing Father in his uniform, but nothing else from when we lived in New York. I do remember traveling on the lakes to get to Marquette, though."

"It's hard to believe Father would be in his seventies now if he were still alive," said Matthew.

"Mother also," said Delia.

They were now at the opera house, and although they easily found seats, the auditorium filled up within minutes after they arrived.

"It seems like we were just here," said Delia, laughing.

"Yes, it does," Matthew agreed, though you would never know the theatre had been transformed into a hotel in France just twelve hours earlier.

They said hello to several people, mostly Delia's acquaintances, who found seats near them, and then they all turned their attention to the program.

At ten o'clock, the veterans marched from nearby Keogh Hall into the opera house to much general fanfare. They made their way up onto the stage, which was dressed with various American, Michigan, and Civil War flags, and took their seats.

Marquette Opera House exterior

Once all the veterans were seated, Rev. H.J. Ellis, the assistant rector at St. Paul's, came forth to give the invocation. Then George Tucker delivered Abraham Lincoln's most famous speech, "Four score and seven years ago...." which strongly reminded all the audience of what had led to Decoration Day becoming a holiday and the sacrifices made by so many to preserve the Union.

Everyone present was disappointed that Colonel Roosevelt had turned down the offer to speak at the service, but the Rev. Bates Burt had gladly taken his place in giving the primary address.

"We are here today, my friends," began Rev. Burt, "to pay high honor to the venerable survivors of that war, and to give reverence to the memory of the dead. The story of their patriotic endeavor cannot be too frequently rehearsed. They were no soldiers of fortune, but soldiers of duty, citizens who dared all that men can dare, endured all that men can endure in obedience to the call of their country. Few of them knew much of constitutional issues—of the theories of states' rights which provoked secession. But one thing they knew—the integrity of the American republic was imperilled, and the national life of a free people was at stake, and they stood ready to make the great sacrifice that government of the people by the people, for the people should not perish from the earth....

"And now, my friends, as we celebrate the achievements, and pay our reverent tribute to the patriotic character of men of the sixties, what lessons may we learn to profit us in these times of peace? What is the legacy that these men have handed down to us, to be by us transmuted into the patriotic adventures of today...?

"The evils of our time will not be eradicated till a sufficient number of citizens enlist in war against them....

"We Americans are proud of our national greatness. We live in a wonderful land. Nature has done everything for us. We have everything given to us in material things that could be desired.

"But these things do not constitute a state. On the shores of the Mediterranean Sea lie the ruins of a number of superb cities that were once centers of dominion and wealth and display. What ruined them? Not the loss of trade, not war or pestilence or flood or fire or exhausted soil. No; the ruin was in the spirit and conscience of the citizens. Not even America, sweet as she is, will succeed where Alexandria and Athens and Carthage and Rome have failed.

"We must then, oh my friends, have honest and clean-minded men in public office, men who will not be influenced by self-interest, particularly where they are chosen to execute the law or to administer justice.

"But most of all, we must have a body of private citizens—a rank and file—frugal, industrious and temperate, who will give unbiased thought and patriotic consideration to all our problems and who will actively and constantly participate in the politics of their ward, city, county, state, and nation, and will lend loyal support to every cause that makes for social righteousness, human betterment, and that helps to establish the brotherhood of man.

"God, give us men who will fight in the nation's battles of peace, as devotedly as you men fought in her battles of war."

The sanctity of the occasion did not allow for applause at the end of Rev.

Burt's speech, but Matthew thought the man had spoken boldly and truly, and despite the inconveniences and difficulties of the newspaper profession, he was reminded that he was doing his part in fighting to keep America a land of integrity by reporting the truth in his stories.

Now, A.A. Cole, the adjutant for the Albert Jackson post—named for a Marquette soldier who had given his life to preserve the Union—stepped forward and read the orders for the day. This ceremony was followed by the members of the Grand Army of the Republic giving their salute to their dead comrades in arms.

Following these solemnities, it was time for a patriotic concert. First, Miss Flora Retallic sang "The Star-Spangled Banner." Then the Marquette City Band played a march. Then Miss Norma Ross, whom Matthew remembered as the star of *Miss D.Q. Pons* a few years back at the opera house, came forward and sang a patriotic ballad that left half the audience in tears. Next, the entire audience joined in a stirring rendition of "America." Finally, Rev. Smith of the Methodist church concluded the ceremony by giving the final benediction.

The audience members now all departed, commenting on what a fine service it had been. Once they were out in the fresh air again, Matthew suggested to Delia that they go get a snack somewhere before walking to the cemetery.

"All right," said Delia, taking Matthew's arm. "I know I said so before, but I'm so glad you're here, Matthew. I hate missing things like this, though I often do because Roger won't go and I can't always get up the nerve to go by myself. And I so appreciate that you're going to the cemetery with me. I would have understood if you had decided instead to join in that golf tournament I read about in the paper."

"I'd much rather go to the cemetery," said Matthew, who had to admit that while the tournament was for the trial witnesses and reporters, he was glad to have a break from concerns over the trial. No doubt he'd find something else to write his next dispatch about. "Playing golf out in the hot sun was never to my taste," he added. "I used to play when I first moved to New York to be sociable, but I never really cared for the game. Should we go in here?"

Matthew was referring to Stafford's Drug Store, around the corner from the opera house on Front Street.

"All right," said Delia, and they turned into the drugstore.

"O for a dish of ice cream that makes
Your lips go smickity, smack, and takes
The glow from out your inner works
Where your ice cream appetite shyly lurks,
And cries aloud with a ravenous shout,
'It's STAFFORD'S for me when the show lets out.'"
— Will S. Adams,
advertisement from the program for his operetta
Miss D.Q. Pons

CHAPTER 19

SEVERAL OTHER PEOPLE WHO HAD attended the Decoration Day ceremonies had had the same idea as Matthew, and so Stafford's Drug Store was quite full. That was all right because it gave Delia and Matthew time to look at the menu board and decide what they wanted.

"'Bull Moose Punch,'" read Delia. "I wonder what Colonel Roosevelt would think of them serving that?"

"I think he'd be more upset about the 'Teddy's Toddy,'" said Matthew, who couldn't help smiling at the offering. "He hates being called Teddy."

"It doesn't sound very appetizing either," Delia replied.

Neither of them opted for these special offerings, but when it was their turn to place their order, Matthew couldn't help asking what made up a "Roosevelt Sundae."

"It's chocolate ice cream," said the soda jerk, "with mint syrup on it in honor of Roosevelt's famous mint patch at the White House, and then it has whipping cream and, of course, a cherry on top."

"Mint's always refreshing," said Delia. "I'll have that."

"We'll take two of them," Matthew ordered. "And we'll have two Coca-Colas also. Ice cream always makes a person thirsty."

"Thank you, sir," said the soda jerk, after taking his payment. "Please have a seat, and I'll bring everything out to you when it's ready."

Matthew and Delia found a little table in the corner where they could watch the crowd of people from the Decoration Day services now streaming in.

"This place must be making a killing with these novelty specials," said Matthew. "I hope Colonel Roosevelt doesn't decide next to sue for misuse of his identity."

"I doubt he'd do that," said Delia. "I'm so glad, though, Matthew, that you had the idea to come here. Roger never will come have ice cream with me. He says he doesn't like it. I don't know how anyone cannot like ice cream."

"I would think he'd at least like rum raisin," Matthew said, smiling.

Delia only grimaced.

As they watched the crowd of ice cream seekers pour in, a few people in line waved or exchanged greetings with them about the weather until the soda jerk brought them their dishes of ice cream and Cokes.

"I don't know if I'll be able to eat all this," said Delia.

"Sure you can," said Matthew, "and we'll walk it off anyway on the way to the cemetery."

Delia stared at him for a minute, making him feel uncomfortable until he finally set down his spoon and looked back at her.

"What's wrong?" he asked. "Not minty enough for you?"

"No," she said, smiling. "I just wish you lived here, Matthew."

"I know. You keep saying that. Well, maybe when I retire."

"I know; I understand. I just get lonely sometimes."

"But you have lots of lady friends," said Matthew. "Whenever you write, it sounds like you're very busy with your social groups."

"I am," said Delia, "but it's not the same as having a brother, and now with Lydia moving out, I'll be even lonelier."

"I'm sorry, Delia," said Matthew, turning his eyes down to his ice cream because he could not face her.

After a moment, Delia tried to cheer herself up by changing the subject.

"Actually," she said, "I think I'll be even busier soon. We're talking about starting our own suffragette society here in Marquette."

"Really?"

"Yes. There are several women interested—Abby Roberts especially, and also Mrs. Schaffer, and Ada Mapes, and Mrs. Blemhuber, and Sigrid Von Zellan and Mrs. Sherwood, and several others. The Lady Maccabees are proponents of suffrage, too, and so are the temperance societies, so we would likely get members from them also. We can't expect the women in the big cities to make all the effort. But don't worry—we're not planning to blow up anything like those suffragettes in England keep doing. It's just that we deserve to be respected and treated like equals."

"You're preaching to the choir, Delia," said Matthew, although he wondered how she would go out and convince other men she deserved to be treated like an equal when her own husband wouldn't treat her that way.

"I really do think it's time," said Delia. "It's the twentieth century, after all. Did you know women in Australia have had the vote for ten years now?"

"Yes, I guess I remember hearing that," said Matthew.

"I've believed in women's suffrage most of my life," Delia continued. "Ever since I was fifteen and Victoria Woodhull came to speak in Marquette."

"I don't even know who Victoria Woodhull is," said Matthew, continuing to spoon ice cream into his mouth.

"Matthew! And you a reporter. And she came when we were still living at home, too. Why, she's the first and only woman who's ever run for president of the United States."

"Seriously?" said Matthew.

"Yes, she ran in 1872, but she came to Marquette a few years after that," said Delia before taking a sip of her Coke.

"I'm surprised Father agreed to you and Mother going," said Matthew.

"I don't think he had a choice. You know Mother could get her way when she wanted to, and Madeleine went with us also."

"Madeleine Henning?" said Matthew. "Her mother let her go?"

"I don't think her mother knew, but you know Madeleine. She always did what she wanted, and she and I were best friends, so whatever one of us did, the other did."

"I'm more surprised that Mother dared to risk Mrs. Henning's anger than that she was willing to risk Father's."

"Well, if Father was angry, he never said anything to me about it," Delia replied.

"Father wasn't really narrow-minded," Matthew reflected, "having been raised a Quaker, but still, I'm sure a lot of the men would have felt emasculated to have their wives go hear a woman speak who thought she could be president."

"The men in the crowd were hideous in how they treated her," said Delia, "and there were hardly any women there, which mother said was proof of how men keep women down. Anyway, a woman can be president if men will just let her. It was the men, of course, who sabotaged her campaign."

"I suppose," said Matthew. "But there are some men in favor of votes for women."

"Hmm," said Delia. "I know Roosevelt claims he is, but I don't remember him doing anything during his presidency to help women."

"Well, maybe the next generation will be different," said Matthew, although from the way Lydia was simpering every time she saw Lysander, he thought women still had a long way to go. "It was a nice ceremony today, wasn't it?" he said to change the subject. "I thought Rev. Burt's speech was very appropriate."

"Oh, that reminds me," said Delia. "We'll have to stop at the greenhouse on the way to the cemetery to buy flowers."

"Yes, I know," said Matthew, taking his last bite of ice cream. Delia had already pushed her bowl away from her with a few bites of nearly melted ice cream left in it. "Are you about ready to go?"

"Yes," said Delia. "I can't eat any more."

Matthew swallowed down the last of his Coke, and then they set off toward the greenhouse.

"I'm glad it's a cool day," said Delia as they started down the street. "I'm not looking forward to the heat this summer. When I think of Father being in the war, I often wonder how he managed to do all that marching down South in a sweltering uniform while toting a gun."

"I believe a lot of the soldiers suffered from sunstroke," said Matthew.

"You," said Delia, "know a lot more about the family history than I do. Do we have any other family members who fought in the Civil War?"

"No, I don't think so," said Matthew, "not since our family were Quakers. Father's family basically disowned him for going off to fight. Quakers are pacifists and opposed to war, you know."

"I guess I remember Mother saying something about that to me," said Delia. "Father never would talk about his family. Was Mother's family Quakers too?"

"Yes," said Matthew. "I think everyone in our family was for generations back to England before they came to New York in the 1600s."

"Didn't you go look up some of our relatives when you first moved to New York?" asked Delia.

"Yes, I found a few of them," said Matthew.

"And are they still Quakers?"

"They were then," said Matthew, "so I imagine they still are, although I got the impression that things had changed a lot for them in recent years. Quakers were always against any form of violence, but when the Civil War began, many of the young men chose to join the Union cause; several like Father, I believe, were disowned by their families as a result."

"That's too bad," said Delia. "I would never support a war started to defeat another country, but a war meant to end slavery is an exception."

"Yes," said Matthew. "I have to agree."

"Still," said Delia. "I think the Quakers have some weird beliefs; don't they think they're God's chosen ones because he speaks directly to them? I've always thought that people who think that must be a little crazy."

"Well, who's to say?" said Matthew. "We can't really understand their beliefs without being them any more than they can probably understand ours." He didn't really feel comfortable talking about his ancestors' beliefs, which he had himself come to believe after visiting his grandfather in New York. He had never told Delia much about it because it had been far too personal an experience for him, so he changed the subject. "What kinds of flowers will you buy for Mother and Father's grave?"

"Oh, something pink for Mother I think, and maybe some red, white, and blue for Father since he was a soldier, depending, of course, on what they have."

They had now arrived at the greenhouse. Fifteen minutes later, they emerged with a box filled with flowers that Matthew tried to carry gingerly so as not to crush any of the blossoms. A few blocks later, they had reached Park Cemetery.

Several other families were already there, busy planting flowers on the graves of parents and grandparents. A few carriages were also there, having brought the remaining Civil War veterans to the cemetery so they could pay their respects to their fallen comrades. Marquette had sent its fair share of its sons to fight in the Great Cause, but now, fifty years after the Emancipation Proclamation, only perhaps a dozen of them were still alive.

"Can you imagine," said Matthew, as he knelt down on the ground to dig with a spade Delia had also bought, since she had forgotten hers at home, "that the entire Civil War generation is almost gone now."

"I know," said Delia. "I hate to say it, but we are now becoming the older generation."

"I hope," said Matthew, taking the flowers Delia was handing to him to plant in the ground, "that after our generation is gone, the next one will come to honor our veterans."

"I hope so, too," said Delia. "But I also hope the generations to come will never know another war."

"Somehow," said Matthew, "I don't think that will be very likely. At least, I don't think it will be in our lifetimes."

Delia didn't reply. She was too busy sorting the flowers according to which ones she'd plant on their parents' graves and which would be for Roger's parents. Once the Newman grave was finished and the flowers watered with water from the pond, they moved on to the Richardsons' graves.

"I don't know why you bother," said Matthew, kneeling to dig up the soil before Roger's parents' stone. "You know Roger will never even come to see the flowers."

"I don't do it for him," said Delia. "I do it for his parents. They deserve to be remembered, and they are Lydia's grandparents."

"I suppose they are," said Matthew.

"Roger's mother was very kind to me when I first married him," added Delia.

Matthew wondered whether, more likely, Mrs. Richardson had pitied Delia. He'd often suspected Mrs. Richardson had known what it was to live with an alcoholic herself—after all, he had heard that the proclivity to drink was hereditary. But he wasn't going to upset Delia about the subject today, so he simply planted the flowers as she directed.

By the time they had finished planting, it was past three o'clock. The sun had been at its height while they were in the cemetery, so the day had now become quite warm.

"I'm ready to go home, sit on the veranda, and have a large glass of lemonade," said Delia.

"That sounds good to me," Matthew agreed.

They crossed Seventh Street and began walking home down Ridge. As they reached the library on the corner of Front, they heard a commotion behind them and saw the veterans' carriages passing them on their way back from the cemetery.

Delia and Matthew stopped to wave, knowing several of the veterans since their childhood. They then continued along Ridge for several blocks, simply enjoying the pleasant day, until they reached Spruce. They were going to turn there to head home when Matthew noticed that the veterans' carriages were lined up in front of George's home. The sight of them made him curious enough to stop in his tracks.

"I know what you're thinking," said Delia.

"Well, Colonel Roosevelt didn't want to participate in the Decoration Day celebrations," said Matthew, "but I guess the veterans wouldn't take 'No' for an answer."

"Go ahead," said Delia. "I know you hate to miss out on a good scoop, and I'm sure George won't mind if you stop by since you're the son of a Union veteran."

"All right," said Matthew. "I won't be long. Just save me some of that lemonade."

And after kissing Delia on the cheek for being so understanding, he scurried down the road.

"We must show, not merely in great crises, but in the everyday affairs of life, the qualities of practical intelligence, of courage, of hardihood, and endurance, and above all the power of devotion to a lofty ideal, which made great the men who founded this Republic in the days of Washington, which made great the men who preserved this Republic in the days of Abraham Lincoln."

— Theodore Roosevelt's Inaugural Address,
March 1905

CHAPTER 20

As Matthew approached the Shiras home, the veterans were still getting out of their carriages, not being too fast at their advanced ages. Matthew stood back on the sidewalk a bit, watching as they stood about in the yard waiting for the last of their brotherhood to exit the carriages. Then they went up the front walk to the house. By then, George was standing on the front porch greeting them as they entered his home. Matthew stood in the back of the line, peering over the veterans' stooped shoulders until George caught sight of him and raised his eyebrows in greeting. Finally, the last veteran was helped up the front steps and made his way inside and Matthew was now on the porch himself.

"Matthew, come in," said George. "Please, join us."

"I don't mean to be rude," said Matthew, walking up onto the porch and shaking George's hand, "but it looked like you were having an open house, and since my father was a veteran, I was hoping I might get a story about Roosevelt meeting the veterans."

Before George could reply, one old soldier, still in the doorway, turned around and said, "Of course you should. What better story could you get?"

"You're more than welcome," said George. "Come inside," and he put his hand on Matthew's back, pushing him toward the doorway that the veteran had now cleared.

"I thought Colonel Roosevelt didn't want to be involved in today's celebrations," Matthew said to George.

"We insisted on seeing him," the old soldier answered, trying to steady his cane as he moved toward the parlor, shuffling in front of Matthew.

"They did," said George softly to Matthew, "and when Theodore saw their determination, he didn't have the heart to turn them down, so he asked them all to come in so he could say a few words to them. He's upstairs making himself presentable, but he'll be down in a few minutes."

Once all the veterans found seats and cleared the way, Matthew was also able to make his way into the front parlor. He saw about a dozen soldiers from the Grand Army of the Republic seated in various chairs, while toward the back of the room stood several middle-aged men, veterans of the Spanish-American War. He also recognized a few reporters from the trial who had somehow caught wind of the veterans' intentions.

"Here comes Theodore," said George, still in the doorway to the room. Hearing Roosevelt's steps in the hall above, George turned to greet his guest as he came downstairs. Meanwhile, Matthew quickly found a corner in the parlor where he would not be in the way as the former Commander-in-Chief of the United States greeted those who had risked their lives for the good of their country.

"I'm delighted to see all of you," said Roosevelt, stepping into the room to address all the men before him. Before he could say another word, a round of applause greeted him. Roosevelt smiled and nodded his head in good-willed acceptance, but then he raised his hands to silence them.

"I hope you all understand," he continued, "that I meant no disrespect to any of you by declining the many gracious invitations I received to participate in your beautiful city's various Decoration Day services. I simply do not wish for my public presence to create any prejudice in my favor, much less against me, during this libel trial I am involved in, and I trust you all understand that. I wish I had thought myself that I might meet you all here privately so that I might thank you for your service to our nation, which I hope to do now."

As Roosevelt spoke, he moved about his hands to give emphasis to his words and further show the delight he felt in having been sought out by the veterans, which was also obvious from his countenance.

"Indeed," he continued, "I realize I am a bit of a celebrity to all of you, but let me say that it is you who do me the honor. It is the rare person who could have so many heroes of our nation seek him out in this manner, and I am very grateful that you have, for I would be quite sorrowful not to express my appreciation to such men on this most sacred of days for our country."

As Matthew listened, he again realized what a great speaker Colonel Roosevelt was, to speak so spontaneously, and yet have the presence of mind to make his guests feel like they were the most important people in the world to him. Although the colonel's crowd was but a few dozen, he spoke with the enthusiasm and vigor he would have given to a crowd of a few thousand. His many references to specific events and battles of the War between the

States made it clear how well he had studied his history of an event that had happened in his boyhood and which he could scarcely remember. He also made mention of the Spanish-American War for those of his comrades from that campaign who were present. More than once as Roosevelt spoke, Matthew noticed one of the grizzled old men in the room looking teary-eyed as he remembered a fallen comrade from his youth, perhaps a beloved brother who had made the ultimate sacrifice for his country.

Colonel Roosevelt concluded his speech by saying, "It was what you did in your golden youth that has enabled us to meet with manly courage and sure steps the problems of today. Your sons, and grandsons, armed with the same courage and devotion and high ideals that took you to the war, are in the forefront of another battle for human welfare and for their country.

"We cannot tolerate a social condition under which men and women are tramped down. It is such a condition that we must fight today, and it must be done by putting in the heart of every citizen the love of his brother and his native land. The contemptible arrogance of the rich man who despises his brother because he is poor and the mean envy of the poor man who hates his brother because he is rich have both the same seed. The same poor man made rich would be arrogant; the same rich man made poor would be envious.

"In the training of our manhood and womanhood we must give them the same noble inspiration you had when you were young—the spirit of justice and kindness and freedom. Train them to service, not to the pursuit of pleasure; for happiness to be worth anything must be a by-product."

Upon concluding his speech with these words, Roosevelt received thunderous applause from all the men. Then he asked them all to come up and meet him individually so he might shake their hands. They quickly formed a line, and Reverend Burt, who had given the Decoration Day address and accompanied the veterans to the Shiras home, began to introduce each man to the former president.

"This," said Rev. Burt, introducing the first man in line, "is Stewart Zryd."

Matthew, upon hearing Zryd's name realized he must be the son of Marquette's favorite violinist, who had played at that party he had taken Frances to so many years ago.

"You're far too young to have been in the Civil War," said Roosevelt, shaking his hand. "You must have served with me down in Cuba."

"I did indeed, sir," said Zryd.

"What's your command?" Colonel Roosevelt asked him.

"I was a private in the infantry," said Zryd.

"Good. It's a pleasure to meet you," replied the colonel.

"The pleasure is all mine," said Zryd. "I'd gladly do it again if I needed to."

"That's the attitude to have," said Roosevelt. "One is never too old to be a patriot and serve his country, as I've found."

Zryd nodded in agreement and then stepped aside so Reverend Burt could introduce the next two veterans.

"These, Colonel," said the reverend, "are the Byrne brothers. Not only did they both fight in the War Between the States, but one fought for the Union and one for the Confederacy."

"Which one fought for which side?" asked Roosevelt, and for just a moment, Matthew could see a bit of concern on the face of one of the brothers, whom Reverend Burt now pointed to and said, "This is Mr. Samuel E. Byrne. He wore the gray."

Without blinking, Roosevelt held out his hand. "I had uncles who wore the gray you know. My mother's family was from the South."

"It was many years ago," said Mr. Byrne, "and my brother and I see eye to eye on most things now."

"And which regiment did you serve with?" asked the colonel.

"The Maryland battery."

"I am most happy to meet you," replied Roosevelt. "And I am happy to see you here with the other soldiers as a sign that the old strife is finally coming to an end. I had two of your men in Cuba with me who were fine soldiers," he added.

"And this is his brother, R.P. Byrne," Reverend Burt continued, "who wore the blue."

"It's an honor, sir," said Roosevelt, shaking the other brother's hand. "Your presence here shows that time can heal old wounds. The two of you are the blue and gray in fact."

As Matthew listened to the two brothers chat with Roosevelt for a minute, and then observed how the colonel went on to greet the other veterans in line, he was again impressed by Roosevelt's general congeniality and his ability to give a special word to each man to make him feel like he was someone truly special. The colonel made it a point to ask each man what his command had been and he shared with them his knowledge of their regiments and the campaigns they had joined in, making each one feel important. Because of

Roosevelt's affability, it took a good hour before everyone in the receiving line was able to speak to him, but no one complained or felt it anything but an honor to be present.

Finally, Roosevelt shook hands with the last of the veterans. He was then about to bid them all goodbye and return upstairs to his room when a reporter pleaded that he come outside where the light was better so he could get some photographs of the former U.S. president with the men who had served their country. Knowing how important it would be to these honorable men to have themselves photographed with him, Roosevelt quickly agreed. He and all the veterans now went out onto the steps of the Shiras house, and Roosevelt posed first with his fellow campaigners of the war of '98, and then with the remnants of the Grand Old Army of the Republic.

Theodore Roosevelt posing with the Spanish-American Veterans. Stewart Zryd is fourth from left.

When the photographs were completed, more handshaking took place, and Matthew himself got a chance now to shake the colonel's hand and remark, "Good luck to you tomorrow, sir."

Theodore Roosevelt posing with the Civil War Veterans

"Thank you, Matthew," said Roosevelt. "The trial will only be a half-day tomorrow, and if it isn't all over then, I am looking forward to going up to Peter White's camp with George. Will you be joining us?"

"No, I'm afraid not," said Matthew, "because my niece is getting married on Sunday."

"Oh, that's right," said Roosevelt. "Please give my best wishes to the bride and groom."

"I'll do that, sir," said Matthew. "Have a pleasant evening."

Matthew now said goodbye to George, thanking him for letting him be part of this very special afternoon. Then he said goodbye to a couple of the veterans he knew before walking down the driveway and heading home.

How lucky he had been to spot the veterans' carriages when he had. A few other reporters had been there, but most of those who were covering the trial had been absent. *Too bad Homer couldn't make it,* thought Matthew, *though I'm sure he was glad to be home with his family for a little while.* Then Matthew remembered Homer said he'd be back this evening in time for dinner.

Matthew looked at his watch. It was just past five. He would have enough time to walk home and maybe have a glass of lemonade with Delia before heading to the dinner being given for all the press men. He hoped Delia wouldn't be upset with him for not eating at home tonight. He'd completely forgotten to tell her he was dining out this evening.

"There should be relentless exposure of and attack upon every evil practice, whether in politics, in business, or in social life. I hail as a benefactor every writer or speaker, every man who, on the platform, or in book, magazine or newspaper, with merciless severity makes such attack, provided always that he in his turn remembers that the attack is of use only if it is absolutely truthful."

— Theodore Roosevelt, Washington, D.C., April 14, 1906

CHAPTER 21

When Matthew walked in the front door and before he could even remove his hat, Delia called to him from the dining room. "Matthew, is that you?"

"Yes," he replied and stepped into the room, where he found Delia, Roger, and Lydia already seated.

"We were afraid you weren't coming home in time to eat with us," said Delia. "Sit down. The food will be out in a minute."

"I'm sorry," said Matthew. "I hope you haven't been waiting for me. I—"

"That's exactly what we've been doing," Roger snapped.

"Now, Roger," said Delia, patting him on the hand, since she was seated next to him, "that's not true. We just sat down, and it's not Matthew's fault we decided to eat a little early tonight."

"I'm afraid I can't stay, though," said Matthew. "I forgot to tell you I'll be dining out this evening."

"Who's the big shot you're ditching us for now?" asked Roger.

"Roger!" said Delia.

"Well, he obviously doesn't want to be spending time with us," said Roger.

At that moment, Martha came in from the kitchen to start serving the soup.

"That's not true," Delia replied. "He spent almost the entire day with me."

"I'm sorry," said Matthew, "but I completely forgot that there's a dinner for all the press men tonight at the Marquette Commercial Club. I didn't know about it until last night, and then I didn't even think about it between going to the play last night and all the other activities today."

"Well, of course, you must go," said Delia.

"Why must he go?" asked Roger. "He's seen more of those other reporters than of us."

"Uncle Matthew, did you get to see Colonel Roosevelt today?" asked Lydia, almost speaking over her father in an attempt to change the subject and keep him from getting more riled.

"Yes," said Matthew. "I just came from the Shiras house. He was speaking to all of the veterans."

"That's nice," said Lydia.

"It would have been nice," inserted Roger, "if the guest in my home had let me know his plans today. I had thought we might go fishing, but—"

"Fishing!" exclaimed Delia. "On Decoration Day!"

"And why not?" asked Roger.

"Father, you haven't gone fishing in years," said Lydia.

"Because I don't know any good fishermen to go with," Roger replied.

"I'm glad you think I'm a good fisherman," said Matthew, but his attempt at appeasement only drew a frown from Roger.

"But, Father, you could go by yourself," Lydia persisted in trying to reason. "I think a lot of people prefer to fish alone. Doesn't too much noise scare off the fish?"

"What do you know about it?" asked Roger. "I doubt that dude you're marrying goes fishing."

"Roger, there's no need for name-calling," protested Delia.

"Well, he is a dude. Look at those suits he wears. Where does he get the money for them?—that's what I'd like to know. You can't tell me he can afford those clothes on a banker's wages, and I find it strange how he has such easy access to cash—"

"Father!" exclaimed Lydia.

"Roger, I thought you liked Lysander," said Delia. "Why are you being so belligerent toward everyone tonight?"

"I just don't like being treated like I don't exist," he replied.

We know all too well that you exist, thought Matthew, *though I, for one, wish you didn't. For too many years, we've tried to ignore your obnoxious behavior.*

"Matthew," said Delia, "you go to your press dinner and have a good time."

"Yes, I better get going," he said. "Roger, if you had told me yesterday that you wanted to go fishing, I gladly would have gone."

"Pretty words after the fact," said Roger, and then he blew on his soup to cool it off.

Delia pursed her lips, but despite her effort, she couldn't help telling her husband, "Matthew and I told you what we were planning to do today and you made no objection, and you know perfectly well you could have gone with us if you had wanted to."

Roger pretended he didn't hear her and started slurping his soup.

Delia was close to tears now.

"Delia, do you want me to—" Matthew began to say.

"You better get going, Matthew," she interrupted, "or you'll be late."

"All right," he replied, seeing that it was better for him to go before he irritated Roger more. "I'll see you all later." He tipped his hat to Lydia and then quickly made his departure.

As he headed back downtown, however, Matthew realized he had lost his appetite.

"What an insufferable little man!" he muttered under his breath. "What the hell is wrong with him?"

And then, after a block of walking at a furious pace, he thought, *I know what's wrong with him—liquor. It's gotten the better of him. Not that he wasn't always obnoxious, even when we were children, but the liquor has made him completely intolerable.*

Matthew could never forget the many past incidences of Roger's obnoxiousness. For a long time when they were young, he had tried to befriend Roger, to try to save the young man from himself, but it had been next to impossible. And he had pitied Roger after that Fourth of July evening when poor Madeleine Henning had fallen out of his canoe and drowned. It had been that event, and perhaps especially how Delia had blamed Roger, that had led to his drinking—although Roger probably would have begun drinking anyway since, as Matthew suspected, his father had been an alcoholic. And Matthew had tried to be forgiving to Roger as a result of his sister's hardness until he finally convinced her to pity him. But as they say, no good deed goes unpunished—as evidenced when Delia's pity turned into her accepting the son-of-a-bitch's marriage proposal.

Only after the marriage did Matthew really begin to understand the man who had become his brother-in-law. Matthew still lived in Marquette then, so he was often invited to Roger and Delia's home for dinner. They still lived with Roger's parents in those years, so Matthew had seen firsthand how Roger's father treated him as if he were stupid. Mr. Richardson never responded to anything Roger said with anything but a sneer. A few times, Matthew had heard Roger make intelligent suggestions about the family business, but his father wouldn't listen to him, and after a year or so, Matthew realized Roger had given up on trying to win his father's approval. Not long after that, Roger started drinking again.

And then Roger's sister, Rowena, had married Reginald Robillard, of the Philadelphia Robillards, a family that had made its fortune in coal. Mrs. Richardson had been one of the Philadelphia Palmers, and so, on a visit back to Philadelphia with her mother, Rowena had met her husband, and what a husband he was. Reginald was the most pretentious man Matthew had ever met, one whose grandiose posing was like water for a dog to lap up, and Roger was that dog—he instantly worshiped his new brother-in-law, who had inherited his family's business at twenty-two and doubled its size and value before he was thirty. The attraction, however, was not mutual; Reginald Robillard saw Roger as a failure; it did not help that Roger's father confirmed that belief. It had been all Matthew could do at one family get-together not to give Reginald a blow to the chin when he remarked how Rowena and Roger's mother had married a backwoods hick. Mr. Richardson was a self-made man who had obviously married above him, but he had done better for himself than most do, through both hard work and a little bullying of those he did business with. Whatever Mr. Richardson's faults, neither Roger nor Rowena deserved to have their father mocked by Rowena's husband.

Matthew had been grateful when he left Marquette that he would not have to deal with the Robillards anymore. They usually only came to Marquette to visit at Christmas, but even that was too often, as far as Matthew was concerned. On the rare occasions when Matthew did visit, he made sure it was in the summer. Of course, the Robillards had been invited to Lydia's wedding, but they had excused themselves from it, saying they had already promised a visit to their friends, the Wideners, in Newport that week. Matthew seemed to recall the Wideners were from Philadelphia like the Robillards and Palmers. He knew a lot about Philadelphia society just from having listened to Rowena talk about it so much whenever he saw her—as if Marquette had no society. As if he even cared about society.

And then Mr. Richardson had died, and Roger must have felt haunted by disappointing his father so much that he slipped further into his drinking. Matthew sometimes wondered how it was that by now Roger had not bankrupted himself since he likely spent half the business day with a hangover. All Matthew could assume was that his brother-in-law had some good and loyal employees—who could say why they would work for such a man? But then, people will do what they have to in order to support themselves. Matthew was sure Martha couldn't enjoy working for Roger, or Mrs. Honeywell either, who apparently always hid in the kitchen, perhaps to stay away from the master.

It's no wonder Roger is such a mess, thought Matthew, *with a father, a sister, and a brother-in-law like that, plus the guilt he probably still feels over Madeleine. He's probably never felt that he could measure up to any other man he's known, myself included, given how he behaves toward me. He's never had a close friend that I can remember. Maybe he was serious about wanting to go fishing; if he had actually asked me, instead of acting like a child, I might have even made the effort. He whines rather than knowing how to ask for something, and then he whines more when he doesn't get what he wants. Still, I have to admit I haven't made any effort to be friendly with him while I've been here. Maybe I can try harder this weekend, especially since it's Lydia's wedding.*

By now, Matthew could see the Marquette Commercial Club's entrance. Several of his fellow pressmen were standing outside, getting ready to enter. It was time to put on his business face and forget about Roger and Delia's marriage problems for a couple of hours. Trying his best to smile, Matthew began greeting everyone as they entered the building. He couldn't help feeling that they were all reasonable and jovial men; sadly, he would have rather had any one of them as his brother-in-law.

Among those present was Philip Roosevelt, the son of Colonel Roosevelt's cousin; he was the correspondent for the *Globe* in New York, and as they all took their seats, Matthew found himself at a table with him, along with Homer Guck and Harry Atwell, a photographer for the *Chicago Tribune*. As they waited for dinner, there was much talk of the newspaper business and their different experiences. An invocation was given by a local minister Matthew didn't know, and then the dinner was served—Lake Superior's very best whitefish, along with green beans, salad, and soup. Of course, plenty of drinks were also downed, no thought given to the abstemiousness that had been the subject of the trial, not that anyone present became intoxicated.

As they ate, Atwell started up a conversation with Philip Roosevelt by asking, "Is it hard for you to report impartially given that you're related to the plaintiff?"

"Not at all," said Philip, "though I admit I'm quite certain my cousin is in the right, as the testimony has proven."

"That sounds prejudiced to me," said Homer, laughing.

"Well, we'll have to wait," Matthew added, "to see whether it is prejudice or good sense, but I have to agree that I also think Mr. Roosevelt is in the right."

"I feel fortunate to get to report on the trial at all," said Philip. "I was concerned my editor would think I couldn't be impartial, and I even raised that concern to him, but he said he knew I would be fair."

"I'm sure your editor picked the best man for the assignment. If anything, your relationship to Roosevelt probably gives you more insight than most of us have into this trial," said Matthew. "As for me, my editor chose me because I'm from Marquette so he thought I could give my stories a little extra flavor."

"I didn't know you were from Marquette," said Atwell.

"I did," said Philip. "Theodore mentioned it me."

"Do you live here now?" Atwell asked Matthew.

"No, I live in New York; I'm the reporter for the *Empire Sentinel*. I've been staying with my sister and her family while I'm in town. In fact, my niece is getting married on Sunday, so I'll be here for the wedding."

"Give her my congratulations," said Philip.

"You're lucky," added Atwell. "I bet you don't have the flea-infested bed I have."

"Where are you staying?" Homer asked Atwell.

"Some little boarding house. It was the best I could get. All the hotels were booked."

"I imagine so," said Homer. "I'm at the Hotel Marquette, and I can't find a single reason to complain about it."

"It's a good hotel," said Philip. "I was actually surprised by how good. It's not the Waldorf, of course, but for such a small city, I've been impressed by the amenities available here."

Talk at the table now turned to newspaper circulation. Homer defended the importance of small town newspapers over the larger papers that had circulations in the hundreds of thousands. Matthew tried to chime in to assist Homer since he had once worked for the *Mining Journal*, but he had to admit that the lack of intriguing news in small towns could make a reporter's job rather dull at times.

Finally, everyone finished eating and the dishes were carried away before the evening's program began. Matthew looked around, seeing that several dozen men were in the room, making the gathering the most nationally representative collection of newspapermen that had ever been held in a Michigan city. Nearly the entire staff of the *Mining Journal* was present; these local newsmen had continually assisted the out-of-town reporters throughout the trial. Also present were the officers of the Marquette Commercial Club, all local businessmen very pleased to have the Queen City of the North in the national spotlight. Matthew noticed that John Van Evera was among the club's officers—Delia had told him how Van Evera had challenged Roosevelt during his campaign stop in Marquette last autumn. Matthew had not seen him in the courtroom, so he was surprised the man had shown up for the dinner, but then again, Roosevelt hadn't been invited to the dinner so Van Evera had no reason not to come. It was odd that he had stayed away from the trial, however—perhaps he was afraid of a bull moose after all.

The Master of Ceremonies for the evening, Mr. Byron Williams, whom Matthew did not know, now stepped forward to begin the program. After thanking everyone for attending, he read the roster of all the men present, asking each one to stand when his name was read so everyone would know who he was—an activity not really necessary since they had all socialized together so much for the past week, but Williams wanted to emphasize the diversity of reporters from so many cities. After the roll call, he was ready to move on to the evening's entertainment segment.

"Tonight," he announced, "we are to have a debate, or rather a mock trial. Our defendant is Chris Haggerty of the Associated Press. Chris, can you come up here, please?"

Mr. Haggerty sheepishly walked up to the room as a few of the men, who already knew what was to happen, booed and hissed him. He covered his face, feigning to be ashamed and taking it all in good stride.

"Now, Mr. Haggerty," said Mr. Williams, "we have a chair here in the center for you to sit at so you can hear all the charges brought against you along with the condemnation of your enemies and perhaps the commendation of anyone daring enough to speak up for you."

Haggerty took his seat in the indicated chair and pretended to look brave as Williams continued.

"Now, the issue at hand is the serious and solemn indictment of Mr. Haggerty for referring, in reports about the Roosevelt Trial, to Marquette as a 'frontier town.' Now, I ask that those members of the Marquette Commercial Club not speak since they are obviously prejudiced and, therefore, would not be acceptable on the jury, but all the visiting newsmen, who have now spent a week in this town which the locals consider 'The Queen City of the North,' may give their opinions as to whether or not 'frontier town' is a proper term to apply to this city. Now, who would like to speak first?"

Homer Guck stood up quickly, much to everyone's surprise, and said, "As a resident of Michigan's Upper Peninsula, I may be one of the most prejudiced reporters here, but since I am not from Marquette but Houghton, I feel I can say that I think Marquette is far from a frontier town. Not that it's as good a city as Houghton, mind you, but I don't think a finer hotel can be found in all the Midwest than Marquette's Hotel Superior, which I have stayed at in the past, save for perhaps the Grand Hotel on Mackinac Island. Marquette is also well-known for its pleasant and temperate climate, the healthy air that blows over it from Lake Superior, and for its prosperous history. We need only look at its grand library, its towering cathedral, and its beautiful courthouse, as well as the pleasantry of its citizens, who never cease to greet you on the street, to see that these are not the uncouth or savage people one might encounter on the frontier, but rather, people who enjoy the very highest benefits and virtues that civilization can bring."

Everyone applauded Homer as he took his seat, and then Philip Roosevelt stood up, inspired by his dinner companion to say his piece.

"I will agree with Mr. Guck that Marquette is far from a frontier town, and I say that based on the appreciation that my cousin, Colonel Roosevelt, has expressed to me for the great hospitality he has been shown here by Mr. George Shiras and all his relatives, who have provided lodging to many of the trial's witnesses, and for the great outpouring of support he has received. I have been on many trips with my cousin, including out West, and I can tell you that there are many places in this country far more deserving of the term 'frontier' than Marquette. I am told that even the local Indians here are friendly, so I have to believe that Marquette is far from a frontier town."

More applause as Philip Roosevelt took his seat.

L.F. Curtis of Chicago now stood up to speak. He was from the Associated Press, and so began by attempting to excuse his colleague.

"As a member of the Associated Press, it is our job to report on a wide variety of information, and unfortunately, we must rely upon the work of our colleagues to collect details. It seems to me that while I will not go so far as to say Mr. Haggerty was correct in referring to Marquette as a 'frontier town,' that he can be excused for his ignorance since he had never set foot in this fine city until this week. He likely could not have even found Marquette on a map before this trial was announced. Furthermore, a few days ago, I was talking to a local gentleman who mentioned to me that Marquette experienced a great fire in 1868. When I responded that it could not have been as large as the Chicago Fire of 1871, which I remember from my boyhood, he admitted that it could not have been, but that the people of Marquette, knowing how devastating such a fire was to their community, were very generous in sending aid to Chicago after its fire. Such warm-hearted people are hardly those who deserve to have their city so maligned, and furthermore, any vestige of this city as a frontier seems to have been erased by that fire of forty-five years ago. All I see now are fine buildings and fine people."

Next spoke Richard Fairchild of the *Chicago Record-Herald*. Then J.H. Dunnewind of the *Detroit Free Press*, and Carroll McCrae of the *Toledo Blade*. All of them spoke of the kindness of the locals, the quality of the hotels where they stayed, the courtesy of the officers at the courthouse toward them, and the fine look of the city.

"Have we heard enough?" asked Mr. Williams when the last had finished speaking. "Are we ready to condemn Mr. Haggerty, this poor excuse for a journalist who does not even do his research before bandying about dangerous and insulting adjectives to describe such a fair city?"

Suddenly, not quite knowing what possessed him, Matthew stood up.

"I would like to say one word in Mr. Haggerty's defense," he announced. Good-natured boos and hisses followed this remark, but Matthew forged on. "We are all assuming that Mr. Haggerty intended to be insulting to Marquette by his remark, but while I now live in New York, I am a former Marquette resident who does not take offense to it being called a 'frontier town.' 'Frontier' has more than one meaning. Not only does it refer to the limit of a nation's territory or a new settlement in a wild land. It is also a word that means the edge of knowledge, the limit that needs to be surpassed. To me, Marquette has always been on the edge of the frontier of knowledge and culture. I came to this town as a small boy just after the Civil War. I remember well that devastating fire of 1868. And I remember what happened after— the city elders issued an ordinance that henceforth all buildings downtown must be made of stone to prevent future conflagrations. I also know that we have never been satisfied here in Marquette with settling for less than being superior—perhaps that's the influence of our mighty lake. In any case, we have always striven to be the best city we can be. We have been proud to be the county seat, proud to be discussed even as the potential capital for a new state if ever we separated from Lower Michigan. We have been proud to have great men here who used the obstacles that the wilderness presented to them to become innovative. It was men from Marquette who helped to create the locks at Sault Ste. Marie. It was here that the first pocket dock was built for hauling iron ore. And it is here that we have had a grand library built, a beautiful opera house, and the Northern Normal School to educate teachers who, in turn, will educate all the populace. Marquette has never settled for being second best. Its residents are innovators, entrepreneurs, hard workers not afraid to get their hands dirty to get a job done, and dreamers who chase their dreams until they become reality for all of us. Yes, Marquette is a frontier town. It is on the frontier of invention, imagination, and ingenuity, and those of us from here hold strong to the belief that anything we put our minds to, we can accomplish. That was true when I first came here nearly fifty years ago, and I believe it will still be true a hundred-and-fifty years from now. Therefore, I thank Mr. Haggerty for having the foresight to see that we are indeed a frontier town."

Thunderous applause ensued as Matthew took his seat. He nearly blushed from the thrill he felt from speaking and the response he had received. When the applause finally diminished, Mr. Williams turned to Mr. Haggerty and said, "How do you plead?"

"Guilty," said Haggerty, "guilty to everything that Mr. Newman just said."

More applause and cheers throughout the room.

"Are you ready for your punishment?" Mr. Williams asked him.

Mr. Haggerty's eyes now grew wide and he pretended to tremble in fear.

"Bring out the punishment!" cried Mr. Williams, and then one of the club officers appeared bearing a coonskin cap that was promptly placed upon Mr. Haggerty's head to much additional laughter and applause.

"Mr. Haggerty, we cast you forth to the frontier," said Mr. Williams. "Go in peace."

Haggerty stood and bowed, dropping the coonskin cap off his head when he did so; it had intentionally been made too large for him so as to make his appearance all the more ridiculous. He snatched it up and tried to walk off, but the club officer and Mr. Williams grabbed him and made him put it back on his head before he returned to his seat to another round of applause.

"Well, that was great fun," said Mr. Atwell to everyone at his table.

"Indeed," said Homer.

Mr. Williams now thanked everyone again for joining them for the evening, ending with, "Now, I am sure you all have your newspaper reports to write for the evening. I wish you all well in all your reporting endeavors, gentleman, and may you enjoy the remainder of your time in this frontier town."

Matthew then rose to go. He shook Mr. Atwell and Philip Roosevelt's hands. Homer then asked him whether he'd like to go get a drink before calling it a night, but Matthew declined since he did not drink, and he wanted to write up a story about how Roosevelt had greeted all the veterans that afternoon.

"I'll see you in the morning then," said Homer.

"See you then," said Matthew. "Good night."

IF YOU ARE A
DRINKING MAN

You had better stop at once or you'll lose your job. Every line of business is closing its doors to "Drinking" men. It may be your turn next. By the aid of ORRINE thousands of men have been restored to lives of sobriety and industry.

We are so sure that ORRINE will benefit you that we say to you that if after a trial you fail to get any benefit from its use, your money will be refunded.

When you stop "Drinking," think of the money you'll save; besides, sober men are worth more to their employers and get higher wages.

Costs only $1.00 a box. We have an interesting booklet about ORRINE that we are giving away free on request. Call at our store and talk it over.

Stafford Drug Store, Marquette, Mich.; Fennia Prescription Pharmacy, Ishpeming, Mich.; City Drug Store, Negaunee, Mich.

— *Mining Journal* ad from May 31, 1913, p. 8, on the same page as an ad for Castle Brew

CHAPTER 22

ATTHEW WAVED GOODBYE TO HOMER and headed back toward Roger and Delia's house.

But before he was a block away from the club, the evening's conviviality began to wear off and he found himself dreading going back.

I wonder what sort of hell Roger made the evening for Delia, he thought. *Of course, Lydia probably had things to do for the wedding to distract her, but she shouldn't have to deal with his behavior any more than Delia does. I guess she's fortunate to be marrying and getting out of there, even if it is to a man like Lysander. Poor Delia, though; once Lydia's gone, she'll be left all alone with that louse.*

Matthew's thoughts were so enmeshed in feeling sorry for his sister and trying to think what he might do to make the situation better for her that after he turned onto Ridge Street, he forgot to turn down Spruce but just kept walking. When he realized his mistake, he was almost to Cedar, so he figured he would turn there.

I don't know what I can do to fix things, he thought as he walked, *but I better stay calm with Roger tonight. He always acts like he can't stand me, so I don't know why he suddenly decided he wants to go fishing with me— it's probably just an excuse so he can hold another fake grudge against me. That said, I haven't been the best brother-in-law to him. I could make more of an effort. Maybe I'll ask him if he wants to have a drink with me when I get home—just the two of us in the smoking room. Not that he needs another drink, but sometimes you have to meet the devil on his own terms. But what would we talk about? I could just ask him about the business maybe.... After all, I am curious how he keeps it going when he's drunk all the time.*

By now Matthew was close to Cedar Street and about to cross the road to head north when he saw Colonel Roosevelt in the Shirases' yard. The former president was sitting alone with a newspaper in his lap, so Matthew didn't want to disturb him. He was just going to walk past without saying anything, but then Roosevelt looked up.

"I didn't think I'd see you again today," said Roosevelt, folding his paper and standing up.

"Neither did I," Matthew replied, stopping but not walking into the yard to intrude. "I'm just enjoying the fresh air as I walk home from the press men's dinner."

"The same here, other than the walking part," said Roosevelt, patting his stomach. "George was just out here with me, but he went inside to make a telephone call to Frances. He misses his wife, and I can't blame him. I miss my Edith."

"I understand," said Matthew.

"You've been away from home for a while now too," said Roosevelt.

"From my apartment in New York, yes," said Matthew. "But Marquette is really home."

"I suppose," said Roosevelt, standing up and walking toward the sidewalk to converse better. "You've never been married, have you? There's no one back home waiting for you to return?"

"No," said Matthew. "No one but my editor." Matthew frowned a bit at this thought; Josiah Pritchard was hardly the person he wanted to have wishing he'd come home since they didn't always see eye-to-eye.

"You look a bit frustrated," Roosevelt observed. "Is the trial not providing you with good enough material for your paper?"

Matthew couldn't help laughing. "No, that's not the case at all, and I'm still hoping you'll be the victor. No, I'm just a bit frustrated with my family is all. You must know what it's like when you go to visit relatives; people can rub each other the wrong way."

"Well, most families do have their problems," Roosevelt agreed.

"Let's just say," said Matthew, not knowing why he said it but feeling the need to express himself and thinking Roosevelt would be sympathetic, "that my brother-in-law and I don't always get along so I needed a break from him."

"I see," said Roosevelt.

And then, because he felt so frustrated, Matthew found himself adding, "My brother-in-law drinks too much, and when he does, he can be very difficult."

"I understand that," said Roosevelt. "Be glad he's just your brother-in-law and not your brother."

"I've never had a brother," said Matthew.

"I did, but I don't any longer because he let the drink get the best of him," Roosevelt replied.

"I didn't know that," said Matthew.

"Yes," Roosevelt continued. "My brother Elliott. Alcohol was his demon. It took possession of him, and eventually, it ended his life. He became completely useless, a spendthrift. I had to become my brother's conservator and help look after his children because he was incapable of handling his own affairs."

"I had no idea," said Matthew. "I'm truly sorry."

"He just couldn't stop drinking no matter how the family pled with him or threatened to cut him off. Eventually, he tried to kill himself by jumping out a window—a botched attempt that didn't kill him but caused him to have a seizure. He then died a few days later. This was back in 1894; we did our best to keep it out of the papers. I trust you won't repeat it. Every family has its black sheep, and I wouldn't want mention of it to get into the press and hurt his children, even though they're adults now."

"I'm so sorry," said Matthew, amazed that Roosevelt would tell him something so private.

"You're a smart man, Mr. Newman," said Roosevelt, "and since you can see how alcohol has affected those you love, I imagine you can understand why I had to go forward with this trial. I've seen what drinking can do to a man. I loved my brother, but I am nothing like him, and I refuse to be compared to someone like him. No one can imagine the pain he put our family through, and especially his wife and children, who suffered the most."

"I believe that," said Matthew.

"There's nothing you can do about it, though, when you have an alcoholic in your family," said Roosevelt. "One thing I've learned is you can't change people; you can't even help them if they lack the willpower to try to help themselves. My brother taught me that the hard way."

"Yes, and my brother-in-law continually teaches me that," Matthew agreed.

"I wish you luck getting along with him for the remainder of your stay then," said Roosevelt. "Hopefully, the trial will soon be over and we can all return home."

"I hope so, sir, and that it ends up in your favor. You don't deserve the aspersions cast on your character, especially after how alcohol has already hurt your family."

"Thank you," said Roosevelt, extending his hand to shake Matthew's. "It's been good seeing you here in Marquette, Matthew. You're a fine newspaperman, and I'm honored to have you covering my story as I seek justice."

"I'm the one who is honored, sir," said Matthew. "And thank you for listening to my frustrations."

"You're welcome," said Roosevelt. "As I've said, I've been in your shoes. Good night."

"Good night," said Matthew.

Matthew turned now and crossed the road, then started down Cedar Street. Meanwhile, Roosevelt returned to his chair and reading about himself in *The Mining Journal*.

A few minutes later, Matthew was back at Roger and Delia's house. After he entered and hung up his hat in the hall, he went into the parlor where he found Delia busy with her needlework.

"There you are," she said. "I was just trying to convince Lydia to have some ice cream with me, but Lydia says it will make her too fat to fit into her wedding dress. She just went upstairs to get her beauty sleep, so I hope you'll join me. It won't be like that Roosevelt mint concoction we had earlier today, but I think we can put some cherries on it."

"Sure. I'd love some," said Matthew, even though he was still full from dinner. "Is Roger having any?"

Delia sighed. "Roger went downtown to the bar."

"Oh," said Matthew. "Oh well, that means all the more ice cream for us."

Teddy Roosevelt's Mint Julep Recipe

Ingredients:

- 10 to 12 Mint leaves

- Splash of Water

- Sugar Cube

- 2 to 3 oz. Rye Whiskey

- 1/4 oz. Brandy

- Sprig of Fresh Mint for Garnish

Preparation: Muddle mint leaves with water and sugar cube in a serving glass. Fill the glass with crushed ice. Top off with rye whiskey and brandy. Garnish with mint.

Taken from http://drinkwire.liquor.com/post/presidential-drinking-four-cocktails-for-presidents-day#gs.6pa9SzM.

"I am more of a Quaker than anything else. I believe in the 'still, small voice,' and that voice is Christ within us."
— Ralph Waldo Emerson

CHAPTER 23

MATTHEW AND DELIA ENJOYED THEIR ice cream without Roger, and then Matthew said goodnight to his sister and went up to his room. He had his dispatch to write, as usual, and he labored over trying to give it just the right tone to describe Roosevelt's meeting that afternoon with the veterans.

Once he had finished writing, Matthew felt exhaustion quickly descending upon him. It had been a long day, and a good one, other than the incident with Roger at dinner. Matthew realized now that he had given that incident too much power because it had really been a remarkable day in many ways—he had spent time with Delia, and witnessed Roosevelt speaking to the veterans, and he had himself made a very good speech at the press dinner, but truthfully, the best part of the day had been that private moment between him and Colonel Roosevelt. To have such a great man take him into his private confidence, telling him of his family's problems—that was an honor Matthew deeply felt and a confidence he would never betray no matter how good of a scoop it might make; he would never want his own family embarrassed by the revelation that there was a drunkard in their family, so he refused to expose them in other families.

As he lay down on his bed, Matthew found himself shaking his head over what a queer mixture of contradictions humanity was. As angry as he had been with Roger, he mostly just felt pity for his brother-in-law. Matthew had long ago learned that you can never fully understand another person; you can't even fully understand yourself. Even the best-intentioned human has weak moments when he will act irrationally; we are all capable of greatness, but just as capable of self-sabotage. Everyone of us is capable of falling into bad behavior when stressed or pushed by others. It takes real courage to stand up to the pressures of society and do what you believe is right when it's not always clear what right is. Matthew wanted to do the right thing by

Roger—he had always wanted that, even when Roger was most obnoxious, but he couldn't do it when Roger wouldn't let him. And he also wanted to do the right thing for himself; he would not help Roger to his own detriment; if he didn't take care of himself first, he wouldn't be able to help anyone.

It had ultimately been for that reason that Matthew had left Marquette all those years ago—to do what was needed to maintain his mental wellbeing. All that winter after Frances had told him she was going to marry George, he had been so depressed that he could barely crawl out of bed in the morning. He had tried to tell himself it was just the cold, the snow, and the dark and gloomy winter days that had him feeling down, but when the spring came, his attitude had not changed. Each week, he had become more depressed, more quarrelsome with Roger, less interested in his work, and just frustrated with his life in general.

When Matthew had confessed to Delia how he was feeling, she had suggested he turn to God for solace. He had then tried to become more involved in church. He had been raised a Methodist, but work and caring for his mother after his father's death had caused him to be absent from church most weeks. Now he committed to going regularly again—and he did for a couple of months, but he found little solace in the services. Then that summer, the minister went on vacation and the Reverend Mordecai Whichgood, whom Matthew remembered from that New Year's Eve party at the Call home, came to town to fill in for him. Reverend Whichgood preached fire and brimstone—which were far from what Matthew had been raised to believe in—and from that day, Matthew knew organized religion was no longer for him. Instead, he read his Bible in the privacy of his home, and he tried to be a good Christian, giving to charities and spreading goodwill to his fellow men. He found he could no longer listen to preachers—not that there were not good ones, but most seemed to know the Bible less well than he did, and how they rambled! As a writer, he could envision their sentences in his head as if on a printed page, and his editorial pen just wanted to slash out whole phrases, clauses, and words here and there that were unnecessary, wordy, bloated, and tedious—flowery phrases and meaningless clichés that mimicked but fell short of what worthier men had said. Sometimes he thought he was just an intellectual snob, but he could not help feeling it unlikely he would find any man wiser than he was about the mysteries of life who could guide him, and consequently, human society became irksome to him. He hoped that would not be the case if he found new sights and new people to converse with, but he feared it would be. Nevertheless, he knew the time had come to leave Marquette and experience the rest of the world—and perhaps still to create a meaningful relationship with someone.

And so Matthew had moved away from home, filled with frustration, filled with a desire to escape everything he felt was holding him back from having the life he wanted—although what he actually wanted he could not yet say.

Then he began to think back to his childhood, to remember happy moments with his parents, whom he dearly missed. He wanted somehow to recapture that experience, but he was not yet ready to return to Marquette. And so, although he had gone to New York City and found a job there working for a daily newspaper, after about a year, he took a few days off and traveled to upstate New York, to the place where he had been born and lived the first few years of his life. He wasn't sure what he hoped to find there—perhaps a family member or two who would remember him or his parents—perhaps something he had long ago lost.

Matthew only had dim memories of his early years in New York. He vaguely remembered playing with his sister in their yard or seeing his mother in the kitchen. The first really clear memory he had was from when he was five years old. It had been an early summer evening, and Matthew had been in the yard with Delia, playing just outside the kitchen window. Their mother had been busy washing the supper dishes. Neither he nor Delia even saw their father approaching until they heard their mother shout, "Joshua!" from the window, and then they turned to look, questioning, wondering who it was. Matthew would never forget seeing the house door open and then his mother practically fly down the road, holding back tears, until she was in their father's arms. For a moment, all Matthew and Delia could do was watch as their parents held and kissed each other, and then Delia started crying, and Matthew took her hand and led her down the road to meet their father, whose arm was now linked in their mother's as he walked toward them. In another minute, their father had let go of their mother's arm and somehow managed to scoop up both of his children. Suddenly, Matthew had felt like everything was right in his world, although he hadn't even realized it wasn't right until that moment.

For the next several days, Matthew hadn't wanted to leave his father's side. He followed him to the barn, to the fields, and about the house, all the while basking in the glow of having a father again. Even when his grandfather came to visit and his father told Matthew to go in the other room, he stood by the door, just out of sight of his father and grandfather, listening and occasionally peeking into the room. He was too overcome by the happiness of being near his father to focus on what they were speaking about, although gradually, he sensed that his father was angry. Had he listened more closely that day, he would have better understood what would happen when they went to meeting that next Sunday.

Matthew had still been too young at five to understand really how the Quaker meetings worked. He only knew he was to be quiet and not fuss but simply listen. It seemed like he had gone all his life with his mother and sister to these meetings, but because his father had been away at the war, he did not remember ever having gone to such a meeting with him. Was that why the meeting on that day felt was so different? Or was it because this meeting wasn't being held on a Sunday?

Everyone was there who was usually present on a Sunday. Each one of them sat in his or her usual seat, but rather than all of them sitting quietly, listening and waiting for the voice of God, the Quaker Elder stood up in the front of the room and addressed Matthew's father from where he was seated with his family.

"Before we begin this meeting, there is business to attend to," said the elder. "Joshua Newman, who was raised in this meeting, has returned to us from the conflict between the States. Brother Newman, before we can permit thou to join us in worship, we must know that thou repentest for thy participation in the violence that recently engrossed this nation."

Everyone was silent, as if fearful of this moment. Matthew felt uncomfortable. He looked at his father and saw the color rise in his cheeks. Was his daddy ill? He wanted to hug him, but his father was seated on the other side of his mother, and his mother was holding him tightly so he could not move.

After a moment, Matthew's father said, "I do not."

"Dost thou not feel shame or guilt over the taking of human life?" asked the elder.

"I would never wish to harm another, but I do not feel guilt over the men I shot or wounded for they would have done the same to me, and they had enslaved, beaten, and tortured, or supported such behavior, toward countless of our brothers in the South."

"Our Lord taught us to turn the other cheek," said the elder.

"He did," agreed Joshua Newman, "but he did not teach us to stand by while others were mistreated."

"Thou cannot worship in this meeting any longer," stated the elder, "unless thou agree to repent for the violence thou hast partaken in."

"I cannot repent for what my own conscience tells me it was right to do," said Joshua Newman, and then he and the elder sternly glared at each other for several seconds before Joshua added, "and, therefore, I will remove myself from thy presence."

Matthew's father had then stood up and walked out of the meeting house. Before Matthew knew what was happening, his mother was standing also, and then she was pulling him and Delia down the aisle until they were once again outside.

"We are a peace-loving people!" shouted the elder as the door closed behind them.

After that—Matthew did not know how his parents came to the decision—his father no longer went to meeting with them. His mother still took him and Delia to meeting, but Matthew noticed more than once that his mother would cry on their way home.

Then one night, when Delia was long gone to sleep, Matthew overheard his parents talking.

"I am a hero," said his father, "and I should be treated like one. The slaves have been freed, which is a cause our brethren spent decades working for, and yet none will speak to me because I broke the Quaker belief in peace."

"Thou art right," said Matthew's mother. "Thou art a hero."

"Thou art my hero, Father!" Matthew had called out then, and he had run from his bed into the sitting room and jumped up into his father's lap, intent upon expressing his loyalty. "I don't care what any of them say. None of them are half as good as thou."

"Thank thee, son," said his father, holding Matthew tightly on his lap, "but thou art supposed to be asleep and in bed."

"What can we do?" asked his mother. "The elders will not go back on their words."

"I wish to leave this place," his father stated. "I cannot stay here among such people who do not follow in the Savior's footsteps of forgiveness."

"But they will forgive thee if thou will just admit thou art wrong," Matthew's mother replied.

"That I cannot do in good conscience," his father replied.

"I know," said his mother, "but then where will we go?"

"To the Lake Superior Country. I hear from our neighbors in Essex County that several have gone there, and it is a prosperous land where I understand there is much work and a fortune to be made. I may not be Moses, but it was Joshua, not he, who led the Israelites into the Promised Land, and I would not be true to my name if I did not do the same for my family."

Matthew's mother agreed to this decision. Matthew's grandfather, Obadiah, however, was not pleased. He was one of the church elders, after all, but while he sympathized with his son, he had not been able to persuade the other elders to change their minds. Nor had he been strong enough to see that everything his religion preached was not black and white. He firmly believed that the slaves who had been freed were humans and had souls, but he also believed the Confederates whom his son had shot had souls just as valuable to the Lord. And so, when Matthew's father told his parents they were leaving, his grandparents chose to remain behind.

Before the next winter set in, Matthew had found himself traveling with his parents and sister to the Lake Superior Country, where they had settled in Marquette. There, after a few years working as a clerk, Matthew's father had bought his own store. There Matthew's parents had lived out their lives, scarcely ever mentioning their former lives back in New York.

But Matthew had never forgotten his grandfather or those Quaker meetings. He had found it strange, once they moved to Marquette, to attend the Methodist church his parents had decided upon. He had grown used to the silence of the Quaker meeting, where you could hear yourself think— where he had been taught that you can hear God's voice. In the Methodist church, all the preaching and singing drowned out any chance of hearing God speak to you—perhaps he had not quite realized that as a boy, but as he got older, Matthew began to realize the logic in the Quakers' way of holding their meetings.

❧

Twenty years after leaving New York as a boy, Matthew had decided to attend the old meeting house in the Quaker community where he had been raised. He arrived there on a Sunday morning. He looked about him for the cottage where he had lived with his parents, but none of the houses looked familiar. Only the meeting house seemed not to have changed. And he could see people entering it. The meeting was about to begin.

As he walked up to the meeting house and entered, a few people looked at him strangely. A couple of them nodded to him in greeting, but none spoke to him or questioned his presence.

And then he sat there for a good long while in the silence with the other members.

It was an uncomfortable experience. He kept waiting for someone to speak. No one did. And then he felt like maybe he was wasting his time just sitting there. He looked around and saw everyone had his or her eyes closed. He had forgotten that was part of the meeting protocol. He closed his eyes. After a minute or two, he thought he might fall asleep if no one spoke. But then he could hear the man sitting closest to him breathing, and that made him pay attention to his own breathing. And he heard one or two people sigh as if in satisfaction, and that made him feel relaxed, and then he quit worrying about whether someone was going to speak or what time it was or who might be in the room. Instead, he began to remember that the whole purpose of this sitting silently was to listen for God's own voice within his heart.

He waited. He tried to dismiss all the distracting thoughts that rushed to his brain. He tried to focus only on his own breathing to quiet his mind. And he continued to wait for God's voice. And to wait…. And he did not hear it. He felt momentarily anxious—impatient even—to hear it, but then he heard someone sigh again and it reminded him once more to stop worrying, and then he thought to say silently, "Speak, Lord; your servant is listening" as the boy Samuel had been taught by the high priest Eli to do in the Bible. Only then had the Lord given Samuel a message.

Yet God still did not speak to Matthew. Or did he? Matthew heard no words, he received no message, but he did feel a bit more at peace.

"I will send to you the Comforter." Matthew recalled that Jesus had said something like that. Matthew felt he could use some comfort; he had spent so much time of late worrying over why Frances didn't love him, and also feeling guilty that he felt jealousy, and then trying to tell himself he must leave Marquette and go to New York if he wanted a real newspaper career. But now he just felt calm. If God said anything, it was simply through that sense of calmness he was experiencing, a sense that all was well and he should just carry on with life where it led him rather than worry so much.

And finally, Matthew heard people stirring; a pew creaked, a footstep fell, and he opened his eyes to see the Quakers all standing up, speaking softly to one another, and departing the meetinghouse.

Matthew felt strange—both sleepy and energized—but he blinked his eyes and stretched his neck, and then he stood and followed the small caravan of worshipers out the meeting house door. Several people were gathered outside and speaking in small groups. One old man, however, stood alone near the end of the walkway. When Matthew looked his way, he saw that the man was staring at him.

"Hello, Matthew," said the man, now approaching him.

For a moment, Matthew was taken aback. How could anyone have recognized him after so many years?

"Am I correct?" asked the man, now standing just a foot in front of him.

"Yes," said Matthew, wondering, trying to see past the wrinkles to recall whom the man might be.

"Thou art the spitting image of thy father," said the old man, "and people said he was the spitting image of me, so behold in me thy future."

"Grandfather?" asked Matthew, and then they were in one another's arms and Matthew felt such joy that it surprised him. He had secretly hoped he might see his grandfather, but he had imagined him long dead by now.

As if reading Matthew's question on his face, when they had separated, the old man said, "I turned eighty last spring. And you must be—maybe twenty-five?"

Matthew nodded. And then he felt his face drop.

"I can see the sadness in your face," said the old man. "Your father...?"

"He died several years ago," Matthew confirmed. "And my mother followed him. But my sister Delia is well and married. No children yet, but they're hopeful."

"And you? Do you have a family?"

"Not yet," said Matthew.

"Come—can you stay? Come have dinner with me."

Matthew nodded his head in assent. They walked across the green and maybe a quarter of a mile to a house Matthew had forgotten, but that he now remembered vividly.

"Your home hasn't changed very much," Matthew told his grandfather as he stood in its doorway, looking about him.

"No, except that thy grandmother is no longer here with me, and so it is not as tidy as it should be," said the old man, taking off his hat and coat and then heading toward the stove.

"I am sorry for your loss, Grandfather," said Matthew. His grandfather then gestured him toward a chair at the table while he put a kettle on the stove to brew some tea. For a few minutes, while they waited for the tea, Matthew told his grandfather about his parents' lives—and their passings—in Marquette and then about Delia and himself.

"So Delia is married then," said his grandfather as he got up to fetch the kettle and fill their teacups. "But tell me why thou are not. Is that why thou hast come?"

"What do you mean?" asked Matthew.

"Thou hast been away for twenty years, and only now do thou come looking for me. Usually, when someone goes looking for something in his past, it's because he can't see the way to moving forward in his future."

"I still don't understand what you mean," said Matthew, uncomfortable with the topic.

"I think thou dost," said his grandfather, sitting back down, having returned the kettle to the stove. "I don't think thou hast come here out of affection for me, as much as I am glad to see thee."

"I'm happy to see you too, Grandfather. I guess I'm wondering—well, do you think Father was wrong to fight in the war?"

His grandfather paused for a moment, and then, shaking his head, he said, "No. When he first enlisted, I did, but it would have been more wrong to let good people remain in chains and give power to others to keep them enslaved. I wish there had been another way to free those people, but I also understand that a man must do what his conscience dictates. I only wish I had told thy father that I understood what he did. I wish I had tried harder to convince the elders to get him to stay here, or perhaps even that thy grandmother and I had gone west with thy family, but thy grandmother, she was already failing then, and I could see it, and I did not think she could make such a long journey to a new place and start all over again. It has been a lonely life for me ever since, and by the time she did pass away, I felt it too late to reach out to thy father. It is a burden I must bear, and even more so now that I know he is gone and can never forgive me."

Matthew could see a tear in his grandfather's eye. "My father loved you," he said. "He never spoke an ill word against you in all the years I knew him. I am sure he forgave you if he ever had need to."

His grandfather wiped away the tear and then said, "That is good to know. That is the best I can hope for now until we are reunited in Paradise, but thou didst not come to make peace between an old man and his dead son. Tell me the real reason thou hast come."

Matthew lifted his teacup, as if to wet his throat to prepare himself for a long speech. However, when his words came out, they were brief.

"I feel lost."

"Dost thou need to be found, or art thou trying to find something?"

"I'm trying to find…I don't know…myself, I guess."

"What has caused this feeling?"

Matthew then told his grandfather how Frances was marrying George—she probably had married him by now, and how he had felt ill-fitted to remain in Marquette with a brother-in-law he could not stomach. And he told his grandfather how he wished to make a difference in the world with his pen.

"Ah," said his grandfather. "The pen is mightier than the sword, as they say, and being a reporter is a good way to bring about change without having to do battle. It was, in truth, the orators and writers—Garrison, Emerson, Harriett Beecher Stowe—and their ilk who brought about the Civil War. I'm sure none of them would have advocated for bloodshed, but their words helped to stir a nation. Who knows what change thou might work through thy words."

"But…I loved Frances, and I had family in Marquette. Now I'm alone."

"Thou just told me thou were not happy in Marquette. That thou wanted to do great things. What great things could thou have done there?"

"I don't know," said Matthew. "I just know that I feel hurt and angry and a little humiliated that she rejected me."

"But thou wishes to do great things. Dost thou want that more than thou wanted to be married?"

"I don't know. I thought I would make Frances proud of me if I did great things."

"Thou cannot live to please another," said his grandfather. "Thou may want to help others, but thou cannot expect their praise and admiration in return. Thou must do it because thou feels a great calling to it, and then it is up to the world how it will receive thy work. Even if the world rejects thee, thou must do thy work, and not for any other but thyself—yes, thou may do it to help others, but in doing it, thou will most help thyself. Are my words clear to thee?"

"I think so," said Matthew, "but doesn't that make for a lonely life?"

"One of my favorite writers is Thomas Carlyle," his grandfather replied. "He once wrote, 'Blessed is he who has found his work; let him ask no other blessedness. He has a work, a life-purpose.'"

"But," asked Matthew, "what if the world does not care about my work, and so I have given up love and happiness for nothing?"

"Carlyle had an answer for that too," said his grandfather, his eyes ablaze as he quoted, "'The work an unknown good man has done is like a vein of water flowing hidden underground, secretly making the ground green.'"

"I'm still not sure I understand," said Matthew.

"It doesn't matter whether the world knows of thy work or not, just that thou do it. The Lord works in mysterious ways, and none of us can determine the power of our influence or rather how and why he uses us in the ways he does."

"If that's true, I wish God would tell me so himself."

"He is telling you now. He is using me as his instrument to say to thou what thy heart would hear were it not too full of confusion because of thy anger. I suspect thou are not really angry that thy friend is marrying the girl thou liked. I think only that thy pride is hurt."

Somehow, after all this time, Matthew had forgotten his grandfather's words—but it had been so long ago now—nearly thirty years.

"My pride is just hurt," Matthew said, repeating his grandfather's words to himself now as he lay in his bed in Roger and Delia's house. "My pride is just hurt." And then for reasons he could not explain, he found himself sobbing. But with the sobbing came a feeling of release, a feeling he could not explain except as freedom from his pain—his body felt light and free, and then he felt a great calmness come over him, and soon, he drifted to sleep.

"A dollar for a telegram! I'll keep the wires hot!"
— *The Prince of Pilsen*

SATURDAY
MAY 31, 1913

"Editor Newett of Ishpeming says he has something up his sleeve. S-h-h-h. Can you keep a secret? It's his arm."

— *The Detroit News*, reprinted in *The Mining Journal*, June 3, 1913

CHAPTER 24

Saturday morning soon came and the holiday was over. It was back to work and back to the trial, even if only for half a day.

Matthew was sorry to go to the courthouse alone. He was sure Delia would have wanted to see the excitement about to enfold since it was assumed Newett would take the stand this morning, but Delia had been insistent she had to stay behind to help Lydia with the final preparations for the wedding tomorrow.

Matthew sent off his dispatch as soon as he reached the courthouse, and then he found his seat beside Homer Guck.

"I hope it's over today," said Homer. "After being home in Houghton yesterday, I realized how much I miss my own bed."

"I don't blame you for that," said Matthew.

The court was now called to order. The plaintiff stepped forward and read several depositions from men who were unable to testify for Roosevelt in person. Each one had signed a written statement swearing to Colonel Roosevelt's general sobriety. The last deposition read was that of Admiral Dewey. Then Roosevelt's lawyers said that they rested their case.

It was time now for the defense. George Belden called forth his client, George Newett, to testify. As Mr. Newett made his way to the stand, the courtroom grew deadly silent. Newett was obviously not well. He looked weak and sickly, his countenance stressed and his brow haggard as he replied to his attorney's questions.

"When and where were you born?" began Mr. Belden.

"On a farm near Janesville, Wisconsin, in 1856," Newett replied.

"How long did you live there?"

"Until I was sixteen years of age," said Newett.

"How and in what manner did you gain your education?"

"In the district schools of that vicinity, attending in the winter and working on farms during the summer."

"When did you come to Marquette County to live?" Mr. Belden continued.

"In 1873."

"Have you lived here ever since?"

"I have lived here continuously ever since."

"When did you begin newspaper work, and on what paper?"

"In 1874, I began to work on the first paper established in the city of Ishpeming, the *Iron Home*, and continued with the paper until 1879, when I engaged in business for myself on my own paper, the *Iron Ore*."

"Will you describe to the jury your weekly paper, the *Iron Ore*, what it covers?" asked Mr. Belden.

"It is a weekly paper, common to enterprising towns of this region, and specializes in mining news, news of local mines, and also deals in news of mining camps throughout the country generally."

"In October, 1912, what was its circulation?"

"From twenty-five hundred to three thousand, as near as I can recall," said Mr. Newett.

"Over what territory was that principally distributed?"

"It circulated principally in Marquette County, probably four-fifths of the publication, and the balance largely in the Upper Peninsula."

Mr. Belden now changed directions in his questioning. "You may state whether or not you use wines or liquors yourself."

"I do not; I am a teetotaler," said Newett, looking both honest and proud to admit it, "and have very strong views on the subject...neither do I use tobacco in any form."

"You may state what offices you have held under the State administrations," said Mr. Belden.

"I was commissioner of mineral statistics from 1896 to 1900. I was appointed first by Governor Rich, and my second term by Governor Pingree."

"State what offices, if any, you have held in the city of Ishpeming," Mr. Belden requested.

"I also held the position of postmaster from 1905 and held that for two years, at the end of which time I resigned. I received my appointment from the plaintiff in this case."

"Have you held any other offices?"

"I have held numerous offices in town, and now I am president of the Ishpeming Advancement Association."

At this point, everyone was surprised when Mr. Belden turned to Judge Flannigan and stated, "May it please the Court, the testimony in this case is of itself of such great importance that Mr. Newett has reduced his testimony to written form, and if counsel on the other side will permit me to give them a copy of this, I would like to have the witness go on and state in his own way the facts relating to this."

Matthew was surprised, but he suspected the questioning had been deemed too much for Mr. Newett given his illness, so his counsel had chosen to introduce a written statement; plus, the statement would ensure that Mr. Newett not fumble his words when making his responses.

Judge Flannigan, without doubt aware of the defense's reasons in this matter, simply replied, "That will be allowed."

Mr. Newett then drew out a few sheets of paper he had prepared. After clearing his throat, he began to read. His voice slightly trembled at first, but it became stronger as he continued.

"Prior to 1912, I had been for many years a strong supporter of Theodore Roosevelt, recognizing him as a great Republican leader, and had frequently published editorials and other articles in the *Iron Ore* commending him and approving his policies, and I had therefore assisted in all his campaigns, not only by personal effort but also by financial contributions. Even in the primary campaign of 1912, I supported him as second choice for the Republican nomination. I mention these facts as indicating the impossibility of my harboring any feeling of personal malice against the plaintiff.

"Sometime before 1912, I began to hear statements from various sources that Mr. Roosevelt was drinking wines and liquors to excess. During this period, I took a trip through the western country, passing through the States of Montana, Nevada, and Arizona, as well as the intervening cities. The statements as to Mr. Roosevelt's excessive drinking were repeatedly made in my hearing in various sections by many persons whom I believed to be reputable, but notwithstanding this I was loath to credit them. I felt that there was a possibility that these persons were mistaken and, therefore, thought the statements probably unwarranted. Late, during the winter of 1912, I took a trip to Florida, passing through Chicago and other cities en route, and spent several weeks at Belleair and other Florida points. During this trip, the same statements as to Mr. Roosevelt's habits were repeated in a very circumstantial way, although no one was able to say that he had actually seen Mr. Roosevelt drink to excess, or personally knew that he did so.

"During this period, I also talked with various reputable people in Ishpeming, and elsewhere than the places before mentioned, who claimed to know the conditions as they existed in Washington and in whose statements I had the utmost confidence, both as to their reliability and their opportunity to know the facts.

"During the spring of 1912, newspapers came to me on our exchange list, various of which contained reference to Mr. Roosevelt's drinking habits. I saw and read these newspaper publications. From the statements so made in these papers and all the information which had come to me from the other sources mentioned, I felt that I could no longer doubt the truth of the statements which had been made, much as I regretted to believe them.

"When Mr. Roosevelt was nominated for the presidency on the National Progressive ticket, I opposed his election, having been a lifelong Republican and believing that the success of that party would be for the best interests of the country.

"In October, 1912, Mr. Roosevelt made a campaign trip through northern Michigan, and among other places spoke at Marquette on the 9th. I was present on that occasion and heard him speak. In the course of his address, he made what I considered a most unjust attack upon our candidate for Congress, who was one of my lifelong friends. This incident, together with the statements which had previously come to my knowledge, confirmed me in the opinion that Mr. Roosevelt ought not to be elected president, and I concluded that it was my duty in opposition to his candidacy to publish the statements which I then believed to be true. I, therefore, wrote and published the article which is here complained of. This publication was intended only as a blow to Mr. Roosevelt's candidacy for the position he then sought. In this publication, I acted in entire good faith, believing that the facts stated were true and believing that as a publisher I owed the duty to my readers to make that statement. After this article was published on the 12th day of October, 1912, neither the plaintiff nor any one in his behalf notified me that he claimed the charges so made were unfounded, nor did they request me to make any correction of the same. On the contrary, this suit was commenced October 25, 1912, and the service of the papers constituted the first intimation I received that the article was complained of.

"After the commencement of this suit, there was nothing for me to do but to prepare to defend it, and I did so to the best of my ability. From that time, I proceeded to investigate the actual facts which could be shown by witnesses who would testify under oath. As I have said, up to the time of the publication, my information had been through persons who have claimed to have knowledge of the statements which had been made, and I went forward to verify those statements and determine the witnesses by whom they would be proven. Additional information came to me from various sections of the country, as this case had been given wide publicity. Both my attorneys and myself went forward with the investigation of all this with great thoroughness, and in numerous places in various parts of the country we found reputable witnesses who were willing to swear that from observation during certain addresses and public appearances of Mr. Roosevelt, they believed he was intoxicated when they saw him. We have been unable, however, to locate or produce witnesses who will swear that they have actually seen Mr. Roosevelt drink to excess. Upon this phase of the case, when the statements attributed to such persons have been sifted, it was found in each instance that the witness did not himself know that Mr. Roosevelt had drank to excess, or that if he had made such claim, he was unwilling to testify. It is fair to the plaintiff to state that I have been unable to find in any section of the country any individual witness who is willing to state that he has personally seen Mr. Roosevelt drink to excess. I have taken the testimony in the form of depositions of more than forty reputable witnesses who have expressed the opinion that on those occasions as to which they testify, he was intoxicated. I believe all these witnesses were honest in making their statements. I have relied upon those witnesses, but have recognized the lesser opportunities they have had to observe the plaintiff and his habits.

"I have been profoundly impressed during the progress of this trial by the nature and extent of the evidence produced by the plaintiff to the extent that he did not in fact use liquor to excess on any occasion. I am unwilling to believe that these eminent men would purposely misstate the facts, or that under the circumstances related by them and their intimate acquaintance with the plaintiff for so many years, they could be mistaken as to his habits. I have, therefore, been forced to believe that those who have given depositions or made the statement that in their opinion on the occasions to which they refer Mr. Roosevelt was intoxicated, had insufficient means and opportunity of correctly observing him, and were mistaken.

"Up to the time of this trial I had believed that the statements made in the article which I published were entirely warranted. But in the face of the unqualified testimony of so many distinguished men who have been in position for years to know the truth, I am forced to the conclusion that I was mistaken. I am unwilling longer to assert that Mr. Roosevelt actually and in fact drank to excess. As a publisher of a newspaper, I have never knowingly done injustice to any man, and neither I nor my attorneys are willing now to make or continue the assertion of an unjust charge against the plaintiff in this case. We have reached the conclusion that to continue expressly or implicitly to assert that Mr. Roosevelt drank to excess or actually became intoxicated as set forth in the article would do him an injustice. Since in publishing the article I acted honestly and in good faith, I propose at this time and throughout the remainder of the case to occupy a like position. My position throughout the introduction of my defense is and will be that in the publication, I acted in good faith and without malice."

Mr. Newett finished reading the statement and then stared straight in front of him, as if to wait to see how his words were received.

Matthew was uncertain what to expect next, but when Roosevelt's attorney, Mr. Van Benschoten, stood and said, "If the Court please, the plaintiff has asked me to ask the Court if he may have the privilege of making a statement," Matthew realized all of this must have been planned behind the scenes. Apparently, the plaintiff and defendant's lawyers had come to some sort of agreement before the trial began today.

Judge Flannigan nodded at Mr. Van Benschoten's proposal and said, "The privilege is accorded."

Colonel Roosevelt then rose to his feet, and from his seat, he spoke loudly and clearly, grinning with satisfaction all the while. "Your Honor, in view of the statement of the defendant, I ask the Court to instruct the jury that I desire only minimal damages. I did not go into this suit for money. I did not go into it for any vindictive purpose. I went into it, and as the Court has said, I made my reputation an issue, because I wished, once for all during my lifetime, thoroughly and comprehensively to deal with these slanders, so that never again will it be possible for any man, in good faith, to repeat them. I have achieved my purpose, and I am content."

Matthew could not help but admire Roosevelt's graciousness at this moment. He could well have asked for much greater damages.

Mr. Newett's attorney, Mr. Belden, then requested, "May I ask the indulgence of the Court to give us a recess of ten or fifteen minutes?"

"It will be granted," said Judge Flannigan.

The recess was brief. No one left his or her seat in the courtroom save the attorneys and Judge Flannigan.

After a few minutes, they all returned and resumed their places in the courtroom. Mr. Belden then said, "In view of the statement made by the plaintiff in this case, we have determined that further testimony will be unnecessary, and we, therefore, rest our case."

Roosevelt's attorney, Mr. Pound, then requested, "May it please Your Honor, not only upon the statement of the defendant himself, and the concession of the plaintiff, as to what he claims, I ask Your Honor to direct a verdict in this case in favor of the plaintiff as matter of law."

It was almost over now. Matthew knew they would have a verdict shortly.

Judge Flannigan turned to the jurors and gave them their instructions. First, he reviewed the case for them, clarifying for them the definition of libel and what a newspaper can and cannot print without violating libel laws. He reviewed briefly the evidence heard and also that Newett had conceded freely that a mistake had been made in his publication. Then Judge Flannigan clarified for the jurors that not only must they determine whether or not the defendant was guilty of liable, but that if he were found guilty, a verdict in the plaintiff's favor of a substantial amount would be warranted up to the sum of ten thousand dollars.

Flannigan then concluded by stating, "But, as the Court is advised by the plaintiff, the object of the plaintiff in bringing and prosecuting this action being the vindication of his good name and reputation, and not the recovery of a money judgment; and he having in open court freely waived his right to the assessment of his actual damages, it only remains for the Court to direct a verdict in his favor for nominal damages, which, under the law of Michigan, is the sum of six cents.

"You are, therefore, gentlemen, directed to render a verdict in favor of the plaintiff for that amount."

It couldn't be more cut and dried than that, thought Matthew. *Of course, the jurors could refuse, but they have basically been told what to do.*

Before the jury could move or speak, Mr. Pound rose and requested, "So that it may appear on the record, I formally ask your Honor to enter an order for the suppression of the depositions not used."

Well done, thought Matthew. Judge Flannigan did not hesitate in ordering that all depositions not read during the trial, by agreement of both parties, be withdrawn from the case's files and destroyed. No one would ever now see the depositions Newett had gathered to aid his side of the trial. Roosevelt's reputation was cleared for all time.

The jury now retired.

"Every American is born lucky."
— *The Prince of Pilsen*

CHAPTER 25

SHORT RECESS OCCURRED. NO ONE left the courtroom because everyone was certain the jury would not deliberate long and no one wanted to miss the verdict.

After the jurors filed back into the courtroom and seated themselves, Judge Flannigan called upon them for the verdict. When half the jurors stood, uncertain of the protocol, Judge Flannigan requested, "Foreman Mathews, what is the verdict?" The other jurors then sat down. William Mathews stood up and gave the verdict.

"The jury finds for Theodore Roosevelt," Mathews replied.

"Is that the finding of the entire jury?" asked Judge Flannigan.

The jurors all nodded their heads in agreement.

"What is the nominal damages assessed?"

"The said defendant is guilty in manner and form as the said plaintiff hath, in his declaration in this cause, complained against him," replied Mathews, "and we assess damages of the plaintiff on occasion of the premises at the sum of six cents."

Judge Flannigan then announced that the court was adjourned and banged his gavel. After he rose and departed the courtroom, everyone in the courtroom jumped up. Colonel Roosevelt quickly walked over to the jury and cordially shook each member's hand.

Matthew and Homer tried to make their way forward. They could not get near Roosevelt, but they ended up in the path of the foreman, Mathews, whom they asked for further comment.

"What convinced you that the plaintiff was innocent of the libel charges?" Homer asked the foreman.

"After Mr. Roosevelt's testimony," said Mathews, "I think we were impressed chiefly with that of Mr. Garfield and Mr. Riis. The statement of Mr.

Newett himself that he could not doubt that Mr. Roosevelt was a temperate man after considering the character of the witnesses was just how we felt."

Matthew and Homer thanked Mr. Mathews and then found a way through the crowd to overhear what Roosevelt was saying to some of the other reporters.

"That's enough. Not a word, not another word, boys," Roosevelt said, but then, as an afterthought, he added, "But you can express my appreciation of the services of my counsel, James H. Pound, William S. Hill, and William A. Van Benschoten." And then Roosevelt saw Judge Flannigan reenter the room without his robes, and smiling while looking at the judge, the colonel said loud enough for Flannigan to hear, "And Judge Flannigan has given us a model of the conduct which should distinguish the conduct of the highest court in the land."

Roosevelt tried to make his way to Judge Flannigan now to shake his hand, but first he was interrupted by the reporter from *The New York Times* asking him, "Are you going down to Mr. Shiras' camp now that the trial is over?"

"I am off to New York at 5:30, if I can get accommodations," replied Roosevelt. "I have to get back to my desk. I am a working man, you see."

Matthew noticed that Shiras was not smiling at this remark, but nor did he look surprised.

"Are you and Newett going to meet?" the reporter persisted.

"Not if the advances come from me," said Roosevelt, looking around and causing everyone else to notice that Newett was departing the courtroom, accompanied by his lawyers and his son, Will. He had taken his defeat like a man, and despite his current illness, he would live to publish many another issue of the *Iron Ore*.

Roosevelt now shook Judge Flannigan's hand and then made his way into the judge's private chambers for a few minutes, perhaps to hide until the reporters left. The reporters started collecting their belongings while the courtroom spectators also began to depart.

"That was quite the experience," said Homer to Matthew as they headed out of the courtroom and into the hall.

"Yes, it certainly was," said Matthew. "I imagine people in Marquette will be talking about this trial for more than a hundred years."

"People all over the Upper Peninsula will," Homer added, as they went down the courthouse stairs. "Well, it was a pleasure meeting you." And he shook Matthew's hand. "Perhaps we'll run into each other again sometime. I better get going now if I want to get a seat on the train back to Houghton this afternoon."

"The pleasure was all mine," Matthew replied. "Have a safe trip home."

"You too," said Homer.

Judge Flannigan

Once they were outside, Homer took off down the courtroom steps toward the hotel to fetch his belongings and catch his train. A few other reporters lingered about. They all came up to shake Matthew's hand and wish him luck with his story, a wish he returned. There was general goodwill among them all, but in truth, they were all lingering about for one purpose—to see whether they could get further comment from Roosevelt when he emerged.

They didn't have long to wait. A few minutes later, Roosevelt came down the steps with his lawyers and Frank Tyree by his side. He did not hesitate but moved swiftly, not wanting to answer further questions, but one brave reporter called out to him, "What do you intend to do with your nickel and a penny?"

Roosevelt stopped, turned around, laughed, and replied, "Six cents is the *price* of a good newspaper."

Everyone present laughed, knowing by now that an issue of the *Iron Ore* only cost three cents.

And then Roosevelt walked to Shiras' automobile and was driven away.

Matthew, feeling exhausted now that the trial was over, decided to go to the library to write his dispatch and get it all down on paper before he forgot any of it, despite the copious notes he had scribbled throughout the morning. He could then go downtown to the Western Union office to send it off since the courthouse would be closing up shortly.

What a morning it had been!

Roosevelt and witnesses leaving the Marquette County Courthouse
Left to Right:
Frank Tyree, John O'Laughlin, Theodore Roosevelt, and Unknown

Letter from Theodore Roosevelt to his sister
Anna Roosevelt Cowles[2]

Marquette

Michigan

May 31st, 1913

Darling Bye:

It was dear of you to write; and tell Hopkinson I was much pleased by his message. But I had all the witnesses I could use; and the libeler finally capitulated. I deemed it best not to demand money damages; the man is a country editor, and while I thoroughly despise him, I do not care to seem to persecute him. I wished once for all to expose the infamy of these slanders, so that never again would I need to notice them; and I have achieved my purpose. The way my friends rallied has been really very touching. We have been very comfortable, for we have been staying in the big pleasant house of George Shiras, who is a trump, if ever there was one.

I am looking forward to a week from Saturday. By the way, I wish to ask Will some questions about the Admirals on the cruise of the battle fleet round the world.

Goodbye, dearest Bye.

YOUR OWN BROTHER.

---

2   Reprinted from *Letters from Theodore Roosevelt to Anna Roosevelt Cowles 1870-1918*. New York: Charles Scribner's Sons, 1924.

CHAPTER 26

AFTER WRITING HIS DISPATCH, MATTHEW was in no mood to head back to Roger and Delia's house. He was still irritated with Roger from the evening before, and since it was Saturday, Roger would most likely be home all afternoon. The thought crossed Matthew's mind that he could suggest they go fishing that afternoon—Delia and Lydia would probably like to have Roger out of their hair while they busied themselves with last minute wedding details—but Matthew also knew there was a chance he could see Roosevelt again at five-thirty when his train would depart, and he wouldn't be doing his duty by the *Empire Sentinel* if he missed any last words Roosevelt might have about the trial. Therefore, he wandered over to the Hotel Marquette to get a late lunch. A few other newsmen were about, planning to leave at various times that afternoon, several of them on the five-thirty train Roosevelt would be departing on. Matthew lingered with them, talking over the trial some more, and then about four-thirty, they all headed over to the depot, most to leave, but a few, like Matthew, just to watch Roosevelt and his party depart.

The train was already at the depot when Matthew reached it, and soon a caravan of automobiles were making their way downtown and parking at the train station. Most of the vehicles contained Marquette's famous visitors, but several celebrity seekers were among them, hoping for a last glimpse of some of the nation's most famous politicians.

Roosevelt arrived in the backseat of Shiras' automobile. He was smiling boldly, appearing completely triumphant, and waving at all the people gathered along the street and around the depot to wish him goodbye.

Besides George, accompanying Roosevelt were James R. Garfield, former secretary of the interior; O.K. Davis, secretary of the national Progressive committee; Lawrence Abbott, president of the *Outlook* company, for whose magazine Roosevelt was contributing editor; William Loeb, Jr., Roosevelt's former secretary; and J. Sloan and Frank H. Tyree, his former bodyguards. They were all busy collecting their luggage and making their way to the train.

The newspapermen also climbed onto the train, eager to find the best seats and make sure their luggage was stored. George was not above helping with the luggage for his guests, and Matthew, farther down the platform and without being asked, happily pitched in a hand by carrying a couple of suitcases onto the train for his colleagues.

Matthew was just stepping off the train when he saw George walking down the platform toward him.

"Matthew, come down to Theodore's car," said George. "The train isn't leaving for another fifteen minutes, and I'm sure Theodore would like to say goodbye to you."

As a gentleman, Matthew would have deferred from troubling the colonel as he prepared to leave Marquette, but as a newshound, he could not decline the invitation. He quickly followed George to Roosevelt's railroad car, both exchanging words about their delight over the verdict as they walked. Matthew was pleased when he reached the car to see a few other newsmen also there.

Roosevelt thought nothing of shaking all of their hands as they entered the car.

"Thank you all for your fair and impartial reporting, especially those of you whom I suspect were prejudiced in my favor," he said, grinning broadly. "Of course, I haven't been able to read all your stories, but I trust none of you would dare to print anything against me now."

A general roar went up among the men.

"We need honest, good-natured, and courageous newsmen," Roosevelt continued. "The press is a vital part of this nation and necessary for it to stay a true democracy, but that can only continue if it reports the truth. When men in power act dishonorably, it is the duty of the press to publicize it so the populace stays informed."

Everyone clapped at these words.

"I'd open a bottle of champagne and make a toast to Marquette for hosting me if I had anything to drink on the train, but I think you all know I don't," said Roosevelt, still smiling and now winking, causing everyone to clap.

Then Roosevelt went around and shook everyone's hand again, speaking a few individual words to each man.

Soon, the train whistle blew, giving its two-minute warning before departure.

Matthew had stepped aside so that he would be last to speak to the former president. Somehow, he had managed to position himself next to George, and Roosevelt, knowing he only had time for a few words, addressed them both simultaneously.

"I envy you folks living here," said Roosevelt.

"Well, I don't live here anymore," said Matthew.

"And I only summer here," said George.

"Nevertheless, I sense Marquette is still your home and always will be. It's a beautiful town. There are good, honest hard-working Americans here, and you are fortunate to be in a place so close to nature. In the big cities, you don't have that connection. Fortunately, I can get away from New York and Washington and be at Oyster Bay most of the time. A man can lose his soul if he doesn't get away to nature now and then. What is it Wordsworth said? 'The world is too much with us'?"

"Very true," agreed Matthew.

"We all need to hold on to that still small voice in our souls that tells us who we are, and we have to fight when the world tries to tell us otherwise," said Roosevelt.

"Yes, you proved that to us through this trial," George agreed. "Well, we better get going. I'm sure I'll see you soon in Washington, Theodore."

"Thank you, Colonel," said Matthew as Roosevelt shook his hand.

"Best wishes to you," Roosevelt replied.

And then, just as they felt the train start to move, George and Matthew disembarked. Roosevelt gave them a wave and then headed for his seat.

"It'll be a long time before Marquette sees another event like this," said George as he and Matthew walked across the platform. "Would you like a ride back to your sister's?"

"Thank you. I would appreciate that," said Matthew, feeling goodwill toward everyone at the moment.

They climbed into the automobile and George started it up.

"I wish Theodore could have stayed a little longer," said George as he pulled out onto the street. "I'm sure he would have loved to see the camp."

"Yes," said Matthew. "He would have really enjoyed it. Do you plan to go out there anyway?"

"I don't know," said George. "I guess not, unless you want to come along."

"I wish I could," said Matthew, "but I have my niece's wedding to attend tomorrow."

"Oh, that's right," said George.

"And then I'll be leaving for New York on Monday."

"I'm going to head back to Washington to see Frances," said George. "I'll probably take the train tomorrow night."

"Why don't you come to the wedding tomorrow then?" said Matthew, surprising himself a bit that he was making the invitation. "You can come as my guest, and I'm sure Delia would be happy to have you."

"Well, I have some packing and such to do, but I might be able to stop by. What time will it be?"

"It's at one o'clock, and the reception will be right after. It's going to be in the backyard, nothing overly fancy…surprisingly."

George laughed. "Why's that?"

"I'm not sure," said Matthew. "I think Lydia would like a big wedding, but I don't think Lysander is a church-going man."

"Just between you and me," added George, "I think the Blackmores have always been rather tight with their money, but then again, I may be wrong in this case since I imagine the bride's parents paid for the wedding."

"The bride's father can be tight too," said Matthew, who couldn't help himself since *tight* could have a double-meaning, although George didn't pick up on his joke.

"Well, I'll stop by if I can," said George, now pulling the car up in front of the Richardson home.

Matthew thanked George for the ride and waved goodbye as he pulled away. He then turned to go up the front walk, but he was stopped before he could climb the steps.

U. P. B. Co.
Marquette

Castle-Brew

U. P. B. Co.
Marquette

Upper Peninsula Brewing Company

The New Bottled Beer in Brown Bottles

*made and bottled in the Biggest, Best and
Most Sanitary Brewery in
Upper Michigan.*

THE HOME
OF
CASTLE-BREW

THE HOME
OF
CASTLE-BREW

In introducing our new beer — Castle-Brew — we do so with every assurance that it will meet with popular favor. We have taken the greatest of care in the selection of materials for the new brew.

It is absolutely right in Flavor, Purity and Excellence of Quality.

With our new and modern equipment, we are able to put on the market a bottled beer such as you can enjoy in your home, your club or your favorite bar.

Try a Case Today.

Upper Peninsula Brewing Company

MARQUETTE

June 2, 1913 *Mining Journal* ad for the Upper Peninsula Brewing Company, commonly referred to as the Castle Brewery.

CHAPTER 27

As Matthew approached the front steps of Delia and Roger's house, the door swung open and half-a-dozen young men, some walking backwards out the door, came tromping out of the house and down the steps. Matthew only barely missed being trodden down by them, and then he realized they were carrying Lysander, who was sprawled out across their arms.

"Oh, pardon me, sir," said the young man closest to Matthew, who had nearly stepped on his feet.

The men were singing, "For he's a jolly good fellow," and sort of tossing Lysander, who was gesticulating wildly with his hands but not seeming to object to his airborne position. As the young men carried Lysander to the street, Matthew turned to watch them, wondering what on earth was going on. Then he heard, "Oh, Uncle Matthew!"

Turning, he saw Lydia coming out onto the porch. "Oh, I'm so glad you're not too late," she told Matthew.

"Too late for what?" he asked as Roger now emerged behind Lydia with his hat in his hand.

"Why, Lysander's bachelor party," she replied. "The boys came to get him—a total surprise. We thought we were going to have a quiet dinner together, but, of course, I can't refuse him his bachelor party."

"Oh," said Matthew, not clear whether Lydia meant he was himself invited to the party, and if so, unsure whether he wanted to go.

"Is the trial over?" asked Roger, coming down the steps.

"Yes," said Matthew.

"And the verdict?" Roger asked.

"Guilty. Newett had to pay Roosevelt minimal damages," said Matthew.

"Quit talking business!" shouted Lysander, who by now had been lifted and placed into a horse and carriage that had just arrived, though with all the singing and shouting, Matthew had not heard it approach. "Let's get going. Come along, old man!"

Matthew didn't know whether the last remark was directed at him or Roger, but either way, he didn't like it. Still, when Roger put on his hat and quickly walked toward the carriage, Matthew could see the future father-in-law was at his future son-in-law's beck and call. *I wonder whether they'll go fishing together*, Matthew mused.

Once Roger reached the carriage, and before he let the young men give him a hand up, he turned around to ask Matthew, "Are you coming?"

"Where are we going?" asked Matthew. But before anyone could reply, two of Lysander's young friends had grabbed his arms and were pulling him toward the carriage.

"Where all good bachelors go the night before they're wed!" shouted Lysander.

"And where is that?" asked Matthew, afraid of the answer. Were there still houses of ill repute down by the docks like there had been in his own youth?

Unable to resist the thrust to his buttocks from the young men, Matthew nearly fell into the carriage, apparently having no choice in whether he would go. Roger was already inside by now, and he scooted over to give Matthew room. Soon, the other men were all jumping in, cramming in between Matthew and the carriage's side; one young man sat on the floor, sprawled out between Matthew, Roger, and Lysander's feet. No one had bothered to answer Matthew's question. He did not bother to ask again. He would have gotten out if he could have moved his legs, but it was too late. The horse had started moving. He was trapped—imprisoned—so he decided he might as well try to have a good time.

Matthew was relieved when the carriage did not turn east toward the lake but rather west and then south down the hill on Front Street and west again on Washington. All the way, the men were singing the drinking song from the comic opera *Robin Hood*, although they barely knew any of the words, save the chorus, which they just kept repeating:

> So laugh, lads, and quaff lads
> T'will make you stout and hail

For all my days

I'll sing the praise

Of Brown October ale.

By Fourth Street, they had grown tired of the song and were instead passing a bottle of whiskey around while a couple of them yelled at the onlookers, "We're holding the funeral services for a bachelor today, ladies!" and "Watch out, mister, or you might be next!"

"Where are we going?" Matthew asked again, this time turning to Roger and practically shouting in his ear.

"The Castle Brewery!" Roger shouted back as the carriage whizzed along, followed by another with several more young men in it whom Matthew didn't know.

"Where is that?" Matthew asked.

"The old Upper Peninsula Brewing Company's beer garden," said Roger. "Everyone calls it the Castle Brewery now that they changed the beer's name from Drei Kaiser to Castle Brew to fit the look of the building."

"Oh," said Matthew; he remembered the structure from when he had lived in Marquette as a young man. "I haven't been there in years."

"You won't even recognize the place now," said Roger. "It looks like a giant sandstone castle. They've got a pond and a beer garden and even some summer cottages for people to stay at."

"And the boys have reserved the whole place for my bachelor party," Lysander added in a lucid moment between the verses of yet another drinking song.

It was well over a mile to the brewery, but they made fast time, the young men driving the horses on at a dangerous speed, but it was evening now and there was little traffic. Matthew thought it less likely they would hit a pedestrian than that one of the young fools in the carriage would fall out and crush his head the way they were all jumping about. At one point, the one who had been lying on Matthew's feet had gotten up and decided it was more comfortable to stand during the ride. Once or twice, though, he nearly toppled over onto Matthew or Roger. By all appearances, the young man was already drunk before he'd even gotten to the brewery.

The Castle Brewery, circa 1913

When the brewery came into view, the men set up another hullabaloo. They were answered by more shouts and cheers from a crowd of young men already at the brewery and waiting for them.

Before Matthew knew it, the carriage had come to a stop and he was being pulled out of the carriage with Roger stumbling behind him. Lysander was again lifted up, this time on a couple of his friends' shoulders—Matthew couldn't help wondering how someone like Lysander could have so many friends. His friends carried Lysander through the door, miraculously not smacking his head as he bent down to make his entrance.

Matthew and Roger followed, or rather Roger followed and Matthew followed him, straight up to the bar where Lysander was still perched on the men's shoulders.

"Drinks on the house!" cried Lysander.

"You ain't paying!" argued one of his friends.

Someone paid, but Matthew didn't see who. Too many members of the bachelor party had surged around him, fighting to get close to the pitcher of beer put out for them. A pretty barmaid glared at them, then picked up the pitcher and gingerly poured out a glass for each of them.

"Music!" someone demanded.

"Yes, music!" several others joined in.

A player piano was in one corner, and one of the young men got it going, sitting down with his beer as if he were playing it with one hand and drinking with the other, and spilling no small amount over its ivory keys.

Then the young men surged out into the garden. Matthew gladly followed, preferring to have more elbow room than could be found in the building itself with all these young wannabe Bacchuses about. The night air was growing cooler by now, and Matthew was glad of it. He set down his beer on a table along the side of the garden where he would be removed from the fracas if things got out of hand. Then he took off his suit coat, which he had worn all through the warm day, having wanted to look presentable in the courtroom and when he said goodbye to Colonel Roosevelt. What a difference an hour could bring. He had just parted from a man who had fought in court all week to save his reputation and prove he was not a drinking man, and here a couple of dozen young men thought nothing of intoxicating themselves as quickly as possible. Was this what the next generation would be like? It made him wish prohibition would become the law of the land.

Matthew sat down and sipped his first beer, while watching the young men guzzle down their seconds and thirds—and Roger was doing his best to keep up with them. They all continued their singing and joking and making impromptu speeches in Lysander's honor; not a few of the speeches had suggestive comments about what would happen on the wedding night with bits of advice for how Lysander should perform—comments that surprised Matthew considering the bride's father was present—was there no sense of propriety anymore? But Roger appeared too sloshed to notice.

Finally, Roger made his way over to where Matthew was sitting. "Is that still your first?" he asked, his voice slurring noticeably.

"Yes," Matthew admitted, although his glass was almost empty now.

"Fill 'er up!" shouted Roger, grabbing the arm of the barmaid as she passed by with the pitcher. Nearly wrestling her for it, Roger managed to get her to refill Matthew's glass—a glass Matthew had no intention of emptying again.

"To my new son-in-law," said Roger, sitting down and raising his glass to clink it against Matthew's. Matthew raised his glass to humor Roger, but after the clinking, he set it back down on the table without drinking from it while Roger downed his.

"You know what you are?" said Roger when he saw Matthew had not drank anything. "You're a self-righteous prig; that's what you are."

"Is that so?" said Matthew, half-snorting at the remark. He was more amused than willing to argue with a drunk.

"Prig. A big, big pig of a prig. Get it? Prig of a pig. I mean pig of a prig. You're a hog—you eat so much priggery that you…that you…well, you can't eat anything else. You're a prig pig, a big pig prig…."

Roger was muttering and looking confused, like it was all he could do to form his words. The rhymes were too much of a tongue-twister for him. And then he reached for Matthew's beer, but Matthew pulled it away from him.

"Prig. A big pig prig, prig," he continued to mutter. And then he laid his head on the table, and in another moment, he was snoring.

Matthew was not a cruel man, but even he could not help feeling tempted to pour his glass of beer on Roger's head to wake him up. Yet he restrained himself.

Once the sky started to darken and the stars became visible, Matthew hoped they would soon all be heading for home. Matthew just sat there, listening to Roger snore and making sure he didn't fall onto the ground. None of the young men spoke to him or paid any attention to Roger. After about an hour of this, as Matthew himself began to feel sleepy, Lysander came over to join Matthew and Roger. It took the bridegroom a minute since his wobbly legs decided to take the scenic route to the table, swishing back and forth like a skier before he finally managed to slalom into a chair beside Matthew.

"Drunk, hey?" he said, looking first at Roger and then at Matthew for a response.

"I guess so," said Matthew.

"He never could hold his liquor," said Lysander.

"I know it," said Matthew.

"Let me tell you something about your brother-in-law," said Lysander.

Matthew raised his eyebrows, not thinking there was anything about his brother-in-law he didn't already know or couldn't guess at.

"You think he's successful, don't you?" said Lysander. Matthew could smell the liquor on the young man's breath from two feet away.

"I guess," said Matthew, "though he inherited the business from his father."

"That might be," said Lysander, "but that man has drunk himself into pauperism."

Matthew's eyes grew large.

"Surprised, hey?" said Lysander. "But it's true. The only thing standing between him and the poorhouse is yours truly."

Lysander reached over for Matthew's still untouched glass of beer and swallowed half of it down. Matthew did not protest.

"Yes, sir," said Lysander. "He's had trouble making his mortgage payments to the bank on that fancy new office he built several years back. Therefore, since I work at the bank, I took it upon myself to befriend him—and his daughter."

Matthew inhaled and then exhaled out of his nostrils before saying, "I'm not sure I should be hearing this, especially not when you're drinking, and—"

"What's wrong, Uncle Matthew?" asked Lysander, setting the glass down hard on the table. "Does the truth hurt? You know your brother-in-law's a drunk. He can barely show up to his office three days a week. His employees do everything for him, and now they know that what I tell them to do is as good as if it came from him. Who do you think has been making the mortgage payments on his office building for the last two years? And what have I gotten in return for it?"

Matthew didn't want to hear what Lysander might say next, but he couldn't pull himself away.

"I've gotten nothing but trouble," Lysander went on. "There hasn't been any profit. No profit because he let himself sink so far into debt that all I've gotten is a lot of hard work with nothing to show for it until now. But now, now we're just about at the breaking even point, and then there will be a little profit for all my troubles. Besides, once I'm married to Lydia, I'll be inheriting everything from Roger and Delia—and I'll make sure the business shows a profit; I've already put men in place to run it properly for me. Yes, sir, your sister and Roger would've been down at the poor farm by now if it wasn't for me. Of course, Lydia doesn't realize it, but only because she shouldn't have to worry her pretty head over business—that's not what wives are for."

Matthew was tempted to ask a question, but he wasn't sure he wanted to know the answer to it. He soon discovered he had no need to—Lysander was drunk enough to reveal all his cards tonight.

"Your sister knows, yes she does, and so does Roger. They know on what side their bread is buttered. Lydia didn't like me so much at first, but now she thinks I'm all kindness because her parents tell her I have a good head for business and her father has taken me on as a partner—and who wouldn't want a banker as his partner? She thinks her father likes me—hah, the man hates me, and I won't deny that the feeling is mutual—I mean, just look at the slobbering idiot."

Matthew couldn't help looking at his brother-in-law then, intoxicated to the point of being unconscious. Lysander was obviously a braggart and probably a bully, but that didn't mean his words were untrue. Matthew had long wondered how Roger hadn't run the business into the ground already.

"Lydia thinks her father likes me so much that he invited me to invest in the company. She thinks I'm a hero for how I've helped her father's business flourish, but she doesn't know I've actually saved it and her whole family from bankruptcy; even so, her parents have praised me so much as a result that how could she not have fallen in love with me?"

Poor Lydia, thought Matthew. *Her father has made a Faustian pact with the devil, and she knows nothing about it, even though she's the sacrificial lamb.*

"Excuse me," said Matthew, now standing up. "I think I better take Roger home."

"Oh, let him be," said Lysander.

"No," said Matthew. "It's getting late and I'm getting tired myself. Roger and I aren't young like you, you know, so I'll take him home."

"Do whatever you want, but you keep your mouth shut about what I just said," said Lysander.

Matthew ignored him and started to nudge Roger awake. Roger groaned but eventually stood up, as if sleepwalking. Matthew put Roger's arm around his shoulders and tried to get him to walk forward, but Roger took one step and crumbled at the knees, falling to the ground.

"Out cold, huh?" said one of Lysander's friends, approaching them. "Here, let me help you."

Lysander simply sat smirking at their attempts as Matthew and the young man struggled to get Roger off the ground. Finally, the young man grabbed Roger from behind and pulled him half up by his back belt loop and onto his feet. Then he pushed Roger's torso up into a standing position. Next, Matthew put Roger's arm around his shoulders again, and with the young man's help, he got Roger outside and into a waiting carriage. After giving the driver directions and thanking the young man, Matthew and Roger were on their way home.

The cool night air felt like a nice breeze as the carriage headed back along Washington Street. Roger was laid out on the seat across from Matthew, groaning all the way. Returning to New York seemed like an even better idea to Matthew now.

When they reached the house, Matthew was grateful when the carriage driver offered to help him with Roger. And it was none too soon because Roger had barely stepped down from the carriage before he vomited all over the front lawn.

That'll be lovely for the wedding guests to see in the morning, thought Matthew.

He then got Roger to walk unsteadily to the door. He'd been basically unconscious for an hour now, and not having had a drink in over an hour, his earlier drinks were starting to wear off a bit.

Matthew didn't know how he managed it, but somehow, he got Roger up the steps into the house. He took one look at the stairway in the hall and knew that attempting to reach Roger's bedroom would be impossible, so he walked his brother-in-law into the parlor and got him to lie down on the couch.

"Good enough," Matthew muttered, and then he made his own way to bed.

"There is not the slightest doubt that Colonel Roosevelt is a mightier and more potent political influence in this country as a result of this trial than ever he has been before. There is no doubt at all that a great many people honestly were of the opinion that they had seen the Colonel intoxicated upon numerous occasions. At the same time, in view of the testimony and in view of the verdict, that intoxication was the exuberance of high nervous tension of a naturally active man. To many who had never seen Mr. Roosevelt in action, his enthusiasm at the conclusion of the trial might easily be mistaken for the intoxication that comes from too liberal consumption of alcoholic stimulants. During the trial he exhibited nervousness all the time and his facial contortions were those of a highly strung individual to whom some kind of action is always necessary to give vent to unusual mental strain. The verdict is proof conclusive that the numerous tales which have been so generally circulated were based entirely upon erroneous premises, in many cases honestly expressed, but untrue nevertheless."

— editorial by Homer Guck, *The Houghton Mining Gazette*

SUNDAY
JUNE 1, 1913

"Town's dull? Well, rather. T.R. was certainly invigorating."
— *The Mining Journal*, June 3, 1913

CHAPTER 28

"**W**HERE'S ROGER?" ASKED MATTHEW WHEN he came down to breakfast.

"He has one of his migraines," said Delia, looking up from her plate.

"Poor Dad was so tired last night he fell asleep on the couch," said Lydia.

"He didn't fall asleep there," said Matthew, taking his seat at the dining room table. "He was drunk. It was all I could do to get him in the house, so I left him there rather than try to half-carry him upstairs."

"He was still there when I got up this morning," said Delia. "I helped him upstairs so he could get dressed. Hopefully, he'll be down soon once his headache wears off."

"It's not a headache," said Matthew. "He has a hangover, and probably a really terrible one."

Lydia changed the subject, having more urgent things to worry about—so much had to be done this morning for the wedding. People had been hired to set up the chairs on the lawn, and Mrs. Honeywell, Martha, and two hired girls were scurrying about in the kitchen to be ready for the luncheon after the ceremony.

"You better get upstairs and get ready, Lydia," said Delia when they had almost finished eating.

"It's only nine o'clock, Mother."

"Yes, but you need to have your hair fixed, and what if Lysander should stop by? It's bad luck for the groom to see his bride on the wedding day."

Right then, the front doorbell rang, and in a second, Martha appeared to say the dressmaker was there as was one of the bridesmaids who was going to help with Lydia's hair.

"See," said Delia. "There's no time to lose."

"What would you like me to do?" asked Matthew as Lydia went out into the hall to show the dressmaker and bridesmaid up to her room.

"Oh, I don't know, Matthew," said Delia. "Maybe you could go outside and make sure everything is set up properly. We need chairs for about one hundred people, and make sure they set up tables for the food and that the chairs are all clean and not damp, and any other little thing you can do."

"All right," said Matthew. "What about Roger, though? He still hasn't come downstairs."

"I'll see to him," said Delia.

"Bring him some coffee to sober him up," suggested Matthew before going outside to help with the setup.

A few minutes later, Matthew found himself enlisted in carrying chairs around the lawn, and then he helped the florists when they arrived. Flower arrangements were far from his area of expertise, but he placed them as needed wherever he was told. The maids came out with tablecloths he helped to arrange, and he went inside to find Roger's keys and move the automobile into the garage so it would be out of the way. When he didn't know what else he could possibly do, he looked at his watch and saw it was eleven-thirty. "I better go change," he said to Martha, entering by the back kitchen door. "The guests will be arriving soon. If anyone asks for me, tell them I'll be down in a few minutes."

He headed for the stairs in the main hall, forgetting he could take the back stairs. He was just about to start up the stairs when he heard someone sobbing in the parlor.

Not wanting to obtrude, but curious, he leaned in just enough to see who was crying without, hopefully, being seen. Even though Lydia was his niece, he didn't think she would want him comforting her, but he thought maybe the girl had finally realized she wasn't marrying the right man.

But it turned out to be Delia, sitting alone on the sofa, with her head in her hands.

"What's wrong?" Matthew asked her, stepping into the room.

She looked up and tried to wipe her tears with her sleeve.

"It's Roger," she said. "He won't even get out of bed."

Matthew's heart broke for her as she stared up at him with big red eyes.

"Here," said Matthew, walking over and handing her his handkerchief. "You can't have red eyes for the wedding."

"There isn't going to be any wedding the way things are going," said Delia, accepting the handkerchief.

"Of course there'll be a wedding," he replied as she blew her nose.

"How can there be," she continued, "if there's no one to give away the bride?"

"I'll go talk to him," said Matthew.

"No, you'll just make him angry."

"Then that will be two of us," said Matthew. "He can't spoil his daughter's wedding day."

"No, Matthew," said Delia. "It's no use. He's impossible when he gets into these moods."

"Well, at least I can try," said Matthew. "Now come upstairs with me. You better get changed and dry those eyes. The guests will be arriving before you know it."

He took her by the hand and somehow managed to get her to stand up. Then he led her to the stairs.

"Oh, what will we do with so many people coming?" Delia fretted.

"I told you I'll take care of it," Matthew repeated. "Now you go get dressed and don't think about anything else."

He walked her upstairs to her dressing room. She and Roger each had their own on opposite sides of their bedroom, and each dressing room had a separate entrance into the hallway. Matthew saw that the door from Delia's dressing room into the bedroom was open so he went into the dressing room with her.

"Oh, I can't imagine the shame if the wedding is canceled," Delia muttered, looking into the bedroom where Roger was sprawled across the mattress.

"The wedding won't be canceled," Matthew repeated. He couldn't help wondering, though, whether Lydia might not be better off if it were, given what Lysander had said to him last night. The insufferable man had acted like Lydia was now his property. Regardless, Matthew said, "Get dressed and I'll see to Roger," and before Delia could say more, he stepped into the bedroom, firmly closing her dressing room door behind him.

For a moment, Matthew didn't know what he was going to do. Part of him wanted to grab Roger by the leg, yank him off the bed and onto the floor, and then tower over him, telling him just how much he despised him for making Delia and Lydia's lives so miserable. But he also knew Delia would hear every word he said, and he did not want to upset her further, so he just sat down on the bed and gently tapped Roger on the shoulder.

"What?" moaned Roger, not even raising his head to see who it was.

But at least now Matthew knew the drunkard was conscious.

"Roger, it's Matthew. In case you forgot, your daughter's getting married today and the guests will be arriving any minute. We have to get you dressed, and you probably need a quick bath too so you don't smell like booze."

That last part sounded mean, but given the situation, Matthew felt he had the right to be a little sharp with his brother-in-law.

"Ain't gonna be no wedding," Roger replied.

"What do you mean?" Matthew demanded. "Lydia's putting on her wedding gown right this minute, and Lysander is probably already on his way here."

"That bastard," muttered Roger.

"What do you mean?" asked Matthew.

"The bastard has bled me dry."

"Well, we can't discuss that now," said Matthew. "We have to get you dressed."

"Get away from me," said Roger as Matthew took his arm and tried to pull him up.

"Roger, please. Don't ruin your daughter's special day."

"I'm not. I'm trying to save her."

"Look," said Matthew. "I know what the situation is. Lysander told me, but there's nothing we can do about it now, and if you get dressed and walk your daughter down the aisle, you'll save yourself a lot of future embarrassment and damage to your family's reputation."

"Go to hell!" said Roger. "You don't know anything about it."

"I know you're blaming Lysander now for what is your own fault. Your constant drinking is what's responsible for bringing your family to this state. Maybe Lysander has taken advantage of the situation, but it's your weak moral character that has allowed it."

"Weak moral character. You're such a fucking prig!" screamed Roger.

For a moment, Matthew saw red at the sound of such vulgarity. He wanted to slap his brother-in-law across the mouth, but instead, he held his tongue, and after a moment of consideration, he gently said, "Roger, please. For Lydia's sake," and he put his arm around him to try to coax him up.

Roger quickly jumped up and let his arms go flying, one smacking Matthew in the jaw so quickly and unexpectedly that Matthew lost his balance and fell down on one knee, just barely stopping himself from tumbling over.

"Leave me the hell alone, you fucking pr—pig—prig!" shouted Roger.

Matthew got back on his feet. As he did so, he could hear Delia crying in her dressing room.

He walked to her door and gently knocked on it.

"What?" asked Delia, starting to turn the handle to let him in.

"Delia, don't come in," said Matthew, holding the door shut. "Just quit crying and get dressed. Then go downstairs for the wedding. I'll be down in a few minutes. I'll walk Lydia down the aisle."

"The hell you will!" shouted Roger, jumping up from the bed and coming at Matthew like a torpedo.

Matthew's reflexes took over, leaving his reasoning behind. His arm reached out to defend itself. His fingers curled into a fist. The fist made contact with Roger's jaw, and then Roger crumpled to the floor.

For a moment, Matthew didn't know what to do. He stood there, in disbelief that he had been violent, but it had been in self-defense. It was better for everyone now that Roger be unconscious. He was clearly still very drunk and hungover. But Matthew didn't want to risk him waking up and coming downstairs to disturb the wedding.

As he pondered what to do, Matthew happened to look out the window and see George on the sidewalk, speaking to one of the florists.

Before he could think better of it, Matthew threw open the window and stuck his head outside.

"George!" he called. "George, can you come up here, please? I need a big favor from you."

George looked surprised, but he did not bother to ask what was needed. Perhaps Matthew's tone or face told him enough to make him sprint across the lawn. He didn't even stop to knock on the front door. Matthew met him on the staircase landing.

"George," he said, "if we were ever friends, please do something for me right now."

"Sure, Matthew," he replied. "What do you need?"

"Roger is a drunken mess," said Matthew, walking back upstairs as George followed him. "He's passed out on the floor in his room, but he's determined to stop the wedding. I can't explain why now, but will you do me a favor? I have to get dressed so I can walk Lydia down the aisle. Can you go sit with him? If he wakes up, try not to make him mad because he might become violent, though being so drunk, he isn't much of a threat. Don't argue with him or try to rile him. Agree with him for all I care. Just make sure he doesn't leave this room. I know it'll mean that you'll miss the ceremony, but I don't know what else to do. I don't want him to ruin Lydia's wedding."

By now, they had entered Roger and Delia's bedroom and George could see for himself that the father of the bride was too incapacitated to perform his duties.

"I heard he got pretty drunk last night," said George.

"Where'd you hear that?"

"Lysander. He's outside. He told me."

Matthew frowned. "It was at Lysander's bachelor party. Anyway, will you do what I ask, please?"

"Yes," said George, looking at Roger sprawled on the floor, "but are you sure he's okay? I mean, he's still breathing, right?"

Matthew almost wished Roger wasn't breathing, but he and George both stood for a moment watching until they saw Roger's body rise and fall just enough to be certain he was still alive.

"I'll tell the maid to bring you some water or whatever you want," said Matthew. "Just don't let him leave this room until the ceremony is over. I hate to ask it of you, George. I know it's not how you wanted to attend the wedding, but—"

"It's all right, Matthew," said George, placing his hand on his old friend's shoulder. "It's the least I can do for you after...."

Their eyes met for a moment. George didn't finish speaking. Matthew wondered what he meant, but he didn't ask because he heard Delia calling for him.

"Matthew!"

"Coming," he said.

"Don't worry about a thing," said George, and after Matthew left the room, George shut the door behind him. A moment later, George had moved a chair in front of the door and sat down on it, taking up his post to make sure Roger didn't depart.

Matthew, meanwhile, met Delia in the upstairs hall.

"I'm ready," she said.

"Good," said Matthew. "Why don't you go see how Lydia is coming along? Let her know I'll be walking her down the aisle. I'll go get dressed."

"What about Roger?"

"Don't worry about it," said Matthew. "I have it under control."

"But is he…?"

"I said don't worry about it," Matthew repeated. "Just go check on Lydia. Let me take care of it, please."

"All right," said Delia, "but don't be long."

"I won't."

Matthew went to his room, which faced the lawn where the ceremony was to be held. He could see several of the wedding guests had already arrived. Lysander was busy greeting them as if he owned the place. *Well, I guess he really does*, Matthew thought as he went into the guest bathroom and washed up. His fist hurt a little from where it had connected with Roger's chin, but there seemed to be no real damage to it.

He cursed Roger under his breath as he changed his clothes, put on the expensive suit he had brought with him just for the wedding, and tied his tie.

Once he was dressed, he felt a lot calmer and more in control of the situation.

"You clean up quite nicely, Matthew Newman," he told himself, looking in the mirror as he gave his hair a last comb.

Someone knocked on his door. He went to answer it, buttoning his suitcoat as he did so.

"We're just about ready," said Delia. "We should go down and greet the guests. Is Roger sleeping?"

"I think so," said Matthew. "I'll go check on him and then join you downstairs in a minute." He didn't want to tell her George was keeping watch over her husband—she might be embarrassed to have someone else know the family secret, and then she might start crying again, and now was not the time for that.

Matthew waited for Delia to go downstairs, and then he gently turned the doorknob into Roger's room.

"He's asleep," said George, quickly jumping up and pulling back his chair from the door. Matthew peeked into the room enough to see that George had somehow managed to get the unconscious Roger back onto the bed—but that wasn't all that surprising; as a naturalist, George had always believed in treating wildlife humanely. "I don't think he'll be getting up anytime soon," said George.

"Good," said Matthew. "Why don't you come down then when you hear the music start?"

"All right," said George, and then Matthew shut the door again. He was just about to head downstairs when he heard another bedroom door open and girls laughing. Then a bridesmaid emerged into the hall, followed by a fluffy, lacey, vision of white.

"Uncle Matthew, I'm ready," said a voice beneath the white vision's veil.

Matthew was taken aback. His niece was beautiful. He wished he could give her so much more than what she would be receiving this day. For a moment, he didn't know what to say. Then he went up to her and gently kissed her cheek. The veil separated them, but Lydia welcomed the gesture.

"Thank you, Uncle Matthew," she said. "I'm glad you're giving me away. You've always been more like a father to me anyway."

Matthew was touched and surprised by the remark. And he wished it was true—he should have made a point of being around for more of Lydia's childhood.

"I'll go down and tell them to start the music," said one of the bridesmaids, brushing past Matthew and heading down the stairs. When she reached the front door of the house, she gave the signal for the small hired orchestra to begin to play.

Matthew had planned to help greet the guests, but it was too late now. He walked downstairs with Lydia, the bridesmaids following behind them. A group of groomsmen were standing in the downstairs hallway; they quickly found their prospective bridesmaids and made their way outside. Then Lydia took his arm.

"Are you ready?" Matthew asked her, thinking how many layers of meaning might be included in that question, but she simply nodded, as if resigned to whatever her fate might be.

They waited until the orchestra began to play the wedding march, and then they started across the lawn. Lysander didn't even seem to notice Roger's absence when Matthew gave Lydia away. His eyes were too busy ogling his property. Matthew could only hope that Lysander would be a better husband to her than Roger had been a father.

Roger made no effort to appear at the wedding ceremony. Halfway through, Matthew noticed George standing off to the side of the lawn where he could watch the front door in case Roger came downstairs and tried to come outside and be disruptive. Once the ceremony was over, Delia began to fret about Roger, so Matthew explained to her what had happened. She then immediately went to George and thanked him profusely, in between apologizing to him.

"No apology is necessary," he replied, "and I promise to be discreet and not repeat anything about it."

"Thank you, George," she said, touching his arm. "You're a good friend. I'll go upstairs now just to check on Roger."

Matthew wished she wouldn't, but she was Roger's wife and would do her duty by her husband, regardless. Later, she told Matthew that Roger had been snoring loudly, which was why she soon returned to the party. Matthew noticed that she ate very well during the luncheon, as if a great weight had been lifted off her shoulders.

Having lived away from Marquette for so long, Matthew did not know many of the guests, and Delia was so busy greeting people and talking to them, and Lydia and Lysander were so busy being photographed, that he found himself sitting alone for a moment. Then George took a seat beside him with two plates of cake.

"Thank you again, George," Matthew said, taking a cake plate from him, though it was obviously not the cake he was grateful for.

"Don't mention it," said George, picking up his fork. "I was happy to help. Every family has its little crises."

Matthew smirked, not imagining that anyone in George or Frances' families would ever behave the way Roger had.

"It gave me something to do," added George when Matthew did not reply. "I always feel awkward at these social events when Frances doesn't come with me."

"I understand," said Matthew.

"How do you do it?" asked George, biting into the wedding cake.

"Do what?"

"Manage to live alone all the time. You must have to go to plenty of things like this by yourself."

"I do," said Matthew, "but being a reporter, you learn how to speak to people so it doesn't seem as awkward."

"But don't you ever get lonely?" asked George.

"No, not really," said Matthew. "I'm usually so busy working. I'm rather a workaholic, and when I'm not working, there's always a book to read, a play to attend, pictures at the art museum to go and admire. I never seem to have a lack of things to keep me occupied."

"Neither do I, actually," said George. "There are always things to do, be it politics or writing or, of course, photography, but at the end of the day, I do like having Frances to come home too."

"You're a lucky man," Matthew replied, before taking a bite of the wedding cake.

"Matthew," said George, casting his eyes down to his plate.

Matthew turned to look at him, waiting.

"Sometimes," said George, "I feel bad. I mean, Frances told me long ago that you proposed to her. I—I'm sorry. I didn't mean to…."

"It was all so long ago," said Matthew. Now that the subject had finally come up between them, he found he felt no anger.

"You see," said George. "I had asked her the summer before I left that year, and she wanted time to think about it, and then I asked her again for her answer around Christmas, just before you did, I believe."

"It's all so long ago," Matthew repeated, "and in any case, it was Frances' decision."

"I had no idea you liked her that way," said George.

"I know."

"I often think if you had asked her before I did—"

"George, it's fine," said Matthew, feeling a tad irritated now by his friend's repetition.

"Are you sure?" asked George, finally looking Matthew in the eye.

"Why ask me after all these years?" asked Matthew.

"Because I haven't seen you in all these years. You left Marquette before I came home the next summer, and you've never been home since then when I've been here. I thought many times about writing to you, but…."

"George, have you been feeling this guilt all these years?" asked Matthew, laughing. "I can't believe this."

"So you don't mind?" asked George, smiling with relief, although looking a little sheepish.

"No," said Matthew. "I quit minding years ago." And somehow he realized that he had. The truth was that Frances and George had barely crossed his mind in the last twenty or so years. It was just being back here in Marquette and seeing George again and all his old familiar haunts that had stirred up the old feelings again.

George now laughed. "I'm glad, Matthew. You always were a trump. It's just—we were close friends back then, and I didn't want to think I had hurt you."

"No," said Matthew. "You didn't."

"Good. I feel silly now," said George, "to have been concerned about it all these years. But I'm glad we've had this conversation. I've missed having you as a friend."

"I've missed you too," said Matthew.

"You should move back to Marquette when you retire," said George.

"Maybe," said Matthew. "I do have family here."

But what a family—a drunken brother-in-law and a niece marrying whatever Lysander was—a bully or a crook or probably both. But there was also Delia, and there was George and Frances. He and George had been almost like brothers at one time. And he would like to see Frances again. They had never really been more than friends anyway—he realized that now. And he had always been his own man—he never would have wanted to be the recipient of Peter White's kindness as his son-in-law, kindness that would have left him stuck behind a desk to run a bank or a real estate company. No, deep in his heart, Matthew was a frontier man, not out blazing physical trails, but blazing intellectual ones—writing his stories and helping to forge a new world with them, encouraging people to fight crime and corruption when he exposed it and to build a better world in its place.

"Well, I should get home," said George. "I have to pack to leave for Washington tomorrow."

"Please tell Frances I said hello and I was sorry not to see her," said Matthew. "I'll give you my address," he added, reaching into his pocket for his pen and reporter's pad. He scribbled his address down, tore off the sheet of paper, and gave it to George. "Write to me or look me up if you're ever in New York."

"I'll do that," said George, putting the paper in his pocket as he stood up. Then he shook Matthew's hand before turning to leave.

Matthew watched George walk across the lawn and stop to say goodbye to Delia. A minute later, he had disappeared from the reception. Matthew now found himself alone amid a lawn full of guests. Not wanting to interrupt anyone's conversations, he went into the house and upstairs to check on Roger. He found his brother-in-law still sleeping soundly like a babe. Matthew felt like tonight he would be doing the same.

Matthew now felt as if the weight of the world had been lifted from his shoulders. Everything had worked out for the best, although he had never realized it until now.

George and Frances Shiras' wedding party
Front: William Gwinn Mather
Seated, left to right: Bess Howe (Sprouk), William Shiras, Carrie Morse (Ely),
Hallie Flint (Cockley), Alfred Jopling, Susan Manning, Ed Wetmore
Standing, left to right: Ed Merritt, Elsie Dyer, Unknown, Nellie Maynard
(Rees), James E. Jopling, Lily Forsythe (Brown)

"And so the famous Roosevelt libel trial has concluded. We can only speculate what difference it will make, but one thing is certain, newspapers will think twice before printing unreliable evidence. We also cannot determine the full extent that Roosevelt's time in Marquette had upon the local residents. It has made them feel more connected to the larger nation, while teaching them to appreciate the advantages they enjoy in their hometown, advantages Roosevelt fully appreciated. One thing is for certain, there are things that happen beneath the surface of visible human events, things that happen in men's hearts and souls, little epiphanies that change a person's life, and we can only speculate upon how the trial changed people in this way. Thanks to Roosevelt's visit, this writer, at least, feels he is not a sadder, but a better and wiser man."

— Matthew Newman, writing in the *Empire Sentinel*,
Monday, June 2, 1913

AUTHOR'S NOTE

WRITING A HISTORICAL NOVEL LIKE *When Teddy Came to Town* is no small task. Although the Roosevelt trial only lasted for a week, I had countless newspaper articles to read, trial transcripts to peruse, and the personal stories of many of the historical people to explore.

Wherever possible, I have directly quoted from the trial transcripts as well as from newspaper accounts. In a few cases, I have had to make up a few lines of dialogue for the courtroom scenes due to lack of materials. I have tried my best to retain the authenticity of all the materials I used, although where information was unavailable, I have had to fictionalize. In a few cases, I have modernized the punctuation of the trial transcripts or corrected a typographical error. I have also avoided quoting from the newspapers regarding the witness testimonies since I could not find their speeches in the trial transcripts, and in some cases, I think speeches were attributed to the wrong witnesses. It seems the newspaper reporters often summarized what was said but presented it as the actual spoken words for the sake of clarity—certainly, in an age before voice recorders and laptops, we can't expect the newspaper reporters to have quoted people accurately, while the court stenographers were more likely to be accurate.

It is true that Frances Shiras was either out East in New York and Washington, D.C. at the time of the trial, or, according to an anonymous manuscript that contains a biographical sketch of Shiras and is in the Northern Michigan University Archives in Marquette, she may have been in Ormond, Florida, where the Shirases frequently stayed. This manuscript captures an interesting little anecdote:

> Roosevelt's characteristic thoughtfulness was instanced on another occasion when Mr. Shiras, entering the library, found his guest busily at work upon a letter. "Shiras," said the latter, "I'll bet you can't guess to whom I'm writing!" "You're writing to your good wife,"

was the reply. "Well, you're right in one way," agreed the Colonel, "except that you've got the wives mixed. I'm writing to <u>your</u> good wife!" Thereupon a charming bread-and-butter letter was duly dispatched to Mrs. Shiras in Ormond.

This manuscript was clearly written for Shiras to be a biographical sketch of his life. Other anecdotes such as the one above were included in the manuscript with the expectation that Shiras would clarify points in question. Unfortunately, I don't believe Roosevelt's letter to Frances has survived.

Frances' daily diaries have survived and are in the possession of the Marquette Regional History Center. Unfortunately, Frances' handwriting is impossible to read so the diaries are nearly useless, and especially are so in the case of the trial since she did not observe it. Her relationship with Matthew is, of course, completely fictional since Matthew is himself fictional. When and how Frances White came to be engaged to George Shiras III is not known so I have had to fill in the blanks about their relationship.

George Shiras tells the story in his book *Hunting Wildlife with Camera and Flashlight* of how when he was a boy he went camping with three other boys ages 9-12. I decided to make Matthew one boy and then Bob Hume another, while adding in Joe Sweet as a fictional character.

Having read the entire transcripts of the trials, I have tried my best to list the witnesses in order as they took the stand, with assistance from the newspaper reports, although it was not always certain who spoke at what time of day, and in a couple of cases, even who spoke on which day. So much of the testimony was repetitive that I have summarized and often skipped over much of it so it would not bore the reader while the snippets I used still provide a sense of the atmosphere of the proceedings.

The local restaurants and drugstores did have specials as described named after Roosevelt, although I had to use my imagination for what might have been the ingredients for the Roosevelt Sundae.

There was a press night held at the Marquette Commercial Club for all the newsmen and they did have a mock trial of sorts over Chris Haggerty referring to Marquette as a "frontier town." The names of all the newsmen at the dinner are accurate, although I had to fictionalize their speeches.

Women's suffrage along with Prohibition were very hot topics at the time of the novel. To the best of my knowledge, the first real suffrage movement in Marquette happened two years later in 1915 when several of the women Delia mentions as possibly interested in forming a society not only did so but sent several women to a suffrage convention. In 1917, the Women Welfare Club, with Mrs. Roberts as its president, had a float in Marquette's Fourth of July parade. In addition, the first female presidential candidate, Victoria Woodhull, really did visit Marquette in 1875, three years after her attempt to be elected. Despite how poorly she was received in Marquette, no doubt many women were interested in women's suffrage in the forty years between her visit and the first suffrage group being formed in the city.

As the photographs testify, the Civil War and Spanish-American War veterans did meet Roosevelt at the Shiras home. Among those mentioned as meeting him was Stewart Zryd, who was my great-great-great uncle. I also mentioned his father Joseph Zryd, my great-great-great grandfather, who was well-known in Marquette for playing the violin. He appears in the party scene at the Call house set back in 1883.

The party scene itself was probably my favorite to write—just to imagine what a party among the wealthy on Ridge Street would have been like in the Gilded Age. All of these families had many connections, both through marriage in Marquette and in the outside world. Constance Fenimore Woolson, the aunt to the Mathers, was a famous novelist at the time, and as Frances and William Gwinn Mather discuss, she did actually meet Peter White in Florence as a March 20, 1880 letter she wrote to her nephew Samuel L. Mather testifies. I have long been her admirer because she was the first author to write fiction set in Marquette—three short stories, two of which feature towns thinly described as Marquette and the other story directly names Marquette. I have searched but never yet found evidence, however, that she herself ever visited the city.

What became of the major fictional characters in this novel after the story ends can be found in some of my other novels since all of my stories about Marquette are very intertextual, meaning characters in one novel often appear in another. That is true as well for *When Teddy Came to Town*. Matthew, Delia, and Roger all first appear in *Iron Pioneers: The Marquette Trilogy, Book One* (2006) where they make brief appearances as Madeleine Henning's friends and are with her when she is believed to drown in Lake Superior. Later, I wondered how that drowning affected them, and so they made a reappearance in my novel *Narrow Lives* (2008), which also includes Lysander and Lydia Blackmore as characters. Lysander first appeared briefly in *The Queen City: The Marquette Trilogy, Book Two* (2006). As for Matthew, the last years of his life, during World War II, are depicted in some of the scenes in my novel *The Best Place* (2013). The snooty Carolina Smith also makes appearances in *Iron Pioneers* as well as in my novel *The Only Thing That Lasts* (2009) and her husband Judge Smith appears in *Spirit of the North* (2012). Many of the historical people mentioned who are from Marquette, including Peter White and Chief Kawbawgam, also make appearances in my other novels. Marquette may not be a large city, but it contains within it a whole world of diverse and fascinating people and stories, and so many people's lives are happening simultaneously in it that I feel it is a never-ending source of viable material for storytelling. I trust my readers agree since they keep asking me for more novels set in Marquette. As I've often thought, Marquette is world enough for me.

As for George and Frances Shiras, they had many more years of marriage. Frances would die in 1938, and then George lived in Marquette until his death in 1942. They are both buried in Park Cemetery in Marquette. They had two children who were both adults and presumably out East also during the time of the trial. Their son George Shiras IV died at the young age of thirty in 1915 and is buried with his parents. Their daughter, Ellen Shiras, would in time marry Frank Russell, the proprietor of the *Mining Journal*. They in turn would have a son, Frank Russell, Jr. who would also own the *Mining Journal* as well as the television station that is today WLUC-TV6.

George Shiras III (it should be noted he preferred "George Shiras 3d") remains well-known today as the "father of wildlife photography." In 2016, a special exhibition "George Shiras, In the Heart of the Dark Night" was on view at the Musée de la Chasse et de la Nature in Paris, France. The exhibit included vintage prints from *National Geographic*, to which Shiras donated 2,400 of his glass plate negatives in 1928. *In the Heart of the Dark Night*, a book of Shiras' photography, was published in both English and French by Editions Xavier Barral in conjunction with the exhibit.

Theodore Roosevelt, despite his breaking with the Republican Party in 1912 to run on the Bull Moose ticket, eventually healed his differences with William Howard Taft, who had been his vice president but whose presidency Roosevelt had thought enough of a failure to make him run against him. The two later met by accident in the Blackstone Hotel's restaurant in Chicago in 1918 where they hugged and made peace with each other. Everyone in the nation knew about their feud, so those in the dining room who witnessed the reconciliation reportedly clapped. As for the Progressive Party Roosevelt had founded, when his party members decided to elect someone other than him for their 1916 candidate, Roosevelt was not happy and decided to rejoin the Republican Party.

Prior to rejoining the party, however, Roosevelt would himself be sued for libel in 1915 when he accused William Barnes, a leader of the Republican Party, of being a party boss. Roosevelt also won that case. Roosevelt would die in 1919, just six years after the trial in Marquette.

Sadly, alcoholism ran in Roosevelt's family. Besides his brother Elliott, father to Eleanor, being an alcoholic, Roosevelt's son Kermit also suffered from alcoholism and depression, leading to his suicide by shooting himself in 1943.

George Newett, despite an illness at the time of the trial, lived for many more years and continued to publish the *Iron Ore* of Ishpeming. He died in 1928.

Judge Flannigan would be appointed to the Michigan Supreme Court fourteen years after the trial for his reputation as an honest and hardworking man.

The Roosevelt-Newett Trial is remembered to this day in Marquette. The Marquette Regional History Center regularly mentions it on its historical bus tours and even has character actors who play Roosevelt. In 1987, a historical marker was placed at the Marquette County Courthouse which notes that it was the site of the Roosevelt trial as well as another famous trial in 1956 which became the inspiration for the novel and film of the same name, *Anatomy of a Murder.*

Other locations featured in the novel have not fared so well. The Marquette Opera House was destroyed by fire during a terrible blizzard in January 1938. The Peter White Home was torn down in the late 1940s to build a modern home by the White descendants, who still reside on the property today.

Numerous biographies have been written about Theodore Roosevelt over the years, but few mention the libel trial in Marquette, and when they do, it is rarely for more than a couple of sentences. Those interested in further reading, however, may consult *Teddy Roosevelt and The Marquette Libel Trial* by Mikel B. Classen, published by The History Press in 2015. The complete transcripts of the trial were also published by Roosevelt's cousin W. Emlen Roosevelt in 1914 under the title *Roosevelt vs. Newett.*

Other books of interest relevant to Marquette and the historical people included in this novel are *The Honorable Peter White* (1905) by Ralph D. Williams, *Hunting Wild Life with Camera and Flashlight* (1935) by George Shiras III, and *Justice George Shiras, Jr. of Pittsburgh* by George Shiras III, the latter being a family history focusing upon Shiras' father, the Supreme Court

Justice. Much of the information about the Shiras family I derived from these books. Several books about Marquette, Michigan, and its history have been written over the years, including Fred Rydholm's *Superior Heartland* and Sonny Longtine and Laverne Chappelle's *Marquette, Then and Now*, but the only one currently in print is my own book, *My Marquette: Explore the Queen City of the North* (2011).

Marquette remains a "frontier" city in the sense that Matthew expressed—a city of innovation and leading-edge thought. It is frequently reported in the media as an All American city, one of the best biking cities in the country, and a top tourist destination, as well as a place where innovative entrepreneurs find means to flourish. It is my great honor to be a seventh generation resident of Marquette and to continue to try to capture the essence of the Queen City of the North in my books.

Tyler R. Tichelaar
May 26, 2018
Marquette, Michigan

ACKNOWLEDGMENTS

So MANY PEOPLE HELP ME in writing my books. Sometimes a stranger will meet me at a book signing and say a sentence that will send me off with an idea for a whole new book, or a simple idea will come to me during conversation with a friend that will shape a chapter or even a character's destiny. It is impossible to thank everyone since I can't always remember in all of these instances whom I am indebted to. However, a few people deserve recognition.

I thank Mikel Classen for writing his own book about the Roosevelt libel trial—he beat me to the punch since I was already well into a draft of this novel when his nonfiction book appeared in 2015, but his work brought to my attention some details I was unaware of at the time.

Beth Gruber at the Marquette Regional History Center was invaluable for taking the time on countless Saturday afternoons to aid me in my research and to scan numerous *Mining Journal* articles about the trial for me.

Diana Deluca and Roslyn Hurley have my gratitude for reading chapters of the manuscript as it was first being written and giving me advice when I went too far off on historical tangents.

Jenifer Brady is a prize proofreader, but most importantly, I prize her continual interest in my books and her enthusiasm for them.

Larry Alexander—what can I say—he designs all my books and puts up with my constant requests for little changes and photo moves until we get it right. I appreciate his patience and his immense talent.

Thank you to Greg Kretovic for his beautiful photo of the Marquette County Courthouse for the cover.

Thank you also to Greg Casperson for the author photo in the back of this book.

And I thank my readers. Without them, my writing would be pointless.

PHOTO CREDITS

Greg Casperson—About the Author page

Greg Kretovic—Cover Photo

Jack Deo, Superior View—7, 12, 106, 116, 117, 150, 324

Marquette Regional History Center—vii, 10, 17, 22, 38, 41, 57, 105, 111, 113, 119, 121, 126, 128, 129, 132, 142, 143, 145, 146, 147, 148, 152, 154, 164, 183, 188, 226, 227, 231, 247, 263, 264, 311, 312, 320, 346

Wikipedia—37, 170

Public Domain—68, 140

A Special Request

If you enjoyed this book, please write a book review for it at Amazon, Barnes & Noble, Goodreads, or another bookseller or booklover website. Authors rely on book reviews and word-of-mouth to sell their books. Readers also rely on reviews to help them make their decisions on which books to purchase and read. Just a couple of sentences from you can have a huge impact. The author thanks you for your time.

BE SURE TO READ ALL OF
TYLER R. TICHELAAR'S MARQUETTE BOOKS

IRON PIONEERS:
THE MARQUETTE TRILOGY: BOOK ONE

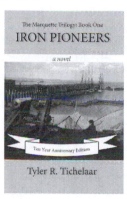

When iron ore is discovered in Michigan's Upper Peninsula in the 1840s, newlyweds Gerald Henning and his beautiful socialite wife Clara travel from Boston to the little village of Marquette on the shores of Lake Superior. They and their companions, Irish and German immigrants, French Canadians, and fellow New Englanders face blizzards and near starvation, devastating fires, and financial hardships. Yet these iron pioneers persevere until their wilderness village becomes integral to the Union cause in the Civil War and then a prosperous modern city. Meticulously researched, warmly written, and spanning half a century, *Iron Pioneers* is a testament to the spirit that forged America.

THE QUEEN CITY
THE MARQUETTE TRILOGY: BOOK TWO

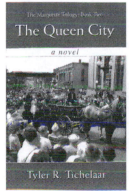

During the first half of the twentieth century, Marquette grows into the Queen City of the North. Here is the tale of a small town undergoing change as its horses are replaced by streetcars and automobiles, and its pioneers are replaced by new generations who prosper despite two World Wars and the Great Depression. Margaret Dalrymple finds her Scottish prince, though he is neither Scottish nor a prince. Molly Bergmann becomes an inspiration to her grandchildren. Jacob Whitman's children engage in a family feud. The Queen City's residents marry, divorce, have children, die, break their hearts, go to war, gossip, blackmail, raise families, move away, and then return to Marquette. And always, always they are in love with the haunting land that is their home.

SUPERIOR HERITAGE
THE MARQUETTE TRILOGY: BOOK THREE

The Marquette Trilogy comes to a satisfying conclusion as it brings together characters and plots from the earlier novels and culminates with Marquette's sesquicentennial celebrations in 1999. What happened to Madeleine Henning is finally revealed as secrets from the past shed light upon the present. Marquette's residents struggle with a difficult local economy, yet remain optimistic for the future. The novel's main character, John Vandelaare, is descended from all the early Marquette families in *Iron Pioneers* and *The Queen City*. While he cherishes his family's past, he questions whether he should remain in his hometown. Then an event happens that will change his life forever.

NARROW LIVES

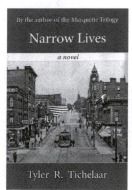

Narrow Lives is the story of those whose lives were affected by Lysander Blackmore, the sinister banker first introduced to readers in *The Queen City*. It is a novel that stands alone, yet readers of *The Marquette Trilogy* will be reacquainted with some familiar characters. Written as a collection of connected short stories, each told in first person by a different character, *Narrow Lives* depicts the influence one person has, even in death, upon others, and it explores the prisons of grief, loneliness, and fear self-created when people doubt their own worthiness.

THE ONLY THING THAT LASTS

The story of Robert O'Neill, the famous novelist introduced in *The Marquette Trilogy*. As a young boy during World War I, Robert is forced to leave his South Carolina home to live in Marquette with his grandmother and aunt. He finds there a cold climate, but many warmhearted friends. An old-fashioned story that follows Robert's growth from childhood to successful writer and husband, the novel is written as Robert O'Neill's autobiography, his final gift to Marquette by memorializing the town of his youth.

SPIRIT OF THE NORTH: A PARANORMAL ROMANCE

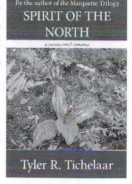

In 1873, orphaned sisters Barbara and Adele Traugott travel to Upper Michigan to live with their uncle, only to find he is deceased. Penniless, they are forced to spend the long, fierce winter alone in their uncle's remote wilderness cabin. Frightened yet determined, the sisters face blizzards and near starvation to survive. Amid their difficulties, they find love and heartache— and then, a ghostly encounter and the coming of spring lead them to discovering the true miracle of their being.

THE BEST PLACE

An irritating best friend gained during a childhood spent in a Catholic orphanage, a father who became a Communist and went to Russia in the 1930s, and 3:00 a.m. visits to The Pancake House. Such is the life of Lyla Hopewell. But in the summer of 2005, when her old boyfriend Bill has a heart attack, her best friend Bel really gets on her nerves, and Finn Fest comes to Marquette, things will change for Lyla.

WILLPOWER
AN ORIGINAL PLAY ABOUT MARQUETTE'S OSSIFIED MAN

There are some stories that deserve to be told. As a young boy, Will Adams' soft tissues were becoming harder, turning him into a living statue. Others faced with such a dark future might have felt sorry for themselves, turning inward. Not so for Will, his disease brought about an amazing creative burst of energy. His story is as inspiring today as it was more than 100 years ago.

MY MARQUETTE
EXPLORE THE QUEEN CITY OF THE NORTH
—ITS HISTORY, PEOPLE, AND PLACES

My Marquette is the result of its author's lifelong love affair with his hometown. Join Tyler R. Tichelaar, seventh generation Marquette resident and author of *The Marquette Trilogy*, as he takes you on a tour of the history, people, and places of Marquette. Stories of the past and present, both true and fictional, will leave you understanding why Marquette really is "The Queen City of the North." Along the way, Tyler will describe his own experiences growing up in Marquette, recall family and friends he knew, and give away secrets about the people behind the characters in his novels. *My Marquette* offers a rare insight into an author's creation of fiction and a refreshing view of a city's history and relevance to today. Reading *My Marquette* is equal to being given a personal tour by someone who knows Marquette intimately.

HAUNTED MARQUETTE
GHOST STORIES FROM THE QUEEN CITY

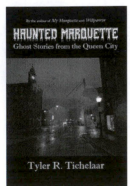

Founded as a harbor town to ship iron ore from the nearby mines, Marquette became known as the Queen City of the North for its thriving industries, beautiful buildings, and being the largest city in Upper Michigan.

But is Marquette also the Queen of Lake Superior's Haunted Cities? Seventh-generation Marquette resident Tyler Tichelaar has spent years collecting tales of the many ghosts who haunt the cemeteries, churches, businesses, hotels, and homes of Marquette.

Now, separating fact from fiction, Tichelaar delves into the historical record to determine whom the ghosts might be, which stories have a historical basis, and which tales are simply the fancies of imaginative or frightened minds.

Hear the chilling tales of:

- The wicked nun who killed an orphan boy, and how the boy continues to escape from his grave

- The librarian who haunts a local hotel while mourning for her sailor lover
- The drowned sailors who climb out of Lake Superior at night
- The glowing lantern of the decapitated train conductor
- The mailman who gave his life so neither rain, sleet, nor snow would stop the U.S. mail
- More ghostly ladies in floor-length white gowns than any haunted city should have

Haunted Marquette opens up a fourth dimension view of the Queen City's past and reveals that much of it is still present.

For more information on Tyler R. Tichelaar's Marquette Books, visit:

www.MarquetteFiction.com

And be sure also to check out Tyler's other titles

THE GOTHIC WANDERER:
FROM TRANSGRESSION TO REDEMPTION

CREATING A LOCAL HISTORICAL BOOK:
FICTION AND NONFICTION GENRES

KING ARTHUR'S CHILDREN:
A STUDY IN FICTION AND TRADITION

THE CHILDREN OF ARTHUR HISTORICAL FANTASY SERIES
Arthur's Legacy: The Children of Arthur, Book One
Melusine's Gift: The Children of Arthur, Book Two
Ogier's Prayer: The Children of Arthur, Book Three
Lilith's Love: The Children of Arthur, Book Four
Arthur's Bosom: The Children of Arthur, Book Five

ABOUT THE AUTHOR

TYLER R. TICHELAAR HAS A Ph.D. in Literature from Western Michigan University and Bachelor and Master's Degrees in English from Northern Michigan University. He is the owner of Marquette Fiction, his own publishing company; Superior Book Productions, a professional editing, proofreading, book layout, and website design and maintenance service; and the current president of the Upper Peninsula Publishers and Authors Association. He is especially proud to be a seventh generation Marquette resident.

Tyler began writing his first novel at age sixteen in 1987. In 2006, he published his first novel, *Iron Pioneers: The Marquette Trilogy, Book One*. Numerous more books have followed. In 2009, Tyler won first place in the historical fiction category in the Reader Views Literary Awards for his novel *Narrow Lives*. He has since sponsored that contest, offering the Tyler R. Tichelaar Award for Historical Fiction. In 2011, Tyler was awarded the Marquette County Outstanding Writer Award, and the same year, he received the Barb Kelly Award for Historical Preservation for his efforts to promote Marquette history.

While Tyler also writes on such diverse topics as nineteenth century Gothic fiction and historical fantasies about King Arthur, he remains engrossed in writing about Marquette and Upper Michigan as microcosms for the greater American story. He has many more books in the works.

Visit Tyler at **www.MarquetteFiction.com**.

92412879R00211

Made in the USA
Lexington, KY
04 July 2018